FEARLESS

MAJOR PUBLICITY AND MARKETING CAMPAIGN

- National review campaign
- Broadcast outreach, including NPR
- Feature and interview outreach, both in print and online
- Outreach to mystery/thriller outlets
- Blog tour
- Major social media campaign, advertising, and promotion
- Multiwave Goodreads promotion and advertising
- Dedicated mystery and thriller advertising campaign including *Book Riot* and *Criminal Element*
- Targeted keyword advertising campaign
- Email newsletter marketing
- Library marketing campaign
- Author website: MWCraven.com

MAJOR STREAMING NEWS TO COME

FLATIRON
BOOKS

FEARLESS

ALSO BY M. W. CRAVEN

The Ben Koenig Series

The Washington Poe Series

The Avison Fluke Series

FEARLESS

M. W. CRAVEN

FLATIRON
BOOKS
NEW YORK

FEARLESS. Copyright © 2023 by M. W. Craven. All rights reserved. Printed in the United States of America. For information, address Flatiron Books, 120 Broadway, New York, NY 10271.

www.flatironbooks.com

Library of Congress Cataloging-in-Publication Data (**TK**)

ISBN 978-1-250-86456-7 (hardcover)
ISBN 978-1-250-86458-1 (ebook)

Our books may be purchased in bulk for promotional, educational, or business use. Please contact your local bookseller or the Macmillan Corporate and Premium Sales Department at 1-800-221-7945, extension 5442, or by email at MacmillanSpecialMarkets@macmillan.com.

First Edition: 2023

10 9 8 7 6 5 4 3 2 1

[DEDICATION TK]

PART ONE

A CITY OF MAGNIFICENT DISTANCES

CHAPTER 1

Six was kind of an insult. It wasn't enough. I thought they were going to need a bigger boat. It's a line from *Jaws*. The sheriff says it when he sees the great white shark for the first time, when he sees how big it is. It's now an idiom for being outmatched. Like how "over the moon" means happy. Or "break a leg" means good luck. So when I saw there were only six of them, that's what I thought. They were going to need a bigger boat.

Then again, it was a small town—maybe six was all they could spare. Maybe six was everyone. And it was an urgent operation. Panicked even. Had to be. If it wasn't, Wayne County wouldn't be doing it. They'd be relegated to cordon control. This had been a hasty phone call followed by an even hastier order: "Do it now before he moves. You don't have the luxury of waiting for reinforcements. In the meantime, we're scrambling everyone we have."

I'm not a huge man—five eleven, weigh a buck ninety—but they approached me like I was unattended baggage. They looked scared. Jittery. Probably never had to do a job like this before. Lived in Wayne County to get *away* from jobs like this. Cold sweat on furrowed brows, faces rigid with tension. One of them had a twitch going on in the corner of his right eye. Probably a nervous thing.

They were doing OK, though. Hadn't tried to rush me. They weren't shouting, weren't giving contradictory instructions. They'd walked through the bar without causing alarm. A ripple of hush followed them. The barman even switched off the music. All eyes turned to me. Not something I was used to these days. They fanned around my booth without getting in each other's way, and then waited. There was no hostility. Just cops doing their duty. If I hadn't seen what was on the TV, I might not have known they were there for me.

It's an oversimplification to say there are good cops and there are bad cops. Cops can be both brave and cowardly, honest and corrupt, and they can be clever and stupid. And they can be all of those things or none of those things. So, to make things easy, I don't trust cops. I don't trust anyone. It's why I'm still alive.

Even before I'd seen them, I'd auditioned several scenarios. None was good. They didn't work out well for me and they sure didn't work out well for them. In the end, it came down to math: When all your options are bad, choose the one that allows you to fight another day. You play the odds.

Before I hit somewhere new, I make sure I'm not walking into a town like the one from the first Rambo film, the one with the sheriff who didn't like drifters.

Wayne County Sheriff's Office covered a large area, and the sheriff was a woman called Diane Long. They had a good reputation. The men in front of me were deputies from the road patrol department. Solid, no-nonsense cops. Not high-profile like the NYPD, but in a small department like Wayne County, the sheer variety of their daily call sheets made them tough and adaptable.

So far, no one had spoken. Their weapons were drawn but remained at their sides. It wasn't a standoff—they were waiting for a signal. A man wearing sergeant's stripes was covering their backs. He said, "Now," and as one, they raised their weapons.

Two were holding Taser X26s. Black and yellow and nasty. When discharged, they launch two probes that attach themselves to the target's clothes or skin, completing an electrical circuit. Hurts like hell. Completely debilitating. They have a range of fifteen feet, and the cops were eight feet away. The ideal distance. I didn't want to be tasered.

The only woman of the group was aiming a shotgun at my chest. I couldn't tell what shells she was packing, but my gut told me they'd be nonlethal. Probably beanbag rounds. Enough to cause a bad bruise and, if I was standing, put me on my ass. Nut-busters, I called them once. Useless, unless you go rogue and aim for something soft and dangly, because with a six-foot-five muscle-head who's in the middle of a Hulk-like meltdown after he's overdone the gym candy, center-mass shots barely tickle. A blast to the balls however . . .

They'd been told to bring me in alive.

That was good.

The sergeant was carrying a standard-issue Glock, though. A serious man with a serious gun. Loaded with 9-millimeter Parabellums. If one of *them* hit me center mass, I wouldn't be getting up. "Parabellum" is taken from the Latin *"para bellum."* It means prepare for war. I've always thought it's a good name for a bullet. The sergeant had a barrel chest, square shoulders, and an even squarer chin. His mouth formed a rigid grimace. His gunmetal-gray eyes fixed on me with no disengagement. The Glock wasn't drawn, but his hand rested on the butt and the holster was unfastened. Although I got the impression he'd been told he wasn't to point his weapon at me, I knew that, at a hint of danger, his hand would shoot out like it was remote controlled. I understood his anger: They were doing someone else's dirty work and, federal order or not, he didn't want his guys getting hurt by some asshole he hadn't heard of until half an hour ago.

The sergeant spoke. "Can you come with us please, sir?"

I said, "You're going to need a bigger boat."

CHAPTER 2

An hour before things went all screwy, I'd been sitting in a hotel bar, nursing a pot of tea. It was good tea. Heavy with tannin. Thick enough to stand a spoon in. My surname is Germanic—my grandfather moved to the States when he was forty, got his citizenship in '46, and dropped the umlaut in König when being German wasn't popular—but my mother is English, and I guess that's where my love of the drink comes from. I like coffee, but I prefer tea.

I'd been minding my own business. Trying not to be noticed. It's what I do. I mind my own business and I try not to be noticed. As a rule I avoid small towns, the kind that remember strangers, but there was a claims adjusters' convention on. And conventions change things. *Everyone's* a stranger during a convention. Towns are crowded and that's good. Crowds are my friend. I can use crowds.

I'd been zigzagging across New York State. Planned to visit Chittenango, the birthplace of *The Wonderful Wizard of Oz* author L. Frank Baum. I'd heard that the town's sidewalks are painted yellow, and when you have nothing to do but keep moving, you may as well go and see things. I was in no hurry, though, and that night I'd ended up in a town called Gosforth, Wayne County. I was hoping to get a hot meal and maybe score a cheap room for the night. I'd been outdoors all week, and although it was warm and I had a one-person backpacker's tent, a bit of luxury never usually killed anyone. Then again, I'm an unusual person.

I was in the lobby bar of the Four Pines Hotel. It was like thousands of other bars: horseshoe booths, red leather armchairs, and round stools at the bar. Shrill laughter and raised testosterone. A disinterested, acne-ridden barman polishing glasses with the rag he'd just been wiping the tables with. Seven mute televisions, all showing the same ball game: Red Sox and the Yankees at Fenway Park. I was sitting in a booth. It was covered in red plastic leather. Pleather, I think they call it. Comes in long rolls and is easy to wipe clean. I checked the menu while I finished my tea.

The first thing that went wrong was the barman putting a bowl of peanuts on my table.

I'd read somewhere that the average bowl of bar nuts contains traces of over one hundred unique specimens of urine. Men and women coming back from the bathroom without washing their hands. And while a different study disproved that, their arguably worse claim was that over 40 percent of ice cubes contain coliform: the bacteria that comes from human feces. I hadn't eaten a bar nut for nearly ten years. Been drinking my Coke warm for about the same time.

I pushed the peanuts back in the barman's direction. "No thank you," I said, then wished I hadn't. Refusing free stuff was unusual. It was *memorable*.

The barman gave me an odd look, then shrugged like it happened all the time. He picked at a spot on the side of his neck and said, "Get ya anything from the kitchen?"

"Burger," I replied. "American Classic with bacon, Monterey Jack cheese, and a double patty, rare. Side order of fries and a chocolate milkshake."

"Good choice," he said. "It's my favorite."

I doubted that. He'd said the same thing to two women who'd ordered mac 'n' cheese not ten minutes earlier.

"It might be a half hour," he added, after he'd made a note of my order. "Everyone seems to be eating now."

Thirty minutes was way too long. I wanted to be back on the road before nightfall. Find somewhere safer than the Four Pines to hole up for the night. I removed a twenty from my roll. "This speed things up?"

"Considerably," he replied, slipping it into his apron pocket. "Fifteen minutes?"

I don't know what my twenty was supposed to buy me, but my burger and shake took longer than the promised fifteen minutes. It actually took longer than the originally offered thirty. When it finally arrived, it was the same barman carrying it over. He made no attempt at an apology. Just put it on the table along with some cutlery. Headed back to the bar and started polishing glasses again. Every now and then he glanced at me but did it like he knew he shouldn't.

He was acting differently, and in my world that's a big, fat red flag.

I had to leave. I didn't know what had happened, but I hadn't survived the last six years by waiting around to see if I was right all the time. It was a pity, but the barman was now openly staring. Wasn't even trying to hide it. It was time to move on. I pulled my backpack closer. It contained everything I owned and was always within reach.

Which was when I saw the television.

It was showing a newsbreak, one of the two-minute updates they have during an innings change. Even though we were in New York State, and the Yankees were playing, no one was really watching the game. I'd been glancing up sporadically to check the score.

The peroxide-blonde anchor was silently reading the last news item before they returned to the game. There was also a rolling banner at the bottom. One of those horizontal text-based displays with the day's headlines and a toll-free number to call. I was too far away to see what it said, but the image on the screen was crystal clear.

It was a photograph. Despite not having seen it for years, I knew it well.

I stared at the screen.

My own face stared back.

CHAPTER 3

It was a photo from my previous life. Almost fifteen years old, but still the most up-to-date one there was. When you disappear, one of the things you need to do is destroy all your photographs, and despite only having had a day's notice, I'd taken the time to do this. Virtually every photograph of me was gone. Either burned or deleted. But there'd been photographs I couldn't access. Ones held in federal databases.

The agency that had supplied the photo on the TV screen was the same one that had taken the photograph: the United States Marshals. I'd finally made their Fifteen Most Wanted list. I was now one of the most sought-after fugitives in the country.

Which didn't make sense. *I* knew why I'd disappeared, but the US Marshals didn't. And even if they did, they wouldn't look for me this way. They would find a different, quieter way. Putting me on the list smacked of desperation, of someone with a deadline.

After what seemed like an age, the channel returned to the ball game. A weak voice cheered at the end of the bar. At least one person was watching the game then. I looked round, feeling exposed. The barman was still watching me.

I had a problem. My face was on a national channel, not a local one, and it hadn't looked like a breaking story. It could have been running for days, even weeks. For six years, no one had managed to get near me. I'd hoped people thought I was dead. That I'd died in some backwater town somewhere. An unnamed John Doe. But the federal government had just announced to every Tom, Dick, and opportunist that I was alive and well.

Hunting season would begin again.

Which was a bit of a nuisance.

I needed to get to the bottom of this. The answers wouldn't be found in Gosforth, though. They'd be found in Arlington, Virginia. That's where the US Marshals were headquartered. Someone there would know what was happening. I still had friends in Arlington.

I grabbed the burger and took a bite. It was dreadful. Canner-grade beef, a thin slice of tomato, and limp brown lettuce. The doughy bun was unbuttered and twice as big as it needed to be. I took another bite anyway. I wanted to be fifty miles away by morning, and I had no idea when I'd next eat again. Never turn down calories or sleep, I'd been taught.

The first indication I was too late was when I checked to see if the street was clear. My booth had a window, and although the curtains were drawn, I'd been pulling them to one side and peering out every now and then. Not for anything in particular—up until the newsbreak I had no reason to suspect anything was untoward—it's just one of those things you do when you're sitting by a window; you look out of it. The last time I'd looked, the street had been busy.

Now it looked like an empty movie set.

It wasn't a coincidence. Without external factors, the street being empty would be a phenomenon. Mathematically implausible.

It had been cleared. There was a cordon set up. Somewhere out of sight. A crowd of onlookers behind a barrier, cell phone cameras at the ready, waiting for something to happen.

It had probably been the barman who'd called the toll-free number. He must have been looking at my photograph all day and couldn't believe his eyes when I walked in. Came over with the bowl of peanuts to make sure. I'd figured his odd look was because I'd turned down some urine-soaked peanuts, but it must have been when he realized he wasn't going crazy. The man in his bar was one of the US Marshals' most wanted fugitives. When I'd ordered my burger, it gave him the excuse he needed to go into the kitchen to make his call. He'd probably been told to act natural, delay me if he could. Give the cops time to arrange something. That was why my meal had taken so long.

Instinct and experience told me that I was about to be arrested. That a team was already outside. No one was getting in or out without their say-so. And if they were already at the door, it meant it was going down now.

I put my hands on the table and sat up straight, like a meerkat.

I didn't want anyone to get hurt.

CHAPTER 4

"You're going to need a bigger boat," I said to the sergeant with the Glock.

He frowned. He'd probably rehearsed what to say when he reached my table and I wasn't following his script. He'd asked me to come with him and I was supposed to stand up. Instead I'd told him he was going to need a bigger boat. Without context, my response was nonsensical. Irrational.

I took a fry off my plate and popped it into my mouth. It was greasy, like the oil hadn't been hot enough when they went in the fryer. I picked up another and held it up.

"Did you know the French and the Belgians are in constant conflict about who invented the fry?" I said. "The Belgians say it's just another case of French gastronomic hegemony. That any Belgian cuisine they liked was assimilated into their own, then *claimed* as their own."

"I didn't know that, sir," he said. His confusion was obvious. I had been talking about bigger boats and now I was talking about French fries.

I shrugged. "Personally I think they're more likely to have been invented in Spain. They were the first European country to get the potato after it arrived from the New World, and they already had a tradition of frying their food in oil."

He raised his eyebrows.

"I used to watch a lot of TV," I said. "And I used to read a lot of books."

"And now?"

"And now not so much," I said. "Anyway, I'm telling you about the provenance of fries, Sergeant, only to demonstrate that things are not always as they seem. Calling something French doesn't make it French." I threw the fry back on the plate. "And putting someone on the Most Wanted list doesn't make them a criminal."

"I'll bear that in mind, sir."

"Am I under arrest?"

"No, sir. But we *would* like to talk."

"There are six of you. Talk among yourselves."

The sergeant didn't crack a smile. Probably heard that joke a million times before. "I need you to accompany us to the sheriff's office, sir."

"You've made a mistake, you know that, right?"

"So you've said, sir," the sergeant said. "And I'm sure it will get sorted out. But not here."

I took another bite from my burger and then wished I hadn't. "No, I meant you've made a *tactical* mistake."

"Is that right, sir?"

"It is," I said. "Is this a teachable moment, Sergeant?"

He didn't respond. The fingers resting on his Glock flexed, though. A warning.

"You've made a tactical mistake because now you have a problem," I continued. "You should have waited until I had left the hotel, or when I was at the bar counter paying my tab. Hell, anywhere would be better than here."

"And why is that, sir?" the sergeant said.

"Are you humoring me, Sergeant?"

"I just want to get this done with the minimum of fuss, sir. Let these fine folk get on with their evening."

"You should never try to detain someone sitting in a booth, Sergeant," I said. "Not if you don't have to."

I lifted the lid of my burger and discarded the patty. Turned it into a lettuce-and-tomato sandwich. I took a bite. It was only marginally better.

"This is a tight booth and the table is bolted to the floor," I said. "I can wrap my legs around the central pillar. Reach down and grab it with both hands, become an immovable object. You can try to drag me out, of course, but the best you can do is put a deputy either side of me. No way is two enough. My glutes are stronger than their biceps. And you can't use your weapons. I'm unarmed. There is no threat to life. And more importantly, right now there are at least ten people filming this with their cell phones, every one of them a potential citizen journalist. So if I refuse to leave the booth voluntarily, dragging me out is your only option. We've already established that won't work, but you have to try, right? Can't have your authority challenged like this."

I pointed at my discarded burger.

"Thirty bucks this cost me. You want to arrest someone, arrest the grill cook," I said. "Anyway, you look like an intelligent man. A strategic thinker. And now you're wondering if maybe I *want* you to try and drag me out. So far you're doing well. You're all keeping your distance. But as soon as one of your deputies is in the booth with me, things change. You wouldn't be so stupid to send him in with a weapon, but this burger's tougher than jerky and the chef kindly sent it out with a serrated knife. In less than a second I could have the blade next to his carotid artery. And now I have a hostage. The lady with the shotgun is blocking your line of sight, and by the time you moved, I'd be out of the booth and using your deputy like a ballistic shield. You look like a stand-up guy. I doubt you'd make the hard call and shoot through him to stop me. I have options now. Maybe I walk him out and take my chances with whoever you have out on the street. Or perhaps I take your deputy into the kitchen behind the bar. Use some of their hot grease to start a fire. Make sure the hotel has to be evacuated. Cause a panic. Slip away in the chaos." I paused and smiled politely. "*That's* why you made a mistake, Sergeant."

To his credit, the sergeant's demeanor barely changed. A slight stiffening of his spine, an involuntary twitch of his trigger finger. He moved a yard to his left. Made sure the deputy with the shotgun wasn't blocking his line of sight.

"Relax, Sergeant," I said. "Despite what you might think, I'm one of the good guys. I'll come with you. But I would like to finish my milkshake." I picked up my glass.

"I really need you to come now, sir." His voice was hard and flat now, his eyes steady.

"I think I'll finish my milkshake," I said. I looked at him over the rim as I took a drink.

The burger might have been a bust, but the shake was cold and thick and creamy. It didn't matter how hard I sucked; it came up through that straw in its own time. I put it down. If I rushed it, the blood vessels in the roof of my mouth would rapidly constrict. I would get a cold-stimulus headache. A brain freeze.

"Well, this is awkward," I said.

The sergeant reddened. In the space of a minute he'd lost control of the situation. Everyone around the booth knew it. The female deputy began to fidget. She had drawn the short straw. She'd been holding her shotgun in the raised position for a while now, and her arms were starting to tire. Holding her arms like that meant she was holding the weight with just one or two muscles. If she'd been a prisoner of war, it would have been called a stress position. Explicitly prohibited under the Geneva Conventions. I wondered what her sergeant would do. If it had been me, I'd have rotated and made sure everyone took a turn. Then again, I wouldn't have tried to arrest someone wedged into a booth.

In the end, it was the female deputy's discomfort rather than the sergeant's embarrassment that forced the issue.

"Come on then," I said. I held out my arms. An old trick perps sometimes try on new cops. They're so relieved the perp isn't struggling they don't consider whether cuffing to the rear would be the better option. To my surprise the sergeant didn't object. Being cuffed to the front was an inconvenience to me, for sure. It would certainly stop me bragging about the size of the last fish I'd caught, but it wouldn't stop me grabbing and using a weapon. The old me wouldn't have made a mistake like that. Then again, the old me wouldn't have been cornered and caught in a bar during convention week. I stood. "We ready?"

"Let's go," the sergeant said.

I edged out of the booth, sideways, like a crab. Stood next to him.

He gave me a calculating look. "You don't scare easy, do you, sir?" he said.

"You have no idea," I replied.

CHAPTER 5

Two minutes later I was in the back of a white Crown Vic. Although the back seat was caged and I was securely restrained, two unarmed cops flanked me, wedging me in. They were both big boys. Bulky biceps strained against the sleeves of their dark brown uniform. Bulky to my lean. Gym muscles rather than natural.

Even though I was secure, they looked tense. Neither so much as glanced in my direction, which was curious. They'd just apprehended one of the top fugitives in the country. It was human nature to want to know what I'd done. All they did was stare straight ahead. I was either in the presence of the most unimaginative people on the planet or, more likely, they were under instructions not to engage with me. A theory that was easy to test out.

Since the sergeant with the Glock had first spoken, no one had Mirandized me. I wasn't under arrest, but I was clearly in their custody. There were subtle clues. I was in the back of a police car. I had handcuffs on. People had pointed weapons at me.

The drive to the sheriff's office took no more than ten minutes and I spent the time studying the terrain. I might have to run through it later. It was very rural. A lot of farms. A big wood. Might even have been a forest. Spring had its foot on the gas and the leaves were packed tighter than broccoli. A million shades of green.

The sheriff's office was in a town called Lyons. I'd walked through it the day before. It was affluent without being ostentatious. Like a lot of towns in America, it had started as a few dwellings either side of the highway and had grown in a linear fashion from there. It was a mile long but only a hundred yards wide. Probably insular in the way small towns are. More interested in discussing people than ideas. I hadn't seen any lawn signs, but I suspected when it came to local elections they were hotly contested, right down to the town dogcatcher. I eventually did see a lawn sign. Someone called David Reisinger was running for supervisor of soil and water conservation. The sign said he was the only person who would protect the town's soil.

"Which side of the fallow debate do you think Reisinger will land?" I asked. I wanted to see if they were under instruction not to engage with me. The deputies didn't answer, which kinda hinted at what they'd been told. "I'm all for leaving land to lay fallow. Good for the wildlife," I added. "How about you guys?"

Still nothing. Didn't even glance at me. Looked like they were making a point of it.

"Well, anyway, he's got my vote," I said before settling back in my seat.

The deputies continued to ignore me and we drove the rest of the way in silence.

The sheriff's office was a large white hexagonal building. Police buildings in wealthy rural counties don't have the throughput that the cities have, so tend to be well maintained.

Although I hadn't formally been arrested, processing someone from the road to the cell necessitated a two-way dialogue.

"Name," the sergeant behind the desk asked.

I said nothing. Giving a false name to a police officer is a criminal offense. Refusing to give one is not. I had no intention of confirming my name. Not until I figured out what was happening.

"Gonna have to search you, sir." It wasn't a request. There were a lot of deputies present, waiting for me to refuse. They didn't want someone like me in their town.

I was expertly frisked. Not an easy job when the perp's in handcuffs, but

I wasn't carrying anything other than a money clip and it didn't take long. The rest of my gear was in my backpack, which had been searched before we left Gosforth. My money was counted in front of me. Three hundred and twelve dollars.

The sergeant said, "I'm going to touch your hair. You're not going to do anything stupid are you?"

I said I wasn't. Checking a prisoner's hair for concealed weapons is standard practice. Needles and small knives can be hidden in hair. I'd even heard of a gun being hidden in a ponytail. But he didn't seem interested in what was in my hair, only in what was *underneath* it. He reached up and lifted the hair covering my forehead, saw my scar and grunted. Although the form on the counter was facing away from me, I watched him write "Ben Koenig" in the "Name of Detainee" section.

The scar hadn't been in the photograph they'd shown on TV. The injury had occurred after it had been taken. But they knew to look for it. To some people, my scar was better than an ID card.

"Welcome to Wayne County Sheriff's Office, Mr. Koenig," the officer said. "We'll take good care of you." He put the money into a cardboard evidence box, signed the seal, and placed it in the station safe.

They'd got their man. And no one had been hurt.

Good result for them, bad one for me.

CHAPTER 6

My cell was the cleanest I'd ever seen. It didn't smell like a toilet. The toilet didn't even smell like a toilet. The walls were graffiti-free. Bodily fluids hadn't been used for finger painting.

There was also a book. A dog-eared Stanley Kubrick biography. Kubrick had directed some of my favorite movies. Back in my old life I'd owned a signed first edition of *The Shining*, by Stephen King. Cost me almost ten thousand bucks, but fair exchange is no robbery.

I wondered if there was a fellow Kubrick fan in the building. In more pleasant times it would have been nice to talk. Maybe discuss his films over a couple of beers. And then I wondered if the Kubrick book being in the cell was a coincidence. I didn't like coincidences. They were a lazy man's explanation. They were the pea under my mattress. They bothered me.

Who had the influence to falsify the Most Wanted list? I'd been out of the game for six years and no longer knew who had access to it. The Lyons cops didn't realize it, but someone, somewhere, was pulling some serious strings.

I picked up the Kubrick book and started to read. I had just finished the chapter on *Full Metal Jacket*, a recap on how R. Lee Ermey, the Marine Corps drill instructor who Kubrick had brought in as a technical adviser, had ended up playing Gunnery Sergeant Hartman in the film, when a deputy looked in on me. Probably a welfare check.

I wondered if they would keep to a schedule. I glanced at the book. I'd read eighteen pages. I read roughly seventy pages an hour. Eighteen is almost 25 percent of seventy. Twenty-five percent of an hour is fifteen minutes. I went back to my book. When I'd read another seventeen pages, the hatch opened and the same face peered through. I waved but got no response. I read a chapter on *A Clockwork Orange*, and sure enough, bang on time, the hatch opened. I now had a way of measuring time.

After a couple of hours a menu was passed through the door. There was no pen or pencil. I figured I was to shout my order through the door. I scanned it and found a cheeseburger. I also found fries, a chocolate milkshake, and some tea. Pretty much the meal I'd left on the table in Gosforth. I walked to the door and spoke through the grille.

Never turn down calories.

A shuffling sound from the other side told me my order had been heard. I suspect they were relieved I was eating. Clearly I was a VIP.

Two welfare checks later and the cell door hatch opened. A face stared through the thick security glass. The glass opened, downward and out on an oiled hinge. A plastic tray was placed on the ledge on my side of the door. Before I could move off the bed, the hatch shut.

I walked over and stared at what was on my tray. I've been in jails all over the country, and the only consistent thing is the food. Greasy, cold, and salty. It's barely edible. But this burger was the real deal. Ten ounces of prime beef, real cheese, fried onions, and a relish with just the right amount of chili heat. Bacon so crispy it was like I was eating a salted fortune cookie. The fries were hot, and the milkshake was cold and made with real ice cream. The tea was dark brown, not milky.

I picked up the menu again. It *only* listed things I liked. A New York strip. Pecos River chili. But the kicker was the milkshake. There was only one flavor: chocolate. *My* flavor.

This wasn't just a menu. And it wasn't just a Kubrick book. It was a message. It said, "We know you."

But who was the messenger?

I'd just finished my meal when the cell door opened. A woman stepped in.

She wore jeans, leather boots with a small heel, and a plaid shirt. Her hair was fashionable but in a no-nonsense kind of way. The type of hair that's easy to fix in the morning. She was probably in her fifties. Her smile was deep, friendly, and reached her eyes. I figured she was the sheriff and that she'd probably been at the station for the entirety of my incarceration. She didn't look stupid. She knew this was unusual. Probably wished I wasn't in her cells, but now that I was, she'd make sure things were done properly.

"Good evening, Mr. Koenig."

I said nothing.

"I'm Sheriff Long," she continued, "and you *are* Ben Koenig." She stared at me for a moment longer than was comfortable, like she was deciding what to do next. She sat on the bed with me. I budged along to give her some space. "Do you want to know how I know?"

CHAPTER 7

Sheriff Long said, "As soon as we confirmed it *was* you in Gosforth, we printed off your apprehension instructions from the US Marshals site." She reached into her back pocket and pulled out a folded sheet of paper. "Do you want me to read them to you?"

My refusal to speak was starting to annoy even me. "Please," I said.

"They're in bullet points, so I'll just read them out as they are here. 'First: this man should be considered extremely dangerous but only'—and 'only' is underlined *and* in bold—'if he feels his life is threatened.'" She looked at me over the top of the page. "Is that correct? Are you a dangerous man, Mr. Koenig?"

I went back to not saying anything.

"'Secondly'—and this is a doozy—'you are not to arrest this man. He is to be detained only.'"

I stood. "I can go then?"

"Sit down, Mr. Koenig."

I sat.

Sheriff Long returned to her sheet. "Third bullet point: 'Ben Koenig might have valid credentials indicating he is someone else. Regardless of what this ID states, Ben Koenig has a one-inch scar above his right eye in the color of a fish bone.'"

She stared at me. Eventually I lifted up my too-long hair and showed her. She nodded and continued: "Number four: When you've detained Ben Koenig you are to call a federal number I'm not allowed to read out, and ask to speak to someone whose name I'm to keep to myself," she said. "I'm wondering why all the cloak-and-dagger stuff, but let me guess: You're saying nothing?"

"I've no idea," I said. It was true.

"I haven't called that number yet, Mr. Koenig, and I'm not sure I want to. Someone is using my department to circumnavigate due process, and I don't want truck with it."

If she was expecting me to agree, I did. Nonetheless, I said nothing.

"The last request is the strangest, and in all my time in law enforcement I've never seen anything like it. Not when I was with the FBI, not in my twenty-three years with the sheriff's department. When we detain you, we are to keep you secure, then give you something to read from a list of books and magazines they provided. Luckily there's a Stanley Kubrick fan in the building. Otherwise we'd have been ruining the bookshop owner's evening."

"And the food? I assume that was part of the last request as well?"

She nodded. "It was. Everything had to be from a PDF menu we had to download."

Which was really very clever of them.

"And what about the bullet point you've not mentioned?" I asked. "Probably number two on your list." The fact she didn't check her paper told me I was right. "The one that says on no account am I to be questioned."

She paused. "It's number three," she said eventually. "In between not arresting you and the scar." She held out her arms. The universal sign of openness.

"So why are you speaking to me?" I asked.

Her face flushed and her lips thinned. "Because, Mr. Koenig, I don't care what you've done. I'm not handing you over to anyone until I know why," she said. "And before you thank me, I have the department's reputation to uphold. Not everyone takes the Constitution seriously these days, but we do here. I'm not breaching it just because someone tells me I should."

I felt her anger, and there was no longer any reason to keep quiet.

As if she'd felt me wavering, she said, "Talk to me."

CHAPTER 8

There are unwritten rules to disappearing. Not using credit cards, bank accounts, cell phones, or anything else registered to your name are obvious ones. Others, like not using old email or social media accounts, are also common sense. Anything with a paper or electronic trail has to go.

If you need to leave without a big bang, then certain things should be done incrementally. If you're a frequent user of social media, become an *infrequent* user. Eventually, when you stop using it altogether, it won't seem like such a big deal. If you have a favorite restaurant or bar, then stop going every week. When you *do* leave your life, it'll be a while before anyone thinks to ask after you.

Moving quickly around the country can be difficult. Unless you have an ID that'll stand up to airport security, flying is out. For the same reason, hiring a car is dangerous. Trains are OK. Buses are better. Walking is best.

All commonsense precautions. Nothing a moderately intelligent person wouldn't think of.

But there are less obvious rules, and obeying them is the difference between long-term success and failure. To truly disappear, there are things that must be done. One of them is getting rid of as many of your photographs as possible. Hard copies and digital. Humans are surprisingly bad at remembering faces. Without visual reminders, people soon forget what you look like.

Destroying my photos was why the one on the news that evening was so old. It was the newest they had, though. The only other remaining photo of me was the one on my Massachusetts driving license, and that had been taken when I was sixteen years old. I was into punk rock then and had the spiky haircut to prove it. The photo they'd shown on TV only existed because I hadn't had admin rights on the mainframe where it was stored. If I had, I'd have replaced it with a picture of someone else.

"Talk to me," Sheriff Long had said. When I didn't, she proved she wasn't an idiot by saying, "Mr. Koenig, judging by our instructions, I don't think you're a fugitive—or if you are, you're not a run-of-the-mill one. I *did* think terrorism, but then it would've been Homeland Security, not the Marshals, we'd be dealing with. But someone sure wants you for something."

"I'm not a terrorist."

"Are you in WITSEC?

"I'm not in witness protection either."

"Have you committed a crime?"

"I almost resisted arrest earlier."

She nodded, like she already knew this. "We found some federally issued handcuffs in your backpack. The serial number says they're from a batch issued to the US Marshals. You want to explain why you have them?"

I didn't. I had my reasons for keeping those handcuffs, and the more people who knew what that reason was, the less use they became.

Sheriff Long shrugged and carried on. "I don't believe you stole them, Mr. Koenig. Given the unusual situation we're both in, I think that they were probably issued to you at some point. I think you're on the run and you have the handcuffs as a reminder of who you once were." She looked at me in expectation. "How am I doing?"

Time to give a little.

"Sheriff Long," I said, "my name *is* Ben Koenig, and I have no earthly idea why you've been asked to detain me. And you're right, up until six years ago I was a marshal. I was with the Special Operations Group. We were the ones who hunted the bad guys. The *really* bad guys." I paused. "And as I never actually resigned, it's entirely possible I still am with the SOG."

I gave her a potted summary of what I'd been doing up until I had to disappear. Not everything. I left out two key events: Gecko Creek and, three years before then, what happened after I'd gotten my scar. Only a handful of people knew about that.

It was a matter of national security.

CHAPTER 9

"Before we made the arrest—sorry, *detention*—I called a friend in the FBI," Sheriff Long said. "Asked him if he could find any record of you. He unlocked the archived file of one Benjamin Koenig, ex–United States marshal, for me."

"You shouldn't have done that," I replied. I might as well have not spoken.

"My friend told me that your record was one of the strangest he'd ever seen." After she'd let that linger, she continued. "He says that your entire career was carefully documented as per the US Marshals' human resources policies. The date you joined, the Special Operations Group training you'd completed, the operations you'd been involved with. Even when you took leave or had sick days." She paused. "Until you were shot in the—"

"Technically I wasn't shot," I cut in. "A bullet fragment got under my hel—"

"—head, that is," she continued, ignoring my interruption. "Then he says your record changed dramatically."

I didn't respond.

"It changes dramatically because it's virtually nonexistent. It's a black hole. In the three-year period between you being shot and you disappearing, there are huge gaps in your service record. They simply say 'other duties.' No explanation what those duties were. He totaled up the time you were on these 'other duties,' and he said it was almost two years. Two years out of three where your actions and whereabouts were unaccounted for. My friend says that type of thing is normally seen on the military records of special forces soldiers. 'Other duties' simply means active service overseas. Usually someplace we're not supposed to be."

She waited for me to respond. I didn't.

"I imagine this is all classified?" she said.

"Highly," I confirmed.

"But nothing illegal?"

"No."

"So what my unit's *actually* been asked to do is detain someone who has broken no laws."

"I'll be on my way then," I deadpanned.

But instead of telling me to sit tight, she surprised me. "Mr. Koenig, I'm satisfied you've broken no laws in my county and that you have no outstanding warrants. I am equally sure that if I were to detain you any further, I would be following an illegal order. As sheriff, I have a responsibility to the Constitution as well as my colleagues in federal law enforcement. I am going to release you, and on behalf of Wayne County I profusely apologize."

There was an attraction to leaving straightaway. Hike through the nearby mountains until I hit a road a long way from here. Pick up a ride, then decide what to do next. It was tempting. But I hadn't survived six years by taking the easy option. I needed to meet whatever was coming head-on, because despite what Sheriff Long had said about not calling it in—they were coming.

"I'm going to respectfully decline, Sheriff Long," I said. "Someone's gone to a great deal of trouble to find me. It would be rude not to see what they want."

"But they've treated you—"

I held up a hand. "Yes, they've been underhanded, and yes, they've probably broken umpteen laws, but there's self-preservation in this. Your guys knew what they were doing. The next bunch—because if I don't sort this out, there *will* be a next bunch—might not be so capable."

"I could make you leave," she said.

"You could," I replied. "But you won't."

"And why's that?"

"Because you're just as curious as I am about who's coming."

"OK. If you're sure, I'll make the call."

I smiled. She was a conscientious sheriff. But she didn't know the tricks of the trade when it came to tracking down fugitives.

"Don't bother," I said. "They're already on their way."

CHAPTER 10

"How can they already be on their way?" Sheriff Long said. "I assure you, no one from this office has called that number."

"You had to download the menu? Couldn't read it until you did?"

"They were the instructions," she replied.

"It was a SOG trap. Soon as it was opened, the team got a notification telling them when, where, and who. They'll have done a confirmation check in case it was nothing more than a bored cop passing time—"

"Nobody's checked with us, Mr. Koenig."

"Not with you, no. This is done on the QT. Standard procedure."

"SOG don't trust the police?"

"They track down mob bosses, Sheriff Long. They don't trust anyone."

"So, how?"

"I suspect it was the chocolate milkshake. The burger could just as easily have come from a bar. It could even have been made at home by someone, then brought in. Milkshakes, not so much. A chocolate milkshake would have to be sourced, and in this town, that means the diner. Someone will have called and asked whether an order containing a milkshake had been delivered to this building. Probably pretended they were coming off shift and needed to confirm the tab had been paid or something. Nothing that would draw attention."

"You used to do that?" She sounded doubtful.

I nodded. "Trust me. They're coming."

The first indication it wasn't the usual crew was the helicopter. Contrary to popular belief, the US Marshals Service does not have a fleet ready to rush agents anywhere at a moment's notice. They have a budget. When we had to travel, we got on a plane, and like every other public servant, we flew economy.

But a chopper had just landed. I don't have an ego, but when I hear hooves, I think horses, not zebras. If it *was* a marshal who'd just landed, they were assistant director level or above.

The second indication was the distinctive footsteps I heard approaching.

Left, right, click.

Left, right, click.

A man with a cane.

I knew of only one person with the authority to requisition a helicopter who also used a cane. The cell door opened, and the man I expected walked through: the United States Marshals Service director himself, my friend Mitchell Burridge.

Mitch was a straight shooter. He'd pushed us hard but played by the rules. Made sure we did the same.

But he'd made a desperate play and fixed the Most Wanted list to find me. It meant something was up.

Something bad.

CHAPTER 11

Mitch was the first Black man to head up the Marshals. He'd come over from the Secret Service twenty years earlier and had a well-deserved reputation for being both uncompromising and ferociously loyal. The guy in the chair before him had wanted to do the headline stuff, the photo op that would make page two of the *Washington Post*. He wanted his demonstration. Wanted to play the hostage role in the shoot house. Watch the guys breach the room, double-tap the bad guys. All action and testosterone. Pretty much what 99 percent of being in the Special Operations Group was *not* about.

Yes, the SOG had a forty-acre tactical training area, specialist ranges, rappel towers, helicopter landing pads, and an urban assault center; even had a warehouse with movable walls so we could vary its internal configuration to suit our needs. And yes, our facilities were better than those of most elite military units. We sent out SOG deputies to Marine Recon to train as snipers. But at the end of the day we were cops, not soldiers. And it was *because* we were cops the unit was needed. SEALs and Delta could do what we did—although we did it more often, so we were better at it, not that they'd ever admit it—but our Constitution doesn't allow soldiers to arrest civilians. Not without martial law being declared. And with the way criminals and terrorists and militias are arming themselves, the SOG *is* needed. I've never been in doubt about that. Sometimes overwhelming force is the safest option for everyone.

But Mitch had been different. Sure, he wanted to see what we were capable of, but not because he needed his ego stroked. He wanted to understand what we could and couldn't do. What our limitations were. I respected him from the moment we met. I trusted him and he trusted me. Came to love him like a father later. We all did. When you know the man at the top has your back, it makes the job a whole lot easier. It also mattered that Mitch had walked the walk. He wasn't an armchair pundit, commentating on a game he'd never played. He didn't talk about the bullet lodged in his hip, the one he'd taken protecting the secretary of state's son during a botched kidnap attempt, but we all knew it was still there. Burrowed in his bone like a wood weevil. It's one thing to say your job is to be a human shield, another to actually do it.

After I'd taken part of a bullet to the head, it had been Mitch who'd overruled the doctors. Allowed me to come back to work. Called in every favor he could so I didn't have to ride a desk.

What was so important he'd had to put me on the Fifteen Most Wanted list just to find me? He'd broken the law, almost certainly for the first time in his life.

He was my friend and I wanted to know why.

Mitch limped into the cell, put his cane against the wall, and sat down on the chair. He turned to Sheriff Long and the deputy who had walked him in. "Could I have a word in private with Ben please?"

Sheriff Long left without looking back. I never saw her again.

"What's up, Mitch?" I said. "Do I owe the coffee fund some money?"

I was a little embarrassed. I hadn't told him that I was leaving. One day I was there, the next I wasn't. Considering what he'd done for me, he'd deserved more. An email, a phone call, even a postcard. He was an intelligent man. He'd have known who had been behind my disappearance. He'd have looked for me. Probably had markers everywhere. And each time a corpse washed up on the beach or someone with concrete boots was recovered from a lake, he'd have sent over my prints, just in case.

I should have let him know I was alive. It would have been the right thing to do. But I hadn't. I hadn't let anyone know.

Mitch didn't respond, just stared at me. He was good at this. He'd perfected the technique over the years. He had a knack for making people feel uncomfortable. When he finally broke the silence, you would feel a rush of gratitude. I knew what he was doing, but I still wasn't immune to it.

"Mitch, come on, tell me."

"Why didn't you come to me, Ben?" he said eventually.

CHAPTER 12

SIX YEARS EARLIER, GECKO CREEK, COLORADO

It was a raid just like any other. We weren't complacent, though. The Special Operations Group didn't get complacent. The people we hunted didn't reward complacency.

We'd watched the house for two days. One of our surveillance experts had placed a bug on one of the windows. Disguised as bird shit, it was a trick of the trade. Eyes on the outside and ears on the inside was good intel. We'd certainly worked with less.

The raid was intentionally low-profile. The gang inside had evaded arrest for so long because they were careful. Outside of the FBI, and now the SOG, no one else in law enforcement knew they existed.

The information we'd been given was strictly need-to-know.

Terrorism would be the usual reason for such a level of secrecy, but these men were no terrorists. Not unless it was terrorism against humanity. Do this job long enough and you think you're immune to the things people will do to each other. This gang was the exception that proves the rule.

I'd heard of gangs who snatched children for the sex trade. For human slavery. Even to fulfill orders made by pedophiles. And everyone knows about pitting animals against each other for money. Dog- and cockfighting.

Badger- and bearbaiting. You name an animal, and someone, somewhere, is trying to make it fight another animal.

But I'd never heard of anyone pitting children against dogs. To the death. It took a special kind of sickness to come up with an idea like that. They called themselves a "special events company." These fights weren't open to the public. They weren't open to the criminal and underground betting fraternity. Your average criminal—even those working in the dogfighting industry—was going to balk at children being ripped apart by a pit bull.

No, this was a bespoke service provided for a very specific clientele. The fights—if you could really call a child of five going up against a starved dog a fight—were only viewable on the internet and were pay-per-view, livestreaming events. Not the thirty bucks we might pay to watch an evening of boxing. More like three hundred grand. For something that lasted less than a minute, I'd imagine.

The FBI had stumbled upon the activity of some its citizens when they were prosecuting yet another Ponzi scheme. The megalomaniac running it, terrified of jail time, threw the FBI a juicier bone. He'd heard of the gang and knew someone who might be able to give them more. A six-month investigation led the FBI to that black hole of depravity: the unregulated dark web. Suicide sites, child pornography, guns, drugs, contract killers, and now, it seemed, pay-per-view child-snuff events.

Posing as a potential customer, the lead officer had been shown a sample film, a snarling dog in a makeshift pit and a terrified child about to be dropped in. Mercifully for the FBI agent, the film stopped at that point. The gang didn't want to show anything that couldn't be explained away as a prank. Or, more importantly, anything that would sate the depraved urges of the potential buyer. The key code to the next live event would follow confirmation of payment. As it was livestreaming, there was nothing incriminating on any computer. If anyone was caught, the best the tech-heads would be able to do was prove that something had been watched and that it had cost them a lot of money. There'd be no way to prove *what* had been watched, what had been paid for. For a successful prosecution, the gang would have to be caught in the act.

The investigation eventually presented information to a special grand jury, indictments were handed down, and federal arrest warrants issued.

After three months of fruitless searching, the request for SOG involvement had arrived on my desk.

Unsurprisingly, the gang didn't stay in the same place for long. One event and they moved on. This was the first time we'd been in the same city at the same time. Normally, we were at least one event behind.

A man called David Placke was in charge. He traveled everywhere with a brutal bit of muscle called Knox. The FBI assumed those weren't their real names. We'd identified three more voices inside the building. At least five men. Two had arrived yesterday. All intelligence pointed to an event that week. Construction work had been heard. Best guess was that a fighting pit was being built. Common sense suggested they wouldn't want it up for long—why risk the exposure? As soon as it was ready, the event would happen. They'd dismantle it, dispose of anything left of the child, and move on to another city. Maybe even another country.

But where was the child? When were they expecting the "package," as they called it? With everything set up inside, the FBI believed they had enough for convictions on every indictment. They didn't need to catch them in the act. But if there was a child out there, I wanted to know he or she was safe before we went in. I didn't want them being used as a bargaining chip.

We'd been listening for forty-eight hours and all we'd heard was the five adult males. And the dog. A poor thing living its last few hours in abject misery. Regularly tormented and starved of food. Occasionally it howled.

The marshal on the ears we'd planted was a woman called Jen Draper. She'd been with the unit for nearly three years, arrived not long after I'd been shot.

I didn't like Jen. Never had. There was just something about her, something not quite right. Like watching a nature documentary narrated by someone other than David Attenborough. That was OK, though, as she didn't like me right back. I thought she was bad-tempered and aloof, and she thought I was conceited and arrogant. In all the time I'd known her, I'd never seen her smile. Not even once. She never attended the team socials and for the most part she kept herself to herself. Do that in a tight-knit crew like the SOG and you get a rep as a poor team player. She seemed to look down on us. I'd tried to get her transferred out on a number of occasions, but Mitch wouldn't hear of it. Said it wasn't something he was prepared to negotiate.

Still, no one could dispute her skills. She was intelligent, deadly with a weapon, and fitter than any man I'd ever met. She was also one of the bravest marshals I'd ever met. Fearless.

I still thought she was an asshole, though.

Without warning, Jen waved her hand to get everyone's attention, before signaling for silence. She shut her eyes and concentrated on the sounds in her headphones.

Everyone froze.

Her eyes snapped open. She looked at me and said, "The child's already here."

I shook my head. It was impossible. We'd have heard something. No child stayed quiet for two solid days.

Jen said, "I've just heard them say they're ready. Someone called Carl was told to wake up the package. I think they've been keeping her doped up. Someone's just mentioned a shot of adrenaline."

My lips flattened. "Shit!"

The team were at the staging area, practicing on a mocked-up version of the floor plan. Portable wooden frames and burlap sacks for walls. Not ideal, but at least it gave an idea of the building's layout. A sense of perspective. I raced over and yelled for their attention.

They gathered around me.

"We're going in now," I said.

Like most elite units, we lifted our breach techniques straight from the British SAS, still the most highly trained special forces in the world. Mitch had sent me to train with them for three months. Their mantra was "Speed, Aggression, Surprise." You go in fast, you make a lot of noise, and you don't tell them you're coming.

As far as I was concerned, the gang had waived their Fourth Amendment protections against unreasonable searches the moment their horrific scheme was hatched. We'd successfully applied for a no-knock warrant, and Mitch had authorized the use of stun grenades.

There were two doors, and I had a four-marshal team on each. One marshal would blow off the door hinges—never the lock—with breaching shells. The 40-gram projectiles, made of powdered steel and bound with wax, would destroy the hinges, then disperse without endangering anyone. As soon as the door was open, the remaining three marshals would breach the house. The shotgunner would ditch his weapon, unsling his Heckler & Koch MP5K, and follow them in to complete the four-person assault team.

Two more marshals covered each window. When the first breaching round was fired, they'd smash the glass and throw in stun grenades. Add to the cacophony of noise and terror we wanted. It was a one-story dwelling, so we didn't need the breach ladders.

I completed a quick radio check, made sure everyone was in position, then joined the team breaching the front door. We crouched together tightly. I was at the back, the front of my right knee pressing into the back of the knee of the man in front of me. Jen was in the number one position. She always was. Being this close together was tactical. It meant we occupied the smallest space possible. More importantly, it removed all doubt. When that door opened, the laws of kinetic energy meant that when I moved forward, *everybody* moved forward. No one could hesitate. They were going in that room whether they liked it or not.

I sensed the tension in the marshal in front of me. He was called Al and he was a good man. He wouldn't let me down. Nerves were normal in situations like this.

I was completely calm. And that was normal for me.

I asked for a final click-check over the comms system and received the right number back.

We were ready.

One of the golden rules of breaching a building is that the longer you are outside, the more chance there is of being discovered. I pulled on my respirator and helmet, and whispered into the built-in mic, "Doors. Move now."

The men with the shotguns in each team had three seconds to move into position. I watched the marshal on my door as he raised his Mossberg 590 combat shotgun. He pressed the muzzle tightly against the door where the top hinge would be. The marshal on the rear door would be doing exactly the same.

"On my three. One, two, three, go."

BOOM!

BOOM!

BOOM!

Six more rounds followed. Nine in total. Three at the top hinge, three at the middle, three at the bottom. No door withstands that.

I felt the noise and shock of the breaching rounds through my gas mask's built-in earpieces. Shouts and screams mingled with the smash of glass. The windows had been breached as well.

The shotgunner kicked in the door, then stepped back to let Jen throw in a stun grenade. I shut my eyes and covered my face with my arm. The M84 stun grenade emits a flash brighter than twenty million candles. Shutting your eyes isn't enough. I still saw the blinding light when it went off. It was disorientating, but that was nothing compared to the bang: 180 decibels. The noise-dampening ear defenders we all wore could only do so much. It seemed to be coming from inside my head.

Still, it was bearable. I was still standing and thinking.

I waited for more of the window grenades to go off.

Six stun grenades in all. Overkill? Probably. I didn't care.

In the enclosed space of the building, the stun grenades would be debilitating. Everyone inside would have flash blindness, confusion, and loss of balance due to inner ear disturbance. They would be staggering around like 1 a.m. drunks.

For at least five seconds. Fifteen if we were lucky.

"GO! GO! GO!" I yelled into the mic.

With Jen leading, we piled into the house. The doorway—known as the "fatal funnel" as it focused attention at the point we were most vulnerable—was cleared immediately. As soon as we were in the first room, like the well-oiled machine we were, we took up positions that allowed our over-lapping arcs of fire to dominate the room.

We were screaming "US Marshals!" but the stun grenades made it doubtful anyone would have been able to hear or understand us. The first room was empty.

Jen peeled left, the second marshal right. The fourth marshal and I moved forward, weapons at our shoulders. A man staggered in. He couldn't see us. He couldn't see anything. I grabbed him and, spinning him round to disorientate him even further, hurled him outside, where the perimeter team would secure him. The room was empty again.

"Front room clear, one hostile neutralized," I shouted into my mic. "Moving in."

At the same time a voice crackled in my ear. "Kitchen clear!"

There were still four men inside.

I heard a bang. A weapon had been discharged. I was about to ask for a sit-rep when a window marshal came on to the air. "Bedroom two. Target down." If one of the gang entered, the window marshals were authorized to take them down using nonlethal rounds. Bedroom two was our team's responsibility.

"Jen, Al, go and get him," I said.

They were already in the hallway, so I couldn't see them, but I knew they'd immediately detour to bedroom two and secure the target with plasticuffs. The window marshals couldn't enter the house. There were eight of us inside, and we all knew where we were meant to be. The last thing we needed was a random ninth. That was how blue-on-blue happened.

Ten seconds later and Jen's voice came into my earpiece. "Bedroom two, target secure. It's not Placke."

Three left. Placke was still inside somewhere.

The shotgunner and I moved into bedroom one. It was empty. "Bedroom one secure," I told everyone.

Three men left and only one room. We'd called it the den. It was a room off the kitchen. It had no windows.

The two assault teams converged on the door.

"My team goes in, team two secures the doorway," I said.

Without further instructions, Jen and Al took the same positions as they'd done when we breached the front door. It would be the same drill as before. Team two moved to give us the room we needed.

I'd have normally called for the shotgun again, but there was a child inside and the internal door looked flimsy. I wouldn't ask anyone else to go through first in this situation. Opening a door knowing armed criminals are the other side was the most dangerous thing we did.

I stepped back and ran. I hit the door with my shoulder, and it flew off its hinges. The forward momentum caused me to fall into the room. A stun grenade followed me in. I didn't have time to cover my eyes with my arm and the flash was blinding. The team stomped all over me as they rushed the room. I could only hear what was going on.

Two gunshots, close together, rang out.

"Hostile Three down! It's Knox."

Jen again. She was having quite the day.

Knox. The henchman. Out of the equation. Two more to go.

The sound of a handgun. A member of the team grunted. He'd been hit. I felt the thud as he hit the floor. Hopefully his body armor would do its job and he'd have nothing more than purple bruises and a story to tell. The unit was too well trained to stop and help. Not until the room was secure.

A sound of a scrabble. Men grunting in my earpiece. Eventually one of them called, "Hostile One down. Weapon secure." Al was getting in on the act. Hostile One was Placke. I couldn't tell if he'd been restrained or killed. It didn't matter.

Not yet.

There was one to go.

And we still hadn't located the child.

I opened my eyes. My vision wasn't great, but I could see enough. The room was smoky. A by-product of the stun grenades. I searched for the last hostile, the one the FBI hadn't been able to identify.

I was still on the ground and could see the makeshift fighting pit. A dog's head appeared intermittently as it jumped. It was howling in fear, little more than a canine psychopath.

A movement in my peripheral vision caught my attention.

A young man, possibly still in his teens. He must have been standing next to the grenade when it went off. Blood flowed from his ears and his eyes were clamped shut. He was staggering wildly.

He was holding the child.

A small blonde girl.

Two more steps and he'd stumble into the side of the dog's enclosure. The plywood walls were about three feet high. He might fall in, he might not. He'd certainly drop the girl. Probably into the dog pit.

Jen realized what was happening at the same time. She raised her MP5, but Al walked into her line of fire. He hadn't seen the hostile and was still scanning the room. She screamed at him to get down, but it was going to be too late.

The guys at the door didn't have the angle.

Sometimes in life, time freezes. Decisions that will be scrutinized for months come down to a fraction of a second's instinct.

I was the one who could save the child.

The *only* one.

Muscle memory took over. I raised my Heckler & Koch, breathed in, held my breath to keep myself steady. The Marshals taught me to aim for the center mass of a suspect, but I'd had subsequent training that superseded that. *Specialist* training. I aimed high and squeezed the trigger, didn't fight the recoil and came back for a second. Both 9-millimeter Parabellums hit their mark. One below the man's right eye and one on the bridge of his nose. Dark red blood sprayed the wall behind him. A classic double tap to the head. Instant death.

The young man fell to the floor. The girl fell on top of him. She began to scream. She was safe.

It was over.

Not *quite* over.

After the FBI had taken over—it was now their crime scene—I grabbed a chance to look around. One of our guys had taken the dog away, first to find a vet, and then, if the traumatized dog could be rehabilitated into a pet, to stay with him. He lived in the mountains, so space wasn't an issue. I was glad. I'd always liked dogs.

The fighting pit it had been kept in was a portioned-off part of the room. Four cameras were set up and running. We'd got there with seconds to spare. A tech was already trying to backtrace links. Seeing if he could identify the IP addresses of anyone who'd paid to watch. I wished him luck.

The agent in charge shook my hand. "Your marshal's going to be fine, I hear?"

I nodded. The man who'd been shot was already up and refusing medical attention like a Viking. I'd go out and tell him not to be stupid in a minute. I needed to take in everything about the crime scene. If I ever had nightmares because I'd killed that young man, I wanted this scene fixed in my mind. They'd been murdering children for money. The naivete of youth doesn't excuse everything.

I'd sleep fine tonight.

"You did well," the agent said before another fed called him over.

"Boss, I need you here a minute."

He'd been taking photographs of the scene and had gotten to the boy I'd shot.

I wandered over. I wanted to see his face. Just because it was justified, I didn't want it to seem normal. Everything about this was horrible. Humans are not supposed to kill other humans.

The boy was younger than I'd thought. The bullet holes were less than an inch apart. Dark blood oozed out of both.

"You were on the floor, right?" the lead agent said. "Lying on your side?"

I nodded.

"And he was moving."

I nodded again.

"Damn, that's good shooting."

I'd taken a life. It was nothing to be proud of.

Then the agent chronicling the scene announced what would become the defining moment of my life.

"Boss, you ain't gonna believe who this dead kid is . . ."

CHAPTER 13

Of course, at the time I didn't know it *was* the defining moment of my life. That would come later. Three days later. Three days after I shot the boy, I'd be given a choice. And much like the choice I'd had then, it was no choice at all.

"Why didn't you come to me, Ben?" Mitch repeated.

I blinked in surprise. "I'm sorry," I said. I'd been miles away. Transported back in time and place. I shook my head. I needed to focus. "You knew?"

"I head up a federal agency," he said. "Of course I knew."

"Then you know exactly why I couldn't go to you. Why I couldn't go to anyone."

He shook his head. "Wrong. It was a SOG problem, not a Ben Koenig problem. It wasn't something you had to do on your own. You didn't have to go all Jack Reacher on us."

"A problem shared?"

Mitch took a silent moment. Then he said, "I never stopped looking for you, Ben. You know that, right?"

I didn't respond. It didn't make sense. Not Mitch looking for me. That made perfect sense. If it had happened to one of my guys, I'd have never stopped looking either. What didn't make sense was why he'd chosen to use the Most Wanted list now. Why wait six years to press the button? What had changed?

Answer: Something was wrong. Something big. Mitch was trying to appear calm, but I'd known him long enough to know something was worrying him. His right foot bounced up and down like there were ants in the cell. He'd picked up his cane and was wringing the stem. And there was something else. The Most Wanted list was always fifteen. Never sixteen, never fourteen. So for me to be put on the list, someone else had to be removed from the list.

It didn't add up. It was illogical.

It wasn't a national emergency. If it were, Mitch wouldn't have come personally. He wouldn't have had the time. A senior deputy would have collected me and taken me to him. If it was something big enough to bring me in by any means possible, then it was big enough to chain Mitch to his desk.

That meant it was personal. It was about him, or someone he was close to.

I studied his face. Tried to read him. The award-winning bags under his eyes were bigger than I'd ever seen them. His shirt collar was loose, and his suit, despite being tailored in London's Savile Row, wasn't fitting right. He was tired and he had lost weight. I wondered if he was ill. He used to weigh 250 pounds, and even with part of that slug lodged in his hip, he had boxed every weekend. Now he looked gaunt.

"What's wrong, Mitch?"

Tears formed in the corner of his eyes. He made no move to wipe them away. He looked down, composed himself, and looked back up.

"Ben, Martha's missing."

CHAPTER 14

The man in the yellow suit had six cell phones, and it took him a moment to work out which one was ringing. It was the phone with only one number programmed. It rang so infrequently he wasn't surprised he didn't recognize the ringtone. He frowned before pressing the receive button. Nothing good ever happened when this phone rang.

He put the phone to his ear but said nothing.

"He's taken a helicopter to Shitsville, New York," the voice at the other end said.

Ignoring the crudeness, the man in the yellow suit said, "Do we know why?"

"We don't. We were lucky to get the flight plan. The pilot's on our pay-roll, but he's not party to whatever's happening."

"Can we get eyes on him?"

"Depends. He might leave before we get there. It's a long way and we have no one useful close. It's a mom-and-pop-store, white-picket-fence kinda town."

"OK. Get someone there ASAP. If he has moved on, he'll have left some bread crumbs."

"Will do. You think it's about us?"

"You don't have children, do you?" the man in the yellow suit asked.

"I don't, no."

"Because if you did, you'd know he'll never stop. Not ever. So yes, I *do* think this is about us. He's getting desperate."

"Fair enough. But she has no link to the town as far as we can tell."

"That's what worries me. I don't like unknown variables."

"He's just one man. He may be some big shot in Washington, but that don't mean shit out here."

For the second time in as many minutes, the man in the yellow suit frowned. Some things, no matter how trivial-sounding, shouldn't be said over the airwaves. Any idiot could eavesdrop on cell phone conversations these days. A few bucks' worth of equipment and you were good to go.

He snapped the cell shut without answering and steepled his fingers. The girl had been a mistake. He knew that now.

Still, the people who worked for him were the best at what they did.

If there *was* a threat, they'd neutralize it.

He wasn't worried.

CHAPTER 15

Cash is king when you live off the grid. You need more than just a fold-up toothbrush. You need a stash and you need to be able to access it without setting off alarm bells. Fortunately, there's a simple answer. When I left my old life, I formed an international business corporation, a kind of offshore company that preserved the confidentiality of the beneficiary. I was the sole shareholder. I transferred all my assets—not that there was much—into the IBC, then issued myself a company bank card. As the shareholders and directors weren't publicly listed, it couldn't be checked, and I could therefore get to my cash whenever I needed. I withdrew the maximum amount possible each time I was at an ATM, and only ever did it when I was ready to leave town. All ATMs have cameras. Any town I withdrew cash from was one I never planned to return to.

The *other* thing my IBC owned was a safety-deposit box. Somewhere to store my driver's license and my passport. My birth certificate and a few photos I couldn't bear to part with. My parents and my sister. Pretty much the last bits of evidence that proved I was still Benjamin Koenig. It was to the safety-deposit box Mitch and I were heading. If I was going to search for Mitch's daughter, then I needed the option of getting on a plane, and that meant photo ID.

* * *

I'd met Martha Burridge several times. She'd visited the SOG barracks with Mitch on some sort of "what my daddy does" project for school. Occasionally I'd been forced to attend Washington functions hosted by various agencies, and after the death of his wife, Mitch occasionally took Martha with him. She'd also visited me in the hospital after I'd been shot.

She was a vivacious young woman and I'd liked her. The whole unit had. She was charming, witty, and not in the least bit stuck-up because her father was an important man. She was in her early teens but mature for her age, the way kids sometimes get when they lose a parent early. Like Mitch, she was intelligent and headstrong. She was studying forensic accounting at Georgetown now, hoping to follow in her father's early footsteps and join the Secret Service. I had no doubt she'd be successful. Some gene pools spawn high achievers.

But now she was missing. Had been for nearly two months, according to Mitch. And when the daughter of the director of a federal agency goes AWOL, people sit up and take notice. None of the usual "there's a mandatory waiting period: file a report and get in line." It's taken seriously.

"What's been done so far?" I asked. We were in the helicopter. It was flying low and hard. Mitch had been briefing me.

"What you'd expect," he replied. "Every three-letter agency's taking an interest. Metro PD has taken it on officially, and the FBI are involved in case it's a kidnapping or related to WITSEC. Everyone else is on board with information sharing. No one wants to think families are in play now."

I nodded. It made sense. If Martha had fallen to foul play, then the cops needed in on it. At a local level, their intel is unmatched. Likewise, the FBI is better at the bigger-picture stuff. Kidnappings and extortion are routine for them. If Martha had been taken across state lines, then it was a federal matter anyway. Might as well be there at the beginning.

"You've told the AG," I said. It was statement, not a question. Other than how he'd tracked me down and what he'd arranged after I'd taken part of a bullet to the head, Mitch usually played it straight. If a marshal was compromised, they were obliged to tell their boss. In Mitch's case, that was the attorney general. His access levels to sensitive material would have been immediately downgraded. Not to the point he couldn't access it, but so that when he did, people would know. It was for his protection just as much as the agency's.

Mitch nodded to confirm he'd told the AG.

"So," I continued, "the people who have taken Martha either didn't know you'd do that, or they didn't care."

He knew where I was headed. I wasn't ready to call it yet, though. Instead I veered into safer territory. "What are our guys doing?"

This was where it would get interesting. The SOG hunts fugitives. It doesn't have much of an investigative role. It's the FBI and the police who investigate kidnappings. Officially, there was no role for the SOG.

Officially.

Unofficially there were things they could do. They had their own intelligence network. Favors could be called in. Snitches could be leaned on. Rumors chased down. And they were *the* experts in surveillance. Sometimes spending months staking out a property a fugitive might use as a safe house.

But none of that needed my expertise.

The SOG isn't, and never will be, a one-man band. Being in the unit is like having your hand in a bucket of water. When it is in the bucket, it is all encompassing, it is all you can think about, but take your hand out of the bucket and it is as if it had never been there. When I disappeared, the next one in line took command. Equally as competent, if not quite as uniquely trained.

And they are an incredibly loyal bunch. Loyal and *proud*. No way did some scumbags get to take the boss's daughter. They'd have been running off-the-book investigations from the moment they heard.

"They've been doing what they can," Mitch said carefully. "But you know how it is. Even for someone like me, there's only so much that can be done. There's no gold service. Everyone gets the same."

I nodded. It was true. It didn't matter who it was, once someone was missing, it was the same agencies doing the same thing. The only difference was how much media attention it received.

"Tell me what you know," I said. Mitch had already handed me a file, but it lay on my lap, unopened.

He sighed and for the first time looked every inch of his sixty years.

"Nothing, Ben. And that's the problem. We have no leads at all. She called me to say she wasn't coming home for spring break. She had some research to do for a paper she was working on. That was two months ago. I didn't think anything of it. She's fiercely independent; has been ever since her mom died."

"Who pressed the button?" I'd asked.

"I did. Her dipshit academic adviser called to ask why she hadn't come back to college. By then nearly a month had passed and the trail was cold."

Mitch was right. A month was too long. Witnesses have forgotten things. Alibis have been bought and fully rehearsed. Forensic evidence is lost. I opened the file and found it full of names and dates. Courses she attended. Clubs she was part of. The names of her roommates and professors. Solid information, but nothing I couldn't have got from Georgetown's admissions office. Still, it was more than I had five minutes ago. I settled down to study and memorize the file's contents.

When I finished, I handed it back. "What do you want from me, Mitch?"

I knew, but needed him to say it.

Color returned to his cheeks and his breath quickened. "Find her, Ben!" He slammed his fist into the side of the helicopter, hard enough for the pilot to turn round to see what the noise was. I glared at him until he went back to flying us east. It was the only direction I'd given him. He'd get the actual destination when we were closer.

"You're an apex predator, Ben," Mitch said, "and I put you through three years of hell for something exactly like this. It's badges-in-the-drawer time."

I nodded. It was what I'd been afraid of.

"I want you to speak to the people who won't speak to the FBI, do the things that they can't," he said. "If she's still alive, you might be the only chance she has."

In the pit of my stomach, I knew she was dead. I knew Mitch knew it too. We'd been marshals long enough to know abduction victims didn't get returned after two months. Not unless it's a protracted kidnapping case. When Mitch said "find her," he meant recover her body. He wanted to lay her next to her mother.

He continued, "If you find the men who had my baby, Ben, you don't hesitate. You do what you have to do. You hear?"

"I hear you, Mitch." He was already referring to her in the past tense.

He stared at me. Looked deep into my eyes. He'd always been able to read me and I knew he was looking for resolve. After a moment he nodded, satisfied. "Then God help them," he said.

It was still dark when we arrived at Bottesford. A field full of sleeping cows woke up in all kinds of a hurry when the Bell 206 JetRanger landed next to them. I'd only told the pilot we were landing a minute before.

"Think Farmer Bob's only getting cheese this morning," I said as we disembarked, trying to lighten the mood.

Mitch replied with an unintelligible grunt.

The pilot wanted to stay with the helicopter. Mitch started walking off. I stayed where I was. He returned.

"What's up, Ben?"

Jerking my thumb at the pilot, I said, "You trust him?"

"Hey, man. Not cool," the pilot protested.

I shut him up with a look. He was a short man with fat arms. Had a bald patch on the top of his head. Probably caused by wearing a helmet all day. It made him look like Friar Tuck.

"Been with me on a few journeys," Mitch replied. "Yeah, I trust him." I didn't.

"Hand over your cell phone," I said to the pilot.

"What the hell?"

Mitch smiled grimly. "I'd do what he asks, if I were you."

The pilot blanched and handed it over without another word. "You get this back when Director Burridge gets back to DC," I told him. "Don't worry, we won't look at it."

Turning to Mitch, I said, "Is your return flight logged?"

He nodded.

"Good," I said, climbing into the cockpit. "You no longer need this then." I removed the hammer used to break windows in an emergency and smashed the radio to pieces.

I climbed back out.

Mitch gave me a look. "What the hell happened to you, Ben?"

We stumbled across the dark field to the road. We'd managed to land near Bottesford's town boundary, so it was only a short walk. It was before 6 a.m., and my bank didn't open until nine, but I knew a place we could go.

Bottesford is like many towns in America's Rust Belt. The heavy industry is long gone, but folks still call it a steel town or a mining town or an auto town . . . After the boom years, the industrial heartland of the nation had shrunk and decayed, the younger population had mostly fled to the coast or more cosmopolitan cities, and businesses had packed up and relocated. They left behind forgotten places. Shells of what they once were. The kind of towns Springsteen sings about. Once proud, now half empty. But there is *always* a diner, and it is always open.

For the second time in twelve hours, I was going to eat when I wasn't hungry. In the Wayne County Sheriff's Office, it had been for something to do; now it was because I didn't know what was going to happen next. Experience said that Martha would eventually be found by someone jogging or walking their dog, buried in a shallow grave or stuffed behind a dumpster. But until that happened, I would keep looking, and to do that I needed energy. The body is a machine, and until this was finished I'd be taking on fuel whenever I had the chance.

We entered Cripkee's on Main Street and took two of the spin stools at the counter. The old-fashioned diner was almost empty. The fluorescent glow spilling from the large windows illuminated the deserted streets, creating sharp angles on the road and the sidewalk. Reminded me of the late-night diner in *Nighthawks*, Edward Hopper's painting of solitude and loneliness.

The sound and smell of sizzling bacon was welcoming, though. I love bacon. Every time I have it, it's like I'm tasting it for the first time. My stomach rumbled. While we waited to be served, I turned and surveyed my surroundings.

The counter I was leaning on was the classic heavy-duty Formica laminate top. Metal-edged with a protective easy-clean finish. A selection of pies and doughnuts underneath clear plastic cloches. Probably there from the night before. The booths were covered in the same red faux leather as the bar in Gosforth. The floor tiles were black and white squares, fashioned in a diamond pattern. Everything was chrome and polished. If the griddle had been out front, it could have been the 1950s.

A trio of men in hard hats and steel-toed boots were seated in one of the booths. Their faces were grimy and they looked tired. They were all about the same age: late fifties, early sixties. I figured they'd just come off shift somewhere. Having coffee and breakfast in the diner so they didn't wake their wives.

A waitress came out from the kitchen. She flipped open her notebook and fixed us a tired smile.

"What can I get y'all this morning?" she asked, handing over two laminated menus. She set down two mugs and filled them with black coffee.

Mitch left his menu on the counter. "Just the coffee," he said.

"No appetite, honey?" She didn't look disappointed. Either too tired or experienced enough to know that sour faces earn small tips.

She turned to me. "Just the coffee for you as well, hon?"

Shaking my head, I said, "Scrambled eggs, bacon, sausage, hash browns, a short stack of pancakes, and all-you-can-eat toast please. And a pot of tea. English breakfast if you have it."

"That ain't gonna be a problem," she replied, writing everything down. She turned to Mitch and said, "Last chance, honey. You sure I can't get you something?"

He picked up his menu. "Goddamn it, Ben. Now I'm hungry. I'll have an egg-white omelet. No cheese."

We handed our menus across the counter and she disappeared into the kitchen again. I picked up a pack of sugar, shook it, and tore it open. "Still watching your cholesterol, Mitch?" I said as I poured it into my coffee.

"You will too, one day," he replied, tracing circles in some spilled coffee.

We fell into silence and stayed that way until our food arrived.

I speared a strip of perfectly crisp bacon and popped it into my mouth, relishing the explosion of salt. With Mitch stuck in another world, I bided my time eating. The waitress wandered over with the coffeepot and refreshed our mugs.

"Getcha anything else?" she asked. The question was clearly directed at me. Mitch didn't seem to be hearing or seeing anything at the moment.

"Chocolate milkshake, please," I replied. After she had returned to the kitchen, I swiveled on my seat and faced Mitch. "This is where we go our separate ways."

That got his attention. He turned and started to protest. "But—"

I held up my hand to stop him. It was time to talk about what we'd avoided before. "You know there are only three scenarios, right?"

I held up a finger.

"One: Whoever took her didn't know who she was and never found out. Got to tell you, Mitch, that's not good." I took a mouthful of pancake, chewed, swallowed, and continued. "But given the amount of time she's been missing, I don't think that's what happened."

"Why not?"

"Because if it was a random killing, a mugging gone wrong or something else horrible, then the chances of Martha's body remaining hidden are slim. Someone would have found it by now. Shallow graves don't remain shallow for long. Something always digs them up."

Mitch grunted and nodded. I wasn't telling him anything he hadn't already thought.

I held up a second finger. "Two: Whoever took her *did* know who she was and they had their reasons. Either revenge for something you did in the past, or some harebrained scheme to force a favor from you."

"And the third?" he asked.

I stared at the glistening fat hardening on my plate. "The third's a little bit of one and a little bit of two. Whoever took her found out who she was after she was taken."

"And Martha wouldn't have been backward in coming forward with that information," Mitch said.

I thought scenario three was just as bad as scenario one.

"Let's hope it's scenario two then," Mitch said. He picked up his coffee and took a sip. He grimaced and looked down into the mug. "Not sure why we're going our separate ways. I thought you'd want to start in DC. Go to Georgetown and see what's been missed."

"I do, and I will," I said. "But if I was involved in this and either knew, or found out, who Martha's daddy was, then I'd want eyes and ears on him. I'd want to know where he was and what he was doing at all times. We caught a break in Gosforth: It's a small town in the ass end of nowhere and you took a chopper. No way can they reach that far, and we weren't there long enough for them to get there before we left. But if someone *is* on the inside—and don't say it can't happen because we both know it can—then they'll get your flight plan eventually. Even if they don't, they'll be watching you like a hawk, and I don't want eyes on me yet. I'll make my own way there."

The waitress brought over my milkshake. It was in a tall glass, ice-cold with condensation dripping down the side. I tore the top off a paper straw and plugged it. Took a drink and sighed appreciatively. That first taste never got old.

There was still an hour until the bank opened, so I took out my notebook and asked for as much background information as Mitch could remember. The stuff that wasn't in the file. Thoughts, suspicions, any theories he or anyone else had. Unsurprisingly, with Mitch being ex–Secret Service and a current US marshal, there was a lot. I filled nearly half the pages. Most of it would be useless, but there's no such thing as having too much intelligence. There was always a chance he'd unwittingly given me the case's silver bullet. After an hour the information began drying up. I could tell it was becoming hard work for him. I snapped shut the notebook.

"That's enough for now. I can get anything else I need myself."

Nodding in appreciation, he drained his cup, looked at his watch, and said, "The bank should be open."

We both left a tip—not big, not small; we didn't want to be remembered—and Mitch paid the tab. As we walked to the bank, I told him what I needed. "Two cell phones, maxed-out credit-wise, one for me and one for you. Mine must be internet-enabled. No numbers to be stored in either and you're never to call mine."

He removed a small but ornate notebook from his inside pocket and jotted it down. "What else?" he said.

"I need a float. Ten thousand bucks." I gave him my numbered account. "I may need to travel and I can't worry about going over my credit card limit. You get back whatever's left at the end."

"At the end of what?"

I shrugged. "At whatever the end is, I guess."

"Anything else?"

"One last thing, Mitch," I said carefully. "You and Martha are like family to me. You know that, right? If you ask me, there isn't anything I won't do."

"I know that, Ben."

"I need to know how far you want me to go then," I said. "How far you're prepared to *let* me go."

He put his notebook back in his pocket. "I'll get right on this. By the time you've got what you need from the bank, the money will be in your account and I'll have a cell phone for you."

"Mitch."

He looked at me. "Do you remember the chat we had when you were in the hospital?"

"The one we had when I was at rock bottom? When I thought my career was over?"

He nodded.

"When I was so low I thought I only had two choices: riding a desk or eating my gun?

He nodded again.

"I'll never forget that, Mitch," I said. "For as long as I live, I'll never forgot what we talked about."

CHAPTER 16

Three years before Gecko Creek, I'd been on a raid that had gone south. I was in a room that had been cleared when a perp ran in, picked up a Kel-Tec hidden in a baby's crib, and managed to get a shot off before someone put him down. He'd missed me, but the bullet had ricocheted off an iron lintel above the door. It had hit me in the head. My tactical helmet had done its job and stopped most of it, but a small fragment had crept under the rim and embedded itself in my skull.

The surgeon removed the shrapnel easily enough, but the neurologist found a shadow she didn't like on the scan. She did a bunch of tests on my brain, then called it: I had a rare recessive genetic disorder called Urbach-Wiethe disease. I'd probably always had it. My right amygdala was calcifying and wasting away. There'd only ever been four hundred documented cases of Urbach-Wiethe.

The neurologist told Mitch it was the end of my career. Although Urbach-Wiethe doesn't lead to a reduced lifespan, one of the functions of the right amygdala is to control the body's reaction to dangerous situations. Virtually everyone with Urbach-Wiethe becomes hypersensitized to fear. *Everything* scares them. Eventually, they can't function in society. When the whole amygdala becomes calcified, they're too frightened to leave the house. The fear cripples them.

But on extremely rare occasions the opposite happens. Instead of becoming hypersensitized to fear, some people with Urbach-Wiethe become immune to fear. They don't feel it anymore.

The neurologist told Mitch that, after reading my service record, she believed that my ability to experience fear had been compromised for some time. It would have been gradual, so no one, including me, would have noticed. She didn't have a timescale, but eventually, I wouldn't feel fear at all.

That should have been the end of it. A man incapable of feeling fear is a liability, not an asset. I offered Mitch my resignation, but he told me no one injured in the line of duty got canned on his watch. He'd find a job for me somewhere, although my days in the field were over.

The thought of sitting at a desk had chilled me. It didn't matter what paper they put on it, I would never be able to sit still long enough to read it. I thanked him but said it was time to go. He'd been good to me and I didn't want this hanging over him. It wasn't his fault.

"We can't let this thing define you, Ben," he'd replied. "Give me a week before you make any decision. Let me speak to some people. See if there's anything we can come up with."

He was as good as his word.

To my surprise, he told me that as long as my condition remained unknown, there was no reason I couldn't carry on as before. He'd spoken to someone in Washington and had come to an agreement. As long as I accepted some safeguards—I'd stay unit commander, but someone would take over my risk-assessment duties—I could remain on active service.

"I'll run all my risk assessments past one of the guys."

"I'll assign someone," he'd replied. "Someone you don't already have a relationship with. Someone who'll tell you no when that's what you need to hear."

"Jacko is good. Might appreciate the chance to step up."

"I said *I'll* assign someone. Not having one of your buddies rubber-stamping whatever you decide. I need someone who'll challenge your thinking. I'll send an email telling the team that it's due to workload commitments."

"OK," I'd sighed. "As long as they're a team player."

"And you have to receive extra training. This isn't just for my benefit,

Ben. It's for yours too. A man with no fear isn't just a danger to others, he's a danger to himself. There's a risk you might forget who you are, what you stand for." He paused.

"What?" I asked.

"It's important you realize that your condition has limitations as well as advantages," he'd said. "The doctors all tell me you've been seeing nothing but green lights for a while now. I need you to understand that there will be times when everyone else sees red. And most of the time, ninety-nine percent of the time, you need to learn how to see red too."

"And the rest of the time?"

"Someday we may need those skills. If it's green-light time, I think you'll know. It's a package deal, Ben: Accept oversight in the field and undertake specialist training. Take it or leave it."

I took it.

Over the next three years, I'd spent almost two of them away from the Tactical Operations Center. I spent time with other organizations. I'd lived, trained, and worked with them. I learned close-target reconnaissance with Marine Recon. Operating in denied areas with the Navy SEALs. Advanced demolition, lock-picking, and close-quarters battle marksmanship with Delta. Specialist breaching and hostage-rescue techniques with a saber squadron of the British SAS. I spent two months in a Detroit emergency room. Instead of the battlefield medicine I'd been taught, I learned how to go into wounds and close them off. I even went to Israel for a month. Spent time with Kidon, the secretive Mossad unit responsible for black ops, learning combat point shooting and, presumably so I'd know what to look out for, "targeted killing techniques," a technical way of saying assassinations.

And every now and then I'd have to go to the Walter Reed National Military Medical Center for a battery of medical and psychological assessments. At the end of each checkup, I'd be given the all-clear and sent on my way.

None of it was pleasant, but it sure beat working behind a desk.

"This is it, Ben," Mitch said, tearing me from my thoughts. "This is what all those years were for. All the money we spent, all the favors we called in."

He still hadn't answered my question. I wondered if he was avoiding it.

I wasn't leaving until I knew how far Mitch was willing to let me go. Just how far was *too* far for someone with my training?

"Mitch?" He knew what I was referring to. I could tell.

It was Mitch the father, not Mitch the agency director, who answered. "If they've crossed that line, if my baby girl is dead, then there's no reprieve. No second chances. They don't get to explain it away as an accident. Do you understand? You provoke a reaction. Make them point a gun at you, Ben." He held my eyes. Didn't waver. "And when they do, you fucking kill them."

CHAPTER 17

I thanked the woman who'd escorted me to the safety-deposit box vault. She waited outside while I emptied the box's contents into my backpack. Bank cards, passport, money, photographs. Few other bits and pieces that proved I was Ben Koenig. I considered asking her to close my account but didn't for two reasons: It still had four years on it—the ten-year lease had been the best fit for my budget and needs—and, more importantly, if Mitch's movements *were* being monitored and they somehow found out about me, I wanted them stretching their resources watching the bank. Shutting the account gained me nothing. In tactical situations every advantage counts.

I returned to the street and walked down the block to meet Mitch. He'd promised to be finished before me, but the small matter of transferring $10,000 had taken longer than anticipated. Eventually he joined me. He handed me a cell phone and a bit of paper with the number of the other one he'd bought. I committed it to memory and destroyed it.

I hadn't owned a phone since I'd disappeared and I wasn't thrilled to have one now. Six years ago, I'd been like everyone else in America. My world had existed through that small black screen. It was the last thing I looked at before I fell asleep, and it was the thing that woke me. It was my personal assistant. It was my calendar, my encyclopedia, and my email system. All my communication had been done through it, and I was contactable twenty-four hours a day.

Mitch must have noticed my expression. He reached across and gripped my shoulder, looked me in the eyes, and nodded, as if to say, "Sorry." He handed me a manila envelope and said, "The ten K's in your bank and ready to use. I've also got you five K cash to get started."

I nodded, shook his hand, and said, "I'm going dark now. I'll contact you only when she's found or I need you. Otherwise assume I'm still out there looking. Now go back to DC and do what you would have done. Don't raise suspicions by relaxing."

Tears brimmed at the bottom of his eyelids. He made no effort to wipe them away.

"I know I don't have the right to ask this of you, Ben. Not after everything I said all those years ago. I warned you about the risk of forgetting who you are or what you stood for. And now I'm asking you to ignore all that. To become the man I never wanted you to be. I'm damning you to hell."

I paused. Looked him in the eye. "Mitch, if hell is where I have to go to find Martha, then the devil himself better start wearing Kevlar. Because I'm coming for him." I paused again. "I'm coming for them all."

CHAPTER 18

I planned to get the bus to Pittsburgh—it'd take about an hour as it stopped off anywhere and everywhere, collecting commuters—and then a Greyhound on to DC. That would take another six hours, so I wasn't expecting to arrive until early evening, which suited me fine. Lots of people going home at that time, other people coming in to take advantage of everything DC had to offer. Crowds had been my friend for the last six years and I blended in. I checked the timetable. I had thirty minutes to wait for the first bus. Time to begin reviewing what Mitch had told me over breakfast. I had reams and reams of information. What Martha was studying, the friends Mitch had met, the friends he hadn't, boyfriends—always a good place to start—lectures she attended, professors, hobbies and social clubs. In short, the usual things young women did when they were starting out in life. Nothing stood out. Georgetown was one of the top schools in the country, and she'd been taking full advantage of campus life.

When the bus arrived, I busied myself with Martha's social media profile. The feds and DC Metro would have been through it with a fine-tooth comb, but I needed to go through it all the same. Start getting a feel for her. She seemed serious and focused. There was none of the bleary-eyed 3 a.m. pictures taken in the Washington bars that the Facebook feeds of her friends were full of. There was the odd comment on some of the more serious pages, but nothing to suggest partying was a large part of her life. It would make things easier. The last thing I wanted to do was spend weeks in DC's bars and clubs with a photo. Metro PD could do grunt work like that. It also made it less likely a sexual predator had randomly picked her up.

An hour after I'd gotten on the bus, it entered Pittsburgh city limits. I exited at the first stop. It was unlikely anyone could have arranged a surveillance operation on anything coming out of Bottesford so quickly—if they were coming at all, I figured they'd still be on their way to Lyons—but why risk it? I wouldn't get out at any bus station where a surveillance crew might be expecting me. I knew how hard it was to track people like that. Over the years I'd seen more tricks than I cared to remember.

I walked the fifteen blocks to Pittsburgh Intermodal Station on 55th and 11th. It took me around forty-five minutes. The station is a large building: modern in style, all chrome and glass, and, for reasons I've never got to the bottom of, a glass tower that stands out like a minaret. I pulled my Sox cap down and joined the longest ticket line; an old trick—the busier the teller, the less likely they are to remember you.

The ticket was twenty bucks, and I peeled off one of Mitch's fresh ones. It felt crisp. I put it back, got out one of my own more worn ones, and handed it over. Anything to make me the gray man. New notes stand out.

The Greyhound's suspension was worse than the go-cart my sister Zoe and I had made out of an old apple crate one summer back in Boston. The bus's seats shook and the windows rattled when it hit the smallest bump. The diesel engine was loud and smelly, the driver louder and smellier. The bus was virtually empty, and I took a seat at the back. It was dulled by years of grease and dirt. It sagged under my weight.

After checking out the three other passengers, an old couple and a hipster wearing a pair of silly striped trousers, I went back to my notes. Read them cover to cover. Went back to the beginning and started again. By the time the bus had passed between Old Stanton and New Stanton, I'd read them three times. When we hit Bald Knob, I was on my fifth read and still hadn't seen anything useful. I tried reading pages at random. Maybe viewing everything through a nonchronological lens might show me something different.

Still nothing.

The bus bypassed another town. The sign said it was called Manns Choice, population three hundred. The Greyhound didn't stop. Maybe some buses did. But not this one. Manns Choice was an odd name for a town. I wondered who Mann was. And why he'd had a choice. And why he'd lost his apostrophe. Then I stopped wondering about that and started wondering why the name seemed familiar. I hadn't been there before. I have a thing for place-names, and I'd have remembered a town called Manns Choice.

I thought it was more recent than that. Something I'd heard in the last few hours. Which meant it would be in my notes. I flicked through them until I found it. It wasn't *Manns* Choice; it was "*my* choice." It was something an uncommunicative witness had said during an interview with Metro PD. "It is my choice," he'd told the investigating detective when he declined to answer questions. A different detective had followed it up a week later, but she'd gotten the same answer: "It is my choice." I flicked through the rest of my notes to check if there had been a third interview. There hadn't been.

I wondered if this was why Mitch had brought me in. To do the kind of third interview that nobody else could. To maybe explain to the witness that yes, it *was* his choice. He could own it. But he'd now have to own the consequences.

By the time the bus had reached Hagerstown, I had a plan. Somewhere to start.

But first I needed to pay someone a visit.

CHAPTER 19

Now I had a solid plan, I spent the rest of the journey sleeping. It was a knack I'd always had. Anytime there was downtime on a surveillance op, I'd eat or sleep. I was like a nurse shark. Unlike most sharks, nurse sharks are exceptionally sedentary. When they aren't eating, they're sleeping. They also existed fifty million years before trees. I know lots of useless stuff.

By the time I woke, we were already at DC's city limits. I stared as the city I hadn't visited in six years rolled past the window. It was a pale evening. Bland and soulless buildings loomed large, their windows reflecting the monochrome gray of the clouded sky.

I've never been a fan of DC. It's a city built on a swamp. A place where lies are told and promises are broken. It's no surprise that, per person, more wine is consumed in Washington, DC, than anywhere else in the country. I figure it's the only way to dull the pain.

When I'd been a marshal, dark suits, black shoes, and understated neckties were the order of the day. Nothing that stood out. Of course there'd also been days when I'd worn flame-retardant carbonized underwear; a one-piece Nomex III assault suit; fireproof knee and elbow pads; an energy-absorbing bulletproof vest, ceramic armor plates to cover my front, back, and groin; and an armored helmet that could all but stop a 9-millimeter round at short range.

But now I no longer worried about conformity. When my life changed six years earlier, one of the first things I ditched was the need to look the part. I wore what I wanted, when I wanted. I no longer glanced at every mirror I walked past. Sometimes I'd get confused with a bum, but that's OK. I had long hair, no job, and drifted from town to town. It was an easy mistake to make. Or maybe it wasn't a mistake. Maybe I *was* a bum. But that's fine. The people looking for me wouldn't think to check in the gutters. In the margins. The fact I'm alive kinda proves my point. No one remembers a drifter's face. And where I was headed now, my untamed hair and five-day stubble would be an advantage.

I exited the bus, left the grand old building, and joined a line for a cab. The chilled wind was rushing up the Potomac and I tightened my coat. The wait was short, though, and I was soon in the back of a yellow Crown Vic. "Where ya going, buddy?" the driver asked.

"Meadowell."

He turned to face me. His brow creased. "You sure, man? Don't wanna be going up the Well this time of night. Not unless you got some shady kinda business up there."

"I'm sure," I replied. Sometimes places like the Meadowell were exactly what was needed. I did have business there. It was just that the person I had it with didn't know it yet.

It was time to go and see Samuel.

To get to the Meadowell, we had to drive through some of the most desirable areas in the country. Streets where a million bucks wouldn't buy you a one-bedroom apartment. Streets lined with the cherry blossoms Washington was famous for.

Inevitably, though, Washington's front yard, the glamorous part seen on shows like *Scandal*, was soon in the rearview mirror, and the much maligned and ignored backyard made an appearance. The smell of coffee and cinnamon gave way to month-old garbage and dog shit. High-end boutiques and restaurants became strip malls loaded with bail bondsmen, pawnshops, and budget liquor stores.

Meadowell is what happens when an area is purposefully ignored. Cracked sidewalks colonized by weeds. Discarded possessions piled high in the yards of bleak red-brick buildings. The main feature of people's homes was the barbed wire they used to hang on to the little they had. DO NOT ENTER signs and ownerless dogs were everywhere.

It looked like the set of an apocalypse movie.

The cab dropped me off on Biddle Street and didn't hang around waiting for a return fare. The street I needed, Fremont Drive, was two blocks over, but I was still being careful. Fremont's rep was such that Metro put intermittent surveillance on it, and I didn't want to be photographed getting out of a cab. A cab could be backtraced to where the fare hopped on. Better to come in on foot.

Hiding in plain sight was best in that part of Meadowell. I adopted the shuffling gait of the desperate addict. That and my appearance ought to be enough. Unfortunately, it came with a drawback. Because there was nothing to steal on Fremont, the only reason an addict would have to be out at this hour was to score. Easy pickings for the people who rolled junkies who'd scraped enough together for a hit.

I'd only walked a few yards when I heard footsteps.

CHAPTER 20

Ignoring the footsteps would be suspicious. I figured that in this neighborhood when you heard footsteps, you turned. That would be the normal response. You might have to run from whoever was behind you. Not turning would be unusual behavior.

So I did exactly that. I turned.

The cadaverously thin man approaching me was in his late thirties. He looked like he only had a few months to live. His skin was jaundiced, and he had a sour smell. Lank hair framed his pallid face. White gunk had collected at the corner of his zit-covered mouth. He had bruised and sunken eye sockets, red-rimmed nostrils, and a permanent sniff. Sweat glistened on his forehead. I figured he had a three-hundred-bucks-a-day habit.

"Yo, man. Gotta light?" he whined, scratching at some invisible bugs in his armpit. He hadn't bothered with the charade of showing me a cigarette. One hand stayed in the right-hand pocket of his stringy jacket. He was standing at an angle, like he was shielding the pocket from me. In my old world that was known as a gun-retention movement. But he was a junkie and I was me. Gun or not, it was nothing to worry about.

"Giving your throat a vacation?" I said.

"'Scuse me?

"'Give your throat a vacation.' It's an old Camel ad. Back in the thirties and forties when doctors prescribed cigarettes."

"What you telling me this for, man?"

"I was just wondering if you'd got the message that the doctors were wrong back then. That smoking is bad for you now."

"To hell with this," he said. He reached into his right-hand pocket and removed a gun. It was a rusty semiautomatic. He held it sideways. Like an idiot.

"Have you ever shot anyone before?" I said.

The junkie didn't answer.

"I didn't think so. I spent some time with the British Army a few years ago. Did you know that when they train recruits on their nine-mil Brownings, they start at two yards. And most of them miss the target at that range." I paused. "I only mention this because you're standing five yards away. On top of that, you're holding your weapon sideways. That means when you miss, and you *will* miss, the recoil will spin you round in a circle."

He looked confused. It seemed I wasn't behaving like I was supposed to. I was supposed to panic. To give him everything I had. I wasn't supposed to give him advice on how to hold his gun. He needed a new plan. A new and improved threat. So he did exactly what I knew he would do: He came in close and pressed the gun against my forehead.

"How about now, bitch?" he said. "You think I'll miss from here?"

"Probably not," I admitted. "But see, now you're *too* close."

I ducked out of the way, grabbing and twisting the gun with my left hand as I did. I struck the ulnar nerve on the inside of his forearm with the knuckles of my right hand. His hand muscles stopped working. My left hand kept twisting the gun until his trigger finger snapped and I felt the click of a broken carpal. After that he didn't want to keep hold of it anymore.

Cold and clinical. Easy as one, two, three. Drunks, criminals, or just plain bad people do occasionally try to roll me. If they're stupid enough to point a weapon at me, I use it on them. A nonfatal warning usually. Call it community service. I thought the junkie could use a life lesson right about now, but I didn't want a gun going off. DC has a series of acoustic sensors called ShotSpotter. Metro PD uses it to accurately pinpoint where gunfire is coming from. He didn't know that, though.

I pointed the gun at his face and said, "See, this is how you hold a gun properly."

He started to cry.

"Are you carrying anything that might hurt me?" I asked. Old habits die hard, and there was no way I would stick my hands in his pockets. The risk of a needle injury was too great.

"I ain't no pincushion, man."

Translation: He didn't take drugs intravenously.

"Crack?"

He nodded just before I grabbed the back of his neck and slammed his face onto my rising knee. Blood erupted from his mouth and nose. He slumped to the sidewalk, limp and still, but, crucially for him, at least, not dead. He started to snore. I did some basic checks to make sure he wasn't in any immediate danger. Breathing, bleeding, breaks, and burns, we'd called it. Later it was ABC: airways, breathing, circulation. Who the hell knows what it is now? He was going to be fine, although his mugging days were over for a few months.

I moved him into the recovery position, then walked off. I didn't hurry, did nothing that would attract attention. The junkie would put the beating down to the cost of business. When rolling people is your day job, you'll occasionally come off worse. There'd be no police or hospital report. The only thing that happened tonight was that ownership of a gun changed.

When I was far enough away, I checked what I was holding. A Beretta. It had seen better days. I removed the magazine. It was empty. Ditto the chamber.

Typical.

CHAPTER 21

It was that strange period of the day. Law-abiding citizens were barricaded indoors and the nighttime people were yet to stir. A few dealers would be working, but the early business had been concluded. In an hour the streets would be heaving again. I wanted to be inside by then.

Moving quickly, but not so quick it looked like I'd just worked out I was in the wrong place, I made my way across to Fremont.

It was more prosperous than Biddle Street but still little more than a ghetto. Chain-link fences protected bleak duplexes and low-rises. One house had blackened bricks—evidence of a recent house fire. The air was heavy and smelled of neglect. It was a forgotten neighborhood. I'd been here fifteen years ago and it hadn't changed at all.

The house I wanted was in between two tired-looking duplexes. It was a two-story home, and even the most unobservant would have noticed the CCTV cameras covering the approach to the door. What they might *not* have noticed was that the ground-floor windows were bulletproof, that smaller cameras underneath the eaves provided 360-degree coverage, that the yard had motion detectors and the metal door had a security grille. Police stations in Chicago's South Side had fewer fortifications.

Samuel's home was in darkness, but I opened the gate and made my way up the yard regardless. If he was in, he'd be watching me. I was on three cameras and had tripped at least one motion detector.

I wanted him to see me.

I didn't know if Samuel had survived. Considering what he did for a living, I gave it fifty-fifty at best. If he was alive, though, he'd still be in this house. There were two types of people in Meadowell: those who wanted to stay and those desperate to escape. Samuel was the former. Born only a block away to his fifteen-year-old mother, he'd scrapped and fought his way to something—in his world, at least—approaching respectability. I'm sure at some point he must have been directly involved in the drug trade, although that wasn't how he came to my attention.

Samuel had stood out among the rest by making things no one else could.

Things I needed.

Everything looked kind of the same as last time. The porch had a different awning—the last one had been red; this was green with white stripes. It covered some chairs and a small table. A place to escape the midday sun or take refuge from the rain. It was promising. Samuel had liked to sit outside on sunny days. There was an ashtray full of cheap cigarette butts, and I smiled as I recognized the brand.

Stopping five yards from his front door, I held out my arms. The message was clear: "I'm not here to harm you."

I counted out three hundred Mississippis. Five minutes.

Nothing.

Time to knock on the door.

I rapped my knuckles on the metal, a quick rat-tat-tat-tat. Like I was sending something in Morse code. The sound bounced all the way down the street. I looked up at the camera. I strained to hear something, anything, to indicate someone was home, but there was nothing. A solitary dog barked in the distance. A man yelled something unintelligible the next street over.

I was about to give it up as a bad job when the door opened.

CHAPTER 22

The man in the yellow suit's phone rang again. This time he'd been waiting for the call, and he answered immediately.

"We might have a problem," the voice at the other end said.

The man in the yellow suit said nothing. He disliked problems almost as much as he disliked unknowns.

The voice continued. "Our man says Burridge picked up someone in Wayne County and together they flew to a town near Pittsburgh."

"Pittsburgh?" the man in the yellow suit asked. "Why Pittsburgh?"

"We don't know. But whoever it was, he was a suspicious son of a bitch. Took our man's cell and smashed up the chopper's comms. That's why we're only getting it now."

"Where did they go then?"

"Burridge flew back to DC. He's back at his desk now."

"And the other guy?"

There was a pause. The man in the yellow suit didn't like pauses either.

"We don't know," the man admitted. "He didn't get back on the chopper."

The man in the yellow suit frowned. Burridge had thrown them a curve-ball. So far they'd predicted, and successfully circumnavigated, everything he'd done. But now, to paraphrase Donald Rumsfeld, there was a known unknown to consider. Still, ten minutes ago, the reason for Burridge's trip to Wayne County had been an *unknown* unknown. Now they knew he'd picked up someone. He supposed it was progress.

Making rash decisions had not got him to the position he held now. He needed more information. "You've sent someone to Wayne County?" he asked.

The man on the other end of the phone confirmed he had.

"OK. Get someone to that town near Pittsburgh as well. They went there for a reason and someone must have seen them together," he said. "Spend what you need, but I want a name. And get me some art. I want to see who this new actor is."

"Consider it done."

The line went dead. The man in the yellow suit stared at his phone long after the call ended. He didn't like this new development. He considered telling management but decided against it. Their response wouldn't be subtle; management's only tool was a hammer, and that meant every problem looked like a nail. To be fair, in their business, it was the hammer that was needed most of the time. But sometimes the surgeon's scalpel was required.

He'd keep it to himself for now.

It probably wasn't anything to worry about.

CHAPTER 23

I hadn't heard anyone move. Samuel must have been waiting on the other side of the door. Watching me walk up the yard, trying to figure out who I was. Whether I posed a threat or not.

Samuel's face peered round. He looked at me blankly. Too many years had passed, and too many things had happened, for him to recognize me straightaway. I recognized him, though. He wore glasses now and was little broader round the waist and cheeks, but the thick head of hair was still there. Glossy, tight black curls, expertly cut.

I could tell an uninvited white man turning up at his house had confused him. Made it hard to place me. "S'up?" he said eventually.

"Aren't you going to invite me in, Samuel?"

"Nah, man. Don't care about the Jesus hair, you're Five-O." He tried to close the door, but I'd already jammed in my boot. A quick shoulder barge and I was inside.

The sides of his shirt weren't level—a telltale sign he had a firearm in his waistband. He went for it, but I was quicker. I held his arm in one hand and removed his gun with my other. It was a Glock 19. The same model the Wayne County sergeant had been carrying. I put it in my jacket pocket.

"Ah, man, that's not cool," Samuel said.

"Stop messing about and shut the door," I said. "We have business to attend to."

"I ain't doing nothing for you, man. Not until you tell me who you are."

"I need some of your stuff. I don't have the time for your best. Just whatever you have ready."

"I told you, I ain't doing noth—"

"You owe me, Samuel."

He stared. Eventually he peered over his glasses and said, "Who *are* you, man?"

"I thought you might have remembered me," I said. "It's only been six years and I did save your life."

A pause. A glimmer of recognition. Then a full-on grin.

"Ben?" he said incredulously. "Ben Koenig?"

"The very same."

"Holy shit!" Samuel lurched forward and wrapped his arms around me. "Ben fucking Koenig! Man, am I glad to see you. I thought you was dead for sure. They brought *The Running Man* down on your ass, man. I figured you'd last maybe a week. Six months tops."

"It has been an unnecessarily exciting few years," I admitted. It didn't surprise me that Samuel knew what had happened six years ago. He was plugged into the criminal underworld more than anyone else I knew. "Anyway," I continued, "I want ten. All on the one card. And one of them has to be for this." I paused to show him a facilities management company website on the smartphone Mitch had bought me. "And I need a gun."

Samuel frowned. "What are you up to?" he said.

I'd always liked Samuel. It was hard not to. He was unrepentant about being a criminal. Said it was what he'd always wanted to be. Put himself through school to become a better one. I trusted him, though. Sort of.

We left his sparse front room and headed into his basement.

From the outside, it looked like the type of room you wouldn't want to go inside. The door was stained with damp, and the clasp and padlock were rusted and looked like they hadn't been opened for years. It was all a façade. Samuel removed a key from a chain on his neck and eased it into the padlock. For something so old and rusty, it sure opened easily. He put the key back around his neck and stepped inside.

Basements all across America are basically places to store the crap until it gets moldy enough to throw out. This one was no different. An old washing machine that was missing the door. Cheap cardboard boxes with labels like BEDROOM and KITCHEN. A bicycle with flat tires.

And a large metal filing cabinet.

Samuel walked over, leaned against it, and grunted. He pushed it to one side. Instead of a basement wall, there was a hole. He squeezed through and I followed.

He turned on the light and I looked round. I hadn't been in this room before. Never had cause to. It was small and modern. Monitors were fixed to one wall, and bits of computer equipment, none of which I recognized, were stacked underneath. One wall was painted white. A plastic seat was up against it. A strong light and a photographer's umbrella were set up.

Samuel turned to me. "Tell me what you need."

CHAPTER 24

Samuel Osborne wasn't just a forger; he was *the* forger. In the greater DC area, for those in the know, he provided the kind of service that made people like me despair. He didn't only provide IDs. With almost unparalleled computer skills, he put information into databases to *support* his IDs. Given enough time, Samuel could provide you with a legend that categorically proved you were who your ID said you were. He was better at it than WITSEC.

His services didn't come cheap, and his clients often wondered why he continued to live in Meadowell. I knew why. It was his home. Where he grew up, where he felt safe. Everything he needed and everything he wanted was there. But also, a master forger hiding out in Meadowell? Come on, man, be serious.

Samuel hid in plain sight.

And he was an invaluable source of information when we were chasing the really bad guys.

The first time I'd met Samuel was when I warned him about a man I was looking for. The second time was when I killed the man I was looking for.

Intel suggested my target had used one of Samuel's IDs in the past and was now burning his bridges, so to speak. After hearing the warning, Samuel had thanked me, but I'd known he hadn't taken it too seriously.

The bridge-burner was ex–Chechen mafia, and he had the resources to clean up after himself. I didn't care what Samuel thought—the Chechen *was* coming for him. Mitch gave me permission and I shadowed Samuel for three weeks. Eventually the Chechen made his move. He'd started shadowing Samuel not far from where the cab dropped me off earlier. I thought he would rush him when he opened his front door. Bundle Samuel inside, kill him, then destroy his computer systems and anything else that could point to his new identity. That's what I thought would happen. What actually happened is that the Chechen took his chance earlier. The street they were walking down, in an almost disastrous quirk of fate, had virtually emptied without warning. The Chechen made his move.

He'd managed to take aim at the terrified Samuel when I stepped out and identified myself. The Chechen wasn't that bright. Instead of living to fight another day, he'd turned his gun on me.

I put three bullets in him. Two in his face, one on his neck.

Samuel and I kept in touch. Grew close even. Well, as close as a crook and a marshal could get, I suppose. I watched out for him. Made sure no one bad went too near him. And in return, if there was a guy Samuel didn't think deserved to be breathing in the free air, he would give me a call. Hint at where this guy might be found. He was never an official source of intel, though. Samuel would rather go vegan than become an official rat.

There *were* other forgers. In the seedier bars and pool halls of DC, for the right price, anything was available. I didn't need to travel to Meadowell if all I wanted was a fake ID. The thing that made Samuel's stand out, his unique selling point, was his bespoke system for disposable ID cards.

Occasionally, having access to multiple IDs is tactically advantageous. And when that's the case, you'd get a load of cheap ones made up. Use the one you need, leave the rest in your desk. No drama. But if you aren't working from a base, if you have to carry them on you, then multiple IDs have a major drawback. If you're apprehended or searched, you're in serious trouble. Multiple IDs get Homeland Security sniffing. Getting caught with multiple fake IDs is considerably worse than getting caught with just one fake ID.

Samuel's solution had been developed in the labs of MIT. His major had been in polymer engineering, with a specific focus on how to bind plastics together without using heat or adhesives. His minors had been in photography and film makeup. A combination of studies not seen before or since. But for Samuel it made perfect sense. He sometimes needed to patch up injuries before clients could be photographed. Sometimes fake injuries or fake tattoos had to be added. Whatever the client needed. Even at that young age he'd known what he was going to be doing for a living.

But it was the polymer engineering that made him stand out.

With his newfound knowledge and specialist equipment, Samuel could produce an unlimited amount of paper-thin ID cards that would stick to each other. They were similar to the peel-off screen covers on new smartphones. Ten of his IDs were about the thickness of a credit card. The huge advantage was that they were interchangeable; you simply put the one you needed on top. The other nine were underneath and hidden. When you'd used one, you peeled it off and put it to the back of the deck. The next one then became the face ID. If an ID card required information on the back as well as the front, Samuel would put it on the back of a different card. As long as you didn't do something stupid, like use an Arizona driving license on the back of a postal inspector ID, it was a flawless system.

I'd asked for ten IDs. It was the optimum size for one card. Anything more and it started to look too thick. Anything less and it was too flimsy.

Other than the facilities management company ID I needed, I had no idea what I would be doing over the next few weeks. I'd leave the rest of the IDs up to Samuel. He'd give me a security consultant, a reporter, and a private investigator as standard, though. They were the kind of jobs that allowed you to poke your nose into places without arousing the wrong kind of suspicion.

He snapped a couple of photographs. We looked at them. My tired face stared back at me. That was a problem. It looked too much like me. IDs are always more convincing when the photograph doesn't look as though it's just been taken. Better to look like it was taken a few years back.

A thought occurred to me. I sat at one of Samuel's spare machines, brought up the website of the US Marshals, and tried to log into the staff-only intranet. My old password would have expired years ago, but I hoped Mitch had possessed the foresight to give me access again.

He had.

The screen burst into life. I went to the Fifteen Most Wanted section. My page had already been removed. Samuel saw my frustration and came over.

"What's up?"

I told him that the photograph they'd shown on TV would have been ideal. It was fifteen years old but still looked like me.

"Move over," Samuel said.

We switched seats, and within a few keystrokes he was logged into an admin section I didn't even know existed. It was unnerving how easily he navigated around my old system. It was almost like he'd been in it before. He brought up an archive database. "When were you on TV?" he said.

I told him. He changed the setting and refreshed the Most Wanted page. Sure enough, there I was. He downloaded the JPEG.

"If you can wait until tomorrow, I can give you some basic cover on your cards," he said. "Put your name on to some databases. Nothing that'll hold up to the cops or the feds, but it'll be enough to fool someone if they only call reception to check you actually work there."

"I'll wait." I couldn't do anything until the next day anyway.

Samuel paused a beat, shook his head, and said, "Thought you was dead for sure, Ben."

I *had* defied the odds. Couldn't deny that.

"And how the hell did you survive?" he asked. "Some scary-ass dudes visit the Russians' website. I know you ain't been living under another name. And you know how I know that?" Before I could answer, he answered his own question. He sounded hurt when he said, "Cuz you didn't come to me for a new gig, that's how."

A gig was what Samuel called his packages.

"Had to leave in a hurry," I said.

He looked at me, stood, and hugged me again.

As I hugged him back, I said. "Speaking of that site, Samuel. You think you can take it offline for a bit?"

It was the other reason I'd gone there. Samuel, when he wasn't making fake IDs, was a bit of a hacktivist. Several times his subversive computer skills had helped to give the voiceless—particularly those who lived in Meadowell—a voice. When a publicity-hungry senator had said that the area's problems were self-inflicted, Samuel had hit his website with a distributed denial of service attack two months before he was up for election. The DDoS had closed his website for a month and stopped almost all his fundraising. The senator lost his seat by ten points. I saw him on TV last year, still bitching about it. I wondered if DDoS attacks worked on the dark web. It might give me a bit of space to work.

"Maybe for a while," he said, nodding. "But you know they'll just close it and reopen another one. How long you need?"

"As long as you can manage."

"I can maybe do a week, tops. Realistically it'll probably just be a couple of days, though."

"Whatever you can give me," I said.

"I'll do some prep now." Samuel pulled up a different keyboard, pressed a button, and a new monitor flickered into life. He typed in a URL from memory. As the site was on the dark web, it was a random series of letters and numbers rather than words. Nothing that could be accessed by accident or found by a surface search engine.

The website appeared. It was the same as it had been the last time I'd looked. A photograph and a load of personal details. It also explained the rules. There was really only one: Nobody was to go through my family. If that happened, the arrangement transferred to the person or persons who broke the rule. It was the only concession I'd been granted. It also detailed what was needed to make a claim.

It wasn't nice.

CHAPTER 25

The man in the yellow suit stared in disbelief at the grainy photograph. He looked up at the man who'd brought it.

His throat had gone dry. "How did we get this?" he managed eventually.

"Bit of luck really," the man said. "There was nothing from Bottesford. He avoided all the cameras, so we're guessing he's been there before. Burridge was on a few, but not him."

The man in the yellow suit steepled his fingers while he waited for him to finish.

"So my man thinks to himself, what's so special about that town? Why bother getting on a chopper in the middle of the night with the director of the US Marshals if you ain't going on to DC with him? The obvious answer is that he ain't going to DC at all, he's going someplace else." He paused, picked up a mug of coffee, looked at his boss's expression, and put it down without taking a drink. "So unless he's still there, which made no kind of sense, he had to have taken the bus. Town's too small for the train to stop there. My man looks at the timetable and sees the first bus goes to Pittsburgh. Takes an hour. So he drives up there and tries to access the CCTV at the station. No doing. Anyway, this guy probably knows enough to stay off them anyway." This time he did reach for the cup. He took a long drag of coffee. Sighed and wiped his lips. "Using initiative we have to give him credit for, he thinks what if he *is* going to DC, just that he didn't want anyone knowing. Getting the bus would be perfect, right?"

The man in the yellow suit nodded.

"He races there. Gets there not long after the bus had arrived. Bungs the driver a few bills and gets a look at the bus CCTV. Bingo. There he is. Reading a notebook and then sleeping. Not a great photo, but at least we have one now."

Silence settled over them both.

The man with the photo asked, "Who is this guy?"

"A ghost," the man in the yellow suit answered eventually. He stopped to think. He was now at the stage where management had to be told. The man in the photograph couldn't be kept from them. He was too dangerous. But first he would be proactive. He wanted to tell management what actions he'd taken, rather than what actions he planned to take.

It was time to start tidying up, and he hated doing that. Not because he was squeamish—he wasn't, he was a stone-cold killer—but because he was a professional, and when the collateral damage mounts, the wrong sort of people take interest. So far, this whole thing had stayed low key.

He was a firm believer in the law of unintended consequences. Who knew what the chain reaction would be when the "tidy" button was pressed? Look at what had happened with the girl. Look at where they were now.

He picked up the black-and-white photograph again and looked at a man who was nothing but trouble. He had no choice.

"Who do we have in DC we can rely on?"

CHAPTER 26

It was 7 a.m. by the time Samuel finally announced he was happy. He handed me my new IDs. I checked them over. They were exceptional. He'd even put the facilities management company ID card used by Georgetown University on top. I looked at the name he'd given me.

"David Decker?" I said. "That how you see me, Samuel?"

He smiled and shrugged. "I only had time to do one name, so they're all David Decker. But he has a social security number, a DC driving license, and, superficially at least, he's on enough of those company databases to beat casual inquiries."

I delved into my backpack for my money roll. My hand bumped against the gun I'd taken from Samuel. I tried to hand it back.

"You keep it, Ben. I can get another."

I turned the Glock in my hand. It was used, but looked serviceable. Felt good in my hand. Reassuring. The weight of it, the textured grip, the polymer frame. I've always used Glocks. They're robust and they're reliable. They have no safety catch, so they're always ready to go. I'd read that the original designer fired his prototypes with his left hand so he could continue drafting new designs with his right if one exploded. I appreciate that kind of commitment.

I spent a few minutes checking it over. I never trust a weapon I haven't personally taken to bits, cleaned, and put back together. Samuel found me a used cartridge case, and I levered out the spent percussion cap. Filled the void with candle wax, put it in the Glock's chamber, and dry fired. Checked the firing pin had made an impression. It had. It was the next best thing to firing a test round.

The barrel's end was threaded for a suppressor. The sights were higher than a standard Glock to make sure it was still useable when the suppressor was fitted. Can-clearing sights, we used to call them. I put it into my backpack. At the top, within easy reach.

I peeled off eighty fifty-dollar bills and handed them over. Four grand. A thousand more than he'd have wanted six years ago. He looked at me quizzically.

"For the gun and some ammo," I explained.

Guns were cheaper than dirt in Meadowell. If he wanted to, Samuel could replace the Glock by the end of day and still be nine hundred up. He disappeared and came back with a box of fifty 9-millimeter rounds. More than enough. He handed me a spare magazine and watched as I loaded it.

"Thanks, Samuel," I said. "And can you get rid of this piece of shit for me?" I handed him the junkie's rusty Beretta.

"Someone round here have a bad day yesterday?"

"He'll live. What about the DDoS attack?"

"The site will be down by tonight," he replied. "It ain't gonna last long, though, Ben."

Our business was almost done. There was one thing left to do. I turned at the door and faced him. He stiffened. For him, the point of departure was always the biggest risk, even with people he trusted. If a customer *really* wanted to cover their tracks, then silencing the only man who knew their new identity was one of the steps they'd have to take. The Chechen had understood that.

"Samuel," I said, "listen to what I have to say very carefully. Before long, those IDs are going to start appearing on systems. It's possible some people may put two and two together and begin to wonder just where I've gotten those IDs."

He nodded. "I knew what I was doing, Ben."

"That site's no joke, Samuel. If you admit to anyone I've been here, if anyone finds out I've been here, if anyone even *suspects* I've been here, then . . ." I trailed off.

"Then what, man?"

"Then you'll be dead, Samuel," I replied. "Simple as that. They'll torture you to find out what you know, then they will kill you so you can't tell anyone else."

CHAPTER 27

The trick to getting into places is to make it look like you have every right to be there. That means no rushing and no dawdling. I was going into the heart of Georgetown, and that meant no admiring the architecture and no asking for directions. I'd studied the campus map before I entered the grounds and knew where I was going.

Martha's professor was called Robin Marston. He was the guy who kept saying "It is my choice" while refusing to answer questions about Martha. The Greyhound bus driving past Manns Choice had reminded me. The Metro PD detective had said Marston didn't believe that Martha had been abducted. That she'd most likely taken a lover and Mitch was abusing his authority trying to track her down. He said it was his choice not to cooperate.

It was something I could use. People with antiauthoritarian leanings were habitually annoyed and easy to manipulate. Now I was on the campus grounds, I switched the facilities management company card for a Metro Police Department ID. I didn't have the badge to go with it, but it would be enough to make Marston think his civil rights were being violated. So far he hadn't cooperated. I think Mitch wanted me to get Marston to change his mind.

The world of academia wasn't something I was familiar with, but once I was inside, it was like any other large building. A bushel of departmental signs, the kind you see in hospitals, pointed me the right way, and I quickly found Marston's office.

I knocked on his door and entered without waiting to be asked.

Marston was a thin man. A corduroy-jacketed, ultraliberal academic. Pampered and soft. His shoulders were hunched, like a heron's. He looked like the kind of man who baked his own bread. Probably had nosebleeds when he was kid. He was wearing a V-neck sweater and a checkered shirt. A threadbare tie wrapped around his bony neck. Hanging on his office wall were framed academic certificates, a poster for a defund-the-police event, and a Che Guevara print.

I could see why Metro PD had struggled to deal with him. He might not be physically or mentally robust, but he looked like he knew how to make complaints. Men like this ruined careers. Men like this *celebrated* ruining careers.

It looked like Marston was in the middle of a group session. Three female students were hanging on his every word. I flashed my phony ID and told the kids to scram. They got up to leave, but Marston wasn't having that.

"Stay where you are, girls," he said. "This man can't make you leave. Remember the discussion we had about the origins of the word 'policeman'?" It was clear none of them did. "It comes from the Greek word '*polis*,' which means city," he continued. "A policeman is therefore a *man* of the city. In other words, this man works for you and me. We don't work for him. This isn't a police state." He looked at me. "Can you please leave? If you want to make an appointment, please speak to my secretary." He faced the girls again. Pretended to ignore me.

Time to raise the stakes.

"Mr. Marston, you have two choices," I said.

"It's Professor Mars—"

"You either ask these lovely ladies to leave, or they can stay and watch you piss your pants. Choose now, please."

"I beg your pardon! I'll do no such thing!"

"Do you know who I am?" I asked.

He regained a bit of swagger. "Well, you *were* Metro PD."

"Wrong."

"And I say *were* because, after making a threat in a room full of witnesses, I'll have your badge . . ." He petered out as his brain caught up with what I'd said. "What do you mean, 'wrong'?"

I didn't have time to argue. I whipped the Glock from my pocket and tapped the bridge of his nose with the bottom of the magazine well. Not hard enough to break the skin, but enough to make it bleed. Make his eyes water. Pain often clarifies just how stubborn you were prepared to be. And the introduction of blood always changes the dynamics in a room. We're wired to see red as a danger color. When we see it, our heart rate increases. Goes back to the days when we coexisted with woolly mammoths and saber-toothed tigers. When we weren't the apex predators we are now.

The girls didn't wait for further instructions. The wild man of Borneo had just hit their professor with a gun. They weren't interested in seeing what happened next. By the time Marston's blood had wet the floor, they were already out the door.

I held up my index finger and said to Marston, "You have one minute to give me Martha Burridge's file."

Holding his nose and tipping his head back, he staggered to his filing cabinet and opened it. He reached in, grabbed a manila file, and handed it over.

I flipped it open. It was empty. I showed him.

"The cops have it all!" he yelled. "Whoever you are, you're too late."

"I've seen the file you gave Metro PD. There was nothing in that either."

He looked away, shifty and sullen. I tapped him on the bridge of the nose again. Hard enough to move gristle this time.

He screamed in pain. "There *is* nothing more!"

I'd made a mistake. He *did* have more, but because he felt it was his civic duty to obstruct the authorities at every turn, the moment he'd realized he had something they wanted, he would have taken it out of his office. Someplace where he could read it at his leisure. Probably the trunk of his car. Maybe his home study.

I should have visited him last night.

"You *do* have a file on Martha," I said. "And for some reason you haven't shared it with anyone. Perhaps it's because you don't want people to see what's inside, or more likely it's because you're an out-and-out asshole."

I racked the Glock's slide. In the quiet office the sound was deafening.

"Which knee?" I asked.

"I'm . . . I'm sorry?"

"Which knee?" I repeated.

He paled. "I don't understand," he whimpered.

"You *do* understand. I'm asking which knee you want to be shot in. It's a binary choice. You're a biped. You only have two. I see by the way your desk is set up, you're right-handed. How about I choose for you?" I took aim at his left knee.

"OK!" he shouted. "I do have a file. But it's at home."

I had a problem. Marston was covered in blood. His students would have already alerted security. No way could I march him across campus without it becoming a newsworthy event.

"Here's what's going to happen, *Professor*," I said. "You're going home this lunchtime and you're going to give me that file. Do that and you'll never see me again. Try to be clever and you'll be looking over your shoulder until I decide to make time for you. Might be a week, might a year, but believe me, I *will* make time for you."

I stared at him. Made sure he believed me. If the dark patch on his trousers was anything to go by, he did.

"Twelve thirty at yours," I said. "Be there."

I put the Glock back in my pocket and left. I didn't run, nor did I dawdle. I could hear running in the distance. Campus security was on the case.

I smiled grimly. Professor Marston would say nothing. I took the campus map from my pocket and got my bearings. Next stop, Georgetown University student halls of residence.

I wanted to see Martha's room.

CHAPTER 28

Copley Hall is one of the oldest buildings on campus. Built in 1932, it's a neo-Gothic gray stone building. Steadfast and proud, it looks more like a museum than dorms. It isn't as old as it appears, but it is impressive nonetheless.

I strolled through the beautiful arched doorway as though I'd been there on a daily basis. I was in a hurry now. The incident with Marston had forced my hand.

Between Marston's office and Copley Hall, I'd switched my ID card back over. I was now David Decker from Innovo (SMG) Facilities Management Services again. At least I'd fit in. Going into Marston's office with long and unruly hair, claiming to be a cop, was never really going to fly. But the man who keeps the toilets flushing? No one cares what that guy looks like.

I made my way to the fifth floor. Martha had shared a room with a girl called Freya Jackson, an overseas student from England. Some of the rooms were open and I had to avert my eyes. The fifth floor was a female-only floor. I was only challenged once, but I flashed my ID and explained that one of the toilets was backing up. Turds on the floor was a real conversation killer.

Martha's was the last room in the corridor and the next to last door. The last door was the fire exit. I knocked and waited. No one answered. I hadn't expected anyone to. Freya Jackson should have been at lectures, and if Martha had answered, then things were about to get weird. I turned the handle and the door opened. I seemed to be in the least security-conscious building in the country. I stepped inside.

The room was small but neat. There were two beds and two desks, and it was easy to see which side was Martha's. Everything had been taken away and a sign had been stuck above her bed asking people to call Metro PD if they had any information on her disappearance. Freya Jackson was still occupying the other half, and she seemed to be making a conscious effort to stop her stuff encroaching into Martha's side. There was a corkboard with photographs of siblings and parents and spaniels—I've always liked spaniels, they seem like the clowns of the dog world—and one of what I assumed was her bedroom back in England. There was also a lot of her and Martha. A selfie taken in a coffeehouse somewhere. They were both smiling goofily. All the other photographs were of Freya in groups of women, all smiles and hugs. Apart from a man I assumed was her father, there were no men in any of them.

As well as the beds and desks, there was a sink, a vanity unit, and a built-in wardrobe. The shelf had a *Star Wars* Chewbacca mug with a toothbrush and paste in it. Just the one. Metro would have taken Martha's for her DNA in case they had to identify a mutilated body later. I opened the vanity-unit door and found nothing of interest. Shampoos, conditioners. The usual things young women kept.

Freya Jackson had been questioned at length about Martha's disappearance. Neither the feds nor Metro believed she had anything to do with it. I'm a natural cynic, though, and Freya Jackson's photographs were beginning to bug me. They were mainly of Freya and Martha. Arms wrapped around each, laughing and smiling. The occasional one where they each had their lips pressed together and their cheeks sucked in. Duck faces, I thought the look was called. Kind of half pout, half self-obsessed idiocy. I suspected Martha and Freya had been doing it ironically.

They were clearly good friends. I wondered how much Freya had told the feds. She probably hadn't lied, but maybe she hadn't told them everything she knew. Maybe she thought she was covering for Martha. Like Marston, but not in a contrary-asshole kind of way. And when it all blew up, when it became obvious Martha was in trouble, maybe she didn't know how to tell the feds what else she knew, not without getting into trouble.

She might speak to me, though. I wasn't a fed. Wasn't Metro. And although I was technically still a marshal, I sure didn't look like one. My hair was so long I looked like a Metallica roadie.

I figured Freya wouldn't be back for a couple hours. I didn't want to be in her room when she arrived, obviously, but I had enough time to conduct a thorough bottom-up search of the dorm. I would then wait outside. Maybe talk to her in her favorite coffee shop or someplace like that. Buy her a meal. See if she knew stuff she hadn't shared yet.

That sounded like a plan.

I'd only just lifted up Freya's mattress when the screaming started and everything turned to shit.

CHAPTER 29

Nothing polarizes Americans more than gun control. Not a woman's right to choose, not a border wall, not even the role of the federal government. Firearms had been a part of my life since I was a boy. My father taught me to shoot and respect weapons as soon as I was big enough to hold one. He wasn't a hunter, but he believed in the Second Amendment. He lived his whole life without firing a weapon in anger and I knew he was happier for it. My father understood what firearms were: a necessary evil.

Although I'm pro–Second Amendment, the fact that American children are the only ones in the world who need to practice active shooter drills is a stain on the national conscience.

Mass shootings in schools and cinemas and malls follow a depressing pattern. A gunman walks in and begins firing. Everyone panics, and the gunman keeps shooting until he eats a bullet, runs out of ammunition, or the cops kill him. He's in a target-rich environment and he's under no illusion he'll walk off into the sunset when it's all over. With very few variations, that's what happens. It's the fight-or-flight response. We can't fight a gun, so we flee or hide. It's hardwired into us. Tens of thousands of years ago, the people who didn't flee danger didn't get to pass on their genes. Simple as that.

I don't have a fight-or-flight response. I don't have the urge to run or hide. So when I heard someone screaming, "Active shooter!" I didn't stop to think. I took my Glock from my pocket and stepped into the corridor to face whatever was out there.

It had been a day for mistakes, and this was another one.

Students were running everywhere, locking themselves in rooms. I could hear them pushing things against the doors. Someone shouted that two people were dead already. I began battling against a tide of terrified students on the stairwell. I figured wherever they were running from was where I needed to be.

In the lobby on the first floor, a panicked student ran straight into me. Knocked me on my ass. By the time I'd struggled to my feet, people were staring. It didn't look good. I had crazy hair and was holding a gun. I'd have probably reached the same conclusion they did.

"It's him!" someone screamed. It was one of Professor Marston's students, one of the girls who had seen me bop him on the nose. "He shot them!"

Before I could protest, a voice from behind shouted, "Fucking psycho asshole!"

I turned to see a huge kid—he had to be the football team's tight end—swinging a fire extinguisher at my head. If I hadn't turned, he'd have crushed my skull. As it was, my reflexes were only good enough to deflect it with my shoulder. I still caught a hefty blow on the temple.

My lights went out like there'd been a power cut.

CHAPTER 30

"Tell me again," the man in the yellow suit said, glaring at the phone in his hand.

"She had a choice: the professor or Koenig," came the patient reply.

"She made the *wrong* choice then."

"To be fair, boss, Marston had just arranged to meet Koenig and give him the girl's file. She had to make a snap decision. She felt it was more important to get the file rather than the man trying to get the file."

The man in the yellow suit frowned. If the professor had a file he hadn't shared with the cops, then yes, of course that needed to be taken care of. But what he clearly hadn't managed to get across yet was this: While Koenig was out there, none of them was safe. It wouldn't matter if they thought nothing linked the girl to them. Koenig would end up on their doorstep sooner or later. Among a certain class of criminal, Koenig was called the Devil's Bloodhound. The man in the yellow suit didn't want the Devil's Bloodhound looking for him.

"Tell me exactly what happened," he said. "Leave out nothing."

The voice at the other end said, "As you know the professor was always a loose end—just because he hadn't told Metro anything didn't mean he had nothing to tell."

Even though there was a thousand miles between them, the man in the yellow suit nodded. Marston had been one of the loose ends he'd wanted "tidied."

"Our woman was on her way to see Marston when Koenig walked out. She didn't know what to do and there was no time to call for instructions. She decided to stay on mission and went straight in to see Marston. Didn't even have to threaten him. Koenig had already busted up his nose, and he'd pissed his pants. He blabbed everything as soon as she showed him her gun. Told her where the file was and gave her a key to his rooms."

"Then she killed him?"

"Yep. And the mall cop responding to Koenig's visit."

The man in the yellow suit grunted. At least something had been done right. "And the file?"

"She has it and there was nothing in it we didn't already know. She'll scan it and email it over when she can. She also destroyed Marston's computer just in case there were backups."

"OK . . . I suppose it wasn't her fault. She did what we asked. Make sure she's paid in full. Throw in an extra twenty as a retainer. I want her ready should Koenig reappear in DC."

The man at the other end laughed and said, "That may be sooner than you think, boss. I haven't told you the best bit yet."

The man in the yellow suit said nothing. He hated guessing games.

"This is where it gets interesting. Campus security initiated their active shooter protocol when they saw the bodies she'd dropped."

"And?"

"And Koenig was in the girl's room over in Copley. Some jock thought he was the shooter and hit him in the face with a fire extinguisher."

"Where is he?" he urged.

"In a DC jail cell."

For the first time since he'd set eyes on Koenig's photograph, the man in the yellow suit smiled. Finally, something was going his way . . .

CHAPTER 31

My thoughts don't usually keep me awake, but for thirty minutes I'd been pondering the fact that to get to sleep, you must first pretend to *be* asleep. You close your eyes and stay still. You slow your breathing. You try to clear your mind. It didn't work. I couldn't get comfortable, and I kept on replaying what had happened.

I was in a holding cell. It was hot and full of flies. Fat bluebottles feasted on something wet and organic on the floor. Vomit or blood. Maybe both. The metal door was gray and spotted with years of water damage. The stench of urine was strong—unsurprising when the only fitting was a metal toilet with no lid. The walls were covered in gang tags. The theme of casual vandalism continued on the bench I was lying on. Messages of hate and proclamations of innocence were scratched into the dark blue paint. I was wearing a paper evidence suit. The cops had my IDs and unregistered Glock. Even if I hadn't been their only suspect in the Georgetown shooting, I wasn't going anywhere soon.

On my way back from hospital, I'd picked up that Marston and a campus guard had been shot. The cops didn't care about Marston. Sure, officially it would be his death that topped the charge sheet, but it was the campus guard they were really angry about. He'd almost certainly been a cop. Campus guards are always ex-cops. It's a universally acknowledged hiring policy. They know what they're doing and they're used to carrying weapons. And as they're normally topping up a pension, they don't need to be paid that much. The confirmation came with what happened at Georgetown University Hospital.

Or rather what didn't happen.

I'd been secured with handcuffs and leg restraints for the ride there. That was expected. It's what I'd have done. But what happened in the ER sealed it for me. I'd been hit in the head with a cast-iron fire extinguisher. I had a possible skull fracture. Despite this, no tests were ordered. No neurologist came by to see me, and no one admitted me or took my name. I didn't even get a chance to lie down. Just sat on the edge of a bed while a bunch of cops gave me the dead eye. Daring me to try something.

At the cops' urging, a junior doctor performed a quick and perfunctory examination. He shone a light in my eyes. Asked me to follow his finger round the room. He quizzed me on who the current president was. He told the cops my pupils were responsive, and I didn't seem confused. Said I was fine, but to bring me back if things changed.

And that was it. I was returned to their custody. Rubber-stamped as fit to be detained and questioned. To be fair to the doc, other than some blurry vision and a splitting headache, I had no other signs that pointed to concussion.

I knew why I'd had an expedited medical exam. Before I got too far in the system, DC Metro wanted payback. And because the holding cell I'd been put in was empty, it would be a prisoner-on-prisoner beatdown. Holding cells are never empty. Not in DC, where there's a constant flow of miscreants.

I couldn't avoid the upcoming confrontation, and as it didn't look like they were going to feed me, I figured I might as well get some sleep. I ran a quick cost-benefit analysis. On the cost side, I thought the chances of them killing me in my sleep were small—they'd wake me first. I was sure of it. It would be more fun for everyone that way. On the benefit side, an hour's sleep after a bash on the head would do me good. It might clear my blurry vision. My headache might ease.

Didn't matter, though. No matter how hard I tried, sleep wouldn't come. I had too much going on in my mind. Marston's murder meant I was pressing the right buttons. Someone hadn't liked me talking to him.

I wondered why. My gut told me he wasn't involved. Something in the file he'd refused to hand over to Metro then, something he was unaware of. He'd have been questioned before he was shot, and he'd have told his killer everything. If it was the file, that was important; it would be long gone. I figured there was nothing I could do until I was back out on the street, so I put my mind to figuring out a way to make bail. Escaping wasn't possible. This was the real world, not the movies. I'd have to talk my way out, and I didn't yet have enough information. I'd try to pick up something at the first interview, something I could tell Mitch when I called him. The way I saw it, it was my only play.

But first I needed to deal with whatever came through that cell door. It wouldn't be long.

CHAPTER 32

The first indication it was about to start was when the cop who had been watching me left the holding area. Said he needed to take a leak. I closed my eyes and concentrated on the noise. A minute later the cell door opened, and some crude and hoarse whispers followed the shuffling footsteps in.

Assaults in holding cells happen all the time. They're regrettable but inevitable. The only way to stop them would be individual holding cells, and no department has the time, space, or money for that. So, cops aren't blamed if inmates fight. Not if they try to break them up. At worst, their knuckles get rapped.

"What we got here then, boy?"

I sat upright and opened my eyes. The cell had been dark when I'd closed them, but the lights were on now. I suspected there were lots of cops watching us. Probably had chips and dips out. A tub of lard leered over me. A skinhead with piggy eyes and popcorn teeth. He had rolls of fat on his neck and hairy shoulders. His lungs struggled and heaved to bring in air before falling under the weight of his own flesh. He looked like a wrestler from the fifties. When being able to squash your opponent was more important than athletic ability. He was wearing greasy jeans and a stained wifebeater. Jailhouse tattoos covered his pale, flabby body. Spiderwebs on his elbows, swastikas on his neck. All black and red and hateful. The numbers 737 were scratched on to his chest, just below the hollow of his neck: 737 is *P*, *D*, and *S* on a telephone keypad. Stood for PENI Death Squad. Meant he was a member of the Public Enemy No. 1 street and prison gang. An asshole, in other words. A man who'd given up on life a long time ago.

Another skinhead stood behind him. His tattoos were equally as vile: A reference to "fourteen words," the rallying cry of white supremacists, and a crucified skinhead that was supposed to indicate he'd spent time in jail or committed murder. His 737 tattoo was on the side of his neck. His nose was running, and his mouth hung open in the way only the truly stupid can pull off. He was taller than his buddy but nowhere near as fat.

I wondered why a couple of Public Enemy No. 1s were in a DC holding cell. They were a California-based gang. I'd gone after one of their top boys in 2014, and I knew that most of their money came from identity theft and methamphetamine. I supposed they might have been in DC on business and had been picked up on outstanding warrants. DC cops decided to use them to settle their scores.

It was all a bit underwhelming, though. Like Metro hadn't really committed to it. Good for me, bad for everyone else.

"Looks like we're getting laid, bro," the fat one leered.

"Yup, nothing sweeter than virgin ass," the tall one replied.

I got to my feet, faced the camera, and shrugged. "Is this the best you can do?" I said. I didn't know if the cell was wired for sound, but the fact I'd turned my back on my potential attackers must have confused them. It sure confused the skinheads. One of them grabbed my shoulder and spun me around.

"I was talking to you, bitch," the fat one said.

"No, you weren't," I said. "You were talking to the idiot catching flies with his mouth. You told him it looked like you were getting laid. If you can't remember, you should probably get medical attention. It was only a few seconds ago, and there is now growing evidence that obesity is linked to brain shrinkage."

"The fuck you say?"

"And that's why I turned my back. I wanted to give you both some privacy."

"You're a dead man!" the skinny one bellowed.

I sighed. The sooner these two morons had been dealt with, the sooner I could get out of the holding cell and into an interview room. Maybe make that phone call.

When I'd trained with the Navy SEALs, they'd given me two bits of advice: No fighting technique is worth spit unless you commit to it totally, and if you have to fight, then you don't wait to be hit. You strike first, you strike hard, and you don't stop striking until your enemy is permanently incapacitated.

I never ignore good advice.

"Are you sure about this?" I asked the fat one. "Are you clear in your mind that this is something you want to do? Do you understand what I'm asking? Or am I speaking too fast?"

He answered by pulling out a shank. It was a plastic toothbrush, filed to a wicked point. Crude but effective. I wondered how he'd smuggled it into a police station. Logically there was only one place. The prison wallet. Lovely. Not only did he want to stab me, he also wanted to add fecal coliform bacteria to the equation. That's quite the escalation.

He smirked.

I smiled.

He frowned.

There are twenty-seven bones in the human hand and they are all fragile. It's why boxers wear gloves. I avoid punching people whenever I can. Hitting bone can cause permanent damage. Far better to strike at softer, more vulnerable areas. The ears, nose, and groin are good. The eyes are better. The eyes elicit a primal response, a desperate need to protect them.

But nothing beats a well-aimed punch to the throat.

Nothing.

It's debilitating. A real showstopper.

Not my problem, though. I wasn't the one who'd brought an ass shank to a fistfight.

I'd practiced the throat punch under the supervision of Ariel Dayan, an Israeli special forces veteran and a Ninth Dan in Krav Maga. He had me hitting a makiwara, the wooden striking post developed in Okinawa, for hours on end. One hundred punches with my left fist, one hundred with my right.

Wax on, wax off.

Turned repetition into muscle memory.

I don't warn people. None of this three-two-one bullshit. Saw that on a TV show once and I never understood why the guy kept doing it. I just go from not fighting to all-out combat like a switch has been flipped. I don't count myself in like I'm launching the space shuttle.

I didn't change my stance or draw back my arm. I just drove my right hand into his windpipe. Aimed for the sweet spot just above the larynx. Felt the punch all the way to my shoulder. Felt his throat cartilage crush.

Game over.

He hit the floor. It sounded like a horse falling over. He was supposed to choke and wheeze and clutch his throat. But he didn't. His eyes just bulged . . . and bulged . . . and then glazed over. It looked like he'd gone from alive to dead and completely skipped the dying part. It didn't look like cardio was a big part of his life, but a throat strike isn't usually fatal. Perhaps he had asthma. Or emphysema. Or one of the other respiratory conditions. Or maybe I'd mashed his carotid artery against his neck bones. It was game over if I had. No coming back from that.

The tall skinhead had changed his mind about cell-based romance. He ran for the door screaming, "Let me out!," but no one was coming to rescue him. No one was outside the holding cell door. When this went down, every cop in the building would be somewhere else. They wouldn't risk their pensions by being caught anywhere near this.

"It's just you and me," I said.

"I didn't mean nothing," he sniffed, wiping his nose on his sleeve. "We was asked to tune you up a little, is all. It was Merl who pulled the shank, not me."

"That's true," I said. "You only threatened to rape me."

"That was a joke, man."

"It was?"

He nodded. Maybe he saw a way out.

"I didn't get it," I said.

"Get what?"

"The joke."

"I don't understa—"

"A joke is something written or said that provokes laughter or causes amusement," I said. "I didn't laugh, which means I didn't get it. Can you please explain the punch line so I can enjoy the joke like you did."

I could have left him alone. It was definitely the more sensible option. Merl was probably dead. His sidekick was no threat to me at all. But people like him were predators. Bullies. They targeted the weak. It wasn't going to be me, but sometime in the future, when today's life lesson had worn off, and after he'd convinced himself it hadn't happened like he remembered, he would go after someone else. Maybe twenty sessions with a renowned psychiatrist might help get to the root cause of his problems, but I prefer a more physical approach to attitude adjustment. A disproportionate, life-changing response. One he'd remember until the day someone pulled an ass shank on him.

Anyway, I could hardly go to sleep with him in the cell. He might tickle my feet. I walked toward him. He panicked and screamed for help again. Scratched at the metal door like he was trying to climb it. I yanked him around and jabbed him in the throat too. Not as hard as Merl. It was mainly to shut him up. I still had a headache. He joined Merl on the floor, mewling and wheezing and clutching his stricken throat. After a minute his eyes had rolled up into his skull. His breathing slowed but didn't stop. He'd survive.

I reached for his left arm. The elbow is a modified hinge joint. It allows limited rotation of the arm bones. If not overused, it can work for decades. And it's very strong. It has to be. If it weren't, we would break it every time we picked up a heavy object. Breaking someone's elbow is hard. It is much easier to target the ligaments, the cartilage that strengthen and support the elbow. They can be easily torn. Particularly if the elbow is bent in a direction it's not meant to bend. I put his elbow over my knee and wrenched it back until the ligaments came away from the bone. It sounded like a carrot snapping. I let it flop back down and did the same with his right. He didn't wake up, which was lucky for him. Even with years of physical therapy, his elbows would never be the same again. Who knows, maybe this would be enough for him to reconsider his life choices.

I sat down and stared at the camera. Now they had a problem. Someone was going to jail for this. It wasn't something that could be ignored.

It couldn't be covered up. Cell CCTV footage can't be deleted. The cops who'd arranged this would be terrified. They'd tried to set up a beating, and now a prisoner in their custody was dead, and another had life-changing injuries.

They'd take me seriously now.

I hoped that would be a good thing.

CHAPTER 33

Four cops rushed into the cell, all white-faced and wide-eyed. They looked like boys who'd fired their daddy's gun by accident. They knew they were in trouble but didn't know how much yet. I was fitted with leg restraints, cuffed to the rear, and walked out of the holding cell. Two paramedics and a uniformed sergeant rushed into it. One of the paramedics was already holding a scalpel for an emergency tracheostomy.

"You shouldn't run with an open blade," I said.

Everyone ignored me.

I was taken to a smaller, single-person cell and left alone. I figured they were still deciding how to explain it. Who they were going to pin it on. It couldn't be me; I was the victim of an orchestrated attack. They would try to blame the two gangbangers. Tricky, though. One of them would soon be bitching about his broken elbows. It would have been better if I'd killed them both. Thirty years ago, the surviving skinhead would have had an accident. Maybe fallen down some stairs. Or perhaps he tried to escape and got shot in the back. Maybe he even hanged himself. Point was, he wouldn't have been around to contradict the official story.

I stopped thinking about it. Wasn't my circus; weren't my monkeys.

After an hour, my cell door opened and I was ordered to my feet. I did the shackle shuffle into a bleak and dark interview room. A strobe light flickered overhead. A camera in the corner of the ceiling blinked red. My cuffs were unfastened, then refastened to the metal ring on the interview table. My leg shackles were fixed to the I-bolt on the floor.

I was left on my own again.

The oldest interrogation trick in the book is to leave a prisoner waiting in an interview room. Turn up or turn off the air-conditioning. Let them sweat or freeze. Give them water, then don't let them take bathroom breaks. Anything to throw them off any rehearsed answers.

I knew this, but they didn't know I knew this.

So instead of getting annoyed, I reviewed what had happened so far. It wasn't the start I'd been hoping for. I'd made a mess of things. I hadn't considered Professor Marston might have removed the Martha file from his office, and I'd let some kid clock me on the head with a fire extinguisher. I had probably killed one of the skinheads in the cell fight. His death didn't bother me, but it would complicate my release. Someone was cleaning up ahead of me, and that meant I had been on the right trail. I needed to get out before it went cold. At some point there'd be a ballistics report that would prove it wasn't my weapon that killed Marston or the campus cop, but my Glock was unregistered and that would be a problem. And at some point my fake ID would collapse. Even if Samuel had been lowballing how deep he'd embedded David Decker into the facilities management company, his ID wasn't going to stand up to a murder investigation.

I hoped Mitch could pull some strings. Hoped he'd be able to call in enough favors to get me bailed. It was unlikely, though. I was in the system now. I'd been caught with a high-quality fake ID. My backpack with my bank cards and passport was still in Martha's room at Copley Hall, so Metro didn't yet know who I was. I was the very definition of a flight risk. Without Mitch's intervention, I would be sent to one of DC's jails until my arraignment.

I needed to hurry things up.

The air conditioner hummed, but due to an uncharacteristic mini heat wave, it merely made the temperature in the interview room pleasant. Which gave me an idea. I slumped in my seat and closed my eyes. Letting me sleep wouldn't be in the master plan. It was the opposite of what they wanted.

Sure enough, within five minutes the door opened. Two detectives ambled in like they had all the time in the world. They took seats opposite me and opened two files. One for each murder presumably. Silently, as if it gave gravitas to what they were doing, they took out photographs of the two murdered men. Placed them faceup.

I never refused free intel. I studied the photographs. Fixed them in my mind. Both men had single bullet holes to the center of the forehead. Good marksmanship. Clearly the work of a professional. Marston had been shot in his chair. The campus cop was lying near the open door. I didn't know for sure why Marston had been killed, but the campus cop had been responding to my unannounced visit to the professor's office. I wasn't responsible for either death, but I was definitely a causal factor in the cop's. If I hadn't busted Marston's nose, he'd be alive. It wasn't a pleasant feeling.

I wondered if they'd been watching Marston or waiting for me. If they'd been watching Marston, why kill him so publicly? And if they were waiting for me, why not take me out? Someone that good could have put a bullet in my head before I knew they were there. I'm good, but I'm not psychic. It didn't make sense.

Unless it was related to the file Marston had hidden. Then it did make sense. It added up. If there was something in it that couldn't see the light of day, then destroying the file wouldn't be enough. Marston would have had to die too. He would know what was inside. He hadn't talked to Metro PD, but he might at some point. Killing him eliminated that risk.

The lead detective, a ginger-haired man with the physique of a someone who drank his meals, had said something. He was visibly angry. Sweat marks stained the armpits of his shirt. They looked like onion rings. He had a mole on his chin that looked like a raisin.

"I'm sorry, I wasn't listening," I admitted.

"Do you have anything to say?" he snapped.

My Fifth Amendment rights meant I had the right to remain silent. I did not have to say anything to assert that right. But saying nothing wasn't going to move this along. I needed to do something. And when you're chained to a table, your only option is your words.

"Your breath smells like a burp," I said.

"What the—"

"And I'd like it very much if better detectives could ask me these questions," I continued. It was rude, but that wasn't the point. The point was to provoke a reaction. Or anger. Even experienced cops can slip up when angry.

"Listen, Mr. No-Name Asshole," Gingernut growled, "we have three girls who've all identified you as the man who burst into Professor Marston's office waving a gun and making threats. We have you in Copley Hall, Georgetown, waving the same gun."

Slipups like that. "Mr. No-Name Asshole" confirmed they didn't know who I was yet. Mitch must have called in a favor and had my fingerprints removed from IAFIS, the FBI's Integrated Automated Fingerprint Identification System. And if he'd had the foresight to do that, he might have also had the foresight to monitor police reports coming out of Georgetown.

Gingernut continued. "And we have two good men in the morgue and—"

"And one bad one," I said. "Don't forget the skinhead you sent to kill me."

Gingernut flushed but rallied fast. "And when the ballistics report comes back, it's going to confirm what we already know: Your gun was used in their murders. Even if we never find out who you are, this isn't a rap you get to beat."

Other than wondering if speaking like Sam Spade had worked for him in the past, I ignored him and went back to studying the photographs. There had to be something in them. I moved from the murder scene and looked at the wider shots. They were mainly different views of Marston's office. One had been taken from inside, shooting out. It had caught a bunch of faculty and staff crowded behind a hastily constructed tape barrier. I committed the faces to memory. If I ever got the chance, they might be worth talking to later.

"Hey, I'm talking to you!" Gingernut barked, slamming his fist on the table. "How long you think it'll take a jury to return life with no parole? I think it'll take less than ten minutes. Bob here disagrees." He nodded in the direction of the other detective. "He says less than five. And you know what, asshole? My momma told me never to bet when the other man's right."

A rookie marshal knows not to interrogate like this. Why wind up the suspect? Attack only has defense as a response. And no one had mentioned the two skinheads yet. Could be they were holding any charges in reserve. More likely they knew they'd screwed up. Knew that the video evidence would look like a prearranged attack on me. Probably hadn't expected one of the skinheads to pull a shank out of his ass. Kind of changed the narrative a bit.

"So I'll tell you what we're going to do here," Gingernut persisted. "I don't know what your beef was with the professor, but you're going to admit you messed up. Write us up a nice little confession. Make it all nice and legal. Do that and we'll put a good word in with the judge. Say you were contrite. That you cooperated. See if we can get you federal time. Otherwise we might get you transferred to Rivers in North Carolina. And you ain't gonna like Rivers. Rivers is a private prison, you see. And personal rights don't mean shit down there."

He said it like he'd thrown down pocket aces.

Bob finally spoke. He was equally clichéd. "That's a sweet deal, my friend. Federal time's like a health spa. Swimming pools, massages. Free health care, big libraries, you might even get yourself an education for when you get out. What you say, friend, you gonna sign this bit of paper?"

"Is this the comedy interrogation, a bit of light relief before the real one starts?" I said. "Are there a bunch of people behind that two-way mirror eating doughnuts and laughing?"

Gingernut went beet red. Looked like he was about to hit me. Luckily for his pension, the door opened with a slam and another cop came in. If Gingernut was angry, this man was furious. He was in uniform and wore the gold of a captain's badge.

"We're not allowed to talk to this man."

Gingernut lurched to his feet, spilling the paper coffee cup all over his groin in the process. "What!"

The captain whispered something in both their ears. One of them whispered back.

"Do I *look* happy?" the captain hissed.

They all stared at me.

Eventually, Gingernut said, "Two more minutes and we'd have had him. You can hold them off that long, surely?"

"No, we have to stop talking to him *now*. You won't believe where this order came from."

"But we still have him for what just happened. He just killed a guy with one punch. The other will never wipe his own ass again."

"Are you insane? No DA in the land will prosecute that. You sent in two thugs to beat the shit out of him, and one of them pulls a shank out of his ass. What the hell was he supposed to do?"

"Hey, that wasn't us, Captain! We were still at Georgetown."

"Get the fuck out, the pair of you. A bunch of people are losing their pensions over this. If I were you, I'd start practicing my story for IA."

"I don't believe this!" Gingernut bellowed. He stormed out of the interrogation room, slamming the door behind him. Bob had to reopen it to follow him. I heard him muttering something along the lines of "I'm not finished with that asshole yet." I think he also questioned whether I'd had inappropriate relations with my mother.

The captain shut the door after them. He turned to me, winked, and reached up to turn off the camera. He pulled the blinds on the two-way mirror.

Maybe this was how it ended? Killed by a corrupt cop in a dingy DC interrogation room. Probably say I made a play for his gun and he had no choice but to put a bullet in my head. Idly, I wondered how he planned to explain me still being shackled tighter than a hatband.

"Are you in charge?" I asked. "Because next time I'd like to be interviewed by real cops. Those two pinheads couldn't organize a one-car parade."

The captain sat down in the seat vacated by Gingernut. He removed a set of keys from his pocket and said, "Hello, Ben. We don't have much time. Now listen very carefully . . ."

CHAPTER 34

"So Mitch *didn't* send you?" It was the third time I'd asked this, but the answer was the same every time.

"Who's Mitch?"

The captain had uncuffed me before leading me through back corridors in the station. He stopped beside a door, opened it, and shoved me inside. It was a small storeroom. Used to keep the Christmas decorations and other nonessential stuff. Meant it was unlikely someone would come in. My clothes and my Glock were waiting for me. I quickly changed. My clothes still had blood on them from the bash to the head I'd taken, but they were better than the paper evidence suit I'd been wearing. I stuck the Glock in the small of my back. Not ideal, but I had no choice.

I knocked gently on the inside of the door and the captain opened it. "Ready?" he asked.

"Ready?" I said. "I don't know what the hell this is. How can I be ready?"

He smiled. "This is your escape from custody, Mr. Koenig."

And with that, he walked off. Nonplussed, I had little choice but to follow him down yet another corridor. Plastered and painted walls covered in photographs of precinct captains gave way to whitewashed bricks and FIRE EXIT signs. We were at the business end of the station. The bit the public never saw.

When we reached the end—a double fire door, one of those with long metal bars that you push down to open—the captain said, "I'm leaving you here. Count to sixty, then open this door. The alarm will sound, but I've made sure the system will be confused for a while. You'll have thirty seconds before anyone works out which door has been opened."

I didn't respond.

"The garbage alley is on the other side of this door," he continued. "Walk out, then turn right. Walk to the end of the block and take another right. There'll be a black Porsche waiting for you. Get in it."

"What the hell's going on?" I asked.

He ignored me. "Remember, sixty seconds. Give me time to get back to my desk. Turn right and then right again." He turned his back to me and jogged along the way he'd come.

"Wait! I don't even know your name."

"No, you don't," he shouted without turning. He went through a door and I was on my own.

CHAPTER 35

Risk-assessment time. Not my strongest suit, but I gave it a go. While I was in the station, a professional hit hadn't been feasible. Too many people would have needed to be involved. Too many cameras, too many people with guns. Too many people sworn to uphold the law. The alley at the back of a police station wasn't the ideal killing ground either, but it was much better than inside. Even if cameras covered the exit, a killer wearing a hat and sunglasses could be a mile away before anyone realized what had happened. The captain with no name had said Mitch hadn't arranged this, and that meant someone else had. Probably a bad actor. Marston's killer was almost certainly still in DC, and the people who'd paid for his hit would know where I was being held.

The "turn right, turn right again, and get into a black Porsche" was a nice touch. Some bullshit to make it seem more real. I'd either get slugged the second I opened the fire exit or as soon as I left the alleyway. I guessed the chances of this happening were between 70 and 80 percent. And it would be a deliberate ambush rather than a snap ambush. Snap ambushes are survivable. They are hastily put together. Deliberate ambushes are unsurvivable.

Two options then. Open the door and step into an ambush or head back into the station. That would almost certainly end with me being back in an interview room facing more amateur dramatics from Gingernut and Bob.

Even as I'd been thinking it through, I'd been counting. I don't even know why I bothered running the calculations. I knew what I was going to do. When I reached fifty, I began a ten-second countdown. On reaching one, I drew my weapon and opened the door.

No one shot me in the head, which I took as a positive sign.

The captain had been right about the alarm. It sounded immediately. It was internal, though. I shut the door and it faded to nothing. I scrunched my eyes from the low afternoon sun, and my nose from the stench. It was overpowering. Black bags reeking of garbage. An overflowing dumpster. Vomit. Excrement. Puddles, oil spills, dirt and grime. It was like any alley in any city in any country. Didn't make it smell any better.

I walked toward the street. Cockroaches scuttled out of my way. I heard the scratching of rats, although thankfully I couldn't see them. I don't like rats. Never have. Was bitten on the ankle by one during a stakeout once. Had to have a bunch of shots.

I reached the end of the alley. If the killer was waiting for me on the street, I'd be shot in the temple the second I stepped on to the sidewalk. Bundled back into the alley before I had a chance to hit the soiled concrete. I'd probably end up in the dumpster.

I stepped out.

Again, no one shot me in the head. Perhaps the captain hadn't been setting up a hit after all.

I turned right.

I was on a pleasant street in an area where the upwardly mobile middle class worked and played. Lots of independent coffeehouses, bistros, and delis. My stomach growled as the smell of Greek gyros hit my nostrils. I willed myself to walk past. Now wasn't the time to root through my backpack for some money.

The block wasn't big and I soon reached the corner.

The black Porsche was exactly where the captain had said it would be. It had tinted windows, so I couldn't tell if there was someone in it or if I was supposed to drive it myself. He had been vague on that point. He either didn't know or he wasn't saying.

It was one hundred yards away and I slowed as I neared it.

Fifty yards.

Twenty.

The driver's door opened. A woman climbed out. Despite the expensive suit and the designer shades that covered half her face, I'd have recognized her anywhere.

It was Jen Draper, my ex–Special Operations Group nemesis.

Her expression was grim. She raised her hand, but she wasn't greeting me. She held a sound-suppressed SIG Sauer. I wondered if it would hurt.

She aimed at my head and pulled the trigger.

CHAPTER 36

The bullet nicked my earlobe. I felt a sharp sting. Warm blood sprinkled on my neck. She'd missed. I found that difficult to believe. Jen had been the best shot in the unit, even better than me. I shouldn't be alive. I didn't bother reaching for my Glock. Jen would get off another three shots before I could reach for my backpack.

Unbelievably, she didn't fire. Instead she lowered her weapon. I wondered if she'd had a stoppage. It hadn't sounded like it. The action had looked normal. A bullet had been fired. The empty casing had been extracted from the chamber and ejected out of the port. I'd seen the slide rack another round. But she'd lowered her weapon anyway. What did she know that I didn't?

Lots probably, if she was working with the people who'd ordered the hit on Professor Marston. Perhaps it was she who had killed him. She was certainly coldhearted enough.

Her bad luck was my good luck. I grabbed my Glock and pointed it at her face. Squeezed the trigger until I felt the bite. An ounce more pressure and I'd put a bullet into her brain. I lowered my hand. Aimed at her stomach. I needed her dying but not dead. In pain but not so much pain she couldn't talk. I had questions for her.

"This *will* hurt," I told her.

A sound behind me made me pull the shot just as I fired. The bullet didn't nick her ear, but it wasn't far off. I saw a puff of brick dust on the building across the road. Thankfully the stray had landed safe. I didn't want more innocent deaths on my conscience.

The sound I'd heard, the one that had saved her life, was the unmistakable thump of a collapsing body. It had been followed by metal hitting concrete. I'd ordered perps to drop their weapons enough times to recognize the sound one makes when it hits the sidewalk.

Behind me was a body and gun.

I turned.

A woman lay dead on the sidewalk, her sightless eyes staring up at the crisp Washington sky. A bullet hole was centered on her forehead. It was small and barely bleeding. She was slight and blonde, little more than a girl really. She wore jeans and a Georgetown Hoyas sweatshirt. If it weren't for the gun beside her outstretched hand, I'd have mistaken her for a student. It was a snub-nosed pistol. A killer's weapon. Fits in a purse and the muzzle blast is little more than a pop. Not much range but deadly up close. The bullet bounces round the skull, turning the brain into ground beef. By the time the victim realizes they're dead, their killer's already twenty yards away.

Jen had needed to shoot through my earlobe to make sure she killed her with one shot. Ballsy move. She jogged back to the Porsche. Before she climbed into the driver's seat, she turned and faced me.

"Get in the fucking car, dickhead," she said.

CHAPTER 37

Her voice was like a starting pistol. I sprinted for the car and jumped in the passenger seat. Before I had a chance to shut the door, she'd gunned the accelerator and joined the afternoon traffic.

"Who the hell was that?" I shouted. "And what the hell are you doing here?"

Jen held up her hand to shut me up. Her cell phone was already between her shoulder and her ear. The phone was hinged in the middle. You had to open it like a clam when you wanted to use it. Looked cheap. Probably a burner.

I listened to her one-sided conversation. I turned to see if we were being followed and noticed my backpack on the rear seats. Jen must have collected it from Martha's room. I wondered how she knew.

"Yes, I've got him," she said. ". . . You're going to have to tidy up a bit, though. I left a body out in the open . . . No choice, she was about to take him out, so I had to do it on the sidewalk . . . Yes, she's still there. Metro will be there soon." She listened a bit more, nodded and said, "Will do."

She snapped the phone shut and turned left at the intersection.

"Who was that?"

She didn't answer.

"Where are we going?" I asked.

"Somewhere safe," she replied.

Didn't even look at me when she said it.

Somewhere safe turned out to be a cabin in some dense woods in Charles County, Maryland.

"What's this place?" I said.

"It belongs to my employer," she replied. "No one will look for you here."

"And who's your employer?"

She didn't reply, but that was OK. I already knew the answer. Mitch had briefed me on what all the old SOG guys were up to now. Jen had left the SOG and transitioned to private intelligence. She'd been working for the Allerdale Group for almost six years now, almost as long as I'd been on the run. They were a small but well-respected company, and I wasn't surprised they could afford a hidey-hole like this. These days almost 70 percent of the government's intelligence budget is outsourced to the private sector.

The word "cabin" didn't do it justice. "Cabin" implies rusticity, a rough-and-ready homestead that offers shelter from the elements but little in the way of modern comforts. This was palatial. Beautifully cut pine logs formed the walls, and polished teak framed the windows and doors. A wraparound porch on all four sides with comfortable outside furniture.

Jen parked the Porsche next to a Range Rover and a red '73 Corvette Stingray. I knew it was a '73 as it had a plastic bumper at the front and a chrome bumper at the back. Best of my knowledge, that's the only year that happened. It had removable roof panels for sunny days and a red leather interior. Not the pleather stuff I'd been sitting on recently. This leather had eaten grass and mooed. I got out of the Porsche and ran my fingers along the Corvette's smooth lines. It really was a beautiful machine.

"Touch my car again and I'll kill you myself," she said.

I followed Jen into the cabin.

"The guest room's at the end of the hall," she said. "Go and take a shower. You smell worse than you look."

"What's going on?" I said, standing my ground. "Never mind showers.

How was my escape from custody arranged? What the hell have you got to do with all this?"

She looked at me. Tilted her head in that same annoying way. "Pout all you want," she said. "I'm not talking to you until you've cleaned yourself up."

"I'm not going anywhere."

"Suit yourself," she said. "I'll be in my office for a few hours. Please don't disturb me."

Ten seconds later I was standing on my own feeling foolish. I decided to do what she'd asked and have a shower. I didn't care that she'd saved my life. I still thought Jen Draper was an asshole.

CHAPTER 38

Twenty minutes later I felt like a new man. The hot water had washed the tension from me. I'd even managed to scrape off my stubble with the disposable razor in the bag of toiletries in the guest room en suite. When I got out of the shower, the dirty clothes I'd heaped on the floor had gone. Jeans and a T-shirt had been laid out on the bed. Clean underwear and socks. I got dressed, slipped on a pair of sneakers, and went to find Jen. If she wasn't going to give me answers, then I needed to move on. She might have all the time in the world; I didn't.

She'd moved from her office to the cabin's living room. She didn't look up from the laptop she was working on.

"Sit," she said.

I did.

"Where are my clothes?" I said.

"They've been incinerated."

"And how did you know to collect my backpack from Martha's room?"

"You'd made a mess. I was tidying it."

I waited for her to expand on that. She didn't. Just carried on tapping at her laptop. In the six years since I'd seen Jen, she'd managed to hang on to her youthful vitality while adding that certain something that turned guys' heads. Tall and graceful, she was like a ballerina on steroids. A grumpy ballerina who no one liked, but a ballerina all the same. Her hair was the color of corn. It was pulled back tight in the style she preferred when working. As I watched, she jutted out her bottom lip and blew an errant wisp from her eyes. Her fingers continued to dance across the keyboard. If I lost nine fingers in an industrial accident, I doubted it would affect my typing speed. Jen wasn't even looking down. Her eyes remained glued to the screen.

"Who's going first?" I asked.

She pressed the return button, and I heard the *whoosh* of a sent email. She looked up and shrugged. "You want to do this now, do you?"

"Do what now?"

"You know what."

I said nothing. I did know what.

"Where the fuck have you been?" she said.

CHAPTER 39

SIX YEARS EARLIER

The immediate aftermath of the Gecko Creek operation was paperwork. And not just paperwork. I'd fatally shot a suspect. There were debriefings, statements made under oath, and questions from pale, stale men with twenty-twenty hindsight. "Had the youth"—because at seventeen, that's what he was—"aimed a weapon in your direction?" "Did you fear for your life?" I almost laughed at that one. "Are you one hundred percent sure the child would have fallen into the dog's enclosure?" "Can you think of any other action you could have taken?" "In your opinion, Deputy Marshal Koenig, was this a lawful shooting?"

I knew protocols had to be followed, just as we all knew that the Office of Professional Responsibility would rule that double-tapping the youth had been the only way to save the child. Although I felt for the family of the kid I'd killed, after a day of bureaucracy, I was bored.

By the end of day two, with no respite in sight, I was crawling up the walls.

On day three I was abducted by the Solntsevskaya Bratva Russian crime syndicate and things got interesting again.

"Abducted" was probably the wrong word. "Strongly encouraged" perhaps. Two goons turned up at my front door and said their boss wanted to see me. If I refused, everyone in my family would die. I might not have been bundled into the back of a van, but the effect was the same.

I knew who their "boss" was. As soon as the dead youth had been identified, the FBI had warned me something like this might happen. They'd urged me to take precautions. Mitch ordered me.

My condition meant I didn't take any of them seriously.

More fool me, I suppose.

The journey to New York took nearly five hours. As we got to the outskirts of the city, smaller buildings gave way to skyscrapers. New York has always been a vertical city. It's now taller than it was before the 9/11 attacks. And not just Manhattan, in the boroughs too. New York symbolizes the American spirit, the "we're all in this together" attitude. It reminds me of a story about Pearl Harbor. The day after the Japanese decimated the Pacific Fleet, a large number of Navajos, a group that had not been treated well by the government, rode their horses to the nearest army recruiting center. Their country had been attacked and they were ready to go to war. It was the same after the towers came down. People wanted to stand a post. After Boston, New York is my favorite American city.

I wondered if we were going to Brooklyn. Maybe a warehouse or basement in Brighton Beach, the traditional Solntsevskaya Bratva stronghold. Or perhaps the abduction of a US marshal would make them careful. Avoid their usual haunts. When the Lincoln pulled up outside a Russian restaurant in Queens, I knew caution had prevailed.

"Inside," one of the goons said, pointing toward the door. "Is open," he added, referring to the CLOSED sign swinging in the window.

I ignored the urge to go on the offensive. The Bratva goons were no doubt battle-hardened, but we were in a car and I'd been taught how to operate in confined fighting environments by the best there was. Headbutts are good; elbow strikes are better. Elbow strikes are short, create a lot of trauma with little risk of injuring yourself. I could kill them easy as pie. Grab a weapon and shoot the rest. Walk into the restaurant and double-tap the man in charge.

I dismissed the idea immediately. The Solntsevskaya Bratva had a long reach. If they couldn't get to me, they'd go after my family. My sister in England wouldn't be safe. My nephews and nieces wouldn't be safe.

So, while the two goons stayed with the driver, I approached the restaurant. The door opened before I reached it, and another goon stepped out to meet me. I was searched again. When he was satisfied I was unarmed, he nodded toward the back.

I waited until my eyes had adjusted to the gloom.

A man in his fifties was having dinner. He gestured to the seat opposite with a fork. After I'd sat down, a waiter put a plate of small dumplings in front of me. I picked up one and bit into it. It was filled with greasy pork. We ate in silence. When the dumplings were gone, a plate of stew arrived. It was the color of blood.

"Borscht," the man said. "My mother's recipe. Made with beetroot and pork. Puts hairs on your chest."

He had an Eastern European accent. Unsurprising. The man I was eating Russian food with was Yaroslav Zamyatin, the second-in-command of the Solntsevskaya Bratva. Recently bereaved father of Bogdan Zamyatin, shot dead by Deputy US Marshal Benjamin Koenig during the execution of an arrest warrant.

I wouldn't live to see what was for dessert.

Zamyatin was an old-school kind of gangster. He believed in civility, even to his enemies. *Especially* to his enemies.

As we sipped jet-black coffee from tiny cups, he got down to business. He didn't follow the script I'd expected.

"My son, Mr. Koenig, was a *durak*."

I had rudimentary Russian, but it didn't stretch to idioms or slang. I shrugged.

"A moron, an idiot," he explained. "My first wife was a beautiful woman, but she was a little too fond of the heroin. Didn't stop when she was pregnant and Bogdan was the result." He waved his arms around, indicated where we were. "This business I'm in. It is competitive."

"I've heard that about the restaurant trade," I said.

He smiled at my joke. "Yes. Very good. If it pleases you, we will keep the analogy. The *restaurant* business is very competitive. There are many other *restaurants* that want our customers and sometimes this results in unpleasantness. My son was not cut out for this. He was too stupid, too reactionary. He was also very cruel."

I took another sip of coffee and watched him over the rim of the cup.

Zamyatin continued. "But this business has been good to me and I did not want to see him destitute or without purpose. A man without purpose is not a man at all. Would you agree, Mr. Koenig?"

I nodded.

"So I gave him—how do you say it over here?—seed money. Told him to go out into the world and make something for himself. I thought some responsibility would turn him into a son I could be proud of. But do you know what that"—he spat out a word I didn't know—"did?"

The question had been rhetorical. I knew exactly what Bogdan had done.

"He gave my two hundred thousand dollars to those fucking animals. Used it to buy a stake," he said. "My life was hard growing up, Mr. Koenig. I have done things I'm not proud of. People have suffered so I could buy things I don't need. But feeding children to dogs? How is it possible to even conceive such an idea?"

He gestured with his cup, and an unseen waiter rushed over with an ornate silver pot. Zamyatin filled both of our cups. He sipped his coffee, added two sugars, then looked at me.

"You put down an animal that day, Mr. Koenig," he said. "Nothing more. He was my son, but he deserved to die. If I'd found out what he'd been doing, I'd have killed him myself. Rest assured, your prison system doesn't have cells deep enough for the rest of those"—he spat out the same word as before. "They'll be dead within the month. You may call this a fact."

Zamyatin drained his second cup of coffee. I hadn't touched mine yet.

"So, to why you are here," he said. "This business of mine in large part is an illusion. We rely on fear to get the things we want. To make sure our people stay in line. And it *is* an illusion, Mr. Koenig. Like the NYPD rely on people obeying the law, we rely on people being afraid of us. If every criminal in New York turned on the NYPD at the same time, well then"—he snapped a small biscuit in two—"the illusion would be shown for what it is: an illusion. There would be no more NYPD."

He stared at me. I knew what he was going to say.

"And if the people aren't living in fear, then we also have no business. And when the son of a boss is killed, there has to be reparation," he said. His voice was neutral. Sad even. "Now you understand that there is not a choice in this. If I want revenge or I don't want revenge is immaterial. It is a business decision. A statement about our unlimited resources and a message to our competitors. If they see it is OK to kill our families, then our families will be killed. We lose our business."

"Only blood can pay for blood?" I asked.

"You *do* understand," he replied. He reached into his pocket and put a piece of paper on the table. He pushed it in front of me.

I unfolded it. It was a screenshot of a website. Writing surrounded my photograph. It was in Russian, but there *was* something I could understand: "$5,000,000."

The Bratva had put a price on my head.

"As a concession to me, my boss—because I too must report to someone—has allowed me the courtesy of explaining this face-to-face."

I turned in my seat, expecting to see someone behind me with a silenced semi pointed at the base of my skull. But the restaurant remained empty. I wondered why Zamyatin had bothered bringing me here. It seemed cruel, and he didn't seem the type. Pragmatic, yes; cruel, no.

"No one will harm you here, Mr. Koenig," he said, "because this is not the only concession I was allowed. I haven't told you the best bit yet."

CHAPTER 40

"He gave me twenty-four hours," I told Jen. "Twenty-four hours from the moment I left the restaurant to the site going live."

She had listened in silence. She'd made a few notes but had otherwise let me tell my story without interruptions.

"I was shown a second sheet of paper. It had my sister's London address on it. Zamyatin explained my choices were limited to two. Either disappear with a five-million bounty on my head, or go after them for threatening a federal agent. If I chose the latter, the fee would cover the elimination of both me and Zoe."

"And here was me thinking you'd just been your usual asshole self," she said after I'd finished. "Left your colleagues in the lurch to go on some bullshit voyage of self-discovery."

"Where do you fit in?"

"Mitch called me. He's been monitoring all DC systems to see if your name cropped up, I think. Told me where you'd be. Said you might be leaving in a hurry. He asked if I had somewhere you could regroup."

"Mitch arranged my escape?"

"I certainly don't have that kind of clout."

"Did he tell you what's happening?"

She nodded. "His daughter's missing. Said he'd used the Most Wanted list to flush you out. Thinks you might be useful. And as you've been cracked over the head with a fire extinguisher, been arrested for double murder, and had to be saved from a contract killer, I'd say his confidence in you is fully justified."

"He's desperate."

"He must be."

She checked her laptop. "I'm waiting on an email on your would-be killer's identity. I assume you're not giving up yet? That you're still aiming to run around like an overstimulated toddler?"

I rolled my eyes. "If you're asking if I still plan to search for my friend's daughter, then the answer's yes. Of course I am."

"The identity of the woman who tried to kill you is the only lead you have then. And while we wait, you're going to tell me how you managed to survive a five-mil bounty for six years. I'm assuming it was dumb luck."

There was no reason not to tell her.

"I didn't have much time. Twenty-four hours to get some cash together doesn't leave a lot of time for emotional goodbyes . . ."

For the next hour I rolled out how I'd survived the last six years. I told her how I'd left Brighton Beach and headed home. After picking up my passport and some other essentials, one of which was the deed to the brownstone, I'd left the home I'd lived in all my life. A home I hadn't seen since.

A friend of mine was a property developer, and I'd driven straight to his office. He'd been joking about turning my house into apartments for years, knowing I'd never sell. When I told him the deed was his for two hundred grand cash, as long as the cash was in my hands within the hour, he didn't know whether to laugh or cry. He asked me about my beloved Super 8 movie collection, the one I'd been building since I was allowed a paper route. I said he could keep it. He said he'd keep it in storage for me. Also said he would turn the brownstone into luxury apartments, but only if I'd let him sell me the penthouse suite for one dollar. Had the paperwork drawn up there and then. I signed it, just to get him off my back. I wasn't coming back. As far as I knew, it was still unoccupied.

One of the hardest men I'd ever tracked, a white-collar fraudster called Arnold Harper, had beat into me the advantage of using an international business corporation to hold your funds. He'd evaded me for a year and that was because we never had any idea where he was. Just as suspects without money are caught accessing their usual support networks, suspects *with* money are caught because of it. ATM photographs, simple electronic trails, even backtracking the banknotes they've withdrawn. Money is always the problem when it comes to staying off the grid. But Arnold managed it. And he'd still be out there if I hadn't discovered his weakness. Just like in *Hannibal*, when Special Agent Starling knew Lecter wouldn't be able to resist buying a Jaguar XJR supercharged sedan when he landed back in the States, I knew Arnold wouldn't be able to stop himself going to the Kentucky Derby. People liked what they liked, and he liked horses. His business had never allowed him the time to attend the Derby before, but I figured with time on his hands and money to burn, he wouldn't be able to stop himself. Two other marshals and I were in our best bib and tucker, mixing with the owners and trainers. When Arnold came in, he actually stood next to me at the bar. I whispered "Gotcha" in his ear, and that was it, his great adventure was over. He served three to five somewhere easy and would be out on good behavior by now.

But the lesson had stuck.

With my money in an IBC, I had a float I could access without giving away my location. To the best of my knowledge, since the bounty went live, no one had intentionally been in the same state as me.

"And that's that," I said. "My last six years. Not particularly productive, but at least my sister's safe."

Jen disappeared and came back with a steaming pot of coffee and two mugs. We retired to the seats by the log fire. It gave a nice glow. Shadows danced and chased each other up and down the wooden walls. We filled our mugs and got down to business.

"What do you need?" she said.

"Access to Marston's file. He was killed only a few minutes after he'd agreed to hand it over."

"Already done." She handed me a paper file and I eagerly took it. "Take a look. That's everything we could find and it isn't much. Someone who knew what they were doing deleted both his home and office computer files. It was unrecoverable. We couldn't find anything in the cloud either."

"The cloud?"

"Luddite," she muttered. "I'll try to put this in words you might understand. The cloud is like a magic box that computer wizards put their spells
in to keep them safe. Is that simple enough for you?"

"Much clearer, thank you."

"I assume you think that the woman who tried to kill you was sent by
the same person who abducted Martha?" she said.

"Unless it's unrelated and she was after the bounty. Bit of a coincidence,
though. Same day a hit is ordered on Marston, a bounty hunter stumbles on
to me after all these years. I'm not buying it."

"Agreed. It has to be connected." Her phone beeped. She checked the
message and said, "That's handy."

She grabbed her laptop and opened an email. She frowned, then printed
it off. She handed the printout to me.

"We've ID'd the woman," she said. "It's not good news."

I took the offered paper and read it. Jen spoke as I did.

"Her name's Catherine Panabaker, or that's the name she's using. She's
not affiliated. Over the last few years she's suspected of having done jobs
for the Italians, the Chechens, the Russians, even the cartels. Basically
anytime someone needs a cute female. My guy says whoever paid her can't
be traced. Sorry."

I wasn't surprised. The main reason to use outside help is to avoid blowback. Secure payment protocols are standard for contract killers. If the Allerdale Group couldn't untangle the route by which Panabaker had gotten
paid, then it was a dead end. Figuratively for me, literally for her.

There was only one lead left. Panabaker had wiped all Marston's computers, but Martha hadn't been taught by him in isolation. She couldn't
possibly have wiped all her other professors' computers. I remembered the
bushel of signs on the way to Marston's office. Georgetown took a holistic
approach to education, and that meant it was likely Martha had contact
with campus services such as accommodation, finance, student employment. Maybe even health and wellness. She wouldn't just be on academic
databases. She'd be on a whole bunch of them.

"Do you have anyone who can get into Georgetown's intranet?" I
asked Jen.

"Not legally."

I didn't argue the point. She'd either help me or she wouldn't.

"Which one?" she said eventually. "There'll be loads."

"All of them," I said.

"Let me make some calls," she sighed. "But you may as well get some sleep. This is going to take a while."

CHAPTER 41

The look on Jen's face when she woke me told me everything. She hadn't found anything.

"I've printed off all the academic stuff for you, but I don't think there's anything useful. I've highlighted every page that mentions Martha, and put everything that mentions both her and Professor Marston at the top of the pile. You might spot something, but nothing stood out to me. The nonacademic stuff is still coming through."

For the next two hours I immersed myself in the stack of paper. Jen was right. There was nothing. Martha had a number of professors, and anytime one of them emailed her, Marston, as the person overseeing the paper she'd been writing, had been cc'd in. When I finished the batch in my hand, I threw it down in frustration.

"This is pointless," I said. "I need to get out there. Start cracking some heads."

"Spoken like a true tactician," Jen said without looking up from her own pile. "You stick with her professors and I'll stay with the nonacademic intranet stuff."

I sighed and picked up the next page on the pile. It was an email to Marston from a professor called Stephen Lind. The subject line was "Complex financial instruments: an academic review of convertible issuances."

"If I'm going to wade through bullshit like this, I'm going to need more coffee," I said. I got to my feet and rolled my shoulders. Rotated my head, tried to loosen some of the cricks.

"This is interesting," Jen said.

I joined her on the couch. "What is it?"

She spun the laptop so I could see the screen. She'd been looking at Georgetown's "Student Living" page. Martha's name was on a list of students who'd requested a room change.

I was silent as I recalled Freya Jackson's part of their shared room. There'd been a lot of photographs of her and Martha. They were friends. Not just roommates, friends. I'd been planning to talk to Freya, see if there was maybe something she hadn't told Metro PD or the FBI at the time. Something she now wished she had.

Now I wondered why Martha had wanted to move rooms. What had happened between them?

I looked at myself in the mirror above the fire. Despite the recent shower and shave, my hair was still a mess. "I need to go back to Georgetown," I said. "I need to speak to Freya Jackson."

"I thought you might say that," she nodded. "But you can't go like that, you look like a bum."

"Can I ask you something?"

"No."

"We hate each other, right?"

"'Hate' is a strong word, Koenig. How about 'strongly dislike'?"

"That's fine," I said. "So as we dislike each—"

"*Strongly* dislike."

"As we strongly dislike each other, why are you helping me?"

"Because I was asked to. I'd have preferred to let Panabaker drop you on the street."

"Which is what I figured," I said. "Only thing that made any kind of sense. Mitch has asked you to help me." I paused, then added, "What are you like with a pair of scissors?"

"Good enough to slice your balls clean off," she said. "And if you ask me to cut your hair, that's exactly what will happen."

"I'll do it myself then," I said. "I saw some scissors in the guest room."

I'd made it to the corridor when she called me back.

"Yes?" I said hopefully.

"If I find a single hair in the en suite's sink, they'll never find your body."

CHAPTER 42

My first pass with the scissors was a bit lumpy, but I found a pair of clippers in the bathroom cabinet so was able to even it out into a buzzcut. There was also a bottle of dye. Chestnut. I think it was meant for women, but I figured it would darken my ash-brown hair. When I finished, I barely recognized myself. I'd even gotten rid of the gray hairs I'd accumulated on the road. My hairline was a bit pale, but I didn't think it would stand out too much in Washington's gloomy weather.

While I'd been hacking at my hippie hair, Jen had gotten one of her employees to bring over a suit, shirt, and tie, and a pair of brogues. He didn't even come in, just knocked on the door and left it all on a porch seat. Apparently, bringing suits for unnamed men at 3 a.m. wasn't an unusual request in the private intelligence business.

"What's your plan?" she asked after I'd tried it all on. Although it fit perfectly, I didn't like it. Didn't like wearing a necktie again. Didn't like the way wearing a suit made me feel.

"I'll catch Freya Jackson on her way to class in the morning," I replied. "Get her while she's still bleary-eyed and yawning. See if I can nudge her memory a bit."

"If the people who hired Panabaker are watching all Martha's contacts, speaking to her in public might put her at risk."

Jen was right. I hadn't considered that. While Urbach-Wiethe was occasionally an asset, it was mostly a colossal liability. It didn't just put me at risk; it dragged others into its gravity well.

"I'll come with you," she said. "We'll talk to her in her dorm. If there's anyone hanging around who looks like they shouldn't be there, we'll abort."

"Thank you," I said.

She raised her eyebrows. Had probably expected me to kick back at her proposal. But other than extending my time in her company, there was no downside, only ups. Jen was an asshole to work with, but she had been an excellent interviewer. Had a knack for winkling information out of the most stubborn witnesses. And as an added bonus, if the campus cops were on the lookout for the loner who escaped police custody yesterday, then having Jen with me was a better disguise than the suit and the haircut.

"Deal," I said. "But we're taking the Stingray."

"No, we're fucking not," she replied.

CHAPTER 43

As a thank-you, I whipped up some eggs for breakfast. Scrambled with chilies, green onions, and cheese: a breakfast of champions. Jen ate hers without comment. We were on the road before seven and in DC within the hour. The sun had already burned through the morning mist. I'd sat in the passenger seat of Jen's Range Rover and fidgeted like a kid in church. I still hadn't gotten used to wearing a suit again.

Jen parked in Georgetown's staff parking lot, and we walked over to Copley Hall. No one gave us a second glance. We took the stairs to the fifth floor and walked to the end of the corridor.

"I'll take the lead," Jen said.

I nodded my agreement. Although I was more presentable than the last time I was there, I was still a man. Freya Jackson might respond better to a woman.

Jen knocked. She didn't bother waiting for answer; she walked in and shut the door behind her. I waited outside. A minute passed before the door opened again.

"You can come in now. She's decent." Jen wasn't using my name, and I wouldn't use hers. Why leave bread crumbs?

Freya Jackson was in her late teens. She had light red hair and join-the-dot freckles, and was looking at us through aqua unisex spectacles.

She looked curious, not worried. She was seated on her bed, and Jen had taken the desk chair. I stood.

"Tell me about Martha," Jen said.

To her credit, she didn't moan when she was asked to repeat something she'd probably recited a dozen times. Her story tallied with the statement Mitch had given me.

When she'd finished, I said, "Now I want to know what it was you didn't tell the FBI."

No lead-in, best way to catch them off guard sometimes.

"I told them everything!" she said indignantly. "She was my best friend here!"

"That's not strictly true, though, is it?" Jen said.

Her face twisted in confusion. "Why, what did she say?"

Jen carried on as if she'd not spoken. "If you were such good friends, why did she want a different roommate?"

Her confusion changed to blankness, then finally understanding.

I had expected excuses at this point. Claims of misunderstandings, of things taken out of context. But she didn't.

She said something else.

"Oh, that. That was nothing to do with me," Freya said. "She just wanted to be in his room for a bit. See if she could get some sort of vibe from it."

Jen glanced at me. I shrugged. I didn't have a clue what she was talking about.

"Whose room?" Jen said.

"Well, Gunnar's obviously. It's on the floor below."

Our lack of comprehension must have been obvious. She shook her head in amazement.

"You don't know about Gunnar Ulrich?"

"Enlighten us," I said.

"I'm not sure how, but I think it had something to do with what she was writing."

The paper—the one thing everyone had been in the dark about. Even Mitch. The only person who'd known was the late Professor Marston. I wonder if that was what he was killed for.

"And this Gunnar Ulrich, he lives downstairs?" I said.

Freya didn't say "Duh," but it was clear she wanted to. "I doubt it. He only died, like, *years* ago."

Jen tapped something into her iPhone. "Got him," she said. "Gunnar Ulrich. Died in a rock climbing accident nearly eight years ago. He and his friend Spencer Quinn were in the Chihuahuan Desert when it happened. Spencer was a student here at the same time."

"And it was definitely an accident?" I used to be a lawman—cynicism is my default position.

Jen read for a bit longer. "Seems so. Ulrich's SLCD failed while he had his full body weight on it. He tumbled down, nearly took Spencer Quinn with him. Staties went to the scene and declared it an accident."

"SLCD?" I asked. I'd never caught the outdoors-sports bug, and although I'd abseiled out of plenty of helicopters, I'd never seen the business end of a rock face.

"Spring-loaded camming device," she replied. "It's a bit of equipment you wedge into a rock crack, and then, when it's under tension, it holds your weight."

I was about to say, "Apparently not," when Freya spoke.

"And that's not all," she said. "Spencer was so distraught at the death of his friend he dropped out of university. Started a business in Gunnar's name down in Texas, near where the accident happened."

"And where might that be?" I asked.

"I can't remember the name, but it's on the internet. I remember Martha talking about it one night."

Jen hit Google again and found it quickly. It was from an old Georgetown press release. She read the headline: "Ex-Student Forms Solar Energy Company in Friend's Name after Tragic Accident."

We talked to Freya for a bit longer, but I wasn't really paying attention anymore.

In my mind, I was already in Texas.

CHAPTER 44

The man in the yellow suit was called Peyton North, and he was standing in front of management. The room was warm and the situation serious. He wasn't sweating. Yet. He knew his worth, and so far events had been beyond his control. That they knew as much as they did was down to him.

But he also knew these men didn't tolerate failure for long. They would soon start pointing fingers.

He'd finished a presentation on what he'd been able to find out. It was basically a risk assessment. Its reception had been mixed. The men he was addressing were not known for their squeamishness, so although the actions he'd taken to silence Marston had been met with tacit approval, the fact that he'd failed to eliminate the main threat had not.

"So this Devil's Bloodhound, this Koenig, somehow killed our asset in DC?" an older man asked. He was nearer eighty than seventy, his face was as wrinkled as a month-old crab apple, and he had rheumy eyes. He called himself Latham, although his real name wasn't known to anyone, and no one in the room was fooled by his age—Latham was one of the most dangerous men in the world.

North nodded. "He didn't pull the trigger, but yes, Panabaker was killed because of him. We don't know how yet, but he engineered an escape from custody. We've recovered footage of the street outside, and it shows that as Koenig walked toward a black Porsche, an unknown woman got out and shot our woman in the face."

"The Porsche's license plate?"

North shook his head. "Not on any database we can get into."

"What about Mitchell Burridge? Is it worth removing him? Koenig is getting instructions from him, presumably."

North was respectful when he answered but firm. "I wouldn't advise that, sir. Killing an agency boss would bring down heat we could do without, but more importantly, Mitchell Burridge and Koenig worked together. I assume Burridge called on him as Koenig used to be his top dog. He had the keenest nose and the biggest teeth. I don't know how close they were, but if Burridge dies, he might go all-out war on us. I'm not sure I can protect us from that."

"He's not El Cuco," Latham said, referring to the bogeyman from Latin America. "He's just a man."

"You're right, sir, he's not El Cuco," North said. "He's the man you send to arrest El Cuco."

Latham's face flushed, and North knew he'd made a mistake. The old man had buried people alive for less.

"I'm sorry, sir, that was rude," he said "But you need to understand. The Devil's Bloodhound wasn't a name the US Marshals gave him. It was our friends in New York who coined it. It didn't seem to matter where they hid or what countermeasures they took, Koenig found them. And don't forget, for six years he's successfully evaded the Russians and every other nut who wants five million bucks. I think we can assume he still has some skills."

"Does he have a family?" a younger man cut in.

The room went silent. It always did when the younger man spoke. Latham might be one of the most dangerous men in the world, but he wasn't the most dangerous man in the room. The young man was.

"I think messing with Koenig's family might be worse than killing Burridge, sir," Latham said. He didn't add that when you're being stalked by a tiger, you don't stick your finger up its ass. "And we'd also have the Russians to deal with. Leaving Koenig's family alone was the only rule on that website."

North's phone rang. He got permission from the younger man to answer it. The room remained silent as he listened. He terminated the call without having said anything.

"That was our source at Georgetown. A man he didn't recognize and a woman who matched the CCTV footage of the woman in the Porsche have left Copley Hall. They'd spoken to the girl's roommate and she's put them on to Gunnar Ulrich."

The temperature in the room lowered. No one looked at the young man. It seemed like it might be a bad time to catch his eye.

"That means he's one step closer to us," Latham said eventually.

North didn't flinch. The old man was right. There was no point spinning it; the phone call had been bad news.

The younger man coughed gently. Everyone turned to face him. "Do you think he'll find us, Peyton?"

North thought for a moment. Considered lying but dismissed it. Eventually he nodded. "I do, sir."

The younger man nodded. "What do you suggest?"

"There are still a few things I can try, but our main weapon will be surprise. When he gets here, he won't know we're expecting him. It won't be hard to slide up next to him in the diner and put a bullet in his head."

Actions spoke louder than words with this group of men. There were nods and mutterings of approval. From everyone except the younger man.

"That's your advice, is it, Peyton? You want to kill an agency director's private investigator. In the very place we want to avoid the spotlight falling on. Does that seem wise?"

North felt the back of his neck redden. "Not when you put it like that, sir. But this man isn't going to quit anytime soon. He *will* find us."

The young man smiled. "Let him come. What's he going to find?"

The room took a collective pause.

"Exactly," he continued. "Does anyone think there *is* anything to find?"

More silence.

"However," he acknowledged, "there's an elephant in the room. We can't have Koenig speaking to Spencer Quinn." Heads jerked toward him. It was a bold thing to say. "If Quinn disappears, then Koenig has no one to talk to and nothing left to investigate. Devil's Bloodhound or not, when the trail ends, the trail ends."

Peyton North coughed. "How would that work, sir?"

The younger man explained his idea.

And by the time he finished, people were smiling again.

PART TWO

ROAD TO NOWHERE

CHAPTER 45

"I want that one," I said for the second time, pointing at the car in the middle.

"My '73 Stingray?" Jen replied. "Are you fucking insane?"

"It's so conspicuous, it's *in*conspicuous, if you know what I mean."

"Of course I don't know what you mean. No one knows what you mean."

We'd discussed, then dismissed telling Mitch what we had discovered. It was probably nothing, but if it wasn't, he was a desperate father and his instinct would be to rush in. Far better to go in quietly. I could always call him later. Once we'd agreed on that, we discussed how I would get to Texas. We settled on driving. I doubted the people looking for me would know we'd made a connection between Martha and Gunnar Ulrich, and therefore had an obvious line of inquiry with Spencer Quinn, but if they had, why make it easy for them? They would assume I'd want to get to Texas as quickly as I could. Driving would take longer, but the extra time would give me an advantage. If they were waiting for me, after a fruitless week of watching the airports, they'd be nervous. Nervous people made mistakes.

"They'll expect me to fly out," I explained. "They'll assume I'm going to get off a plane and into a rental car. That means they'll be on the lookout for Toyotas and Chryslers and Chevrolets. They might miss a Stingray. You can't hire a car like that anywhere."

"That's such bullshit," Jen said after I'd finished. "You just want to drive the Stingray. There are fifty cars that don't look like rentals. I'll get you one of them."

"Nothing white, nothing silver, and nothing black."

"I know how to do this," she snapped.

"Fine. But the sooner it arrives, the sooner we can part ways."

"I'll make a call and get one here within the hour. Are you going to be OK on your own until then? I won't come back to find the cabin's burned down?"

"Where are you going?"

"I was asked to help you," she replied. "And as far as I'm concerned, I've gone above and beyond. I've saved your life. I've fed, clothed, and hidden you. And I've just helped get you a lead. Now I need to go back to work."

She gave me a strange look. Looked like she was about to offer me her hand. Instead she shook her head and walked to her front door.

"I'd be lying if I said it's been a pleasure, Ben," she said. "You're still a self-centered asshole, but do me a favor: Try not to get killed."

The rental car arrived twenty minutes after Jen had left. It was a blue BMW 4 series. It wasn't the flavorless sedan I'd feared, but it still looked like a hire car. It had barcodes in the window and didn't have dealer markings. Dead giveaway if you knew what to look for. Worse, it actually managed to look like a rental that was trying to *not* look like a rental. Back in my SOG days, it was the kind of car we used to look out for.

Jen had taken her Porsche. The keys to the Stingray and the Range Rover were still in the fruit bowl on the kitchen bench. I would take the Range Rover instead. It wasn't ideal, but at least it didn't look like a rental. It had dealer stickers in the window and had enough scratches and dings to look like a family car. It would have to do.

I went back into the cabin, grabbed my backpack and some bottled water. I walked over to the fruit bowl.

My hand hovered over the Range Rover keys.

CHAPTER 46

"You stole my fucking car?" Jen yelled. "What are you, a juvenile delinquent?"

Her anger didn't surprise me. I had indeed stolen her car. Although I'd always wanted to drive a Stingray, I hadn't taken it for completely selfish reasons. The BMW she'd hired for me wasn't suitable, and neither was her Range Rover. There was nothing special about them. The Stingray, though, that was a spectacular car. Anyone watching the road would notice it. They'd remember it. If someone asked them later on, they'd be able to talk about at it length. They'd be able to describe the deep, rich red paintwork. They'd talk about the polished chrome taillights. They'd rave about the sleek lines. But if they were asked about the driver, they'd likely come up a blank. The Stingray would be the only thing they could remember.

So, no, Jen's anger didn't surprise me. I'd have been angry if our roles had been reversed. No, what surprised me was the fact we were speaking at all. This was the first time I'd stopped since leaving her cabin. Hadn't even stopped to use a bathroom or top up with gas. Before I'd even gotten the keys to my motel room, the clerk's phone had started to ring.

"It's for you," she'd said, trying to pass me the phone.

"Can't be for me. What name did they ask for?"

She'd whispered into the handset, then asked me, "Are you 'the dick-head driving a '73 Stingray'?"

"Pass me the phone," I'd sighed.

"How'd you find me so quickly?" I said.

"Never mind that!" Jen snapped. "All the things I've done for you and this is how you repay me? You really are the most self-absorbed man I've ever had the misfortune to meet."

"The rental you got me had barcodes in the window."

"You should have scraped them off then! Or at least stolen the Range Rover."

I told her my theory about how anyone watching the roads would only remember the car, but not the driver.

"Go to hell," she said.

"How'd you find me?" I asked again. Jen knew where I was headed, obviously, and she could probably take a guess at the direction I'd take. But I'd avoided I-81 and taken a bunch of smaller roads. And yet as soon as I'd walked into the hotel, the clerk's phone had started to ring. Something didn't add up.

She paused, then sighed. "I've had that car since I was a teenager. It used to be my dad's. My mom made him give it up when they had me, but instead of selling it, he put it in storage without telling her. He gave it to me on my sixteenth birthday. I had it LoJacked the moment they released their model for classic cars."

"I'll look after it like it was my own," I said.

After another profanity-laced tirade, she hung up. I put the phone back in the cradle and said to the clerk, "Does your handyman have a toolbox I can borrow?"

An hour later I was hot and sweaty and dirty. I was also more than a little perplexed. I removed Mitch's cell phone from my backpack and powered it up. I dialed a number from memory.

It was answered with a "Yo."

"I need you look into something for me," I said.

CHAPTER 47

There's an old saying: "Never ask a man if he's from Texas. If he is, he'll tell you, and if he ain't . . . then there's no need to embarrass him." It kind of sums up the state for me.

According to Texans, there are only two states in the USA: Texas and TAFT—and TAFT stands for "This Ain't Fucking Texas." It's a bat-shit crazy, wild, and beautiful state. It was labeled a rebellious province by Mexico in 1836, and it's been rebelling ever since. It's the state that put a man on the moon but couldn't get a president down a street. It's twice the size of Germany, has a town that renamed itself DISH just to get free cable, and it built its own power grid just to avoid federal regulation. Texans are straight-talking and self-reliant, and it would surprise no one if they eventually seceded and became an independent sovereign state again. They've been threatening to do it for years.

I've always liked Texas.

The road was burning hot and deserted. Any chance I got of re-upping on water and gas I took. Sensible precautions.

Gauntlet, the place I'd been driving to for five days, was in Brewster County. Part of the Trans-Pecos region west of the Pecos River, Brewster County was sparsely populated, but bigger than Connecticut. Gauntlet was thirty-five miles from the Mexican border and was an oasis in a sea of hills and desert. Driving to Gauntlet was the same as rowing out to a desert island. There was nothing else on the way to the town, nothing after it, and everyone could see you coming.

Each night, after checking into a motel and having a meal and a shake, I'd find a computer and check the shared email account Jen had set up. We were using the tried-and-true method of not sending anything, just leaving it all in the draft messages folder. Nothing sent, nothing to track. It isn't foolproof, but these days nothing is. Even air-gapped computers can be hacked now. It's done via high-frequency sounds apparently.

Although Jen was still mad as hell about the Stingray, and although she began every message with the salutation "thieving dickhead," she was sticking to her promise of providing me with up-to-date information.

Most of what she sent was background information.

Gunnar Ulrich was Danish-American. His parents moved to the States in their late teens, and he'd been born a few months later. He'd won a scholarship to Georgetown on the back of some original research he'd conducted at high school on climate change. He planned to study ocean law, sustainable development, and global security.

His roommate, Spencer Quinn, had been even more studious. He had studied international economics, in many ways the polar opposite to what Gunnar was studying. On paper, there had been no reason for them to have been friends. They'd been thrown together as roommates because Spencer had registered late and Gunnar, on a scholarship, was more restricted with his choices.

But from what Jen had been able to find out, they'd hit it off immediately. Possibly because they were both serious students, but more likely because of their shared love of rock climbing.

The state police's report on Gunnar's death was unequivocal: Gunnar's spring-loaded camming device had failed, and he'd fallen sixty feet onto solid rock. Cause of death was massive internal hemorrhaging. His distraught family had tried to sue the makers, but they didn't get far. The SLCD was old, and the manufacturer's information clearly stated it had to be replaced every twelve months. And he was definitely dead. This wasn't an attempted faked death. His family had identified the body. His open-casket funeral had been attended by faculty, staff, and students.

Spencer returned to Georgetown a different person. To the surprise of no one, he dropped out. But instead of moving back to his family in Delaware, he relocated to the desert town of Gauntlet and started a business that now employed a quarter of the town. In an article in a young-entrepreneur magazine the year before, he had told the interviewer that it was a business he knew Gunnar would have approved of. That he would have enjoyed the irony of a solar energy company succeeding in a fossil fuel state.

I'd hoped that Jen would dig up whatever it was about Gunnar that had interested Martha. Something that might spark a memory in Spencer Quinn. But as the days passed, those hopes faded. Gunnar appeared to be what he looked like: a big, daft, lovable Dane. Why he was part of the paper Martha was writing remained a mystery.

Four days on the road and I had nothing.

That all changed on the fifth.

I'd finally made it to Texas and had found an out-of-the-way motel to spend the night. It was forty miles from Gauntlet. I like the number forty. It's the only spelled-out number in the English language that's in alphabetical order. I'm thirty-six now, and in forty months I'll be forty myself. Next year I'll be forty-one, and "one" is the only number that's spelled in reverse alphabetical order. My mind likes facts like that.

After taking a shower and eating at the nearby diner, I used the motel lobby's computer and checked the draft folder in our shared email account. There was a single unsent email from Jen. The subject heading turned the food in my stomach to concrete.

SPENCER QUINN MISSING, KIDNAP SUSPECTED!

I clicked the link in the email's body. Nothing happened and I cursed the motel's slow Wi-Fi. Eventually it opened. It was a one-paragraph news item in the *El Paso Times*—a hasty summary of the breaking news. In-depth reports would follow.

The town of Gauntlet was in shock today after self-made millionaire Spencer Quinn was abducted at gunpoint. Footage from Quinn's home security cameras show that Quinn was in his home office when two masked men broke in. After a severe beating, Quinn was dragged unconscious into the back of a Ford Transit cargo van. It later transpired that the van's license plates had been stolen from a similar van in Houston. GU Solar Energy Systems' spokesperson Peyton North said, "The whole company is in shock. Quinn is the lifeblood of this company. It was his bold vision that transformed this town into what it is today. We will not rest until we secure his safe return."

At the time this report was posted, no ransom has been demanded and no one has claimed responsibility.

More to follow.

I reread the article, then read it again. My heart sank. I was too late. They'd got to Quinn first. There would be no ransom note.

Spencer Quinn was dead.

And so was my only lead.

CHAPTER 48

With Samuel's *Washington Post* ID card face out, I drove into Gauntlet as bold as a bear.

It was early, but the sun was already beating down like a jet engine. The ground smoldered; the air was thick and hazy. The lizards were sheltering anywhere that wasn't hot enough to roast them, and I was regretting taking a car with leather seats to one of the hottest states in the country. I was glad I wasn't wearing shorts. Even with the Stingray's roof panels off and the wind rushing through my hair, sweat was stinging my eyes and rolling off my nose.

Gauntlet sat in the low, rolling hills of the Chihuahuan Desert. Jen's research had shown that the town's population had doubled since GU Solar Energy Systems had been founded. The newer homes weren't hard to see. The original part of the town had an easy charm, an eclectic collection of whitewashed buildings loosely lined up and down Main Street. Clean storefronts, a wooden church, a couple of restaurants, and the obligatory diner. Flags flew on all public buildings. White picket fences separated well-kept yards. The sidewalk was spotless.

The new houses looked rushed, like getting them up had been more important than getting them right. Cheap wood rather than whitewashed stone. Shared yards. They had a transient look, like they wouldn't be there long.

Prior to GU Solar Energy Systems setting up shop, Gauntlet had been too far off the beaten track to attract tourists in any great number. The surrounding hills offered decent hiking and climbing, but so did other, more accessible places. The town hadn't been geared up for a large increase in its population. The new homes would no doubt be torn down and replaced by solid stone structures eventually, but for now it was all a bit higgledy-piggledy. I wondered if the town's original residents resented the intrusion. Dynamics like that are useful to understand. They can be helpful sources of intelligence.

I drove down Main Street, realized Gauntlet ended when the street did, and turned back around. I'd grab breakfast at the diner, always a good place to hear the most recent gossip. I parked right outside and walked in like I didn't have a care in the world. Before I'd left the motel that morning, I'd found a store that sold cheap T-shirts and I bought one with the New York Dolls emblazoned across the front. My Glock was hidden, but easily accessible, in the small across-the-shoulder utility bag I was carrying. I looked every inch the hipster metrosexual the people in towns like this expect big-city reporters to be.

The diner was bustling. Either the energy company worked around the clock, or everyone started work early. Maybe it was the latter: Before long, it would be too hot to do anything. Either way, the only seats free were at the counter. Photographs of ugly children and a warning about checking your change were taped behind the till. I could smell bleach, stale grease, and burned coffee. A sign above the grill claimed that their Mexican food was "The Only Choice In Town."

The atmosphere in the diner was subdued, presumably because of what had just happened to their chief executive. Shock at his kidnapping mixing with concerns for their futures, no doubt. Now probably wasn't the best time to be a stranger in this small town. But that was fine. I expected hostility. I could work with hostility. It's not just dumb cops who say things they shouldn't when they're angry.

The SOG adopted a number of guises to get close to suspects, and I'd been a fake reporter before. I'd found there's a universal rule: The people who say they hate talking to reporters, like it's beneath them somehow, in reality desperately want to talk to reporters. Even if it's just to tell them they don't want to talk to them.

I checked out my fellow diners. A couple of good old boys were eating pancakes and drinking coffee. They looked retired. Skin as tough as saddles, faces like maps of the world. A young woman was feeding her baby some mashed banana. Most of the customers were workingmen and -women, though. Some were white and some were Latino. I guessed GU setting up in town had changed Gauntlet's demographics, maybe for good. The call would have gone out for manual workers, and I wasn't surprised to see so many Latinos had crossed the border. Jen said GU paid above industry-standard wages.

The diner served a combination of traditional American and Mexican breakfasts. Serious Mexican food, not the crap found in Taco Bell. Tamales, chile rellenos, and taquitos. A few other dishes I didn't recognize. A waitress approached. She had the leathery skin of a sun addict, the stained teeth of a chain-smoker, and a smile like a coffin lid. She pushed a mug in front of me. Filled it with lukewarm coffee.

"I'll freshen that real soon," she said. "What can I get you?" She pronounced "get you" as "getchu." She sounded bored *and* harassed. Quite a skill.

I ordered the "Chimichanga de Huevo y Chorizo," a deep-fried burrito filled with egg and spicy sausage, and a pot of tea.

"Think we got some of that fancy-ass chamomile in the back. That do ya?"

"Chamomile is a herbal infusion," I said. "It isn't tea."

She put her hand on her hip and scowled. "Look, mister, I ain't got time—"

"Just the coffee then," I said. "But if you wouldn't mind telling me about your fine town, there's a big tip in it for you."

She eyed me shrewdly. "How big?"

Using two fingers, I reached for my billfold and slung a hundred-dollar bill on the counter. I put my hand on it.

"For real?" she said hopefully.

"A hundred bucks buys me some information?"

She nodded.

"And a chocolate milkshake?"

She nodded again. Stared at the money like a dog stares at cheese.

"OK then," I said, releasing my grip on the bill. It was whipped away and in her apron faster than the eyes could follow.

CHAPTER 49

I sat at the counter with a plate of spicy chimichanga and a freezing-cold chocolate milkshake. Marlene was being super helpful. She must have figured I might be ripe for another hundred.

She was right. I was. I never discount idiots as a source of intelligence; they usually don't know when to shut up. I slapped another hundred on the counter and Marlene skipped over. She fixed a tight smile and gazed at me. Before she could grab the money, I placed my hand over it.

"Spencer Quinn's kidnapping, tell me what you know."

For the first time she looked uneasy. "What you want to be sticking your nose in that for, mister?" she said, staring at the money.

"It's my job to ask questions like this. If I don't, my editor will want to know why."

"You're one of them reporters. Like I see on TV?"

I nodded.

Sweat formed on her powdered brow. She looked over my shoulder conspiratorially. Checked there was no one in earshot. "You didn't get this from me, y'hear?"

I could have said I never revealed my sources, but that might have been too much, even for someone like Marlene. I settled for a curt nod.

"Well, I know it ain't no kidnapping like what the papers is saying. Any fool who believes that ain't no sharper than a cue ball. Way I hear it, that boy just pissed off the wrong people."

I picked up my milkshake and took a sip. Silence worked better than questions on people who had an emotional need to gossip.

"See, that boy came to town a few years back now. Had a load of fancy ideas with his sun-farm thing. Wasn't enough white folk in Gauntlet, so he had to bring in a load of Mex'cans just to run the damn thing. Had to build them all homes and a school for their kids. Pissed some people off, I can tell you. And before long all the sun-farm people are making money, while us Gauntlet folk still ain't got a pot to piss in or a window to throw it out of."

"Did none of the locals take jobs?" I asked.

"Well, sure, some of them did. But what about people like me? I applied for a job in the office, but I was told I didn't have no qualifications. Who the hell needs qualifications to lick a goddamned envelope? Discrimination, that's what that was."

I took a slurp of my milkshake. It was good. Helped loosen my dry throat.

"Anyway, a young boy getting all rich like that," she continued, "it was bound to go down the crapper. He might have thought he was ridin' a gravy train with biscuit wheels, but when that type of money starts rolling in, no way he's gonna be left alone to spend it. Too many greedy sons of bitches gonna want a piece of that pie."

"You got anything to back that up?" I said, ignoring the overuse of food metaphors. "Another hundred in it if you have."

She scowled, and it was clear she didn't. Someone a few stools over rapped his knuckles on the counter, and she slouched over.

Marlene's bitterness aside, someone wanting a piece of Quinn's business had to be considered. Had he been forced out of his own company? GU Solar Energy wasn't publicly listed, so it would be almost impossible to legally engineer a change in ownership. Of course, in business, just like everything else, there are a number of illegal ways to force the issue: threats of violence, corporate sabotage, espionage, blackmail. An endless list.

But that didn't make any kind of sense.

Jen had researched what GU was doing in Gauntlet, and it was nothing new. They weren't using proprietary technology, and they weren't inventing the next big thing in clean fuel. Everything they used could be bought from a catalog. And although the oil industry is sometimes known as having an iron fist in a velvet glove, I couldn't see them being involved. To them, the clean energy market was like the *T* in "tsunami": irrelevant. Texas was a fossil fuel state. Always would be. A bunch of wannabe Greta Thunbergs wasn't going to change any of that.

Something more organized perhaps? Probably not in Texas. There were gangs, but none of them had the resources to engage in high-end white-collar crime. An individual then. The Russian mobster Yaroslav Zamyatin told me six years ago that people had suffered so he could buy things he didn't need. Some people could never have enough. There were definitely men and women out there who wouldn't see a young man doing well; they'd see an opportunity. Some low-hanging fruit.

It seemed unlikely, though. Jen had already looked into the tax returns of GU Solar Energy Systems. If something had been amiss, she'd have found it.

I ate my breakfast and stared into space while I thought it all through.

It all came back to Gunnar Ulrich.

He'd been the subject of Martha's paper and she was missing. Marston had refused to hand over her paper and he was dead. Quinn had been there when Gunnar had fallen to his death, and he was now missing, presumed dead. I'd asked some questions and a contract killer had tried to kill me. These were facts.

But what connected a rock climbing accident eight years ago to the more recent events?

Whatever it was, it was worth killing for.

CHAPTER 50

I finished my milkshake, left the diner, and stepped onto the burning sidewalk. The sky was a perfect cerulean blue, not a hint of cloud. The only blemish was the scar of a passing airplane. As Marlene might have said, it was already hotter than a blister bug in a pepper patch. I'd always loved the desert and I loved the people who made it their home. There's a harshness to the desert folk not found anywhere else. A fierce independence that said: "You think humans can't live out here? Well, sir, guess again."

The key to the Corvette was in my hand, but as beautiful as it was, I was sick of sitting in a metal box. I yearned to put in some hard yards. Get back on my feet and hit the sidewalk, even if it was just for a short while.

I needed more information. It shouldn't have been difficult. People in small towns can get addicted to spreading gossip. And while I could have done without the kind of bitter snark that Marlene spewed, there were always people who knew how to put what they were told through a common-sense filter before they passed it on. The kind of person used to separating the wheat from the chaff. Someone with a naturally curious mind, someone used to finding out things.

In other words, I needed to speak to an ex-cop.

Cops never retire. Not really. They never lose their inquisitiveness, their need to know what is going on. And they love to talk. It doesn't matter where you are, a city like New York or a town like Gauntlet; cops have a knack for seeking out their own kind. It's usually a bar, a place they can regroup when their shift has ended. The kind of place where closed cases are celebrated and deaths are mourned. And after they pull their pin, the cop still drinks there. Every town in America has a cop bar; most have several.

I couldn't see a bar, though. Not one that was open anyway. So I went for the next best thing. I scanned the storefronts for the traditional sign, one that's been in use since the Middle Ages. I saw the pole with a helix of colored stripes at the end of the street. I smiled. A barbershop. The perfect place to get the name of an ex-cop. The guys who spend their days in a barbershop know everything about everyone. I rubbed my chin. It had a couple of days' stubble. Maybe it was time for me to have a shave.

A man in his late fifties had just switched on the barbershop pole when I arrived. It was now rotating, which turned the helix into a visual illusion. The stripes now looked like they were traveling up and down the pole rather than around it. I watched it for a while.

"What can I do for you, sir?" the man said. He was wearing a pair of worn jeans, a checkered shirt, and an easy smile. A rock-solid, no-frills American. I glanced at the window display. Everything was neat, symmetrical. Everything where it needed to be. Kind of habit you carried over from a life in uniform. Didn't even realize you had. There was also a small Project K-9 Hero sticker in the corner of the window. It was a charity that raised money for retired military and police working dogs. I'd had a ten-bucks-a-month standing order, back when I'd had a regular bank account.

"This your place?" I asked.

He looked me down and up, not up and down. Hands before face. Paid special attention to my hips and the bottom of my jeans. Looked for the sagging pocket, the oversized shirt. With a response like that, I figured the guy was ex-police rather than ex-military. Cops engaged people up close, and they did it every day. Checking for the telltale signs of a concealed weapon was second nature.

"It is, sir," he said. "How can I help you?"

"Straight-edge shave?" I said.

He nodded. "John Travis," he said, offering his hand, "but everyone calls me J.T."

"Decker," I replied. "David Decker." We shook. His hand was calloused, his grip firm and dry.

J.T. showed me into the waiting area. "Five minutes to boil the water?"

I took a seat. It looked like every barbershop I'd ever been in. Smelled of
oil, soap, and coffee. A recliner seat in front of a low, wall-mounted wash-
basin. Had an arched cutout at the front for the back of the neck. Kinda
looked like a guillotine block. Retro posters advertised Brylcreem ("Just a
little dab'll do ya!") and Camel cigarettes ("Every inch a real smoke!"). It
was nice. Like stepping back in time.

There was a stand-alone chair, larger than the one in front of the sink.
It was rich burgundy leather and fully adjustable, sort of like an upmarket
dentist's chair. A brown stool was beside it. I figured this was where J.T. sat
while he did the wet shaves.

"I'm fixing myself a coffee," J.T. said. "You want one? It's Turkish. Black
as hell. Kicks like a mule."

"Sure."

Turkish coffee is something else. Like a 90 percent cocoa chocolate bar,
it's dark, bitter, and very, very strong. Guaranteed to keep you awake for
thirty-six hours straight.

While he rattled away in the back, I picked up a magazine. I wasn't
interested in reading, but someone staring into nothing made other people
nervous. The first magazine was some sort of celebrity-nonsense infomercial
kind of thing. A drunken idiot photographed leaving a nightclub at 3 a.m.
A faded sitcom star doing a cabbage-soup diet. Someone I didn't know was
having an affair with someone else I didn't know. I dropped the magazine
back on the table and rifled through the pile until I found something useful.
GU Solar Energy Systems evidently produced a quarterly employee magazine, something we hadn't been aware of back in DC. I opened it.

Company magazines always have a vanity quote from the CEO on the
inside page and GU's was no different. The all-American, perfectly formed
smile of the kidnapped Spencer Quinn topped his column. He was in his
late twenties and looked every inch the successful entrepreneur he'd been.
The photograph was the same as the one on GU's website. A headshot,
with Quinn looking off-center rather than directly facing the camera. A
three-quarters shot.

The short paragraph underneath thanked staff for their hard work and made it clear Quinn linked the company's profits to their efforts. Some more spin about how the price of oil was hitting the clean energy markets, but that GU was bucking the trend. I doubted Quinn had written it, but the message was clear: "We're a close-knit business that values our employees."

I flicked through the rest of the magazine. It was mainly technical, and although I can navigate the basics of a smartphone, I'm essentially an analog man in a digital world. Most of it was way beyond my understanding.

J.T. came back carrying a traditional Turkish *cezve*, a small, long-handled pot with a pouring lip. He sat opposite me and filled a couple of small white cups, the kind with handles you pinched between your fingers. Demitasses, I think they are called. Means half cup in French. J.T. heaped a spoon of brown sugar into his. I left mine as it was. He raised his eyebrows. I took a sip, put down the cup, and added some sugar of my own. It was the bitterest thing I'd ever had in my mouth.

J.T. grinned.

While he waited for his coffee to cool, J.T. picked up a pearl-handled straight-edge razor and began running it up and down the leather sharpening strap fixed to the table. He saw me looking and handed the razor over.

"My daddy had that with him on Utah Beach in '44. Blade's eighty years old and still holds an edge sharp enough to cut the nuts off a stink bug."

The handle was warm and worn smooth. I loved the simplicity of the design: a blade, a hinge, and a handle with a safety groove. That was pretty much it. The way they were made hadn't changed for decades. No need to. I handed it back to J.T., who went back to sharpening it.

"The towels will be ready soon, then we can get started," he said without looking up.

I wasn't sure if "soon" meant five minutes or five hours. He didn't seem to be in any kind of hurry. I picked up the GU employee magazine again.

"You were reading about our lord and master?" J.T. said.

Nodding, I opened the magazine to the inside cover and showed him the picture of Spencer Quinn. "Must have been quite a shock in a town like this?" I figured the organic approach would work best. Flashing cash like I had with Marlene would get me hauled out onto the street.

"Damn shame if he comes to harm," he replied carefully. "That young man put Gauntlet on the map."

Which sounded like a prepared answer.

"You knew him?" I asked.

J.T. nodded. "I did. Him and that friend of his came in here for a shave just like you. It's the straight-edge razor, you see, not many of us left doing it. It's a bit of a novelty."

"You saw him with Gunnar Ulrich?"

J.T.'s eyes narrowed. "You ain't from a newspaper?"

I shook my head. "No, sir."

He narrowed his eyes. "Because I used to be Chicago PD and I know when I'm being questioned."

He said "ex-CPD," but I heard "tough SOB." Parts of Chicago had a violent crime rate almost 1,000 percent higher than the national average. It was in Tornado Alley, had winters that went down to minus thirty, and their baseball team went 108 years without winning the World Series. "Tough" didn't really do Chicago justice.

There was no point lying to a man like J.T. He'd either help me or he wouldn't. I'd hit the fish-or-cut-bait moment: I either walked or told him a bit of the truth. Not all of it, but enough.

I held my hands up in surrender. "I'm an ex-marshal doing a favor for a friend. Tracking down his missing daughter. Trail's brought me here."

"Decker your real name, son?" he asked.

The smile he'd worn before hadn't returned, and I got the impression I was one smart-ass comment away from being thrown out on the street. I couldn't give him my name, though.

"What precinct did you work out of?" I asked.

J.T. frowned. "Twelfth before I got my shield," he said eventually. "Moved to Violent Crimes. Did my twenty-five, 1990 to 2015."

I did the math in my head. Worked backward. I'd been in Chicago in 2014. Followed a nasty perp called Dawson Root all the way from Lake Superior, where'd he'd murdered a store clerk for a six-pack of Coors Light and a pouch of Virginia tobacco. He'd been from the Windy City originally and I'd called upon Chicago's Criminal Investigation Division's Fugitive Apprehension Unit for assistance. A cop called Steve Hogben had been the one who'd actually traced and arrested Dawson Root. I asked J.T. if he knew of him.

He nodded. "Worked with Steve in Central for a while. Good police."

He pronounced it "po-leece." We all did. Guess we all watched the same TV shows.

"That he was," I said. I told him about Dawson Root and how Hogben had used intelligence-led policing way before it became all the rage.

"You want another coffee?" J.T. asked.

The *cezve* still had some left, but I figured he wanted to go into the back to think for a while.

"Love one," I said.

He was gone five minutes, and when he came back, he stood before me and studied my face. When he saw what he was looking for, he offered his hand again.

"Nice to meet you, Mr. Koenig."

CHAPTER 51

Turned out Steve Hogben and J.T. more than knew each other: They were buddies who still kept in touch. J.T. called him from the back of his shop. Hogben was still with Chicago, civilian staff now. He'd told J.T. that if the man in his shop had a fish-bone-colored scar above his right eye, then I *was* an ex-marshal, but I was called Ben Koenig, not David Decker.

It's how ex-cops worked the world over. They spend their whole careers in one city, but when their pensions are banked, most of them scatter like roaches under a spotlight. The blue grapevine extends way beyond the fifty states. It's a law enforcement intelligence network that rivals anything I could formally access. Everyone knows someone somewhere, or if they don't, they've got a "buddy" who did.

So much for staying under the radar.

"Steve didn't tell me why you quit," J.T. said.

There we were. Nosey needed to know. The blue grapevine died without gossip.

"Not sure I ever did quit, J.T."

"Your business, I'm sure."

"And I'd appreciate it if you called me David when we're not alone." I showed him my David Decker *Washington Post* ID. "I'm trying to stay under the radar."

"Discretion's my middle name," he said.

"So you're J.*D.*T.?"

"Funny," he said. Didn't smile, though.

"What brought you this far south, J.T.?" I asked, changing the subject.

His shoulders sagged a little. "The wife. She had bad lungs, and we hoped the desert air might dry 'em out a bit."

"And it didn't?"

"Reckon we were a day late and a dollar short. She died within a year of getting here. That was nine years ago. Retirement's no fun without the person you'd planned to spend it with."

"Sorry to hear that," I said. It was a sad story but not a new one. It was surprising how many cops and cops' partners died not long after leaving law enforcement. My own thinking was it had something to do with rigid routines and tight camaraderie being whipped away. Replacing the life they knew with the one they've dreamed about. Ending up with neither.

"We'd planned to spend our days hiking and our nights drinking white wine and eating barbecue," J.T. said. "I opened this place for the company. Few of the fellas will start coming in later. Couple of them are ex-cops. Three of them never stop banging about how they were marines back in the day. My advice is don't ask them where they served, you'll be here the rest of the day and most of tomorrow. They'll spend a couple of hours drinking my coffee and moaning about their wives." He shook his head. "And that's enough of me feeling sorry for myself. What can I help you with, Ben?"

It felt insensitive to get down to business with him still thinking about lost futures, but if he did indeed have the "fellas" coming in, I didn't want to waste time.

"What can you tell me about Spencer Quinn?"

J.T. took a seat beside me. Looked as though he was thinking about how to describe him. Eventually he said, "Sometimes, when I take some milk from the refrigerator that's maybe been open a couple of days, I'll take a sniff, make sure it hasn't turned. And every now and then, and despite what my nose is telling me, I'll throw what seems like perfectly good milk down the sink. It might seem OK, but for some reason it just don't feel right. You ever get that feeling, Ben?"

"More than you'll ever know," I replied.

"Now it may be that old J.T.'s just a cynical son of a bitch, but that's how I feel about Spencer Quinn and his solar energy company. It might have looked like chocolate and it might have tasted like chocolate, but it still smelled like a turd to me. Nothing tangible and nothing I could ever go to someone with."

"Cop's intuition?" I never dismissed it. "Intuition" was just another word for experience.

"Damn straight."

"You think Spencer was running a front?"

"If it is, I've no earthly idea what for. And if you get out into the solar fields, you'll see an awful lot of folk out there sweating. Polishing those panels, keeping them dust-free. Not ideal location, you see. Gauntlet's in a basin and it's a bit too windy. He'd have been better off going east a short way. It's a bit more sheltered there. Wind equals dust, and dust equals lost energy."

I filed "wrong location for a solar energy farm" for future analysis. "So, the workforce are all gainfully employed?"

"Seem to be," J.T. said. "If you come back after I close, we can take a drive out if you like. See the solar field firsthand."

Satellite photographs and company brochures are fine, but nothing beats getting your own eyes on something. I was about to thank him when J.T. glanced over my shoulder. "Uh-oh. I think we're about to get some company. That puckered asshole Bryson's outside."

I turned. Saw a man in a cop's uniform. Looked like a typical small-town deputy. A paunch overhung his belt. His face was whiskered and his nose was bulbous. Comfortable having a job that didn't challenge him. We watched as he shielded his eyes and looked through the window. As soon as he saw me, he opened the door and entered.

He nodded at J.T. and approached me.

"Been a complaint, sir."

J.T. stood. Put himself between us. "What's this about, Earl?"

"Man's illegally parked."

J.T. nodded thoughtfully. "And that's a problem all of a sudden, is it? There ain't a NO PARKING sign anywhere in town. How can he be parked illegally?"

Earl peered round him and said, "Gonna have to ask you to come with me, sir."

I stood. I'd been there less than two hours and I'd already caused waves. I called that progress. Earl's cruiser wasn't outside. He saw me looking.

"We'll just take a walk down to your automobile if you don't mind the heat?"

As civilized as Earl was trying to make it seem, I could taste his tension. The man was scared. Something was about to happen.

I turned to J.T. and winked. "I'll be back for that shave, J.T."

"I close at four," he replied.

CHAPTER 52

Earl wasn't in the mood to talk on the walk back to the Stingray. The closer we got, the more nervous he became. His hands were damp and shaking. He rubbed them on his trousers. They left a dark stain. I didn't think he was scared of me, though. At least not directly. His holster would have been unfastened if he had been.

Jen's Stingray was where I'd left it. There wasn't another car on the road, and it wasn't blocking anything. I'd expected nothing less. There was a little play being acted out now. Everyone knew their roles, but I was the only one who didn't know who the actors were.

Earl spoke for the first time since leaving J.T.'s. "Gonna have to write you a ticket, sir," he croaked. He flipped open his pocketbook but didn't bother reaching for the pen in his breast pocket. I leaned against the passenger door and waited for whatever was about to go down. Earl was too scared to notice, but I'd slipped my hand into my utility bag and onto my Glock. It was broad daylight, and we were in the middle of Main Street. I doubted it was about to get noisy. But if it did, I'd start firing immediately. I wouldn't even take the gun out of my bag. The first person to point a gun at me would get a 9-millimeter Parabellum wrapped in satchel canvas in his gut.

Act one finished and act two began. A well-heeled man wearing a pale yellow suit sauntered out of the diner. He was tall and lean and tanned.

Had an easy smile, white teeth, and designer stubble. The smile and the suit made him look like the entertainment manager at a summer camp. Until you saw his eyes. They were the eyes of a rattlesnake: cold, calculating, missing nothing.

He was a better actor than Earl; he looked unruffled. In a voice that was cotton wool wrapped in steel, he asked, "What are you doing, Deputy?"

Earl visibly gulped. "The man's illegally parked, Mr. North. Just writing him a ticket."

North looked up and down the empty street. "Is his car causing problems?"

"No, Mr. North."

"We're hospitable to strangers in Gauntlet, Earl. Now, I'm sure Mr. . . . ?" He paused and waited for me to fill the gap.

I cleared my throat, put on my best Sidney Poitier. "They call me Mr. Decker," I said.

"Of course," he said. "I'm sure Mr. Decker will be happy to move his car to the lot over there. How about you just put that notebook back in your pocket and we'll forget all about this?"

"Yes, Mr. North." Earl managed to leave without bowing, but only just.

"Peyton North," North said after he'd gone. He offered his hand.

I took it. Squeezed hard to see if he'd react. He didn't. "Please, call me David."

"I must apologize for our deputy. His wheel turns, but the hamster's dead, if you get my drift."

"Bad time to be a stranger?" I asked. There's never a bad time to gather intel.

He nodded. "You're referring to Spencer Quinn?"

"I am."

"The police know who they're looking for," he said dismissively.

"I hadn't heard that."

North smiled as if he was in on some big joke. "A couple of amateurs took him. I'm sure Spencer will be back at his desk by the end of the week."

I doubted it. I thought Spencer Quinn was already buried in the Chihuahuan.

North didn't want to linger on Quinn, though. "No harm done with Deputy Earl?"

I told him there wasn't.

"Let me apologize on the town's behalf anyway," he said. "No excuses, Mr. Decker, I'm buying you dinner tonight. There's an executive dining room at GU. I'll book it for tonight. How does eight o'clock sound?"

I didn't need to use a dynamic risk assessment to know this was a setup. "Perfect," I replied.

North beamed a smile. He pointed toward a nearby foothill. "If you drive back out of town, you'll see a private road on the left about half a mile up. Press the gate intercom and tell them you're Peyton North's guest. Park anywhere and I'll meet you in reception. How d'you like longhorn steak?"

I thought longhorns produced some of the stringiest beef in the country. "Love it," I said.

He beamed at me again. "Eight o'clock then."

CHAPTER 53

Apart from a trip to get some suitable clothes for dinner, I spent the rest of the day at J.T.'s. Finally had my shave. The hot towels opened my pores, and the straight edge removed the stubble and the road grime. Before long I'd nodded off. When he'd finished, J.T. gently shook me awake.

"Sorry," I said, rubbing my eyes.

"Don't worry about it. Happens more often than you'd think."

He had a few "fellas" in and out during the day. None of them was impressed by the solar energy plant. Solar energy was un-Texan, they said. And so was Spencer Quinn.

At a quarter to four, J.T. flipped the sign to CLOSED and I helped him clean up. We were soon in the Corvette and headed out of town. I saw the private road North had mentioned. A modern-looking gate system controlled egress and access.

"Lot of theft round here, is there?" I said idly.

J.T. shrugged. "That place has always been locked up tighter than a frog's asshole," he said.

I twisted in my seat and craned my neck. "I can't see anything. Maybe I can ask for a tour tonight. The worst they can do is say no."

"Thought you said you used to be a marshal." I said nothing and he continued, "What's the most valuable tool a marshal has at his disposal?"

I turned to face him and instantly knew what he was getting at. "Local knowledge."

"Local knowledge," he agreed. "I'm local and I have knowledge."

"You do?"

"I know a place," J.T. said.

The "place" was a twenty-mile drive in one direction, then fifteen in another, the last three bumpy enough to stress-test the Stingray's suspension. I winced at the thought of what Jen would do to me if I damaged the car's alloys. By the time we'd reached the summit of the foothill J.T. had pointed out, I was a little seasick.

J.T. got out. I followed him. We were high up but in a natural hollow, like an open-topped cave. I figured a hundred million years ago, back when *T. rex* prowled Texas, it had once been the top of a waterfall. We were shielded from the sun by Texas ebony trees and flanked at the sides by red sandstone. The hollow was about the size of a double garage and was partly in the shade. Probably would be for half the day. I couldn't have picked a better observation post if I'd been allowed to design one on paper.

I followed J.T., and he pointed toward a low-hanging branch that acted as a seat. It gave us both a perfect view of the vista below us.

"Hell's bells," I said.

Because Gauntlet was a small town, I'd unfairly expected any business based there to be small as well. A town full of mom-and-pop stores would have a mom-and-pop major employer, right?

Wrong.

I'd seen photographs before I'd left DC, but they hadn't done justice to GU Solar Energy Systems. It was a massive operation.

With the vast Texas sky behind me, I looked beyond the hills and trackless, barren desert and saw a futuristic landscape, a glittering oasis stretching as far as the eye could see. Hundreds, possibly thousands, of mirrors filled a natural, horseshoe-shaped basin. Cliffs and mountains encircled them. In the distance, the town of Gauntlet sat at the horseshoe's opening.

I got to my feet and approached the edge of the hollow. I leaned over and checked out the cliff face. It was jagged but sheer. Easy to climb up, not so easy getting down. I couldn't quite see where it met the desert floor, so I leaned out a bit further. Balanced on one leg and looked down.

"Are you crazy!" J.T. said, pulling me back.

"What?"

"That's a two-hundred-foot drop onto solid rock. A gust of wind could have blown you off!"

I peered over the edge again. "But it didn't," I said. "And it's not windy."

"No, it's not," J.T. admitted. "But anyone with a lick of sense wouldn't have risked it anyway." He gave me a look. Shrewd, like he knew something but wasn't sure whether to say it. In the end he said, "Come back to the ebony tree, Ben. You're making me nervous standing so close to the edge."

CHAPTER 54

We spent the next hour looking at mirrors.

Each one was about the size of a regular garage door. They were mounted on complicated plinths. A tall tower structure sat in the middle of the basin. It looked like a lighthouse. The mirrors surrounded it. Raised cable ran from a box-shaped building at the base of the tower to a modern building pushed tight against the cliffs on the opposite side of the basin to where we were seated. The mirrors slowly moved as they tracked the sun's journey across the horizon.

From our lofty vantage point, the central tower and the circular arrangement of mirrors made the whole setup look like a giant, unblinking eye. The mirrors were the iris, the tower was the pupil, and the cables were the veins.

"The heliostats reflect the sun onto that tower," J.T. explained. "The heat produces steam, and that drives a turbine in the building underneath. The turbine creates the electricity, which is piped along to that eyesore over there." He pointed toward the glass-and-chrome building pressed up against a cliff.

"And that's where I'm going tonight?" I asked.

"That's the place," J.T. replied. "You think it's a trap?"

I shrugged. "Possibly."

"Your funeral, I suppose. Anyway, you get a chance, ask if you can have a look out of their top-floor window. Best view of Gauntlet bar none, I've heard."

"Better than here?" I grunted. "Find that hard to believe."

"Yep," J.T. replied. "Because it's the only view of Gauntlet that doesn't have that goddamned building in it."

I laughed. "I had no idea it was this big," I said, gesturing at the sea of glass in front of us.

"It isn't," J.T. said. "Not as far as these things go, least ways. And because the mirrors are in a natural basin, it looks like there are more than there are. Compared to some of the projects in California and Vegas, this is tiny."

"How much energy do they produce?"

J.T. shrugged. "Enough for the whole town, that's for sure. Anyone who wants it can sign up and get cheap electricity from GU."

I raised my eyebrows. Asked the question.

"What, am I crazy?" he replied. "Of course I did. Slashed my bills by nearly eighty percent."

I whistled. "How can they afford to give it away like that?"

"Spencer Quinn said it was a thank-you to the town for putting up with the change in lifestyle. Sort of a quid pro quo thing. GU sells their excess to the grid, and that's where they make their money."

"So there wasn't much protest when he arrived?"

"A bit. Some of the old-timers, me included, don't like change. Some of the younger ones, and some of the families with children, welcomed it. Means they can live in Gauntlet if they want. Most of our youngsters have to move to Houston or San Antonio, even Dallas, to find work. Now they can go off to college, get an engineering degree, and come back to guaranteed employment."

As we watched, a flatbed drove along one of the myriad arterial service roads. The truck had a team of three, all seated in the front. They stopped beside a mirror and got out. They spent time removing a mirror from its plinth before setting it carefully on the ground. They climbed into the bed of the truck and untied a fresh one. Half an hour later it was on the plinth and hooked up to what looked like a portable diagnostic device. The new heliostat was soon facing where it was supposed to. They secured the old mirror on the flatbed and drove back to the GU building. I looked at my watch. The whole thing had taken an hour.

I followed the truck all the way back to the building in the rocks. A hangar door to the far left of the main door opened. The flatbed drove inside and the door closed behind it.

There was nothing suspicious about what I'd been watching.

Nothing at all.

So why was my antenna up?

CHAPTER 55

The drive to GU Solar Energy Systems headquarters didn't take long. J.T. had insisted I bunk with him for however long I was in Gauntlet, and I'd gladly accepted. The cantankerous old cop was good company and he knew almost everyone in town.

We spent the rest of the early evening discussing Spencer Quinn and GU Solar Energy Systems. We also skirted around how Martha's bread crumbs had led me to Gauntlet. I couldn't tell J.T. everything, but he was a good enough detective to fill in some of the gaps. Eventually we got around to the man I was having dinner with, Peyton North.

"Stone-cold psychopath," J.T. said immediately. "Comes in here for a shave sometimes and I always come away with the feeling I've just had a tiger in the chair, if you know what I mean? That I was just one careless remark away from being gutted like a tapir."

"That's weirdly specific."

J.T. shrugged. "I like the Discovery Channel."

"Deputy Earl sure seemed terrified of him," I said. "I wonder why a solar energy company needs someone like him."

"Not just him," J.T. said. "He sometimes has a seven-foot-tall mute with him. A dead-eyed lump of gristle going by the name of Andrews. Spitting image of Red Grant, the henchman in *From Russia with Love*. Showed up about the same time North did."

"Your use of 'henchman' was not unconsidered, I think?"

"Listen, Ben," J.T. said, his voice newsreader-flat. "I don't know what you're really up to, but my advice is if you have to go up against Andrews, you don't mess around. You put a bullet in his head and you do it from a safe distance. North is a psychopath, but Andrews is a sadist."

"It's only dinner," I said.

"My ass it's only dinner. North might wear a silly yellow suit, but he's a thinker. And that means tonight's invitation is to his benefit, not yours."

"I'll be careful," I promised.

"You got a cell phone?"

"I have."

"Pass it over."

I did. I'd been deleting any calls I'd made and anything I'd googled. The cell phone was as data-free as the day Mitch had handed it to me. J.T. wouldn't see anything he shouldn't. He opened the SMS app, entered a cell number, and composed a message. He handed it back.

I read what he'd written. It said: "DON'T WAIT UP, I MIGHT BE LATE."

"If you think things are about to go south, you hit that send button. Second I get that text, me and the boys will storm GU like a geriatric SWAT team."

"I appreciate the offer, J.T.," I said. "But even if North does have ill intentions toward me, he won't try anything tonight. Too many people know where I'm going."

"Like a geriatric SWAT team," he repeated. He stood, like the discussion was over. "I'm making a sandwich, you want one?"

"I don't. But while you're busy, do you have a computer? I need to check my emails."

"Down the hall," he said.

I logged into the shared account and went to the draft emails. There was a new one from Jen. I read it, then cursed. Samuel's distributed denial of service attack on the Russians' website must have been fixed. I had a $5 million bounty on my head again. I hoped it wouldn't interfere with what I was doing.

I composed a new draft email and brought Jen up to date. I asked if she could check out Peyton North and Andrews. Said I didn't know if Andrews was his first or last name, but he looked like a Bond villain, if that helped.

The clock in the top right of J.T.'s computer said it was coming up to 7 p.m. I logged off. Time to grab a shower and put on my new clothes. If something was about to go down, it wouldn't be while I was wearing dirty underpants.

CHAPTER 56

I stopped at the CCTV-covered gate, pressed the intercom, and told them who I was and who I was there to see. A security van appeared in the distance and I watched it drive to my location. The welcoming committee. A man in an ill-fitting uniform, sweating despite the cooler, sweeter night air, got out and punched some numbers into a keypad on the other side of the gate. It slid open without making a sound.

"Good evening, Mr. Decker," he said. "Follow me, please." He didn't wait for a reply and got back in his van. As soon as I was inside, the gate closed behind me. I did what I was asked and followed the security guard. We were on a proper road, wide enough for two cars with a white line separating the lanes. After a mile the road split in two. The left led to where I'd seen the flatbed head into the hangar. We turned right and into the public face of GU.

The van drove to a discreet parking lot to the side and stopped. The guard pointed at the space next to him. As soon as I'd killed the engine, he drove off. I got out and headed toward the well-lit main entrance.

GU Solar Energy Systems' headquarter building rivaled that of any *Fortune* 500 company I'd seen. It was wider than it was tall, and taller than it was deep. Effort had been made to make it fit in with the cliff it nestled under. Matching sandstone made up the frontage, and although the building

was almost certainly propped up by steel and concrete, from a distance the
I added to the illusion of it having grown right out of the desert.

Up close, however, it was unapologetically modern. Several large, steel-
framed windows jutted out from the sandstone front, their lines geomet-
rically clean and straight. The building's flat roof acted as a mechanical
floor. From J.T.'s bluff I'd seen a whole load of equipment up there: satellite
dishes, whip-thin aerials, fans, air-conditioning units, and a bunch of other
stuff I hadn't been able to identify. I'd even seen a large *H*, and J.T. had
confirmed he'd seen helicopters land there.

A drive circled a modern water feature. A fountain danced and the
colored spotlights sent water shadows flittering across the manicured lawns
like bats. Despite the arid climate, lush green gardens surrounded the front.
A gardener sat on a marble bench enjoying a late supper.

But as expensive as it all looked, I understood what J.T. had meant
when he said any view that didn't have GU's headquarters in it was a better
view than one that did. The landscaping was classy yet somehow not classy.
Like a Vegas hotel. All that was missing was a couple of guys handing out
flyers for call girls.

As I neared the front door, Andrews the giant stepped out. J.T. hadn't
been yanking my chain. He looked like a human pit bull. He was at least
three hundred pounds, a full head taller than me, and bulked out with muscle. His sleeves were so tight they acted like tourniquets on his biceps. He
was bullnecked and cauliflower-eared. The backs of his hands were matted
in thick black hair. He didn't need to have "personal bodyguard" tattooed
on his forehead; everything about him screamed it. J.T. was right. The only
way to win a fight against Andrews would be to shoot at him from distance.
His neck was so heavily muscled not even a throat punch would work. It
would be something to think about over dinner. An intellectual exercise.
How do you beat someone who physically outmatches you in every single
department?

Andrews had large and surprisingly graceful strides. He was soon on
me. Unlike the junkie in Meadowell, he stopped at a safe distance. Instead
of the "fee-fi-fo-fum" I'd expected, he gestured for me to raise my arms.

I kept them by my side.

The giant didn't look annoyed. He didn't look happy. He didn't look anything. He simply waited for me to comply. I recognized a test when I was in the middle of one.

For two minutes neither of us moved.

Eventually the front door opened again and a smiling Peyton North stepped out. He seemed to have a variety of smiles. None of them reached his eyes. He was still wearing a yellow suit, although it was slightly more vibrant than the one he'd worn earlier. Probably his fun nighttime suit. The one he wore when he was drowning kittens. He had white loafers on his feet, and his shirt was a crisp white, unbuttoned with no necktie. I was glad I'd made the effort and bought something suitable.

"You'll have to forgive Andrews, Mr. Decker," North said. "He doesn't speak, and Mr. Quinn's kidnapping has got him rattled."

"Can't speak or won't speak?"

North inclined his head in a "you appraise me and I'll appraise you" kind of way. "Does it matter?"

"Not to me."

He turned to the giant and said, "Everything's OK, Andrews. Please let Chef know my guest has arrived."

Andrews left without a backward glance.

"One of your scientists?" I said.

North laughed politely. "Hungry?" he asked.

"Starved."

"Good," he said. "Follow me."

CHAPTER 57

GU's private dining room was designed to make a strong first impression. A polished mahogany bar ran the length of the room. A barman in a beautifully cut white tuxedo waited on our orders. Original watercolor desertscapes hung on the wall. Some depicted the breathtaking natural beauty of Texas's flora and fauna; others were of the two things with which the state was synonymous: oil and cattle. The furniture was sandblasted wood, and the chairs were rich brown leather.

It was expensive, and unmistakably Texan.

It seemed over the top. Unnecessary. Who were they hoping to impress? Who demanded this level of luxury? I marked the dining room as "interesting" and put it in the same file as J.T.'s comment about the heliostat field being in the wrong location.

A maître d', also in a white tux, seated us. He asked for our drinks order. I wanted a frosty beer—it had been a long day and my throat was dusty—but North beat me to it.

"Bottle of Don Julio Real," he said.

North had just ordered a four-hundred-buck bottle of tequila. I wondered why.

"Reef and beef tonight," he said after the maître d' had left. "The steaks will be with us soon, but chef has some Moonstone oysters in the seafood fridge. We'll start with them. They're flown in from Rhode Island. Best there is."

It was a good way in. "That where you're from, New England?" I asked. Made it seem polite, nothing more than idle chitchat.

North didn't answer. Instead he said, "Ah, the drinks are here." The maître d' had returned with the tequila and two expensive shot glasses. Even if you knew nothing about liquor, the Don Julio Real looked classy. The squat bottle was wrapped with ornate, brushed-steel leaves that made it look like it was being grasped by skeletal hands. North uncorked it and poured two generous measures of the oily golden drink.

"Got to have this neat," he said. "None of that lime-and-salt crap." He took a sip, held it in his mouth for a few seconds, then swallowed. He finished the rest in a single gulp, then handed me the bottle to inspect.

I took it from him. Gently swirled it. The tequila clung to the inside, leaving a string-of-pearl pattern. I set it on the table and picked up my shot glass. Took a sip. Swished it round a bit, let it reach all parts of my mouth, swallowed it. It was extraordinary. Brutal yet sophisticated. Peppery but mellow, with a long, complex finish. Undeniably Mexican. It had been a day of imbibed firsts: the bitterest coffee and the most expensive shot. Like North, I drank the rest in one go.

I glanced at North. He was watching me, a smile dancing across his lips.

"Good?" he asked, reaching for the bottle and refilling our glasses.

I nodded my appreciation. "You were saying where you were from," I said.

"Was I?" he replied. "That was careless of me."

I tried a different approach. "What's your job here, Mr. North?"

"Peyton, please."

"What's your job here, Peyton? You don't look like a solar engineer."

"Operations," he said, waving his arms expansively around him. "All of this needs . . . managing. Not the type of strategic management the board does, but the more immediate issues. Supplies, staffing problems, union issues, that kind of thing." He leaned forward and looked straight me. "Basically, I fix things before they become a problem."

"You're a project manager then?" I said, ignoring the threat.

"Of a kind," he replied. "But enough about me, what about you? What brings you to our dusty old town?"

"There's interest in this place back in DC," I said, looking right back at him.

"That right?"

"Spencer Quinn's kidnapping. His link with DC was enough for my editor to send me on a trip."

North took a sip of his tequila. Considered what I'd said. "That's a long drive. How long did it take you?"

"Five days."

"And yet Mr. Quinn's kidnapping wasn't reported until yesterday."

I shrugged. "Guess I'm psychic."

He smiled.

The conversation was halted by the arrival of the oysters. Two dozen, still in their shells and on a bed of crushed ice. I reached for one and threw it down my throat. I'd always thought oysters were the culinary equivalent of the emperor's clothes: a big joke on the diner. The aquatic equivalent of raw snails. These ones were bigger and meatier than the few I'd had in the past. I had two just to be polite. North had twelve. He ate with gusto, wiping his mouth with a cotton napkin after each one. The maître d' replaced it with a clean one when he removed his tray of empty shells.

"Has a ransom been demanded yet?" I said.

"You'd have to ask the police."

"I'm asking you."

North shrugged. "Not to my knowledge."

"But you don't appear too concerned."

"'The life of man is solitary, poor, nasty, brutish and short,'" he said.

"Thomas Hobbes," I replied.

"You know your philosophers, Mr. Decker."

"I know lots of things, Peyton. Earlier today you said you were expecting Spencer Quinn to be back behind his desk in a week. Now it sounds like you think he's dead?"

"It's my job to think things like that," he said. "I have a responsibility to this company and its employees. A multimillion-dollar business cannot be allowed to collapse because of the actions of one misguided individual."

"I thought there were two kidnappers?"

"Slip of the tongue."

North refilled our glasses.

"To Spencer Quinn," he said, raising his glass. "Genius. Visionary. Friend."

"To his safe return," I replied, raising my own glass. I took a sip but let the drink fall back in the glass. I wouldn't have any more. I didn't want to feel light-headed. "Tell me about him," I asked.

North paused while he gathered his thoughts. Finally he said, "Spencer Quinn was the finest man I've ever known."

CHAPTER 58

Longhorn prime beef is an oxymoron. It's a Texan tradition to pretend it's the best steak in America. It isn't. It's too lean. Doesn't have the right marbling. Unless it's cooked low and slow, it's inedible. By the time I was halfway through my porterhouse, I had aching jaws.

As we ate, North gave me a potted history of the company. Some of it I knew; a lot of it I didn't.

Spencer Quinn had been in Texas with Gunnar on a climbing holiday. They'd wanted to climb a rock face in every county in the Trans-Pecos area. When Gunnar Ulrich's SLCD failed—or slipped; it was never established—he'd fallen from a bone-smashing height where the chances of survival were negligible. Quinn had been underneath on the same rope, and Ulrich had hit him on the way down. He'd been knocked unconscious, but his SLCD had held firm. By the time he'd regained consciousness and climbed back down, Ulrich was already dead—cause of death: massive internal hemorrhaging.

I'd known most of that. The stories in the press were comprehensive, and North stuck largely to what had been written. There'd been a bit more color to why the two boys had been in Texas to begin with, but rock climbers, especially those who live in a city, always have to travel. The rocks won't come to them. It's kind of part of the deal.

It all seemed straightforward. What happened next wasn't.

I could understand the motivation behind Quinn doing something in his friend's name. People had certainly started things for worse reasons. It was a little twee, but that sort of made sense. How Quinn had achieved it didn't.

Not the starting-a-solar-energy-company-in-the-desert part. That did make sense. No point setting one up anywhere else. It would be like putting a wind farm inside a barn.

It was how he'd raised his capital that was interesting.

Most people, when faced with a funding shortfall for their all-consuming passion, will start tugging on people's heartstrings. Get donations flooding in. Maybe get a bit of crowdsourcing going on. Try to get some momentum. It was a protracted but risk-free way of funding projects like the one Quinn had in mind.

But Quinn hadn't been interested in that. Instead he had gone directly to the banks, asking for a loan of $30 million. According to North, banks were permanently on the lookout for solar energy investment opportunities. The government underwrote large parts of their loans, making it virtually risk-free.

Still, none of the main banks would touch him. He was technically still at school, wasn't studying the right field, and didn't have an entrepreneurial background. But Quinn refused to give up. Eventually he found a bank willing to back him. Banco Nacional de Coahuila, a small Mexican bank with a scattering of branches stateside, was the one that finally agreed to fund the project in his dead friend's name. Quinn hired North to help him during the difficult early days.

"And were they?" I said.

"Were they what?"

"Difficult early days."

"You saw the sun today, Mr. Decker. Solar energy is a business that can't fail. And Spencer was clever. He built up the business slowly. Spent almost half the thirty mil on the heliostats and the tower, another ten on the infrastructure needed to turn heated water into electricity, and a bit more on linking it up to the grid. Came in a million under budget. Paid back the first installment eight months before it was due."

"And it's profitable."

"We're a small plant compared to the fifty-megawatt beasts out there, but yes, it *is* profitable. And that means we're able to expand exponentially. Every year we get bigger." North drifted into a prepared speech about how the sun had enough energy to power the universe for five billion years, and that more solar energy fell on the planet in one hour than could be consumed in an entire year. How it was both an environmental and economic tragedy that the sun's awesome power wasn't being harnessed to anywhere near its full potential. I didn't know if he understood the subject or had just memorized the talking points. I was starting to get bored when he finally said something interesting.

"Hey, when the sun goes down, the hard work begins. There's a full shift on tonight. You want to see how electricity is made, Mr. Decker?"

CHAPTER 59

As we walked down into the plant, I asked North what GU would do if it turned out Spencer Quinn was dead.

"Recruit a new CEO," he said. "Solar energy's the new kid on the block. It won't be difficult to get someone with the right credentials."

"That's not what I meant," I said. "GU isn't publicly listed and Mr. Quinn is the sole shareholder. If he's dead, he can't be a shareholder. Corporations can't be owned by dead men, they have to be passed on to someone."

North frowned.

"My editor will want to know," I added.

"That would be an issue for the board," he said eventually. "I reported to Mr. Quinn on operational matters only. I have no idea how the company is structured."

We walked the rest of the way in silence. Along corridors and down flights of stairs. Outside the dining room and the immediate passage to it, the building was perfunctory in its decor, like the administration areas of any factory or plant.

We stopped at a secure metal door. North pressed a buzzer and looked up into a small modern camera. A click and the door unlocked. I followed North down a well-lit corridor and onto a gantry overlooking the workshop floor. Men in protective clothing and face masks were fussing round a central machine. One or two employees glanced up, but no one seemed concerned by our presence. We walked down some metal steps and onto the shop floor. A man whose protective clothing covered a suit, a middle management giveaway, met us.

"Jim," North said, shaking hands with the man, "this is Mr. Decker. He's with the *Washington Post*. Can you give him the five-minute tour?"

"Sure," Jim said. He turned to me and said, "What do you know about solar energy, Mr. Decker?"

I shrugged and glanced at North. "More than I did an hour ago."

"You've seen our solar field?"

"Not yet," I lied.

"No matter," Jim said. He walked over to a computer terminal and pressed a couple of buttons. A live feed of the heliostat field flickered into view. It was dark outside, but it was a high-quality image. Using a track pad, Jim dragged a progress bar back a couple of hours. The screen became bathed in light.

"There are two ways to get electricity from the sun, Mr. Decker," he said. "One way is to use solar panels made up of photovoltaic cells, like the ones that power calculators. They're dark in color and convert sunlight into direct current electricity."

"But those things out there are mirrors," I said, pointing at the screen.

"Indeed they are," Jim said. "They reflect an extremely hot beam of light on to the central receiver in the solar power tower. A heat-transfer liquid takes the energy to a boiler on the ground. The steam spins our turbine and the electricity is sent here. This is technically a substation. We send some to the town for immediate use, and the rest goes to the grid."

"Fascinating," I managed to say before turning to North.

He was talking to another man and studying footage on the screen. I looked over his shoulder and saw a picture of the flatbed truck I'd seen earlier. The one that had replaced the presumably malfunctioning heliostat.

"Has Jim finished with you?" North asked.

I nodded and pointed at the screen. "Do you repair the heliostats on-site, or do they have to go away?"

Annoyance flashed across his face. I had no idea why. For once I'd been asking a genuine question. Some of Jim's enthusiasm must have rubbed off on me.

"We have a small workshop here, but major repairs and servicing are done off-site," he said.

"Why's that?"

"Why's what?"

Sometimes investigations move forward by tugging on the most unlikely of threads, and for reasons unknown North was finding the off-site repair questions difficult. He was stalling.

"Why can't you do it here? Has to be cheaper."

"Mr. Decker, our heliostats are state of the art. They can't be taken apart in a dusty environment, and maintaining a *sterile* environment here would cost more than it does to ship the units to Austin. We have a regular servicing schedule, which means we ship at least two units a day there. If we attempted to do that here, the costs would be astronomical."

"Mind if I see?"

"The workshop in Austin? Sorry, out of the question. It's strictly controlled."

"I meant the workshop you have here."

There was no obvious reason to say no. "I can give you five minutes, but this is a work night, Mr. Decker. You've already been a distraction."

He turned on his heels, and I hurried after him down another corridor and through yet another security-controlled door.

This workshop was nowhere near as impressive as the one we'd just left. There were no men in suits and face masks and no expensive machines. It looked like an auto shop. High roller doors, storerooms, inspection pits, and wooden pallets to transport the heliostats. Power tools and wheeled spanner sets. Nothing unusual. Grease monkeys yelled and hollered at each other. A man in a forklift waited for a team cutting thick protective plastic from an enormous bale and wrapping a heliostat with it. When they finished, the forklift driver lifted the wooden pallet it was secured on and loaded it onto the back of a flatbed. Someone climbed on top and strapped it down. One of the roller doors opened and the driver carefully drove out.

"He off to Austin?" I asked.

North nodded curtly. "It's getting late, Mr. Decker. If you have any more questions, I'm sure our communications and marketing director will be able to answer them."

"Thank you," I said.

North mumbled something in return, but I didn't catch it. My mind was already on what I had to do next.

CHAPTER 60

A phone rang in a dark room. The young man answered on the first ring.

"How did it go?"

"I had to take him to workshop two. Couldn't be helped. If I'd refused, he'd have got suspicious."

"Did he see anything?"

"What's to see?"

"Fair point."

"And I had to tell him about Austin."

The young man paused. North didn't like that. People had a tendency to die after one of the young man's pauses.

"And?" the young man said at last.

"He didn't pick up on it."

"You're sure."

"I'm sure," North said.

"On reflection, was tonight worth it, Peyton? Did you get what you needed?"

"Yes, sir. Couple of beauties."

"And what about him? What was he like, this Devil's Bloodhound?"

"He was . . . interesting."

"How so?"

"I can't quite put my finger on it, sir. There was just something about him that didn't ring true."

"He's here under false pretenses, Peyton," the young man said. "Nothing about him rings true."

"That's my point, sir. I knew he wasn't a *Washington Post* reporter. And he knew I knew he wasn't a *Washington Post* reporter. Yet he came anyway. Didn't seem like he had a care in the world. Got the impression he was enjoying himself."

"He's reckless then."

"Even reckless people crap their pants when they see Andrews for the first time. He still gives me the chills. Koenig didn't blink. And it wasn't like they were having a pissing contest, I genuinely think Andrews didn't bother him. Koenig sort of weighed him up, then dismissed him as irrelevant. Like he didn't matter. The guy must have ice running through his veins."

The young man considered this. "I don't like this new information, Peyton."

"Nor me, sir."

"He can't be scared off then?"

"I don't think so."

"What do you suggest?"

The young man knew if North was calling about a problem, he'd also have a potential solution.

"Do you remember that website I told you about, sir?"

"The Russian bounty one? The one you couldn't open a few days ago?"

"My guy tells me it was a DDoS attack that shut it down, an attack that was likely orchestrated by Koenig himself."

"He's a resourceful pain in the ass, isn't he?"

"That he is, sir," North said. "Anyway, we have good news on that front. The site's back up. As of six hours ago, Ben Koenig has a five-million-dollar bounty on his head again."

"Oh dear," the young man said. "Imagine what would happen if the wrong sort of people found out he was in Gauntlet."

CHAPTER 61

"And you have to hijack a truck?" J.T. asked for the third time.

"I need to get into that workshop," I replied. "He might think he hid it, but he didn't want me knowing about their operation in Austin."

"So why *did* he tell you?"

"I'd asked the question. He had to say something."

"Maybe he's pointing you there so you don't look someplace else?"

"It's possible. He's certainly clever enough."

"But?"

"I don't think so. It wasn't like it was part of my master plan. I only asked about where the mirrors were serviced to keep them all talking. I sort of said it while I was thinking of something better to ask."

We were in his den. Drinking beer and eating chili-covered nachos. There was a ball game on the TV, but the sound was off. I'd told J.T. about my dinner with North. He was envious that I had gotten to taste the Don Julio Real, but relieved he hadn't had to eat the longhorn steak. "Like chewing a tire that's been through a cow's asshole," he'd said. I didn't ask how he knew that.

"Why don't you just drive there?"

"Has to be in a GU truck," I said, shaking my head. "If the security in Austin's a fraction of what it's like in Gauntlet, it's the only way I'll get in."

"How you gonna stop one of their flatbeds, though? A lot of the folk who work at the plant are regular working-class Americans, Ben. Peyton North aside, I can't let you hurt anyone."

"I'll persuade one of their drivers to lend me one, J.T. Other than a bruised ego, no one will get so much as a scratch."

"How?"

I grinned. "You think those friends of yours might be up for a bit of a caper?"

"Does the Tin Man have a metal dick? Of course they'll be up for it. What do you have in mind?"

I ran through what I would need. When it came to operations like this, simple was always best. I looked at the snacks in front of us. Thought about the best way to stop a truck. Remembered something I'd read one time. "Is that canned chili on top of those nachos?"

J.T. laughed. "This is Texas, Ben. We make our own chili here. We certainly wouldn't serve canned crap to a guest. Mrs. J.T. only used fresh produce, so now that's what I do."

"So, no tins at all in the house?"

"Even my beer's bottled."

"I guess I'm going shopping then."

I slept well that night. I thought I was making progress. To what, I had no idea. North definitely knew what had happened to Spencer Quinn, though. He'd hinted he'd been killed to stop him talking to me. "A multimillion-dollar business cannot be allowed to collapse because of the actions of one misguided individual," he'd said.

Gauntlet had a secret and secrets are like swamp bubbles. Eventually they rise to the surface. North was in an escalating cycle of whack-a-mole right now. Martha and Quinn were both missing, almost certainly dead. Professor Marston was definitely dead. North wasn't panicking, but he was making rash decisions.

I wondered what he'd do when he found out I'd been to Austin.

It was past eight when I woke, the sun cutting through the gap in the curtains like a laser. J.T. had already left for the barbershop. He'd left a piece of paper on the kitchen table, a list of stores where I could get what I needed. I fixed some eggs, then headed out. I figured the stores would be open now.

At Karsten's Sporting Guns I got five military shemaghs, the heavy-weight square scarves used in the Middle East to protect the face from sunburn and sand.

At the general store I got eight cans of Wolf Brand Chili.

At Mike and Sons I got twenty-five feet of nylon paracord.

And outside Lynne's Bakery I got zapped in the neck with a Vipertek VTS-989 stun gun.

A mixed bag of a morning then.

CHAPTER 62

Cause: The Vipertek VTS-989's spiked prongs penetrated my collar and delivered thirty-eight million volts into my neck. And effect: The neurological impulses that control my voluntary muscle movement were disrupted. My blood sugar was instantly turned into lactic acid. The shock overwhelmed my nervous system, causing my muscles to lock up.

By the time I realized I'd been attacked, I was already in the trunk of a Dodge Charger. I was still dizzy, nauseated, and weak. I figured it would be fifteen minutes, at least, before I had recovered from the early effects.

Two men stood over me. The sun was behind them and it was hard to make out their features. They were little more than silhouettes. I sat up as best I could. Changed the angle of the sun. My captors were about my height and build. One had a handlebar mustache, a wannabe Sam Elliott. The other was clean-shaven but gaunt. He had hollow cheeks and a haunted look, like he'd seen something he wanted to forget. He reminded me of Tom Hanks at the end of *Cast Away*. I would think of them as Sam and Tom from now on. It was how my mind worked. They were both wearing Stetsons and shirts with metal collar tips. Aviator shades and boots with pointy toes and decorative stitching. Dressed like ranchers but had never been on a horse in their life. I didn't know who they were, but I knew their kind.

Bounty hunters.

My time on the road had dulled my keen edge. No way would these two yahoos have gotten the drop on me six years ago. I felt like the veteran bomb-disposal guy, the one with a lifetime of making IEDs safe, getting killed by a pull-the-pin-and-throw grenade.

Perhaps I was being unfair. Sam and Tom might look like Village People extras, but they had me in the trunk of their car. No one else had managed that.

Tom leaned over and squirted a stream of tobacco juice through a gap in his teeth.

"That stuff'll kill you," I said.

He ignored me. I wondered why the trunk was still open.

"Look sharp, he's here," Sam said.

I heard footsteps, slow and unhurried, and then a face I knew well joined them at the back of the Dodge.

Peyton North.

He glanced up and down Main Street. I don't know why. No one would dare say anything. They'd be out of a job for sure. Might even end up in the trunk of a car themselves.

"Do it away from here," he told the cowboys.

"We know a place he won't be found," Sam said.

"And the Stingray?"

"We'll come back for it when we're finished. Drive it to Fred's Yard. Turn it into a Rubik's Cube."

"Shame, though," Tom said. "That car's a looker."

"He disappears," North said. "And so does the Stingray. I hear anything otherwise and Andrews will want to know why."

"That won't be a problem," Sam said. "And the bounty?"

"Like I said, the five mil is all yours."

"We'll be on our way then," Tom said. He touched the brim of his Stetson. "Much appreciate your business, Peyton."

North looked down into the trunk. He smiled, but I got the impression he wasn't happy. Like he'd been enjoying the game and was disappointed it had ended so quickly.

"Goodbye, Mr. Koenig," he said. "I suppose it was always going to end like this."

He shut the trunk and I was plunged into darkness.

CHAPTER 63

Escaping from a Locked Trunk 101.

Method one: Pull the release catch. All American cars made after 2002 have a release catch inside the trunk. It's an anti-kidnapping feature and it's the law. Lady called Janette Fennell campaigned for it after she and her husband were forced into the trunk of their Lexus at gunpoint. The release catch usually has a glow-in-the-dark handle.

I couldn't see it.

I reached up to where I thought it was on a Dodge Charger. Felt the sheared plastic instead. I ran my hands up and down the roof of the trunk just in case they'd forgotten that the release catch was attached to a release cable, but it had all been removed. Sam and Tom knew what they were doing.

Method two: Use tools to pry open the trunk's latch. Or use a tool to punch through a taillight. Signal for help or pop the bulb. Hope a traffic cop gets bored enough to stop the car. There were no tools, no tire jack, not even a loose nail. The trunk was emptier than the inside of a Ping-Pong ball.

Method three: Bludgeon through the back seat and crawl into the passenger compartment. It was a poor third choice. It would be slow and noisy. Sam and Tom would have plenty of warning. I spent a minute getting myself into position anyway. I got my back against the taillights and my feet against the rear of the back seat for maximum leverage. The trunk of the Dodge Charger is one of the biggest on the market, and it didn't take long. When I was ready, I gradually increased the pressure, turned my body into a jack. Nothing moved. I increased the pressure until I couldn't press any harder. It didn't budge an inch. They either had something very heavy on the rear seats or, more likely, it had been retrofitted that way.

I didn't think I was the first person to have taken a ride in the trunk of their Dodge. It was a mobile prison. They knew what they were doing.

Method four isn't really a method at all. It's more of a tactical reality. And it's not even a good one anymore. With old cars the kidnapper had to physically pop the trunk. They had to turn a key in the lock or push on the mechanism. When the trunk opened, the kidnapper was standing right there. It meant the kidnappee could explode out of the trunk and grapple with their kidnapper. It gave them a chance. But modern trunks are opened by pressing a button on the key fob. The kidnapper can open the trunk remotely. He can stand ten yards away. Or twenty. Or fifty. Far enough to be safe.

I couldn't do anything about this now. I would have to wait until we got to wherever we were going. See what happened then. Sam and Tom would either make a mistake or they wouldn't. With my options explored, the only thing that remained was to conserve energy. Let my body shake off being zapped with a stun gun.

I got as comfortable as I could and went to sleep.

CHAPTER 64

"Is this asshole asleep?"

"I think so."

"How the hell can he be asleep?"

"Maybe we stunned him too hard?"

"Nah, that ain't it. Stings like a bitch, but it don't knock you out for an hour. Hey, asshole, wake up!"

I had been asleep but had woken when the engine had stopped. I sat up and opened my eyes. Blinked away the sun until it didn't hurt so much. As I'd suspected, when the trunk had popped open, Sam and Tom were a safe distance away. Sam had a combat shotgun trained on me. It had a pistol grip rather than a stock and looked a bit like the one Schwarzenegger used in *Terminator 2: Judgment Day*. I thought it was probably an Ithaca 37. It would be a sensible shotgun for Sam. The 37 ejected expended shells downward so were popular with southpaws. Most shotguns ejected to the right, which was a problem if you were left-handed. Meant they were coming back at your face. Tom held a Desert Eagle. Big gun. Too much for a man like him.

"Get outta the trunk, asshole," Sam said.

They hadn't tied my feet, so getting out was a case of getting my legs over the lip of the trunk and letting my body follow. I'd been in the fetal position for an hour, and I spent a few seconds rolling my shoulders and getting the cricks out of my back and neck. Did a bit of the boxer's shuffle while I took stock.

We were in the desert. No surprise there. We hadn't been driving long enough to be anywhere else. I couldn't see any road. Couldn't even see the shimmer of one. Again, no surprise there. North had said I was to disappear, and that meant I was going in a hole. And as hiding bodies in the desert is almost a cliché, even the most dull-witted highway patrol cop was going to wonder what was happening if they saw someone digging a hole by the side of the road.

"You know what's about to happen, right?" Tom said.

"You're going to kill and bury me," I said. I looked around me. "Probably here. Looks like easy digging. No trees and no obvious rocks. Just loose dirt. Shouldn't take long to dig a grave."

"That's right."

I didn't respond.

"But you went to sleep," Tom said, fascinated.

"I had a long night," I said. "And you zapped me as I was getting my coffee." I yawned. "Saying that, car sleep is never as satisfying as bed sleep, though, is it?"

"What the hell's going—"

"He's an asshole," Sam cut in. "Don't worry about it."

"I'm not worried. But neither is he. Why is that?"

Sam frowned, then said, "Guess we'll never know." He turned his attention to me. "Walk to me," he said. I did. When I was ten yards away, he said, "Stop there. Get on your knees."

Again, I did.

Tom skirted around me and got something from the back seat of the Dodge. A long-handled shovel, the kind gravediggers use. An Irish shovel, I think they're called. I'd wondered why I was still alive and now I knew.

They wanted me to dig my own grave.

Which was stupid of them.

CHAPTER 65

Shovels work in tandem with the body to form a simple machine. The shaft is the beam, the shovel head is the load, the hand in the middle of the shaft is the fulcrum, and the hand at the top is the force. It doesn't matter how loose the dirt is, you can't use a shovel if your hands are tied together. The machine can't work. The fulcrum and the force are too close together. It's basic physics.

They would have to untie me.

And that meant they'd have to get up close.

Unfortunately they had planned for this. It wasn't their first rodeo. Tom threw me a folding knife. It had a bunch of tools, like a Swiss Army knife. "Cut yourself free, then throw it back," he said.

I found a blade and sliced through the zip tie. I rubbed my wrists to get the circulation going.

"The knife, asshole," Tom said. I threw it back. It landed at his feet. He picked it up, put the blade back in its groove, and slipped it into his pocket. He then threw me the shovel. "Dig," he said.

After an hour I stopped for a rest. I'd dug down more than two feet and my shirt was wet through. Now I was knee deep in my own grave, the cowboys had kind of relaxed their guard. Sam was smoking and watching the sky. Tom was scratching his balls and complaining about his prickly heat.

"How you going to spend the money?" I asked.

"Shut the hell up," Tom said.

"I was just making conversation. I thought we could be friends."

"I'm so sick of your bullshit it ain't even funny."

"I haven't spoken for an hour."

"You know what I mean," he said.

"I really don't."

"Your whole 'I don't give a shit' act. You ain't fooling no one, asshole."

"Potty mouth," I said. "And it's not an act."

"What the hell do you know that I don't?"

I shrugged. "Lots of thing, I imagine." I picked up the shovel. "Anyway, best not dawdle. How deep you want me to go? I guess at least another foot. Anything less and it'll be a shallow grave. The critters will find me and then Andrews the giant will find *you*. That's a lose-lose situation."

I started digging again. Tom was overthinking things. Right now, he was his own worst enemy. He was already twitching like a tweaker. Truth was, other than trying to get some sort of an edge on the shovel, I had no plan, no expectations I would survive this. The first time the shovel bit into the dirt, I'd uncovered a round, fine-grained rock. Looked like it had once been a river stone. Tom and Sam obviously didn't feel like digging today, so they had given me a gallon bottle of water so I could finish without keeling over. Every time I took a drink I splashed some down by my feet. Turned the river rock into a whetstone. Anytime they weren't paying me too much attention, which was happening more and more as the day got hotter, I sharpened the shovel using small circular strokes. Tried to keep an angle of thirty degrees. Thirty degrees is a good compromise between durability and cutting ability. If I could give the shovel an edge, I'd have an improvised hacking weapon. It would work like a glaive, a single-edged blade on an elongated staff. The glaive had been an important weapon in the fourteenth century as it meant foot soldiers could engage with cavalry. It was long enough to keep the horse at bay, and the blade was heavy enough to cleave through armor. It was a futile gesture, though. Even if I could sharpen it, I'd still be the man who'd brought a shovel to a gunfight.

Still, it kept me busy.

CHAPTER 66

A couple of years back I'd watched a Kirk Larsen movie called "Dig Your Own Grave." It was short, only thirteen minutes or so, but it sure packed a punch. There were two people in it, Reggie and Dan. Dan was the guy digging his own grave, and Reggie was the guy holding the gun. After some black comedy in which Dan complains that the ground is too hard and Reggie has brought the wrong shovel, Dan scoops up some dirt and flings it into Reggie's face. Reggie's gun goes off and the bullet ricochets off Dan's shovel, right back into Reggie's femoral artery. He bleeds out, and Dan buries him in the grave he'd dug for himself. The end. Good movie. Funny.

I figured a bullet from Tom's Desert Eagle implausibly bouncing off my shovel and killing them both in some freak accident was my best shot of getting out of this. I'd considered filling my pockets with dirt, but I'd missed my chance. I should have done it when I was moving the powdery stuff on the surface, as the dirt I was digging now was too gravelly. It wouldn't spread and get in their eyes like I needed it to.

"That's enough," Sam said.

The grave was almost four feet deep. I thought he was right. It was enough. I climbed out and dusted myself down.

"Now what?" I said, resting on my shovel.

Sam read something on his phone. His lips moved. "Says we need fingerprints and DNA," he said. "And either a verified film of his death or the location of his body. I say we film you shooting him in the head. We then take prints and get some blood for the DNA. We can send them a GPS location of the grave if they want to check we ain't stiffing them."

"Who the hell would try to stiff the Russians out of five mil?"

"No one with the sense God gave geese, that's for sure. You ready?"

Tom said nothing. He looked uneasy.

"What's up?" Sam said.

"Why do I got to shoot him?"

"Because you have a Desert Eagle and I have a shotgun. If I shoot him in the face, then he ain't got a face no more. How those Russians gonna be sure it's him and not just some punk that looks like him? We've been through this."

"But look at him? Dude don't have a care in the world."

"Maybe he don't," Sam said. "Maybe he's just plain tired of running. Got to come a time when it just ain't worth it anymore."

"And why is it Peyton wouldn't do this job himself?" Tom said. "Why was he so quick to give up five million bucks?"

"Hell if I know."

"I'm telling you, something ain't right. I got a bad feeling about this. A real bad feeling. I think we're being watched."

"Who by? There's no one around for miles."

"You ever heard of drones? And we're in a dip so we can't be seen from the road. But that means there's a million places for a bunch of snipers to hide. You were in the marines. Tell me I'm wrong, tell me there's no way for a sniper to hide."

Sam looked around. Saw the rolling dunes, the rock formations, the shrubbery. "No, you ain't wrong." He paused. "But that's a five-million payday standing right there."

"And I'm sure you'll spend it wisely," I chipped in.

"Shut the hell up, asshole! This don't concern you."

"Well, it sort of does. A little bit anyway."

Sam pumped his shotgun. "What's going to happen if I point this at your gut?"

I shrugged. "Nothing good."

He took a couple of steps toward me. "What the hell's that supposed to mean?"

"Means he's an undercover cop, man!" Tom yelled. "Peyton's ratted us out for that Arizona job. There's a whole team of them out there, just waiting for us to point a weapon at him."

"Get a fucking grip!"

"Can't you see it, man? It's why he's been so calm all this time. He knows he ain't in any danger. He went to sleep in the goddamned trunk! I'm telling you, you raise a weapon to him, you'll have so many red dots on your chest it'll look like you got the pox." Tom hurled his Desert Eagle as far as he could. It passed over my head and disappeared into a pile of rocks. He dropped to his knees, raised his hands, and shouted, "I'm surrendering!"

So I swung my shovel as hard as I could.

I aimed for his head but caught his neck. Hacked a chunk out of it, right where it met his shoulder. Tom fell into my grave and started filling the bottom with blood. It was deep red, not oxygen-rich pink. I'd severed a vein, not an artery. Probably the exterior jugular vein seeing as my shovel had shattered his clavicle at the same time. He was twitching and jerking, like he was touching a live wire, but that wouldn't last long. It wasn't a survivable wound, not out here.

Sam Elliott stared in horror. "You ain't no cop!" he said.

"Never claimed I was," I replied.

He took another step toward me and raised his Ithaca.

CHAPTER 67

Cut and thrust: an idiom. A lively debate. An enthusiastic exchange of ideas. John enjoyed the *cut and thrust* of politics.

Cut and thrust: a fundamental fighting technique that uses both the point and the edge of a blade. Sometimes called slashing and stabbing.

Bladed weapons cause harm in four ways: thrusting, cutting, hacking, and impact. Thrusting was out—the shovel didn't have a pointed end—and an impact blow would be like dinging him with a frying pan. Might work, probably wouldn't. Hacking had been effective against Tom, but only because he was unarmed and on his knees.

Cutting was most effective against close-contact weapons. A baseball bat, a knife, a crowbar. It didn't need the skill or pinpoint accuracy of the thrust. It didn't target the internal organs. Cutting wasn't about killing; it was about stopping. But it was no use against range weapons like spears, arrows, slingshots, and boomerangs.

Or guns.

Sam Elliott had a gun, but he'd made a mistake. By getting in too close, he'd turned his range weapon into a close-contact weapon.

I gripped the shovel tight and went to work.

Sam Elliott tried to swing the shotgun in my direction, but I was quicker. I slashed at the inside of his left forearm. The edge of the shovel sliced through his flexor muscles, severing the mechanical connection between muscle, tendon, and bone. Without muscles working his tendons, his left hand was no more use than a bubble. He could no longer grip anything or work his fingers. Defanging the snake, it was called it in the Philippines. I'd trained there one summer. It rained for fifteen days straight. Before Sam even knew what had happened, I'd brought the shovel back around and cracked him on the right elbow.

He yelled and the shotgun fell to the desert floor. He took a couple of steps back and bled for a while. We stared at each other. The blood pitter-pattering onto the desert floor sounded like rain. It smelled organic. Out of place in such a harsh and sterile environment. Sam gripped his forearm with his right hand, tried to stem the flow. It turned his hand slick and red.

He looked at me shrewdly. I was surprised. The change in his fortunes hadn't taken the fight out of him like I'd hoped. It looked like he was figuring out what I'd do next. He knew I was on top, but he also knew it wasn't over yet. A fighter like him will always have a chance. He didn't have the shotgun, but neither did I. He thought I had two options: I'd either use the shovel again, try to bludgeon him into submission, or reach down for the shotgun.

It wouldn't be like it was with Tom, though. If I aimed for his head, he'd be expecting it. He'd step inside my swing and block the shovel with his arm. He'd then have a range of options. Biting, headbutting, elbow strikes, punching with his right hand. Nothing lethal, but enough to put me down for a while. Long enough to fire up the Dodge Charger. Either get the hell out of there or, more likely, drive over me. Turn me into road-kill.

And if I reached for his dropped shotgun, he'd run up and kick me in the face like he was shooting for a field goal. He'd only need to do it once. A kick like that is all about kinetic energy and momentum transfer. My head would be like the last ball in a Newton's cradle.

This would be bad. Very bad.

Aiming for Sam's head or reaching for the shotgun weren't good options. They would be the quickest way to snatch defeat from the jaws of victory. I needed a third option. One that would allow me to pick up the shotgun without exposing my head. I considered throwing the shovel. Distracting him long enough to get hold of it. But throwing the shovel was kind of a one-shot deal. Like a spear. Or a disposable anti-tank weapon. Once it was gone, it was gone.

Or I could discard the shovel. Throw it behind me. Engage Sam in hand-to-hand combat. One of his hands was useless, but thirty-eight million volts had just messed with my nervous system. He'd been resting and I'd been digging a grave. I still figured my chances were good, maybe sixty-forty in my favor.

There was a better way, though. One that Sam wouldn't have thought of. I'd never tried it before, but the mechanics were sound. I adjusted my grip on the shovel so I was holding it at the end of the shaft with both hands. I spun around and swung it as fast as I could, like I was throwing the hammer at the Olympics. Sam threw his arms up, like I knew he would. That was a mistake. I wasn't targeting his head; I was aiming for his quadriceps, the large muscles that cover the front and sides of the thigh.

He took a step back. Another mistake. It meant the edge of the shovel slashed both legs instead of the one. I'd only expected to get the side of his left thigh. I thought the left thigh would protect the right. Instead the shovel glanced off the front of the left and hit the side of his right. Cut them both through to the bone. The quads work together to help you stand. Without them you can't support any weight on your legs. Your knees will buckle the second you try to move.

Which was what happened to Sam. He collapsed in a heap like a dropped puppet.

To his credit, he didn't cry out. He didn't try to beg for his life, not even when I picked up his shotgun and pressed it against his forehead. He smiled, like he'd always known his life would end this way.

"What would you do in my situation?" I asked.

"I dunno, man. Think I kinda saw all that green and lost all sense of perspective. I ain't ever done nothing like this before."

"Give me a number," I said.

"A number? I don't understand."

"Sure you do. The trunk of your Dodge has been retrofitted. It can't be opened from the inside. And it's a custom job, not something you did last night with duct tape and chewing gum. Means you've done this before. So give me a number. How many people have been in this trunk?"

Sam Elliott didn't answer. He closed his eyes.

"That's what I thought," I said.

I pulled the trigger and made his head explode.

CHAPTER 68

Tom was dead. He had blue lips and shrunken eyes. There was so much blood in the bottom of the grave it looked like an oil spill. I thought I'd only severed a vein, but his shattered clavicle must have nicked an artery as well. Probably his subclavian. It would have kept pumping out blood like a busted faucet. Death by exsanguination. It's a compound of two Latin words. "*Ex*" means out and "*sanguine*" means blood. Literally translates as "out of blood." Tom had tried to surrender and now he was out of blood. Guess my rules of engagement had changed since my SOG days. It was frontier justice now. I didn't like how comfortable I was with that.

I dragged Sam over and threw him into the grave as well. I spent ten minutes backfilling it. I didn't think anyone was going to be hiking here anytime soon, but hiding their bodies cost me nothing. I pushed the shovel into the loose soil and kicked some dirt over it. Made sure it couldn't be seen.

I kept the shotgun, though. I could use that later.

The fob to the Dodge Charger was in the central console. I pressed the starter button and the engine growled into life. I followed the tire tracks onto the road and was back in Gauntlet in an hour.

I parked it where I'd got in: outside Lynne's Bakery. Guess it was my lucky day. Peyton North had just stepped out. He had a takeout coffee cup in one hand. It was brown with a cardboard sleeve. In his other hand he held a bag of pink conchas, the Mexican sweet bun. Looked a bit like a seashell. I don't have a sweet tooth, but I like conchas. Soft and cottony in the middle, sweet and crunchy on the outside. North stopped and stared as I got out of the Dodge Charger.

"I hope they weren't friends of yours," I said, throwing him the car keys.

I wandered into J.T.'s barbershop five minutes later, slurping on the chocolate milkshake I'd bought from Lynne's. Apart from J.T. it was empty.

"Damn, Ben, it's almost two o'clock," he said. "Where'd you go for that chili, Reno?"

He chuckled at his own joke, then stopped when he took in my disheveled state. He raised his eyebrows. "You OK?"

"Bumped into some folk who knew me."

"And are these folk still breathing?"

"Not so much," I said.

"North's men?"

"He was there, yes."

"Well, let's hope he doesn't find out they're dead."

"He already knows."

"How?"

"I told him."

"You told him? Why would you do that, Ben?"

"It sort of came up."

J.T. paused. Gave me another of his shrewd looks. Eventually he shook his head and said, "You know, when I spoke to my friend in Chicago, he said there was a rumor about you. Something about a death wish."

I paused a couple of beats, then said, "Cops do like their rumors."

"Yes, they do," J.T. said carefully.

"And now you've met me, what do you think?"

"You've got something, Ben, but it sure ain't a death wish."

"Your friends still up for later?" I said, keen not to get bogged down. "We'll need to leave soon."

"A dog with two dicks couldn't be more excited," he confirmed. "You get everything you wanted?"

"I even managed to pick up a shotgun," I said.

CHAPTER 69

Ned Allan was not having a good day.

He'd argued with his supervisor about who was doing the Austin run that night. It wasn't supposed to be him. He'd already put in a twelve-hour shift, but his supervisor claimed the regular guy had called in sick. That was total bull crap. Ned knew the other guy just wanted an early start on his fishing trip.

Ned Junior, his eldest boy, had been picked to play point guard for the Gauntlet Falcons that night. Ned loved basketball almost as much as he loved his son, and being forced to work when Junior was playing made him feel like he was missing a limb.

And finally, he was running late. Mr. North didn't like tardiness. Everyone at Austin was waiting for the heliostat. His job was to deliver the one in the back of the truck and collect its replacement. It was a simple task and he'd done it many times. Four hundred miles. An eight-hour drive. Give or take. The turnaround would be quick. It always was. There'd be barely enough time to take a piss and grab a coffee before his truck was loaded with the replacement heliostat.

So when Ned saw the rock pile in the only part of the road he couldn't drive around he felt like crying. What were the odds? The canyon road he'd been driving through had been clear for miles and miles, but as soon as the cliffs closed to form the only tight squeeze on the journey, some goddamned rocks had to go and make him even later. It was the only place he couldn't go off road, drive around them, and let some other sucker move them.

If he'd been carrying anything other than a heliostat, he'd have been suspicious. They were expensive pieces of equipment, but they were useless to anyone outside the solar energy industry. Still, Ned answered to Peyton North and that meant he was always cautious. He took out the ignition keys, put them in his pocket, and climbed out of the truck's cab. When he was on the tarmac, he unfastened his holster, removed his sidearm, and approached the obstruction. He looked round, but there was nowhere to hide. After putting his gun back in his holster, he set about moving the pile of rocks. Ned had never been afraid of hard work, and it didn't take him long. Five minutes later he was back in the cab. He grabbed the keys from his pocket and started the engine. A couple of macho revs later and he was back on his way.

For less than a hundred yards.

This time it was a rattle that stopped him. It was coming from the back of the truck. He must have missed a rock somehow. It certainly sounded like he'd bumped the exhaust. Using curse words Ned Junior would have gotten the belt for, Ned climbed out of the cab again. He hurried to the back of the truck and looked down.

"What the hell . . . ?"

Instead of the hanging exhaust he'd expected to see, some joker had tied a bunch of empty chili cans to the rear bumper. They must have done it while he'd been moving the rocks. Although he processed this in under a second, by the time he realized his mistake, it was too late.

He heard the snick-snick of a round being pumped into a shotgun and felt the cold steel of a barrel pressed up against his ear. His arm was twisted sharply up his back, and he was forced to his knees. His ID card was ripped off. Without realizing, he let out a low moan.

A scarf-covered head bent down and whispered into his ear. "Relax . . ." The man checked the ID card he'd just taken. ". . . Mr. Allan, I'm not going to harm you."

Ned's shoulders slumped in relief.

The man spoke again. "But I am going to need your uniform."

CHAPTER 70

The hijacking had gone down without a drop of blood being spilled. J.T. had asked why the plan had needed to be so complicated. I'd asked if he'd ever tried to drag someone out of a car. "It's like trying to uproot a tree," I'd explained.

I left Ned Allan in the care of J.T. The friends of his who'd been acting as lookouts were now back in Gauntlet. They'd only been gone an hour. I'd discarded the shotgun and showed Allan my Glock. Made sure I knew what to expect when I got to Austin. The satnav in the truck was already set up, so finding the location wasn't an issue. I'd been concerned there'd be a code word on arrival, but I'd been overthinking it. Allan was just a deliveryman. If there was criminal activity going on, he was oblivious to it.

I drove ten miles, then parked in a small gully. Searching vehicles and their loads was something I'd been good at. If there was something in the truck, I'd find it.

For two hours I pored over every inch of the truck. The usual hiding places were empty. So too were the more creative ones. I checked the spare tire and the door panels. I shone a light into the gas tank and I checked the air-take box. I measured the vehicle's dimensions to check for false compartments.

There was nothing.

The flatbed was clean.

I moved on to the cargo. I carefully removed the heliostat's protective wrapping and searched the mechanical mirror. Nothing. I unscrewed the control panel and looked inside. Again, nothing. I found a way to lift the mirror slightly and I shone my flashlight behind it. There was a small gap, presumably to allow for heat expansion during the day, but it was empty.

I photographed everything with Mitch's smartphone and emailed the pictures to Samuel. Asked him to check with someone in the industry. See if there was anything out of the ordinary. I knew he'd alter an email account so it looked like the request came from someone in the trade. Probably do something like switch the modern English *a* with the Cyrillic *a* in the sender's email address. Different letters, but they look identical.

Satisfied I wasn't carrying contraband, I got in the cab and raced along to Austin. Tried to make up some of the time I'd lost searching. I would still be late, but I hoped that would work to my advantage. Whoever was at the other end would be rushed. They might be less likely to worry about an unfamiliar driver. The satnav said my destination was seven hours away. I pressed the gas to the floor and was in Austin by 11 p.m. exactly.

CHAPTER 71

Austin: The laid-back soul of Texas. The drunkest city in the United States. The live-music capital of the world. It's been said that the cities of Texas are one big dysfunctional family. If that's the case, then Austin is the kooky aunt, the one who smokes weed and doesn't wear a bra. I'd spent time there when I was younger. Drank and ate on Dirty 6th. Stood on Congress Avenue Bridge at dusk and watched over a million bats emerge. I'd played Chicken Shit Bingo at Ginny's Little Longhorn Saloon.

I love Texas, but I *really* love Austin.

But the city had changed recently. Its cultural reputation and an influx of tech firms had altered the socioeconomic landscape. The cost of living had skyrocketed. Austin's inner core had gentrified, and the city's poor had been pushed to the outer rings. It wouldn't be long before the locals would be priced out completely. And when that happened, Austin would become like all the other bland, corporate cities in the US.

The industrial park I needed was off I-35, in the northeastern part of the city. Even if I hadn't had the satnav, it wouldn't have been difficult to find. The industrial park was in a sensible location. It had good access for eighteen-wheelers and was close to the airport.

GU Solar Energy Systems' workshop was the end unit on a block of modern factory buildings. It was the only unit with lights on. The doors rolled up as I approached. I was expected. I braked at the door, and a man with a baseball cap marched up to the flatbed's cab and looked up at me.

"You're late," he said.

"There was a rockslide on the road." I showed him my bleeding and calloused hands. I'd refused to let anyone help me hump them onto the road for exactly this reason.

"Shoulda called in."

I said nothing.

"You been here before? I don't recognize you."

"Should have been Ned tonight, but he's watching his kid play basketball. Got my eye on a new bass rod, so I needed the OT."

"Asshole," he muttered eventually. He stepped away from the cab and waved me inside.

There was only the one bay in the workshop and I put the flatbed in it. It had raised platforms on either side. An empty trolley jack was on the driver-side platform and a reconditioned heliostat was ready to go on the other.

I got out the cab, stretched, and looked around. It was just another workshop, similar to the one in Gauntlet. There was a small area with a few tools, but the workshop was little more than a one-room garage. It had a couple of doors off to the side, but nothing wide enough to take a heliostat. The sophisticated sterile environment described by Peyton North was bullshit. It looked like a place to load and unload heliostats. Nothing more. If they were being fixed, it was someplace else.

"Hey, man," I called to a man on a trolley jack. My heliostat was halfway off and he was waiting to load the repaired one. "This gonna get fixed here?"

He stared but said nothing.

"Suit yourself," I said. "I hear Torchy's has the best tacos in town. That right?"

The man in the baseball cap came over. "Hey, no talking! You know the rules. And it's goddamned midnight, you asshole. Torchy's is closed." He reached for a package on the bench and threw it over. "Here's your meal."

I opened it. There were two vacuum-packed sandwiches, a pack of chips, and two warm sodas. "What the hell's this?"

"You don't leave the building. You drop off and you pick up and you don't stop anywhere. You need a leak, the can's over there," he said, pointing at a small door. "Otherwise you wait in your cab."

I did as I was told. It wasn't long before the cab pitched up and down as the new load was maneuvered onto the back. Baseball cap man walked up to the driver's window. He looked at his watch. "It's one a.m. now," he said. "You should be back by eight at the latest. I'll let them know what time you left. I suggest you don't dawdle this time." He turned his back on me and began yelling at the men in the shop. I started the engine and backed out.

In the yard in front of the shop, I did a U-turn and headed back the way I came. As soon as I was round the corner I parked up and got out. I ran back to the workshop, but the door was already shut. I got settled in some landscaped shrubbery and waited an hour. Nothing happened. No one came out and no one went inside.

I got back in the flatbed and left Austin. The truck hadn't left my sight, so I knew I wasn't smuggling anything in it. The new heliostat, however? I couldn't shake the feeling that I wasn't going to find anything.

Stopping as soon as it was safe, I dismounted and checked in the same places I had earlier. Halfway through my search, Samuel texted me. Said an expert had looked at my photographs of the heliostat and nothing was amiss. I carried on with the rest of the search, but knew I was going to come up short.

I'd taken nothing there and I was taking nothing back.

One thing was certain, though: Something was going on. For some reason, GU was doing two five-hundred-mile round trips every day, and it had nothing to do with repairing heliostats.

It had happened right under my nose, but I had no idea what it was.

CHAPTER 72

We untied Ned Allan and gave him his truck back. He was terrified of any repercussions and swore blind he wouldn't say anything. I believed him. He couldn't identify his hijackers anyway. J.T. hadn't spoken, and we'd both hidden our faces with shemaghs. I'd been exposed at Austin, but I doubted I'd made enough of an impression for anyone to bother checking up on me.

Despite being younger than J.T. by a good twenty years, I excused myself and went to bed first. I'd been concentrating for nearly twenty-four hours. My eyelids felt heavy and my mind was a mash of crunching gears and grinding cogs. Something had been bugging me about the journey back from Austin, and I couldn't help feeling I'd missed something important. Forcing it wouldn't help. I'd have to come at it from the side, and sometimes sleep was the best way to help it along.

It was midday when I woke, and I could tell J.T. had been waiting for me. He fixed me a coffee and we sat down.

"What's next, Ben?"

"I need to lie low while I figure something out, J.T.," I replied. "If I stay here, North is just gonna send more and more goons. They only have to get lucky once, I have to get lucky every time."

"What do you need to figure out?"

"The trip back from Austin. There's something that wasn't right about it."

"What?"

"I don't know. But it's like having a pebble in my shoe. I can't stop thinking about it."

"I have a buddy in San Antonio. I'm sure he'll put you up for a few days. You want me to make a call?"

"I think I'll head back to the bluff," I said. "Time spent on reconnaissance is seldom wasted and all that. Maybe something will jolt my memory."

"When you gonna be back?" J.T. asked.

Surveillance is an all-or-nothing job. You either do it properly or you don't do it at all. You don't dip in and out whenever you have a spare ten minutes. "When I have a plan," I said.

As ex–Chicago PD, J.T. knew this as well as anyone. "I'll get some food together," he said. "Got some barbecued brisket left over. Good old-fashioned brain food. I'll fix you a few sandwiches."

"Appreciate it," I said. The brisket had been hot, greasy, and delicious the day before. It would be just as nice cold.

"And when this is all over, you and me are going largemouth bass fishing. One of the fellas has a cabin at Caddo Lake. Real quiet. I spend a week there every year. This time you're coming with me. No arguments. You clearly need a vacation . . . from whatever it is you do."

"I dunno, J.T., isn't Caddo Lake where the Texas bigfoot lives?"

"You want to invite him, be my guest. But gotta tell you, Ben, that hairy asshole ain't bunking with me."

I smiled. A week away with J.T. didn't sound terrible. He was good company, he made me laugh, and he was right: I'd been on the road for far too long. I did need a vacation.

"Deal," I said.

"Look at Andrews, Ned," North said. "It's no fun if you don't watch."

Ned Allan had never felt pain like this before. It consumed him. It dominated him. It owned him. His vision was a swirl of violent colors. The pain was somehow constant *and* pulsating. He'd stopped screaming but kept up a low moan. He was at the back of the workshop, and although others would hear what was happening, he knew no help was coming.

Two minutes before North's giant had broken his leg as casually as he'd have swatted a bug, he'd been hearing all about how Junior had acquitted himself in the basketball game he'd been forced to miss. Did well by all accounts. There'd been lots of backslapping and handshakes when he'd arrived at the workshop. When his supervisor had told him he was wanted out back, he'd marched there with his head held high. He reckoned a man could feel proud after his son had played a game like that.

Despite the problems of the night before, he was in a good mood.

That had ended with the swing of a baseball bat.

"Ned. Please look at Andrews."

He'd been on the verge of losing consciousness, but North's syrupy-smooth voice brought him back to the present. He didn't want to look at Andrews. Knew that when he did, the baseball bat would come swinging down again. But refusing to look would be worse. He knew he'd never walk again, but if he did what he was told, he might get to see Junior play basketball.

He opened his eyes.

Andrews's face was expressionless. He could just as easily have been waiting for a bus. He raised the bat, and Allan watched as it reached its upward arc, slowed, stopped, then picked up speed as it came back down.

The bat was hard and his leg was no baseball.

He felt his bones splinter and shatter. Blood sprayed into the air as a fragment of bone tore through his thigh and overalls. The giant stepped back to avoid the mess. Ned Allan screamed.

North knelt and watched as the arterial spray covered his yellow suit. He raised his fist and punched down into Ned's inner thigh. The bleeding stopped like a faucet had been turned off. North leaned in and whispered into his ear. "Do I have your attention, Ned?"

Allan nodded weakly. The small movement caused another wave of crushing pain.

"Good," North said. "Now, I'd like you to tell me all about last night."

CHAPTER 73

Peyton North knew he was close to finding out what a sandy hole felt like from the inside. The men he was standing in front of were going to make someone pay, and he didn't have anyone to throw to the wolves.

Not yet. But he was working on it.

The young man appeared calm, but that only made him scarier. "So now he's been to Austin." It wasn't a question. The facts of the hijacking had been laid out for them.

North said nothing.

"Do you think he found anything, Peyton?"

There, at least, North had some good news.

"The timings don't support it, sir. Even if he drove flat out, he'd have had no more than an hour at each end to have a proper look. And Vincent says he was never out of his sight when he arrived. He asked a couple of questions but was told to shut up."

"And the driver . . . what's his name again?"

"Ned Allan, sir."

"He wasn't going to say anything?"

"No, sir. It was Vincent who put it all together. Said the lateness of the delivery was worth checking with us at Gauntlet."

"What are we doing about Allan?"

"Already dealt with, sir," North said. "The autopsy report will show he was crushed between two flatbeds. Femoral artery was ruptured, and he bled out before help could arrive."

The young man nodded in satisfaction. "Send flowers to his family. Make sure they don't starve."

North didn't utter a sound. His boss was strange like that. He'd happily get rid of anyone who threatened them, but he'd also attend their funerals and would seem genuinely upset at their loss. He was obviously a sociopath. It was why North was so worried.

"Where's Koenig now?" the young man asked.

"We don't know, sir. He got in his Stingray and left town."

"Maybe he's finally got the hint," Latham said.

The old guy's eyes were weak and rheumy, but they scared the hell out of North nonetheless. They missed nothing. They saw everything. He had to tread very carefully. "I don't think he's the kind of guy who takes hints, sir," he said. "But I do have an idea."

He turned and faced the young man. Waited for permission to continue. The young man nodded.

"I think it's about time we sprang the trap we set for him that night he came for dinner."

He told them his idea.

When he finished, the mood in the room lightened considerably.

CHAPTER 74

The big Texas sky had uncluttered my mind. Unrestrained by houses and people and noise, it was going wherever it wanted to. And right now it wasn't thinking about the flatbed or the trip to Austin or what North might do next; it was thinking about shadows. There's something melancholic about shadows. What they represent. The unfulfilled potential. Light that has traveled ninety-three million miles from the sun is stopped from reaching the ground by me.

The light that made the ground was a different matter, though. That light was fulfilling its potential and then some. J.T.'s bluff trapped the heat like a grill tray. There was no breeze, no shade, no respite. It was unrelenting. The rubber on my boots glistened like warm cheese. My hair was stiff with salt. Sweat stung my eyes and rolled from my nose. I'd gone through half my water just replenishing what I'd lost, each sip feeling like luxury.

I hadn't moved, though.

The secret to surveillance is to either hide or blend in. In urban areas hiding in plain sight is best. The more blatant, the better. Sometimes all I'd ever needed was a hi-vis jacket and a clipboard. After a while you became background noise. I'd once had a perp approach me on the street to ask me if I'd seen anyone watching his house. In rural areas you use cover, natural or man-made. Trees, the natural contours of the land, vegetation. Camouflage sometimes. I'd once used a pickup truck loaded with Christmas trees. Even managed to sell one to the ex-wife of the guy I was looking for.

But out in the open you need to stay still. If you don't know how to stay still, the wildlife will give you away. Spooked birds. Running rabbits. Things going quiet when they should be noisy. Things going noisy when they should be quiet. All indicators something is there that usually isn't.

I'm good at being still.

I was so good at being still that for the last ten minutes a western diamondback rattlesnake had chosen the same rock as me as a basking spot. It had crawled over the lip of the ridge and nestled between my sneakers. Like a spaniel might. It was a heavy-bodied snake, malevolently handsome. A triangular head at one end, alternating rings of black and white at the other. Diamondbacks are habitually hungry and mean and can hit a target in as little as fifty milliseconds. The human blink takes over two hundred. Diamondbacks can literally strike within the blink of an eye. But it seemed this one just wanted to chill out. Like it was on vacation. I'd had an irrational fear of snakes when I was a child. A phobia they'd call it these days. And now I was sharing a rock with one of the most dangerous snakes in the country. Go figure.

I turned my attention back to the heliostat field. There was nothing happening. No human activity for the last eighteen hours. Not even a flatbed doing maintenance. But that was OK. Nothing was what you watched for 99 percent of a stakeout. Hurry up and wait. Eventually something would happen—I was sure of it.

The diamondback must have gotten warmed up as it flicked its tongue out a couple of times, then slithered off in a series of S-shaped loops. It wasn't long before a group of collared lizards had appeared out of the cracks and crevices in the surrounding rock piles. They were blue-green with a mosaic of honeycomb scales. They were so bright and colorful they looked like a tattoo of a lizard. They'd made themselves scarce when the rattlesnake had appeared but were back now to feast on the bugs scuttling around J.T.'s bluff. A colony of ants had gathered around my feet, attracted by the crumbs from my brisket sandwiches, and the lizards were darting in and snatching them up.

I turned back to the heliostat field. A pair of jackrabbits hopped into view and began grazing on the woody vegetation near their warrens. They wouldn't normally venture out during the day, but nothing else was moving out there. I closed my eyes and breathed in deeply. My brain was telling me I had all the information I needed. That all the data was there. It was now a case of putting everything together in the right order. I was sure it was something to do with the heliostats they were transporting every day. It had to be. There was an anomaly that hadn't registered yet. Something that hadn't seemed important at the time.

I unwrapped another sandwich as I ran through the sequence of events again. The heliostat was loaded in a workshop in Gauntlet. It was driven to a workshop in Austin. A different heliostat was secured to the flatbed, and this was driven back to Gauntlet. The flatbed had been free of contraband. The heliostat had been free of contraband. Ned Allan had been free of contraband. North had told me the heliostats were being serviced in Austin as it was cheaper to maintain a sterile environment in the city than in the desert, but that was a crock of nonsense. It was a lie. An untrue statement with the intent to deceive.

To quote Winston Churchill, it was all "a riddle wrapped in a mystery inside an enigma." And it was giving me a headache. I put my half-eaten brisket sandwich on my blanket and grabbed the bottle of water. My throat was dry and starting to get sore. I could feel dry gunk forming at the corners of my mouth. I took a swig of the water. It was hot, like I'd filled the bottle from a recently boiled kettle. Water was water, though, and it washed away the dryness in my throat. I splashed the rest into my hands and rubbed it into my face. I reached for the sandwich.

Then stopped.

I caught my breath.

CHAPTER 75

My brisket sandwich was crawling with ants. But that didn't bother me. I could brush them off. And even if I missed one, ants were protein anyway. I'm told they taste sweet and nutty. The UN Food and Agriculture Organization say there are almost two thousand species of edible insects and that in fifty years we'll all be eating them.

It wasn't the thought of eating bugs that had stayed my hand, though. It was the juxtaposition of my last two sandwiches. They were beside each other on my blanket. One was open, half eaten; the other was fresh and wrapped.

A riddle wrapped in a mystery.

Wrapped.

Unwrapped.

Kind of like the heliostats.

They'd been wrapped.

And then, like an arm sweeping across a messy desk, my mind cleared and all that remained was the solution. Something so unimportant I hadn't even bothered to check it.

It was the wrapping that had been the pebble in my shoe.

The wrapping was the anomaly.

The outgoing heliostat, the one I'd transported to Austin instead of Ned Allan, had been wrapped in protective plastic. Heavily wrapped. That made sense. The heliostats were valuable pieces of equipment. But the heliostat I'd collected in Austin and taken back to Gauntlet hadn't been so well protected. It had been wrapped, but not to the same level.

Which was the wrong way round. It was topsy-turvy. The repaired heliostat should have got all the protective wrapping, not the broken one.

But what if it wasn't truly the heliostats they were transporting? What if the whole purpose of the journey was taking the wrapping from Gauntlet to Austin? The heliostats were the camouflage. The wrapping hid in plain sight. You don't see it as once it's removed, it becomes garbage. It was the one thing that mattered, and I'd put it on the side of the road while I wasted hours examining the flatbed and the heliostat.

I had one half of the GU Solar Energy Company Systems puzzle now. The other half didn't make any sense at all.

But it would.

I would solve the other half of the puzzle.

I would find out why Martha had to die.

And then I would kill everyone involved.

CHAPTER 76

It was the reappearance of the western diamondback that finally helped me understand the other half of the GU paradox.

I'd been stress-testing my theory, and there was only one weak point. Everything else fitted tighter than an egg. I had North's methodology. I knew what he was doing, and I knew how he was doing it. But the location didn't make sense. And that meant none of it made sense. Until the rattlesnake showed up again, it had been like looking at M. C. Escher's impossible cube. The one with parts that appear to be simultaneously in front and behind other parts of the cube.

Prior to the rattlesnake reappearing, the collared lizards had been binge eating the ants around my feet. They had a stuttering, stop-start gait. Run in. Stop and look up. Look down and eat. Run off and stop. Look up again. Rinse and repeat. The ants either hadn't realized they were under attack or didn't care. Maybe it was the latter. Ants seemed like a task-focused insect.

The diamondback came back to the exact same spot. It spread itself out, then looked at me like I was sitting in his favorite armchair. I didn't move. The diamondback didn't move.

The collared lizards sure did, though.

The second the snake reappeared, they scattered like buckshot. Some just put their heads down and ran for the hills, but the majority disappeared into the cracks and crevices of the myriad rock piles on J.T.'s bluff. One scrambled into a crack at least ten feet above my head.

Having a good startle response was an essential survival trait out here, I thought.

The bluff emptied in less than five seconds. It was like watching water disappear through a sieve. The collared lizards squeezed into any hole that would fit them, the smaller and tighter the better. There were plenty of places for them. The bluff was fissured and cracked like a dried-up riverbed. A natural mosaic. No logic to it. Some of the fissures were crumbly and less than an inch thick; others were cleaner and deep enough for the lizards to disappear into entirely.

I found myself staring at one of the cracks. It was an inch high and three feet wide. Deep enough for a bunch of the collared lizards to escape into. Sometimes my mind stays coiled. Quietly processing data at its own speed, making neat and logical conclusions. At other times it's capable of making huge intuitive leaps.

An answer to the "why Gauntlet?" question began to unfold. I tested it against the facts as I knew them. It worked.

It was happening in Gauntlet because if it didn't, it couldn't happen at all.

CHAPTER 77

I needed to speak to Jen. I opened my backpack and reinserted the battery into my cell. Pressing the contacts icon, I scrolled down and found her. She answered on the first ring.

"You better not be calling to say you've dinged my car, asshole."

"Your car's fine," I said.

I told her everything that had happened since I'd arrived in Gauntlet and what I thought I'd figured out. She was skeptical, but that was OK. So was I. She was interested, though. I could tell.

"You're not expecting any blowback for hijacking one of their trucks?" she said.

"I don't think so. The driver has a vested interest in keeping quiet, and it didn't seem like a big deal that I turned up instead of him at Austin."

She didn't respond.

"What?" I said.

"Nothing. Anyway what's this got to do with me? You've already stolen my car. What do you need now? The sock monkey my mom made me? My yearbook? My baby teeth?"

"Nothing so dramatic. I need to see the market value going back the last ten years. I want you looking for a pattern."

"Fine," she sighed. "I'll call some people and ask them to send the data over. Keep your phone on."

"It would be better if you could analyze it for me?"

"I'm not your indentured servant, Koenig. I have my own work to do."

"Please, Jen. You're better at this stuff than me."

"A pat on the back from a self-centered asshole. Yeah, that's exactly what I was hoping for when I woke up this morning."

She ended the call. I took a moment and wondered how long it would take her to get back to me. I expected a quick turnaround. And if there was, another piece of the Jen Draper puzzle would slot neatly into place.

When it came, the blowback for the truck hijacking was brutal and decisive. It was blitzkrieg, a devastating play designed to remove me from the board and destroy my will to fight. North had actually made his move the day before, but I only found out when Jen called me back thirty minutes after I'd called her.

"That was quick, even for you," I said.

She didn't answer.

"What's up, was I wrong about the market value?"

"It's not the market value, Ben."

"What is it then? And are you feeling OK? You called me Ben. You usually address me as 'asshole' or 'dickhead.'"

She didn't respond.

"Seriously, Jen. What's up?

"It's J.T.," she said. "He's dead."

CHAPTER 78

I closed my eyes and concentrated on the guilt. I didn't want to miss this part. It would be important later. It was my fault. No excuses, no "he knew what he was getting into." I hadn't killed J.T., but he was dead because of me. The moment North had found out about the heist was the moment he knew who had been involved. My inability to recognize danger, to even consider there might be consequences for others, had sealed J.T.'s fate. I'd put a target on his back, then driven off into the sunset without a backward glance, and while I was watching the lizards and the snakes and the ants, J.T. was cooling in a morgue with a cardboard tag tied to his big toe.

I hadn't known J.T. long, but he had been my friend. The first real human connection I'd made in six years. But to North that meant nothing. He hadn't seen J.T. as the ex-cop who'd tried to do right by his sick wife by leaving his beloved Chicago for the drier climate of Texas. Didn't see a man who'd dedicated his life to public service. All North had seen was a means to an end.

"How?" I asked Jen, the first time I'd spoken in almost ten minutes.

"He was found at home. His throat had been slashed wide open."

"Anyone else?"

I was thinking about the others involved in the heist. J.T.'s friends hadn't had direct contact with the truck driver, but North would know who they were anyway. At least three people had been involved that night, and if he was going to war, he'd try to take out everyone at once. He'd have his own Night of the Long Knives.

Jen paused, then said, "Ned Allan, the truck driver you kidnapped, had an accident. He got caught between two trucks and bled out. Dead before the ambulance got to him."

Two innocent men, both dead because of me. With Professor Marston and the campus cop that number rose to four. I didn't count the fat skinhead.

"It's not your fault, Ben," she said. "And you know if it was I'd tell you."

They were words I'd said myself after shootings when marshals had been injured or killed. It was never the fault of the marshal. It was always the fault of the person who pulled the trigger. But my own words sounded hollow. There was a direct evolutionary line between the actions I'd taken and all these murders. They were all down to me.

"That's not all," Jen said. "The murder weapon was left at the scene."

"Let me guess, a straight-edge razor?"

"How'd you know?"

I ignored the question. "And I imagine my prints have already been matched with some found in GU's executive dining room. That they now know my real name."

North handing me the tequila bottle to inspect had been a fingerprint trap. I didn't know if he'd had anything in mind at that point, but he'd clearly been thinking ahead.

"There's a BOLO out on you. You're officially a person of interest in the murder of John Travis. They have art. A security camera in GU snapped your face. It's all over the news. Every cop in the state is looking for you. The *real* you. The story in the early press says that a drifter murdered J.T., one he'd taken in. It doesn't make good reading, Ben. I think you need to come back to DC. Wait at the cabin while we get this sorted out."

She went silent. I didn't break it.

I thought back to my training with the Israelis. They had a saying: "Anger is motivating. Anger is optimism." They believed that the only way Israel could exist was if it channeled that anger into positive action. I had never understood what that meant. I had always thought that anger was debilitating. It was emotion. It bypassed the rational part of the brain. I understood now, though.

Anger is good.

Anger is energy.

Anger is *permission*.

I breathed out and counted to one hundred. Let the anger wash over me. It felt almost physical. Everything else faded into background music.

Until all that was left was a monstrous calm.

I had made a mistake, but North's mistake was worse. He thought I would have to run. He thought that by framing me for J.T.'s murder he was being proactive. North didn't know the meaning of the word.

But I did.

And I was about to show him what being proactive really looked like.

CHAPTER 79

I had a twenty-four-hour wait before I could go into Gauntlet. Apart from a trip to a town fifty miles away to collect supplies, I remained on the bluff. I didn't see the diamondback again.

Before Jen gave me the go-ahead, she offered one final chance to back out. "You sure you want to go through with this? We can regroup and find another way."

"I go in at six o'clock tonight," I said.

At 5:15 I got into the Stingray and drove to Gauntlet. At 5:45 I parked sixty yards away from the sheriff's office. In the distance a patrol car approached. The day shift was finishing. The night shift would already be inside. The patrol car drove into the sheriff's parking lot. A deputy got out and entered the office through the back door.

After a final check, I got out and walked toward the front door. The sheriff's office was set back from the street. A nice white stone building with modern sliding doors.

I stood on the street, waiting. I didn't think I'd be there for long. Someone would come out soon. Who it was didn't matter.

The front door opened and I stifled the urge to laugh. It was Earl, the deputy who'd pretended to give me a parking ticket. He was checking something in his notebook and didn't see me.

"Deputy Earl," I said. "I hear you're looking for me."

His head snapped up. He recognized me, panicked, and fumbled for his service weapon. If I'd been looking for a fight, he'd have been dead already.

"On your knees, Koenig!" he screamed. He grabbed his radio and shouted into it.

I got to my knees and put my hands in the air, like I was crossing a river with a weapon. Earl being there had been a bonus. He'd already met me. This was good. He didn't need to go through the mental process of matching my face with the one on the BOLO bulletins. Humans are surprisingly bad at checking faces against photographs. The one thing I hadn't been able to control was getting some dope who didn't know who was standing in front of him.

Earl approached me but kept to an as-per-standing-orders safe distance while he waited for backup. I kept still. I didn't want him to shoot me.

I heard a vehicle behind me. The emergency squeal of brakes. I saw fear in Earl, and I turned to see what he was looking at.

A black van had screeched to a halt on the sidewalk. The side door slid open and a man wearing a George W. Bush mask leaned out. He pointed an automatic rifle at Earl and gestured for him to lay his weapon down. Earl did. I swiveled on my knees so I could face both threats. Used my peripheral vision to keep one eye on the guy in the van and one eye on Earl. I kept my hands raised. There was nothing else to do. I didn't have a weapon anyway. Getting into a shootout had never been part of the plan.

As we all stared at each other, a new threat emerged.

I heard someone running.

And then I heard the snick of a trigger being squeezed.

And then I heard a shotgun blast.

And then there was nothing.

PART THREE

A SPECIAL KIND OF MADNESS

CHAPTER 80

Yaroslav Zamyatin's meal breaks had been getting longer and more frequent since the death of his son. He knew he was still mourning Bogdan, and he knew his self-indulgence was only barely being tolerated. The head of Brighton Beach was already muttering about him "taking some time off," Bratva code for retirement. He wouldn't have dared say that publicly if the bosses back home weren't already muttering the same thing. Perhaps they were right. His decision about Koenig had shown a softer side he hadn't known he had. Before that his code had been simple: You kill one of ours, we kill all of yours. There were no exceptions to this rule. It was only because Bogdan had been involved in killing children that the twenty-four-hour grace period had been authorized.

But six years later, and with Koenig still in the wind, his softer side was starting to look like weakness. Weakness wasn't tolerated for long in his business. There was always someone more ruthless looking to step up. And if he were honest, his heart wasn't really in it anymore. He missed Russia. He missed the cold and the vodka and the food. He missed the company of Russian men and women. New York was too hot, too smelly, too liberal.

But until he decided to go home, he *was* still a boss. It surprised him therefore when his associate approached while he ate. He was holding an iPad and clearly had something that needed his immediate attention. Despite almost being Zamyatin's equal, he stopped at a respectful distance and waited to be beckoned. Zamyatin sighed and put down the fork he'd been using to stab his *pelmeni*. The dumplings had gone cold and greasy anyway. He picked up his napkin and wiped his lips before signaling for the man to sit down.

Zamyatin had never been known for his tolerance of fools, and that aspect of his character hadn't changed since the death of his son. The man with the iPad knew this, so he didn't waste time on small talk.

"Someone's trying to claim the contract," he said, putting the tablet in front of him and showing him.

Zamyatin's heart jumped. He didn't know if he was excited or disappointed. Over the years, he'd come to grow fond of Ben Koenig. When he was given updates on how the contract was running, he'd found himself rooting for the quarry rather than the hunters.

It was all very un-Russian.

He looked at the screen on the immaculate white tablecloth. He saw an encrypted email. Communications on the site were automatically encrypted for everyone's protection. It contained a number of files. The man leaned over him and pressed the first one. It was a video file.

It had been taken from the inside of a vehicle. Probably from the driver's seat, judging by the angle. It showed a man on his knees with his arms raised. He was half facing a cop with a drawn weapon. The cop was shouting something into his radio and pointing his weapon at the man. Something must have happened off-screen as the cop put his gun on the ground and raised his arms as well. Someone wearing a mask entered the screen from the left. They ran up to the man on his knees, removed a sawn-off shotgun from under a long coat, and blasted him in the back of the head at point-blank range. The man tumbled forward and lay still. Blood pooled around his head.

The video kept playing as the killer dragged the dead man in the direction of the vehicle. The film stopped when the angle didn't work anymore, but it was clear the dead man had been pulled into the vehicle.

"Could be anyone," Zamyatin grunted, although the fact there were more files to view indicated the killers knew more proof would be needed.

The man pressed play on the next film. It showed a man wearing a George W. Bush mask, propping up the dead man for the camera.

The victim's eyes were sunken and milky, his skin waxy and gray. Dark blood matted his hair. He was very clearly dead.

"Is it him?" the man asked.

Zamyatin said nothing. The last time he'd seen that face had been six years ago. In the same restaurant he was in now. At the same table. The irony wasn't lost on him. He hoped the extra six years he'd given Koenig hadn't been wasted. That he'd found time to enjoy some of them.

"Yaroslav?" the man said softly. "Is this the man who killed that fine son of yours?"

Zamyatin couldn't look at the dead man anymore. He picked up his fork and stuffed a cold dumpling into his mouth. "It is," he said after he'd finished chewing. He jabbed his fork at the screen. "But I want more proof before I spend five million dollars," he said.

The man swiped on to the next video. This time it was Koenig's hand being pressed up against a piece of clear plastic. The plastic was then held against the congealed blood on the side of Koenig's head. The plastic was placed in an evidence bag and sealed. The bag was placed in an addressed envelope before the film showed someone leaping out of the back of a van and posting it. It was all done in one continuous shot. At no point was anything out of sight.

The man removed the same envelope from the bag he was holding. He said, "We received it this morning, ten minutes before these videos were posted. We rushed it past our contact in the FBI, and he confirmed the fingerprints were of missing US Marshal Benjamin Koenig."

He took a document from his bag. It was a lab report. A fast-tracked DNA summary sheet.

"What is this?" Zamyatin said.

"The DNA profile from the blood on the plastic. Also matched to Koenig's profile." Zamyatin didn't answer and his associate continued. "We have a video of his murder, which has been cross-referenced with the town's on-street CCTV. We have a close-up of his face and you've given visual confirmation. We've matched his DNA to blood collected at the scene and we have confirmation of his fingerprints. I think it's enough, but you have the final say, Yaroslav."

"Where?" Zamyatin muttered.

"Texas. Town called Gauntlet."

Zamyatin raised his eyebrows. Why had Koenig ended up there? "When?"

"Three days ago," the man said.

"Do we know what happened?"

The man frowned for the first time. "It all got a bit . . . metaphysical," he said. "Apparently Koenig was wanted for the murder of a local. The cop in the film has made a statement saying it looked as though he was trying to hand himself in."

Zamyatin said nothing. A murder? That didn't sound like the Ben Koenig he knew. Still, six years on the run would do funny things to people. Now it was over, he didn't know how he felt. He'd almost achieved what the Americans called closure.

He stabbed the final dumpling and held it in front of his eyes. The grease had congealed, but it was still a thing of simple beauty. The food of his ancestors.

"Yaroslav," the man said, "can I release the money? Are you satisfied?"

He jammed the dumpling into his mouth. "*Da*," he said. "Give them their damn money. It's over. Ben Koenig is dead."

CHAPTER 81

Peyton North was a relieved man. The plan to run Koenig out of town hadn't worked, but the end result had been even better. He'd just finished playing management the films that had been uploaded to the Russians' site as proof the contract had been successfully claimed.

"There's no doubt?" Latham said.

"None at all, sir. The Russians have released the five million. We assume the fingerprint evidence the killers sent checked out. And we collected some blood from the sidewalk. It matches Koenig's DNA. It's him."

All eyes turned to the younger man. They waited in silence for him to make a decision.

"Are we expecting federal activity?"

"Not as much as you might think, sir. Local cops are still officially investigating the John Travis murder, but I'm told they're not looking beyond Koenig."

The younger man seemed satisfied. He pointed at the paused screen. The Gauntlet deputy was front and center with his arms raised. "I gather Koenig was trying to hand himself in?"

"Yes, sir." It was the one point Peyton North was worried about, the one part that didn't fit. Everything else made sense. Koenig being wanted for murder in Gauntlet had caught the attention of a professional crew. They'd made the trip to Gauntlet and had got lucky straightaway. He was trying to find out something about who'd claimed the contract, but he wasn't holding his breath. But still he wondered why. Koenig knew he hadn't killed the barber, so he had to have known he was being set up. North had used the barber's own razor. Koenig must have handled it as his prints were all over it. That and some fabricated eyewitness testimony would have secured a conviction.

He'd looked Koenig in the eye. There was something not quite right about him, but the man was no fool. He'd survived an international contract for six years. Peyton North had two choices. He could voice his concerns, which, given the upbeat mood in the room right then, would probably have been ignored, or he could keep quiet and accept the plaudits.

He chose option B. He kept quiet.

It was probably nothing to worry about.

CHAPTER 82

From GU Solar Energy Systems headquarters building, the young man had only a short walk to his apartment. He'd stayed a while longer after North had been dismissed. He had wanted to reassure the other men in the room. He'd noticed the look of concern in North's eyes. There was something the man wasn't telling him. He would ask him tomorrow. There was no point making everyone nervous again. The threat—and regardless of how much North had downplayed it, Koenig had been a threat—was neutralized. There was just one more thing to box off before the whole thing could be consigned to history.

The girl.

From start to finish that had been managed badly. But now the Devil's Bloodhound was out of the picture, she could be disposed of properly. No more temporary measures. Not acting decisively the first time had gotten them into trouble, and he wasn't the kind of man who made the same mistake twice.

His apartment was never locked. No one visited without being summoned or without calling ahead. It was in darkness. The Koenig situation had kept him away for a few days. He opened the door and picked up the pad that controlled everything. He pressed a button and the gentle hum of air-conditioning began. Another button shut the drapes. He arranged for the subdued evening lighting to come on before making his way to his kitchen. He fixed himself an ice-cold mineral water and headed to his family room. The room was spacious, airy, and minimally decorated. A huge television hung from a wall. A La-Z-Boy recliner was aimed at it. He set his drink on a carved wooden coaster he'd had commissioned from an artist in Austin and relaxed into the seat. The room was in darkness. The control pad had been configured to ignore this room when the evening lighting came on. Any light caused a glare on the television screen. He had the beginning of a headache, and for a minute he did nothing but massage his temples. Eventually, he reached for the control pad and pressed the television's on button.

Nothing happened.

He must have pressed the wrong button. Removing his cell phone, he found the flashlight function and lit up the control pad. This time he made sure he pressed the green power button.

Again, nothing happened.

He frowned and got up. He hoped the TV wasn't broken. He had a small one—if a fifty-six-inch curved-screen 5K Ultra HD television could be classed as small—in his bedroom, but he'd wanted to relax in the La-Z-Boy for the rest of the night. He knew nothing about how televisions worked, so he hoped turning the power off and on again at the wall socket would resolve whatever bug it had. He reached round the back and fumbled for the power switch.

He couldn't feel the plug.

His cell phone was still in his hand and he hadn't disabled the flashlight. The television was on an adjustable wall mount. He tilted it and shone his light at the socket.

He smiled. That was why the television wouldn't switch on. The plug wasn't fitted. His cleaner must have removed it. He replugged it and turned round.

He gasped.

A man was now sitting in his La-Z-Boy. He was in silhouette, but the young man could tell he was completely bald. He must have found his control pad as the lights came on.

"Oh, God," the young man cried out. Didn't even realize he had.

The bald man smiled and said, "Not quite."

He saw what the bald man held in his other hand. It was a semiautomatic.

The gun fired, and the young man's right kneecap turned into a mess of bone and gristle. He collapsed to the floor screaming. The man pointed the gun at his head, his expression cold and merciless. He said, "Stop."

The young man did.

For a moment they stared at each other. The only things moving in the room were the beads of condensation trickling down the glass of mineral water.

The young man couldn't contain himself. "But you're . . . dead."

"And you're missing, *presumed* dead," the bald man said. He aimed the gun at the young man's left knee and fired again.

This time the young man heard as well as felt his other kneecap explode. He screamed out in pain again. The bald man put his fingers to his lips and said, "Shhh."

"What do you want?"

Ben Koenig looked down at the sniffling mess on the floor without compassion or pity. Peyton North might have been responsible for the recent murders, but sure as eggs in April, the young man pissing himself on the floor had given the order.

With an eerie calm, Koenig said, "Everything, Mr. Quinn. I want everything."

CHAPTER 83

Sometimes WITSEC, the United States Marshals Service's Witness Security Program, has to protect a witness who, to put it bluntly, cannot be protected. They usually fall into one of two categories: someone who is about to expose something and needs to be stopped, or someone who has already exposed something and needs to be punished.

When deciding what level of resource to put into their protection, WITSEC works on a grid-type risk assessment. It's a complicated tool, but it boils down to two questions. The first is: Does the person who poses the threat actually have the motivation to go after a federal witness? It's the easier of the two questions, and there is usually a direct correlation to what damage a living witness can do to them. The second question is more complex: Does the person who poses the threat have the *means* to go after a federal witness? Are they well resourced? Do they have a history of corrupting public officials? Do they have access to specialists? How far are they willing to go?

If they score highly on both, more resources are pumped into the witness's protection. Witness relocation, new identities in new states, live-in protection. Nothing is ruled out.

It's a system that's worked for decades.

But on incredibly rare occasions, even that isn't enough. If a hostile foreign power poses the threat, for example, even the highest resource available couldn't guarantee the witness's safety. Trying to protect witnesses against state-sponsored assassination puts marshals at risk.

WITSEC computers are stand-alone systems, isolated from the internet. They are heavily encrypted and coded. The only way to discover a witness's level of protection is to sit at a WITSEC terminal and log on to the database. If a witness does have the very highest level of protection, then realistically there is only one way to get to them: go through a WITSEC marshal. Although WITSEC marshals are subject to rigorous vetting and frequent psychometric testing, when all's said and done, they're human. They can be threatened and they can be bribed. This is negated as much as possible by having WITSEC marshals working in silos. They don't have carte blanche access to every witness on the database, just the ones they are personally responsible for. But theoretically it would be possible.

To the best of my knowledge, there's only ever been one witness exposed to a level of threat that meant that the protection system, despite all the resources, despite all the measures, was *almost certain* to fail. And on that occasion, special measures were needed.

And that was where I had come in.

Mitch had liked to plan for all scenarios. A couple of years before Gecko Creek he'd asked me to come up with a plausible, realistic, and, most importantly, *convincing* way of publicly faking someone's death. My time spent with Kidon in Israel gave me the seed of an idea, and within a month I had a working theory. It was too dangerous to test, and when I put it to Mitch, he thanked me, then told me to forget all about it.

Which I did.

A year later, someone who only ever used his first name approached me. I assumed he was CIA or NSA. He never told me and I never asked. He wanted to know if what I'd theorized could actually work. I told him what I'd told Mitch. It could. The "victim" would need nerves of steel, the "killer" would have no room for error, and external variables would have to be in everyone's favor. But I thought it was possible.

He asked me to give him a percentage. I told him seventy-thirty.

"In favor of surviving?"

I shook my head. "No, I think it's likely that the person would die."

I assumed that would be the end of it. It wasn't.

I didn't have the security clearance to know why the woman had to "die," but I do know she had balls of steel. Didn't flinch once, not even when I pressed the gun to the back of her head. I'd dragged her to the waiting van myself, checked her for injuries. It had worked flawlessly. To this day, to the best of my knowledge, only I, the driver of the van, and the man who'd arranged everything know she is still alive.

That's how to really hide someone. You get people to stop looking.

And when I'd figured out that Spencer Quinn's kidnapping had been staged, it made me realize that, if I wanted to avenge J.T.'s death, if I wanted to find out what had happened to Martha, I would have to die.

I knew how.

But I couldn't do it by myself.

CHAPTER 84

It *is* possible to successfully fake someone's death. No-body drownings can be staged. Bodies can be disguised. Faces can be destroyed beyond recognition. Records can be altered. Fire can be used. So can acid.

And so can shotguns . . .

But for the people whose job it is to hunt for other people, all this does is raise alarm bells. It's just too . . . convenient. A no-body, no-face death never puts off the determined tracker. The *only* way to fake someone's death is to do it publicly, with independent witnesses.

Like shooting them in the back of the head at point-blank range.

On CCTV and in front of a bunch of cops.

With supporting DNA and fingerprints.

That isn't so easy to stage.

When Mitch asked me all those years ago, I came at it from the only angle that mattered: What would convince me? I made a list of the things I'd need before I declared a perp dead and called off the hunt.

I'd definitely want to see the corpse. If I couldn't, then photographs were OK. Videos were good. A video of the *death* was better. But even if the visual evidence was compelling, I'd still want fingerprint and DNA analysis. Dental records. I'd inspect the scene. If I had all that, I'd consider, only consider, declaring someone dead and canceling their arrest warrant. In my sixteen years in the marshals, it had never happened.

But I had an advantage.

The people hunting me couldn't claim their money without my corpse.

They couldn't leave it for the cops. They'd have to take it with them.

I had spent an hour grieving J.T., then gone to work. I called Jen back.

"Do you have that market share information yet?" I asked.

"I do. You were right."

I didn't ask how she'd gotten that so quickly. That was a conversation for another day.

"You have a plan." She wasn't asking a question.

"I need to die."

"Okaaaay."

"It's the only way to identify all the players," I said. "And that's not all. I want it to be you who kills me."

She paused, then said, "I thought you'd never fucking ask."

I told her what I needed to happen. She didn't try to talk me out of it. Instead she asked for specifics. She wanted to know exactly how I wanted it to go down. Who would do what and at what time. She asked about the odds of success.

"Seventy percent chance it'll kill me for real."

"A plan with no drawbacks then."

Finally, she asked if it had been tried before.

"No," I lied. "But the theory is sound."

"This is a two-person job."

"It is."

"Do you have anyone in mind, or should I find someone?"

I gave her a telephone number. "Ask him. He might help."

"Who is it."

"Man called Samuel."

"Do you trust him?"

"With my life, yes," I said. "With my wallet, no."

I got in the Stingray, backed out of J.T.'s bluff, and headed away from Gauntlet. I kept driving until I found a midsized town 150 miles away.

I had a bunch of stuff to buy.

From a medical supply store I got a parietal bone teaching aid. From a pharmacy I bought condoms, an insulin syringe, some adrenaline, a razor, shaving gel, and a solar charger for my cell phone. I wanted a wig, but there wasn't a theatrical supply store. There was a playhouse, though, and after I'd spun a stagehand a tale about doing something for an ex-cops' charity, she let me root through some old stuff they had in storage. I found a wig that sort of matched my own hair color, and the same stagehand was kind enough to give me a tube of hair adhesive. I was in Texas, so the shotgun cartridge I needed was the easiest thing of all to buy. I bought a field medical kit while I was there as well. Prepare for the worst, hope for the best.

I checked my mental list and found I'd ticked off everything. I jumped back in the Stingray and headed back to the bluff.

Some tasks had to be done at the last minute, but there was a certain amount of prep to be getting on with. First off was shaving my head. Not easy when you're out in the desert. I'd forgotten to buy scissors, which was a bit of a drag, and when I'd finished, the razor was blunt and I was covered in cuts and scratches. That was OK, though. I wasn't auditioning for *Kojak*. After the bleeding had stopped, I tied a handkerchief around my head. My skull hadn't seen the sun for a long time, and I didn't want to get burned.

Next up was the shotgun cartridge. I pried open the end and emptied half the shot into the condom. I threw the rest away.

After the cartridge was the parietal bone teaching aid. The parietal bone is the roof and side of the skull. It wasn't ideal, but the occipital bone went too far down the back of the head. It would be seen. I began gluing the parietal bone to the inside of the wig. After a bit of trial and error, I had it fitting like a skullcap, which it kind of was. I hacked at the wig until it looked like the hair I'd shorn off a few minutes before. I checked in the Stingray's chrome wing mirror. It was slightly darker in color, but from a distance I thought it would fool anyone who didn't know me that well.

I left a four-inch strip unglued at the back. The final stage could only be done at the last minute. I carefully set the wig and bone to one side and went back to watching the arid desert. There was still nothing happening.

I figured that was all about to change.

CHAPTER 85

As the hour arrived, I made my final preparations. I took the syringe, found a vein in my arm, and withdrew the full amount. I emptied it into the condom and repeated the process until the condom was half full. When I thought I had enough, I tied the end and triple-bagged the blood with two more condoms. I tested it for leaks. It held.

I lifted the unglued section of the wig and gently eased the condoms between the hair and the bone. I glued it in place, then held it firmly for five minutes until I was sure it was set. I tried it on again. A quick check in the mirror showed the external appearance hadn't altered much.

I looked at my watch. It was time. I glued the wig-bone-blood-condom to my head, checked it one last time in the mirror, then left J.T.'s bluff for what could well be the last time.

I had done my bit. It was up to Jen now.

It's funny how you can trust someone you dislike.

Samuel had been driving the van. When he'd screeched to a halt, he'd pointed a weapon at Deputy Earl. The camera was fixed to a bracket on the driver's window, and it was already filming. Samuel said when Jen shot me, I'd collapsed facedown, and it had looked so real he'd thought something had gone wrong. That they hadn't removed enough charge from the shotgun shell, and some shot had penetrated through the teaching aid bone and had entered my skull for real. It wasn't until Jen dragged me into the van that she could check my pulse. I was unconscious but alive.

They drove to the next town over, and Samuel got cracking. His training in film makeup meant it was easy for him to make me look like a corpse, a significant upgrade on the CIA job I'd done all those years ago. He'd even brought some contact lenses of his own creation, cleverly colored to look cloudy and shrunken. A waxy solution to make my face look pallid, and I was ready for the second video to be filmed.

When I woke, we viewed what we'd done. I was happy. Job done. The film and evidence would have fooled me.

But would it fool Peyton North?

CHAPTER 86

"Wake up."

Spencer Quinn and I were in a rented garage in Fort Stockton. Far enough from Gauntlet to avoid the inevitable searches, but not so far we couldn't get back in a couple of hours. Jen had rented it through the Allerdale Group. She assured me we wouldn't be disturbed. She and Samuel were back in Washington. Samuel had volunteered to stay and help, but I didn't want anyone around for the next bit. Jen hadn't offered, which I thought was odd. Her Stingray was still in Gauntlet, so she left me the rented sedan she and Samuel had traveled down in. I'd driven to Fort Stockton with Quinn in the trunk.

He was unconscious when we arrived. His complexion was pale and clammy. I dragged him out of the trunk, tied him to a workbench, and fastened a couple of thigh tourniquets to stop him bleeding out.

With Quinn down and out, I took the chance to check myself over. Getting shot is like being hit with a sledgehammer. The back of my head was bruised and tender, my neck clicked when I turned it, and a few bits of shot had penetrated the parietal bone teaching aid. They were under my skin but hadn't penetrated my skull. They felt like grains of rock salt. Nothing I could do about that now. They would have to wait. I opened a blister pack of Tylenol and dry crunched as many as I dared.

Quinn had slept for long enough. I emptied a bucket of cold water over his face and he spluttered into consciousness. He immediately began screaming for help.

Pointing my Glock at his groin, I said, "Keep it up and the next bullet goes there."

He whimpered to a halt. Just sat there panting. Staring at me, wide-eyed in terror.

"I won't waste time with introductions, Mr. Quinn. You know who I am and I know who you are," I said.

"But how . . . ?" he said.

"How did I know you had faked your own kidnapping? A diamondback rattlesnake told me."

He frowned. Tried to make sense of what I'd just said. He shook his head and said, "No, I meant how are you alive? I saw you die."

"You saw what I wanted you to see, Mr. Quinn." I paused a beat, then added, "I assume you've realized just how precarious your position is right now?"

Quinn said nothing.

"No? Then allow me to explain. I'm officially dead. I was shot in front of a cop. My murder was filmed. Legally I can no longer be held accountable for anything that happens from this point to the next. Whether I kill you now or later, there will be no comeback on me whatsoever. I could shoot you in the middle of Fenway Park during a Red Sox game and no one would look for Ben Koenig."

His predicament dawned on him. North thought I was dead. He would know someone had abducted Quinn for real this time, as I'd purposefully left his house in a mess, but he wouldn't have any place to start looking. He would think there was a new bad actor in Gauntlet, someone who had yet to identify themselves. Quinn's face, already white from the blood loss, turned gray. The sweat that had beaded on his forehead began to roll down his cheeks. He clenched his teeth and he stared at me with hatred. "What do you want?" he said eventually.

I looked him in the eye and said, "I've already told you: I want everything."

Silence. I didn't break it.

"Who are you with?" he croaked.

I ignored him. "I'm going to start asking you questions. If you hesitate or if I think you're lying, I shoot. Understand?"

He didn't respond.

I sighed. "Allow me to demonstrate."

I lifted the Glock and another bullet spat out. This time into his ankle.

Quinn howled in agony.

I waited until he stopped. "Next time I ask a question, you answer, because quite frankly I'm running out of places to shoot you."

"You're a fucking psychopath!" he spluttered.

"I think you're wrong about that. Psychopathy is a neuropsychiatric disorder characterized by a lack of empathy and poor behavioral controls. I'm doing this partly because of my friend J.T., partly because of the truck driver you had murdered, and partly because of my friend's daughter. I believe that shows empathy. And I've successfully faked my own death and managed to resist shooting you in the head. I believe that shows I am in full control of my actions. No, what I am is *resolute*."

"Asshole!"

"And that's subjective," I said. "I imagine if I asked the son and widow of Ned Allan who the asshole is here, I might get a different answer."

He hurled a few more creative curse words, but eventually we were able to get down to business.

For the next half hour I laid out what I knew and what I thought I knew. What happened on that rock climbing trip, the funding of GU Solar Energy Systems, the plastic packaging, everything. He didn't contradict me. I think he was surprised at how much I'd figured out.

Eventually I got to why I was in Texas. My raison d'être. "Why did you take Martha Burridge?"

He shrugged. Still unwilling to incriminate himself.

"Mr. Quinn, let me explain something. I was asked to investigate her disappearance, to recover her body, and then punish anyone who was involved with her death. I can't think of a single reason to let you live."

I studied his face. I wanted to make sure he understood he was expendable.

But something else was happening. Something I'd said had surprised him. He blinked owlishly. Lies and deception would be the tools he lived by, but the pain and blood loss must have been affecting his ability to mask what he was thinking. Right now, he had all the guile of a five-year-old.

His expression had shifted when I'd mentioned Martha being dead. Like he thought he might actually get to live through this. That was unexpected. Everything I knew about abductions told me she was dead, and everything that had happened since I'd met with Mitch had only confirmed it. Quinn and North were ruthless when it came to eliminating threats. Now I wasn't so sure.

"Is Martha Burridge alive?" I said.

Quinn didn't answer. A gleam of hope had sparked in his eyes. He was now wondering what to tell me. I moved the hand holding the gun. Jammed it into his groin.

"She's alive!" he screamed. "But not for long, asshole!"

CHAPTER 87

Martha being alive changed everything. All my plans had been predicated on her being dead. I had intended to get the names of everyone involved and pick them off one by one, leaving North to last.

Things were different now. I'd need proof of life, of course, but if Martha was alive, I had to tell Mitch. This scenario wasn't something I could manage on my own. The FBI did this for a living. They would know what to do next.

A surge of energy flowed through me. "Where?" I snapped.

"Gauntlet."

"Be specific."

He told me. His answer was bad. Very bad. I couldn't tell Mitch after all. I couldn't tell anyone. Not even Jen. The FBI couldn't get to where Martha was. An army wouldn't be able to reach her. And even if they could, she would be killed before they got anywhere near. No point leaving a living witness. Not when you could make a dead one disappear forever. She might as well not exist where they were keeping her.

But I could get to her.

"Why's she still alive?" I said.

Quinn didn't hesitate. Not this time. Not when he had good news to share. "We didn't know who she was when we took her," he said. "And by the time we did, there was a federal search on. We were waiting until it had died down."

I thought about that. It sort of made sense. They couldn't kill her, not until they knew how exposed they were. What she knew and who she'd told. And they'd dragged her back to Gauntlet as they didn't have the infrastructure in DC to do the questioning there. They'd feel safe in Gauntlet. Untouchable. But when they discovered who her daddy was, they had a real problem. How could they dispose of her? If she simply disappeared, Mitch, the director of the oldest federal law enforcement agency in the United States, would never stop looking. Never. And if she was found in Texas, he'd never stop asking why. No, there was only one thing they could do with her.

"You were going to take her body back to DC," I said. "Dump her in a crack house or something like that?"

At least Quinn had the decency to look embarrassed. He scrunched his eyes and nodded. That was good news. It meant Martha wouldn't have been harmed. Evidence of torture wouldn't fit with a drug overdose. By now Quinn was slipping in and out of consciousness. I jabbed my Glock into his shattered knee. He yelped.

"Why did you take her in the first place?"

"That paper she was writing," he mumbled.

I frowned. "Explain."

"It was about us." He realized I still didn't understand. "My funding," he added. "She found out that Banco Nacional de Coahuila had no history of investing in solar energy."

"I thought banks were desperate to lend money to clean energy?"

"Taking on business outside your normal range of expertise can indicate money laundering. Banks avoid it when they can."

I nodded. Martha planned to specialize in forensic accounting and would know this. It probably started with little more than idle curiosity. The tragic story of the boy who'd lived at Copley Hall and lost his friend in a climbing accident. Started a clean energy company in his name and turned it into a multimillion-dollar business. I wondered how long it had been before she'd spotted the inconsistencies. If she was anything like Mitch, it wouldn't have been long at all.

How long before she voiced those suspicions to others?

How long before someone at GU heard a whisper someone was looking into them?

And how long then before they became proactive?

"Who's your fail-safe?"

He looked confused by the change in direction.

I explained. "Mr. Quinn, your business partners don't like to share. For you to have survived this long means there's a document lodged with someone, something that will bring GU crashing down, that it is to be released if you die."

Quinn stared at me in shock.

I pointed the Glock at his uninjured ankle. "I'll ask you again. Who's your fail-safe?"

He told me. Not a person. He was using those businesses that send emails to your loved ones after you die. You can tell them the things you couldn't when you were alive. What you really thought of them, where the treasure's buried, that type of thing. Quinn had accounts with two different providers. Thirty emails with attachments ready to go in the event of his death. His account was arranged so that he had to call them every week with a code word. And so that his business partners couldn't simply eavesdrop on him, he was given the next week's code word only after he'd successfully given *that* week's code word. He also had a duress code word. Give the duress code and the emails were sent immediately. Give the wrong code word, and after a short period to remember the right one, the emails were sent. Don't contact them for seven days and a minute and they're sent.

Very clever. If I'd been on the other side of all this, I doubted I could have thought of a way around it.

"When did you call them last?"

"Two days ago."

"I imagine your friends will be keen to hear from you then?"

Quinn nodded.

I smiled grimly. I could see the sketchy outline of a plan. More of a bargaining position. A way to negotiate Martha's release.

I removed some field dressings from the field pack I'd bought and packed Quinn's wounds. I could have got all fancy and gone inside and tied off some of the bigger blood vessels. It might have saved his legs later on. But this was the man who'd ordered the death of my friend. Not letting him bleed was as generous as I was feeling. I put a cannula into the back of his hand and fashioned a drip stand out of a wire coat hanger and a broom handle. The field kit included bags of saline, and I forced one into him and set up another on a three-hour drip. It would keep him alive. I jabbed a double dose of morphine into his thigh muscle and he drifted into a peaceful sleep. I estimated it would be at least an hour before he woke, and I had things I needed to do before then.

CHAPTER 88

"Who am I speaking to?" I said into the laptop.

Peyton North leaned into the screen. "Everyone's here, just as you asked, Mr. Koenig."

"Who's in charge?"

"I am," North replied.

"No, you're not," I said. "I know exactly who you are, Mr. North. Who's in charge?"

North frowned. "Mr. Koenig, I don't know what you think you've found or what you think you're doing, but as far as I'm concerned—"

"This is the last time I'm going to ask," I said. "Who's in charge?"

North shouted. "No one's in charge! We haven't recruited anyone yet. I told you all of this when we had dinner."

A bubble of noise accompanied him. I waited until it subsided.

"OK . . . How about I just give you your old CEO back then?"

Deathly silence. I seized the advantage and angled the computer so that Quinn's prostrate form was visible. He was unconscious but clearly alive.

The older man in the room took over. "You have our attention, Mr. Koenig."

"Mr. Quinn and I have been having a nice chat, and although he won't tell me what's going on in that damn town of yours, he has told me that you have a friend of mine. He also tells me that if he doesn't call his fail-safes, then whatever it is you're doing down there finishes. By my calculations, you have five days to get him back. Is that right?"

"What do you want?" North said.

"Proof of life. In one hour I want to see Martha Burridge holding today's newspaper and saying the following words: 'Everything will be all right.' When I call, I want to see that, Mr. North. If I do, we can move on to the next part. If I don't, then Quinn dies and you're looking over your shoulder for the rest of your life."

I quit the video call before anyone could respond. The screen went dead. If Martha was alive, they'd do what I asked. They had no choice. It was the only play they had left. Swap Quinn for Martha. They needed him back at all costs. If he died, it was all over.

While I waited, I called Samuel and asked him to get me a phone number. I committed it to memory. If he was curious why I wanted it, he didn't ask. The number was for someone I never thought I'd speak to again.

But I'd thought through every angle and it was the only way.

I was about to end the call with Samuel when he said, "I did that other thing you asked me about."

"And?"

"I don't know how the hell you knew, but you were right," he said. "That lady's keeping some dark secrets, man."

I looked at the unconscious Quinn.

"I have time," I said. "Tell me what you found, Samuel."

He did. It took him almost an hour.

"She's a monster," I said when he'd finished. "But at least it explains why she hates me. She probably hates everyone."

CHAPTER 89

Martha came into focus. Dark rings underscored her eyes, and her face was thinner than normal, but she still had that spark of defiance I'd always liked. She was in a dimly lit room that offered no clues as to her whereabouts. She was holding the local newspaper in front of her. Someone off camera spoke, and Martha turned the paper round and read the headlines. She put on her best newscaster voice and gave a sarcastic rendition of the fall in the price of beef. The paper was snatched back by her unseen, and now annoyed, captor.

"Hey," she protested. "I hadn't read my horoscope yet."

Martha listened to someone to her right, then said, "Everything will be all right."

The screen went black for a moment; then North came on screen. He looked at his watch. "That video was taken thirty minutes ago. Are you satisfied?"

"For now," I said. "Of course she needs to stay that way if you want Mr. Quinn back."

"We're aware of the stakes, Mr. Koenig," North said. "What happens next?"

"Can I assume that, as you're running a legitimate solar energy project alongside whatever it is you're doing, most of your staff aren't involved in your side business?"

I could see North trying out my question. Trying to see the angle I was playing. Eventually he said, "Yes, you can make that assumption."

"Here's what's going to happen then. All noncombatants go home until this is over. Make up whatever reason you want, but they all get a few days off. Paid. Forty-eight hours after the plant's clear, I'll surrender myself to your custody."

"You're coming to GU?" North said after a short pause.

"I am."

"Even though you know we can't let you leave?"

"That's right."

"Then—"

"Why am I prepared to do this?" I interrupted. "Because, although I think you're a psycho with mommy issues, North, unfortunately I *do* think you know what you're doing. And I know Martha. If you explain that her father dies if she talks, she'll keep your secret."

"And you?"

"You can't let me go, North. I'll never stop coming after you. You know that. The only way Martha can live is if I die."

"And you're happy with this?"

"Happy is stretching it a bit."

"OK. Then what happens?"

"You'll take Martha to the address I'll give you when I arrive, and hand her over to a friend of mine. They'll call me when Martha's safe, and then, and only then, do you get the location of Spencer Quinn."

"Then what?"

"Then I'll try to escape, obviously."

North turned to the other men in the room and they whispered among themselves.

"We find those terms are acceptable, Mr. Koenig," North said after a few moments. He didn't sound happy.

I nodded. "Calm down, Peyton. In two days all this will be over."

CHAPTER 90

Now I had a timescale, my planning could get serious. And so could my hardware acquisition. I had *some* equipment, obviously—one piece in particular was key to everything—but as North had agreed to my terms, I now knew exactly what I needed.

Firepower. Lots of firepower.

Quinn's part was almost over. I was only keeping him alive in case a contingency plan was needed. I jabbed another double shot of morphine into his buttocks and sent him back to sleep. His wounds were looking bad, and I figured he had three days max left before toxic shock took him. I hooked him up to another bag of saline.

For the last couple of hours he'd been too weak to reach the bucket he was using as a bathroom. If he made a break for the door, the wounds would open again and he'd die. He wasn't going anywhere, but I secured him with the handcuffs I kept from my old life, the pair Sheriff Long had been so interested in the week before. I taped his mouth shut as well. He moaned but didn't wake. The morphine was becoming less and less effective. I didn't care. Quinn had been responsible for the deaths of six people: J.T., Professor Marston, the campus cop, Ned Allan, the female contract killer, and the skinhead in the DC holding cell. All on him.

And they were just the people I knew about. There'd be others, of course. Lots of others. Some innocent, some not so much. The inevitable cost of a business like his. I wasn't about to lose sleep over leaving him on the garage floor whimpering in pain, soaked in his own blood, piss, and shit.

I had a problem. I needed guns, and although Texas doesn't have a mandatory waiting period, federally licensed firearms dealers can't sell directly to people from out of state, and all Samuel's IDs were for DC.

Buying privately was legal *without* ID. All I had to do was promise not to commit a crime. Didn't even matter if my fingers were crossed. Still left me with a problem, though. The type of people who advertised private gun sales were usually enthusiasts. I could maybe pick up a couple of items, but they wouldn't have the stuff I wanted.

I needed another kind of seller.

If I had enough time, I'd have hit the bars and pool halls of Houston. See if anyone had a name. A guy who knew a guy. Hope I didn't stumble into some undercover cops. After a few days I'd have what I needed. I didn't have a few days.

So it was a problem.

But luckily in Texas, one man's problem is another man's chance to make a buck. I knew exactly where I needed to be.

There are five hundred gun shows every year in Texas. There were two that day. The nearest was in Rockdale, Milam County. It was day one of a two-day event. If I couldn't find the person I was looking for, there was another one a bit farther away in Waco.

The show didn't start until eleven, so I stopped for bacon and pancakes at a roadside grill. Even managed to get a shake. Felt like it had been ages since I'd had one. Although the BOLO had been canceled when I'd been shot in the head outside a police station, I wore a loose disguise anyway. A long-billed baseball cap with a duck logo on the sides and wrap-around shades. I didn't think it would be needed, but just like with Jen's Stingray, people would only remember the cap and the shades, not the man wearing them.

Rockdale was technically a city, but with just five thousand residents, it was little more than a small town. It was nice. Mom-and-pop stores rather than chains. The gun show was in a hotel. I paid the five-dollar entrance fee and walked into the function room.

There were five rows of tables. The first two were for dealers. I couldn't get guns from them without a Texas ID, but an item I hadn't seen before caught my attention. It was a fifty-cent coin that pulled apart to reveal a hidden blade. The laminated flyer said they were ideal for covert escapes. I picked up one and studied it. It was indistinguishable from the real thing.

"Neat, huh?" the dealer said. "Just don't get caught trying to get on a plane with one."

The sticker said forty bucks. I peeled off a couple of twenties and bought one. In all my years in the Marshals, I never once thought to check the coins from someone I'd arrested.

I moved on to the rows for the private dealers. It was extraordinary the things people thought it was OK to sell. Dozens of AR-15s, H&Ks, and AK-47s. Handguns of makes and models I'd never even heard of. Thousands and thousands of rounds of ammunition.

I picked up a new AR-15. The vendor walked over to me and said, "Nice machine. Easily configured to fully automatic."

"That legal?" I asked. I knew it wasn't.

The man shrugged and moved on to a different customer.

I'd been wandering the aisles for an hour before I saw what I had come for. Gun shows always have a third type of seller. He's not a dealer and he's not a private vendor. He doesn't have a table, but he has items for sale nonetheless. He normally walks around with a weapon of some kind and a FOR SALE sticker hanging from it. Most of these men, because they are nearly always men, are legitimate sellers.

But some aren't, and I reckoned I'd just found one.

He was carrying a small revolver and almost, but not quite, belonged. It wasn't that he was acting suspicious, because he wasn't, but he stood out nonetheless. Most private sellers, especially the ones in the third group, aren't 100 percent sure that they aren't committing a felony. Even though the law is clearly on their side, selling a weapon to a stranger without any checks feels illegal. So, although most sellers are law-abiding citizens, they look as though they aren't.

The man I was looking at didn't seem to have a care in the world, though. He wandered up and down the aisles. He looked at nothing, but he saw everything. It looked like he had something to sell, but only if the money was right, and only to a certain kind of customer.

A customer like me.

CHAPTER 91

A woman approached the man and asked about the gun he had for sale. He shook his head and moved on. That was suspicious. The woman had wanted a small purse-sized revolver, and the man was selling a small purse-sized revolver.

I approached him from behind and said in his ear, "What you selling?"

He turned casually and stared. He was clean shaven with a thatch of sandy hair. His eyes bore the beginnings of crow's feet. They were full of mistrust. Eventually he said, "Nothing."

"I'm not police," I said.

"Never said you were," he said right back.

"I'm after something . . . a bit different. This is too vanilla."

He didn't respond.

I opened my pocket and let him glance in. I'd brought ten thousand with me.

"Got any ID, man?" he asked.

Samuel's pack of ID cards came out. "Any particular one in mind?" I said, peeling off one ID after another. As a way of demonstrating criminal intent it was perfect.

"Name's Odell," he said. "Come with me."

He led me back out into the parking lot. "Coffee?" he asked.

I nodded and followed him to a small restaurant. It was full of folk taking a break from the gun show, but we found a table near the restrooms. Odell looked round to make sure we couldn't be overheard. An old couple were seated at the nearest table studying menus, each holding a glass of red wine. The noise level was high.

After we'd gotten our drinks, we got down to business. He wouldn't have anything with him, but it would be within driving distance.

"I need a SIG Sauer MPX with ten thirty-round magazines," I said. "If you can get the MPX-K compact version, that's even better." The machine pistol was a weapon I'd used before. I liked it. Short enough for close-quarters combat, but not so short you lost power or accuracy.

Odell nodded like this happened every day. Who knows, maybe it did. He took out a small book and made a note. "What else?"

"A suppressor for a Glock 19 and five magazines."

He made another note.

"Five M84 stun grenades and one medium-sized, level-three-threat hard-armor protective vest." The vest would be stiffer and heavier than Kevlar but would stop almost any small-arms round fired at it.

Odell raised his eyebrows. "That all?"

"Five hundred nine-mil Parabellums and a tactical gas mask with electronic ear defenders. Don't need the version with a built-in mic." I stopped talking and waited for him to finish writing.

"And?"

I slid across a piece of paper. I'd written this part of the order down as there was a lot of chemistry and I doubted it was something he'd be familiar with. "And ten of these," I said.

Odell read the note and let out a small whistle. "Are these . . . ?"

"They are," I nodded. North had all the advantages. It was his home turf, he knew when I was coming, and he had overwhelming firepower. I needed to reduce those odds.

Odell took out his cell. He punched a few numbers and put it to his ear. When it was answered, he repeated what I'd asked for and listened. "How long?" he asked. He was silent while he waited for an answer. Eventually he looked at me and said, "Three hours. Eight grand in total. That includes five hundred rounds. And I can only get two M84s."

"You get the money when I see the goods," I said and got up to leave. "Back here?"

He nodded. As I passed, he gently grabbed my arm. "There must be some crazy dudes after you, man."

I shook my arm free. "You have that the wrong way round, my friend."

I returned to the gun show and waited in line to show my entrance ticket. I hated the term "waiting in line." I much preferred the British version: "queue." Much more succinct. It's also one of the few words in common use with four consecutive vowels. And the only one I could think of where the last four letters were redundant. Didn't need to be there. The first letter did all the work. Funny what you think of sometimes.

Once I was inside, I made quick work of buying the remaining items on my list: A shoulder holster for the Glock—I'd cut out the bottom to accommodate the suppressor later. I also bought a tactical sling for the SIG. At a survivalist's stall, I bought some nuts and jerky. Also got some military gum, the type that gives you a shot of caffeine when you pop a piece. Anything that could give me an edge.

I paid fifty bucks for some secondhand boots. It was steep, but they were sturdy with big grips. Wore well. I didn't know exactly where I was going to end up, but a good pair of boots never hurt anyone. The guy must've had a pang of guilt as he sold me a small canvas backpack for ten bucks. I'd need it to carry all the extra gear I'd asked for.

I was about to leave when I passed a table I hadn't noticed earlier. It was selling combat knives, and one in particular caught my eye. It was a Fairbairn-Sykes fighting knife and had /|\ stamped on the handle side of the cross guard. It was the "broad arrow" stamp of the British Army, sometimes called the crow's foot. I suspected it was one of the original knives issued to their commandos ahead of the Normandy landings. And if it was, it was entirely possible it had shared a battlefield with J.T.'s dad's straight-edge razor. It had a knurled and checkered brass handle and came with an oiled leather scabbard.

I didn't believe in fate, but I sure as hell believed in not ignoring omens.

I picked it up and examined it. Everything about it was precise. The double-edged, slender blade was tapered and razor-sharp. It was over six inches long, the ideal length for thrusting and slashing. A killer's knife. It was perfectly balanced. When I held it, it seemed like it was an extension of my hand.

"How much?" I asked.

"Six hundred," he replied. "It's an original."

There are times to haggle and there are times to simply pay what's asked. This was one of those times. I handed the man six one-hundred-dollar bills.

He even threw in a sharpening stone.

CHAPTER 92

Odell was not alone when he returned to the restaurant's parking lot. He had two friends with him. They wore combat fatigues and baseball caps. I quietly racked my Glock. Edging my way out of the snug seating area, I paid for my food, then made my way outside.

Odell took the lead. He signaled to one of the men, who unhooked the trailer gate to reveal a large canvas bag. Odell unzipped it, stepped back, and gestured me forward to take a look. Before I could open the bag, he said, "The price has gone up a thousand bucks. I need nine now."

I'd been expecting something like this. Had even factored it into my budget. Odell wasn't in the gun trade because he had a yearning for public service. I raised my eyebrows anyway.

"Open the bag and you'll see why," he said.

I'd asked them to get me a SIG Sauer MPX, preferably the compact variant, the MPX-K. It had a four-and-a-half-inch barrel rather than the standard eight. It was less accurate but easier to conceal and was closer to what I needed. But Odell had gone one better. He'd gotten me an MPX-SD. It had built-in sound suppression, and although the barrel was a couple of inches longer than the compact version I'd wanted, the sound suppression more than made up for the additional length. It was brand-new. The selector switch had the automatic fire setting as well as the semiautomatic. Illegal in every state in America. I wondered where they'd got it.

I slotted one of the curved magazines and checked the action. It seemed solid. No surprise there. It doesn't matter whether it's machine pistols or cuckoo clocks; Swiss engineering is always reliable.

"Thought you could use the help," Odell said.

I said nothing while I checked the rest of the equipment I'd asked for. Everything was there. The protective vest was a bit loose, but that wasn't Odell's fault. He'd got me the size I'd asked for. I should have asked for small. They're normally worn over bulky fire-retardant one-piece suits, and I was wearing a Springsteen T-shirt. Not to worry, it wouldn't get in the way. The gas mask fit perfectly. The ten specialist items I'd asked for were also there. I zipped the bag closed again.

Turning to Odell, I said, "You thought right." I removed my billfold and counted out $9,000. Odell watched me carefully but not greedily. As soon as I handed him the money, all three men got in the pickup. I barely had enough time to grab the canvas bag before they were driving out of the parking lot. Odell tipped an imaginary cap in my direction as they passed.

I had my guns, I had my stun grenades, and I had some stuff North wouldn't be expecting. I even had an original Fairbairn-Sykes fighting knife.

I was ready.

It was time.

CHAPTER 93

I drove back to Fort Stockton without stopping. Quinn was still unconscious when I got there. It was unclear whether this was because of the morphine or his injuries. He had started to smell sour. Sepsis had set in. Septic shock would follow, sure as U follows Q.

I forced another bag of saline into him, then popped the trunk of the sedan. I lifted Quinn up and manhandled him in. The irony of him being locked in a trunk wasn't lost on me. One of his knee wounds burst open, but there was nothing more I could do about that. He needed urgent medical attention and he wasn't going to get it. He'd either survive the journey back to Gauntlet or he wouldn't. The only reason I wasn't leaving him in Fort Stockton was there were city cameras that might have caught the sedan Jen had hired, and I didn't want them linking her with Quinn's corpse. Better I took him with me and left him for the caracaras. The fierce-looking falcons would strip him down to his bone faster than a river full of piranhas.

The journey was uneventful, and I was back at J.T.'s bluff just after seven. I parked under the heavy canopy of the Texas ebony tree cluster. If North looked for me by air, they'd need specialist equipment to find me.

I unloaded Quinn. He was circling the drain. I thought he had maybe twelve hours left, a day at the most. After I got him out of the trunk, I removed the handcuffs and sat him under a tree. I didn't bother restraining him; with no knees he wasn't going far. In the garage he could have banged on the door, maybe called for help. Out here he could either fall off the cliff and tumble to his death or crawl ten miles across the baking desert. I put a bottle of water next to him and loosened the cap.

I began by preparing my kit and weapons. The first thing was a noise check. I put it on like I was a packhorse, then jumped up and down. There was a *tink* from the canvas backpack. The pin on an M84 grenade wasn't taped down. I fixed it and jumped again. This time one of the Glock magazines had a small rattle, probably had a bit of grit in it. I discarded it and jumped up and down again. Nothing. I took it off and set it down carefully.

I put some water on for a last cup of coffee. While I waited for it to boil, I tore a page from my notebook and pinned it against a tree. I paced back fifty yards and scratched a mark on the ground with my boot. I collected my MPX-SD, returned to the mark, and snapped off three two-round bursts. The suppressor was excellent. The noise was about the same as an air pistol. And as the subsonic ammunition was designed to travel below the speed of sound, there was no sonic boom either, no high-pitched crack all the way along the bullet's flight path. I walked over and examined the piece of paper. The grouping was high and right. I adjusted the rear sight, walked back, and fired another group. Bang in the middle.

With the weapon zeroed to fifty yards, which was the maximum range I expected to engage anyone, I drank a cup of strong coffee, then took a "caffeine nap." I set my alarm for ninety minutes. It would be long enough to take me through one full cycle of sleep and bring me out in the REM cycle. The caffeine would clear my body of the fatigue-causing chemical adenosine, but because it would take a while getting into my system, it wouldn't stop me getting to sleep. A Navy SEAL had taught me that.

I was woken by the whump-whump of a helicopter. I checked my watch. It was almost 9 p.m., when my alarm would have woken me anyway. The helicopter was a couple of miles away. I could see a green light, which meant it was flying left to right. It was heading to GU. North must have hired it in case they had to collect Spencer Quinn in a hurry. Or maybe to take Martha somewhere safe. I watched it all the way onto GU's roof. After a minute the whump-whump stopped, the rotors slowed to a standstill, and the lights went out. The helicopter's silhouette was hunched and ominous, like a bird of prey.

I turned back to my final preparations. I melted some butter into the last of the coffee. The fat would prolong the caffeine hit. I gulped it down, then ate some nuts and jerky for energy. I wouldn't be taking water with me as it would be too noisy, so I drank a whole bottle. The last thing I needed was dehydration cramps.

The sun was low enough to cast long shadows across the desert floor. It was time to move. A final kit and weapons check, and I was ready. I glanced at Quinn. He was watching me. I checked the sky. It was dark but not too dark. I walked across to the edge of the bluff and peered over. I could still see a route down.

"What are you doing?" Quinn said. His voice was thin and scratchy.

"I'm climbing down this cliff face, then I'm walking across the heliostat field, then I'm going to get Martha," I replied. "Anyone who gets in my way will find out we're playing with live ammunition tonight."

"Where's your rope? Where's your harness? You don't even have a belay device."

"Why would I need all that? It's not steep and there are plenty of hand-holds."

"Are you crazy, it's pitch black! And even if it wasn't, you can't climb down there without specialist equipment."

"Why do you care?"

"Because when you fall and break your neck, I'll be dead before anyone finds me."

"Almost certainly," I said. "But I won't fall."

"Peyton was right," Quinn said. "There's something not right about you. He couldn't put his finger on it. Said you must have ice in your veins. I thought it might be that you were reckless, but it's more than that, isn't it?"

I didn't answer. I was barely listening, truth be told. My mind was elsewhere now. It was running through scenarios, thinking about contingencies and counterattacks. I was picturing the heliostat field and the layout of GU's workshop. I was mentally going through my close-quarters battle drills.

I walked past Quinn and stood at the edge of the cliff. I looked down.

I watched the view fade into purple and gray shadows. For ten minutes I planned my route down. I could just make out the heliostat field. Bright specks in the matte black sky provided a sliver of light. I thought it would be enough.

It was twenty-four hours until I was due at GU headquarters.

I planned to be there in five.

CHAPTER 94

They were never going to let Martha live.

Never.

How could they?

Martha might accept a threat against her father as a reason to keep quiet, but how could they be sure?

They couldn't. There would always be doubt. And Mitch was an old guy. At some point he was going to succumb to the inevitable. I knew Martha, and I figured by now they did too. The second Mitch passed on to whatever came next was the second Martha made the phone call that brought the roof crashing down on North and Quinn.

So, no, they had no intention of letting her live.

And I'm pretty sure they knew that I knew that.

The way I figured it, North had three needles to thread. Getting Quinn back was his priority. Killing Martha and dumping her in a DC crack house was a close second. The third needle was me. He needed me dead, but not until I'd given him Quinn's location. And not before he found out how much Quinn had told me and who I'd passed it on to.

Neither of us was in a strong position.

Both of us knew the other was lying.

So when I asked for the heliostat field and workshops to be cleared of anyone not involved, I knew North would do exactly as I asked.

But that didn't mean they would be empty.

Far from it.

There were twenty-four hours until the deadline, but I knew North wouldn't leave his approaches unguarded. He didn't know what I had planned, but he'd know I was planning something. His sentries would have been there within an hour of me calling. Maybe working in six-hour shifts to keep them fresh. I hadn't seen any, but I wouldn't expect to. North would only use professionals tonight.

Finding North's sentries would be useable intelligence. Their saturation would help me understand how many he had at his disposal. If, at five miles out, they were spaced every fifteen yards, then North had an army at his disposal and I was in trouble. But if the outer cordon was only lightly protected, then the number of men who could hold a gun was finite. He'd hold his best men in reserve, of course. I wouldn't meet them until I was inside the building. There would be a crowd of them, all tough, battle-hardened, and loyal. It was where North and Andrews the giant would be. But that was OK. It was why I'd brought some surprises with me.

I glanced back at Quinn. He looked dead. I didn't care. I checked my weapons and equipment one last time. Everything was either secure or within easy reach. One last jump to make sure nothing rattled.

I was ready. As Marine Recon would say, it was time to advance to contact.

It was time to take the fight to North.

I turned around and lowered myself into the darkness.

PART FOUR

ADVANCE TO CONTACT*

---

* Military; a purposeful and aggressive operation designed to gain or reestablish contact with the enemy.

PART FOUR

ADVANCE TO CONTACT

CHAPTER 95

Climbing down a rock face is harder than climbing up. It's difficult to see footholds, and the tendency is for your eyes to stay closer to the rock. It takes courage to lean back far enough to see where to place your foot next. Gravity exaggerates even the tiniest mistake. I'd heard of experienced mountaineers freezing climbing down a route they'd just climbed up. Climbing down gets in your head.

I don't have problems like that. Even carrying a load of weapons and equipment, I reached the bottom in under a minute. The rock face was steep but not vertical, and it was cracked like a broken windshield. There were plenty of foot- and handholds, and when there weren't, I moved across until I found one. I heard a rattle halfway down and I wondered if I'd just been warned off by my old friend the western diamondback.

As soon as I reached the bottom, the SIG Sauer MPX-SD was in my hand.

I stood still.

In the basin of the desert, away from the lights of distant Gauntlet, the darkness was absolute. I strained my eyes, but could barely see my hands.

I needed to wait thirty minutes. That's how long it takes for the human retina to start producing "visible purple," the chemical that helps the eye make out blacks, whites, grays, and general outlines when there isn't much light. I hadn't been able to produce visual purple at the top of the bluff as

GU's lights were too bright. While I waited, I moved my arms directly out to my front, then separated them slowly until they were stretched all the way out either side of me. I wriggled my fingers but couldn't see them. I repeated the exercise half a dozen times until I could see my fingers move. It's a technique called wide-angle vision. It improves peripheral awareness.

Gradually the unending blackness transformed into a monochrome landscape. I could make out shapes. They were blurry, like I was looking at them through the bottom of a bottle, but it showed my retinas were up to the task. I mentally prepared myself for what I was about to do, and by the time the silhouettes of the heliostats were the color of a sepia photograph, I was ready to move off into the shadowless world ahead.

CHAPTER 96

I'd identified their blind spot the first time I'd been on J.T.'s bluff. Back then, it had been an intellectual exercise. Something to do while I whiled away the hours. In forming a defensive position, the heliostats were a significant disadvantage.

North had told me that the costs involved in laying pipe capable of transporting electricity were prohibitive, so the solar tower, the big light-house the heliostats aimed the sun's energy toward, had been situated as close to the headquarters building as regulations permitted. The outer heliostats were therefore less than fifty yards from the building. And because the desert's vast horizons meant the sun didn't disappear until the curvature of the earth blocked it, and because the heliostats *followed* the sun, at the end of every day all the heliostats were facing the same way: west. When they finally powered down for the night, they were almost vertical. Anyone facing the heliostat field from GU would be looking at a wall of mirrors.

I thought I could walk between them all the way up to GU headquarters. There was virtually no defense to it. Searchlights wouldn't work. It would be like shining a light in Scaramanga's house of fun, the one with all the mirrors in *The Man with the Golden Gun*. Infrared wouldn't work either; I wouldn't be in their line of sight. Heat-seeking devices couldn't be used as North had his own men out there. He wouldn't know which of the yellow blobs was me and which were his men. He couldn't even use dogs;

they were only effective in enclosed spaces. Let a dog loose in the desert at
night and you'd never see it again. A dog wouldn't have the biggest teeth in
the desert. If the coyotes didn't get it, the rattlesnakes would.

By coming in through the heliostats, I'd made North virtually blind,
and unless I stumbled into one of his sentries, I knew I could get close. It
was a small advantage, but sometimes that's all you need.

With my night vision as good as it was going to get, I stepped off.
Sweeping each foot for obstacles, and testing each footstep for noise before I
put my full weight on it, I reduced my noise to zero. Moving quietly at night
is a laborious process. I was headed for a small ravine I'd seen from the top
of the bluff. I hoped to pick up a bit of speed there. Moving slowly in the
open is the right thing to do, but when there's natural cover, there's no harm
in cautious speed.

When I got to the ravine twenty minutes later, I was drenched in sweat.
I was pushing muscles I didn't use much. My calf muscles were tight and I
knew they would cramp later. I took a five-minute break, then set off again.
The ravine wasn't as deep as it had looked from the top, but with a crouch I
was able to cut a couple of hundred yards off my open approach.

By the time the ravine ended, the outer limit of the heliostat field was
less than thirty yards away. I completed another kit check and switched
the MPX-SD for the silenced Glock. Short weapons were better than long
weapons in enclosed places. I press-checked, a never-ending habit that anyone whose life depends on guns picks up. It involves pulling the working
parts back slightly and checking there's a round in the chamber. No one
wants to hear a dead man's click. By the time I'd got to GU headquarters,
I'd have press-checked a dozen times I reckon. Wouldn't even remember
doing it.

The climb out of the ravine was noisier than I'd hoped, but it couldn't
be helped. Although noise carries further at night, I was confident I was
still coming in under their radar. Using the sweep-and-test walk, I approached the relative cover of the heliostat field.

Which was when I heard something.

CHAPTER 97

I froze. What I'd heard had been no more than a rustle, but it was sound when there shouldn't have been any. I strained my eyes, but despite my night acclimatization, I couldn't see anything. Another small noise had me raising the Glock. I crouched into the standing-horse stance, the one I'd learned with the Israelis. Legs shoulder-width apart, knees bent, elbows straight and locked. I took a deep breath, released half, then held the rest. If I had to shoot from distance, I needed to do it from a stable position and that meant no breathing. I took one last deep breath and released half of it. I held the rest and waited.

Two minutes passed. It felt like ten. I didn't breathe, and I kept the Glock pointed in the direction I'd last heard the noise.

Without warning a young black-tailed jackrabbit broke cover and darted out from the darkness, its white tail bobbing furiously as it kicked across the rocky ground. I tracked it with the Glock, but within seconds its earthy coat had blended into the gloom and it had disappeared. I almost laughed. All that for a rabbit. On the off chance it had been spooked by something I couldn't yet see, I waited another five minutes before moving off again.

Three minutes after that and I was in the relative cover of the heliostat field.

And a second after that I realized I'd made a mistake.

* * *

Two mistakes. Not one.

The first was the all-encompassing cover of the heliostat field. Once I was in, I had no way of seeing where I was going. It was like being in a maze. I couldn't see GU headquarters and I quickly became disorientated. Putting the North Star on my right would point me west, but that wasn't good enough. I needed to leave the heliostat field at the closest point to GU headquarters.

I was still figuring out what to do when my nose told me what my second mistake had been. The heliostat field was a double-edged sword. It didn't just provide me with cover. It also provided cover for sentries.

And I could smell tacos.

CHAPTER 98

Staying hidden in the dark means more than just choosing good cover and keeping still. It means being careful with what you eat and what you wash with. Spicy food can be a dead giveaway. Literally. It was why I'd eaten nothing but nuts and unflavored jerky.

I couldn't see him yet, but I wondered if it had been Taco Man who'd disturbed the jackrabbit. Not enough to startle it—it hadn't been panicked—but enough to make it want to be someplace else. It didn't matter. There was an obstacle in front of me that needed to be dealt with.

Marine Recon had drummed into me that obstacles you didn't want to engage should be boxed around. It doesn't matter if the obstacle was a Russian battle group or a lake. You march on a series of ninety-degree bearings for a mile at a time. Four ninety-degree turns later and you've boxed around the obstacle and are headed the same way you were. It's a maneuver all special forces use.

Boxing around Taco Man wouldn't work for me, though. I didn't have time and, more importantly, it would be an implausible coincidence to have walked into the only sentry in the heliostat field. Far more likely, North had a number of men guarding the outer perimeter, and because I had no idea how tight he'd drawn his net, boxing around one sentry would only bring me into contact with another. And the next one might not have eaten spicy food.

Tactically, it made sense to pierce North's net here.

I had a problem, though. I knew Taco Man was there, but I couldn't see him. Other than the faint smell of cumin, there was nothing. Not even a patch of darkness that was maybe a little too dark. I bent into a squat position to see if the lower angle created a new silhouette. It didn't. Taco Man was well hidden and wasn't moving. If he hadn't eaten something spicy, I wouldn't have known he was there at all, and because sound travels farther at night, the chances were that by the time I'd gotten close enough to see him, he'd have been ready and waiting.

Wherever he was, he had to be dealt with, and dealt with quietly. That meant getting up close. And I couldn't do that until I knew where he was. I wasn't moving until he did. I settled my breathing, set my eyes to search, and waited to see how good Taco Man really was.

Turned out he was OK. Not the best, not the worst. Just what North had available. It was twenty minutes before he made a mistake. But it was a doozy.

At night, human eyes can see a candle at thirty miles. It means you don't use flashlights, not even ones fitted with red filters. You don't use any electronic gizmo that lights up or glows. You certainly don't smoke. It's called maintaining light discipline.

Because I thought Taco Man was a professional, the flare of the match took me by surprise. Instinctively I shut my eyes to protect my hard-earned night vision. After I'd given him enough time to light up, I opened one eye. It was enough to see while allowing my rod cells to keep producing visual purple.

The smell of cigarette was unmistakable. A rich heady aroma. I kept watching where the match had flared, and sure enough, the tip of a cigarette began to glow. I watched him suck in a deep draw. The tip of a cigarette is 1300 degrees Fahrenheit, and it gives off a red light. It was enough for me to see his face. He was a white man in his early forties. Had a noticeable slouch. A bit paunchy but otherwise fairly nondescript. Probably had strength but not much stamina. No more than hired muscle. Brought in especially for this task.

He was near enough for me to put two bullets in his head, but as I didn't know where the next sentry was, I needed to control his fall.

This would need to be done the old-fashioned way.

CHAPTER 99

I tightened the SIG's sling, holstered the Glock, and unsheathed the Fairbairn-Sykes fighting knife.

Taco Man was thirty yards away, and each step was going to be a mission. I'd been traveling silently before, but I needed to be in close-target reconnaissance mode now. It's where the guys in the SAS and Navy SEALs observe the enemy up close. *Real* close. Ten-yards-away close. The close-target reconnaissance walk is different to the standard sweep and test. Each step involved lifting my foot high enough to clear any stiff grass, twigs, or anything that might make a noise. Keeping my weight on my back foot, I used the toe of my front foot to feel for obstacles. If there weren't any, I'd lower my heel to the ground and gradually transfer my body weight from the rear foot to the front foot. That's how you move in total silence.

It took an hour.

Every inch of that thirty yards was a leap of faith. In the absolute silence of the Chihuahuan, even the rustle of dry grass would give me away. If that happened, I'd have no choice but to shoot from distance.

Eventually I was close enough to hear him breathing. I could also hear faint chatter coming from an earpiece I couldn't see. Made sense. They had to keep in touch somehow.

Approaching from the front was out. I'm quiet, not invisible. I aimed

to Taco Man's left, my right. I'd box around and come at him from his
rear. Unfortunately, this was a kill mission. It's OK in the movies to knock
someone out by hitting them with the butt of a gun, but in the real world
there's no such thing as a stun setting on a blunt instrument. If I crunched
him on the skull with the butt of my Glock, one of two things would
happen: He'd die slowly of a brain hemorrhage, or he'd holler out in pain.

I got to less than a yard away, and for the first time I hesitated. Should I
just walk past him? Head toward GU without letting him know how close
he'd come to dying? I could do that. It would be the humane thing to do. Not
everyone had to die. I looked at Taco Man's hand and saw he was wearing
a wedding band. He was married. Might even have kids. Even hired thugs
have personal lives. Perhaps allowing him to live was the right thing to do.

I was still in two minds when he answered his radio. Probably some
routine check-in.

"Twenty-three, all clear," he muttered into a mouthpiece I'd missed
earlier.

That settled it. If Taco Man was twenty-three, it was reasonable to assume that one to twenty-two were out there as well. And although I hadn't
approached the heliostat field from the center, I wasn't at the edge either. It
was unlikely twenty-three was the highest number out there.

North had more goons at his disposal than I'd imagined.

There were now two reasons Taco Man had to be taken out. The first
was simple numbers. If I let him live, he'd be directly behind me. When I
went from quiet to noisy, he'd be the closest person to my rear. Removing
him from the playing area might buy me precious seconds.

But the main reason was to give the rest of the outer perimeter sentries a
reason to sit out the fight. Fear is a great reason. The best reason. If you fear
what you're running toward, you might not run as fast you're able. You might
dawdle a bit. Let someone else get there ahead of you. Maybe stop and tie
your laces. Maybe not bother at all. Decide you don't get paid enough.

A colleague not answering a radio check would start the rolling waves
of fear. Someone would be tasked to see why Taco Man wasn't answering
his radio. They'd find him dead and know the man who killed him was
still out there. Waiting in the darkness. Maybe he was close. Maybe he
was watching.

Nobody wants to be on their own with creeping death.

It wouldn't work on everyone, but it would work on some.

Killing Taco Man had to be done. It was necessary.

My resolve turned to granite. Ignoring the sweat running down the back of my neck, I raised my Fairbairn-Sykes.

There are two ways to kill someone quietly with a knife. Both involve clamping your forearm over the victim's mouth to cut off the initial cry of panic. The first way is to repeatedly drive the knife into the victim's back. It's effective but not foolproof. Sometimes the victim is wearing body armor. Sometimes the guard gets snagged on clothing. A misplaced strike can result in the knife sticking in bone. It's not uncommon for the blade to break off in someone.

But unless you're wearing medieval armor, the throat is *always* unprotected . . .

I didn't hesitate.

I catapulted from my crouch, slammed my left arm across Taco Man's mouth, and pulled him back into my chest with as much force as I could. He yelled in terror, but it was stifled. I wrenched his head back, exposed his throat, and slashed the Fairbairn-Sykes's blade across his neck. Aimed for the intersection where the jugular veins and carotid artery are closest. His skin sprang apart like it was elastic. It was a mortal wound, but I didn't stop. I needed him dead quickly.

In a sawing motion, I sliced back and forth across his throat, the razor-sharp blade cutting through flesh, muscles, and arteries like they weren't even there. Violent jets of arterial blood sprayed into the crisp night air, a new one for each beat of his heart. I kept cutting until I'd severed his windpipe. A rush of air escaped, the scream trapped in his chest finally coming out as a bubbling gurgle. My hands were bloody and wet, and the handle was becoming slippery, but I kept going until the blade jarred against his cervical vertebrae. I stopped. I didn't want his head to come off.

I held Taco Man as he died. Blood continued to leave his body. At first the pulsing gushes were thick and strong, but they slowed and weakened as his body emptied itself. The circulatory system works on hydraulic power. When it doesn't have enough fluid, it fails. This is at about 40 percent for humans. About half a gallon for someone like Taco Man. I figured there was more than that on the desert floor.

The blood stopped. Taco Man was dead. It had taken less than twenty seconds.

I held him for another minute before I lowered him to the ground. I found his water canteen and cleaned my hands, arms, and the Fairbairn-Sykes. I drank the rest.

The radio was fixed to his belt. There was nothing leading to his earpiece, and I assumed it was the wireless kind. I fastened it to my belt and removed the ear- and mouthpieces. A quick rub on my shirt to get the worst of the blood off, and it was in my ear.

Now I had ears as well as eyes.

CHAPTER 100

I didn't think I'd meet the next layer of security until I reached GU head-quarters. I still had some distance to cover, and it was time to pick up the pace. North's sentries were disciplined when it came to keeping radio silence, which was unfortunate. I needed them to discover Taco Man before I arrived. Not to worry. I could always call it in myself.

Using the heliostats as cover, I continued in the general direction of the GU headquarters complex.

I suspected I'd have something to navigate by soon.

It was an hour before my handiwork was noticed. The first indication was a double click in my earpiece. I'd been on enough covert stakeouts to know it was a signal. Someone had pressed the send button twice as a prearranged message.

I stopped and listened.

The replies started coming in. Every man seemed to have his own way of informing base things were OK where they were. They all had a number, though. I waited until they got to number twenty-three.

One to twenty told whoever was on the other end that everything was fine.

Twenty-one agreed with twenty, and twenty-two said there was "squat happening out there."

I didn't answer. Fear of the unknown trumps all.

"Manny, where are you?" a man said.

It was North. I'd have recognized his voice anywhere. He sounded frustrated.

More silence. Manny wouldn't be answering today.

North wouldn't panic. Manny could be having radio problems. He could have fallen and knocked himself out when he'd taken a leak. A rattler could have gotten him. Or he could have had his windpipe severed by the person he'd been charged with looking out for.

To be fair to North, he didn't waste time. As soon as he realized Manny wasn't answering, he took action. He didn't get angry and he didn't panic; he got practical. He did what I'd have done: He asked someone to check on him.

Without thinking, my hands ran over my equipment, making sure it was secure. I holstered my Glock and unhooked the SIG Sauer MPX-SD. Press-checked and fixed it in the combat-ready forward position. The bulky silhouette of the sound-suppressed muzzle looked ominous, even to me.

I hunkered down and waited for chaos to erupt. It didn't take long.

A shout erupted over the radio: "Oh, Jesus H. Christ! Manny's dead, boss!"

More silence.

"You should see what he's done to him, man. Asshole's almost cut his head off."

North came on. He was calm. Probably glad it was finally happening. Hated waiting. "His radio?"

"Boss?"

"Is his radio there?" North urged.

"Gimme a minute." The crackle of someone who'd forgotten to take his finger off the send button followed. A few more seconds of someone searching a body. "It's gone, boss."

"Everyone in now," North snapped. "Secure the inner perimeter."

The lights at GU burst into life. Action stations.

I finally had a bearing.

I started to run.

CHAPTER 101

It had taken three hours to reach the halfway point. I completed the second half in ten minutes.

As I reached the last lines of heliostats, I slowed. Before I assaulted the building, I wanted my breathing under control.

While I waited, I laid out the kit I'd need to hand for the next phase. My stun grenades. My silenced Glock. My SIG. My *surprise*. Made sure they were either to hand or on top of my backpack.

I found a good view of the complex and sat down. I could afford to wait some. The people behind me would be cautious.

None of them wanted to be the next Manny.

There were a number of doors where the men North was holding in reserve could be waiting. And they'd be core men. Seasoned mercs probably. One dead sentry wouldn't stop them. I needed to create a bottleneck and I needed to create confusion. Six years ago, I'd have just told someone to cut the electricity. Plunged the place into darkness, then moved in while they all shouted at each other. Couldn't do that here; they generated their own.

I raised the SIG and waited. After a minute, one of the workshop doors opened. A man stepped into view. He was bearded, wearing jeans and a checked shirt. He carried an AR-15 in the ready position. He scanned the immediate area and then stood his post. I figured he was there to let the returning men inside.

I needed to beat them to it.

Raising from my crouch, I sprinted across the open yard. I was twenty yards from the workshop door before the sound of my boots alerted him. He turned and gawked, his face a rictus of fear and shock.

I stopped, raised the MPX-SD, and aimed for his T-box. It's the area that goes from one eye socket to the other, then down the bridge of the nose to the upper lip. Forms a natural T. Shoot someone in the T-box, and it guarantees a complete and instantaneous loss of consciousness and life. Flaccid paralysis, it's called. No involuntary spasms. Meant he wouldn't fire a burst from his AR-15 as he went down.

I held my breath and squeezed the trigger. The recoil made the SIG move in a natural arc. I didn't fight it. Brought the sights back on to his head and snapped off another round. Did it so quickly it sounded like I'd set the selector to fully automatic. Both bullets hit him in the middle of the face. Blood, bone, and bits of skull exploded from the back of his head. As he crumpled to the ground, the expression of shock remained on what was left of his face, frozen forever. My brass hit the concrete floor at the same time he did, a puff of pink mist hovering where his head had once been.

Although the sudden silence was shocking, I was no longer in a covert action. In all the training I'd done over the years, every single unit had told me that when you're forced to go from quiet to noisy, you go from quiet to *very* noisy. Noise adds to the confusion. It's terrifying. It makes it harder for the enemy to locate and engage you. When your numbers are small, noise is your friend.

And nothing is noisier than the M84 stun grenade.

Using the garage wall as cover, I pulled on my gas mask. I could hear men running and shouting inside. I'd made no attempt to pull their friend into cover. As soon as they reached the door, they'd see his body.

I pulled the pin on the grenade and threw it inside.

There was the obligatory two-second pause.

Then a flash of light brighter than twenty million candles, and a bang louder than a Boeing 747 taking off. Even with my eyes clamped shut, I saw the outline of my retina in the back of my skull. The noise almost knocked me off my feet.

It was louder than war.

And I'd been expecting it.

Five to fifteen seconds, the SAS reckon. Five to fifteen seconds of complete incapacitation for anyone on the receiving end. As the screeching bang faded, I raised my SIG and entered the workshop.

It was a scene from hell. Men were holding their heads. Covering their eyes. Staggering around, bumping into each other. Bleeding from the ears. Screaming. Vomiting. Not even thinking about taking cover. But like Colonel David Hackworth once said, "If you find yourself in a fair fight, you didn't plan your mission correctly."

SEALs and Rangers can go their whole careers without firing a shot in anger. In the Special Operations Group live action was an almost weekly occurrence. My unique training program, my old job, the Urbach-Wiethe, and my motivation for being there meant that right then, in *that* environment, against *that* enemy, I was the perfect killing machine.

Remorseless.

Fearless.

I began firing. Bullet after bullet. Unerring accuracy. Each one punching a hole in someone's head. The SIG an extension of my body, a combination of muscle memory and concentration bringing it up to the next firing position, even as my eyes were focused on the last target. Old habits die hard. At the range I was firing from, I didn't need to bother with double taps, but I did anyway. Two bullets to the head of each man.

Fire and move.

Acquire a new target.

Fire and move.

Targets fall when hit.

Maintain ammunition discipline. Count the rounds.

Shock and awe.

Running hard, keeping low. The *phut-phut* of the double taps. The jangle of hot shells on concrete. Shattered glass and screams. Floor wet with blood and piss.

Absolute chaos.

Perfect.

Because the SIG's sound suppressor was superbly engineered, and because the stun grenade had caused a smoky fire, I wasn't even sure that the living knew I was in among them yet. Or maybe they'd been told not to return fire. Killing me was the same as killing Quinn. One man either didn't know or didn't care. He even managed to snap off a shot. It went high and right and pinged off the metal beams in the roof. Before he could shoot again, I'd shot him twice in the face. One bullet removed his nose; the other went through his cheek. Came out through his ear. He dropped to the workshop floor, his AR-15 stitching a line into the wall as he fell.

Two more opened fire from behind a toolbox, one of those tall ones with wheels, but they were scared and couldn't shoot for shit. They were all ready, fire, aim. Spray and pray. Their bullets gouged the walls and sent splinters of wood flying through the air like shrapnel, but nothing hit me. I'd seen storm troopers shoot straighter. Winning the firefight isn't about shooting from cover. It's about getting into a fire position, looking through your sights, and engaging the target. All the two men were doing was wasting ammunition. I waited for their magazines to empty, then walked over to the toolbox. They were frantically trying to reload. I leaned over and shot them in the top of the head. Like shooting fish in a barrel. If the barrel was a toolbox. And if the fish were bad men cowering behind it.

I turned and looked for my next target. Found one more. He was staggering around like he was four-fifths into a quart of bourbon. He had fluid coming from his ears. Must have been close to the stun grenade when it went off.

Phut-phut. One less bad guy.

I searched for someone else to kill. Couldn't see anyone. It wasn't over, but this part was. It was time to move on.

The workshop looked like Christopher Nevinson's *Paths of Glory* painting, the one that showed dead soldiers at the Western Front. The one the British War Office tried to censor. Like in Nevinson's painting, North's men lay where they had died. No one had survived long enough to crawl away. Some were draped over each other; others had died alone. All of them had horrific head wounds.

Shattered glass covered the floor like hailstones. I could hear it crunch under the treads of my heavy boots. The smoke from the stun grenade fire was thick and oily and noxious. Blood mingled with the rainbow colors of spilled gasoline on the workshop floor. A faint smell of cordite got through my gas mask. I tightened the straps. I couldn't afford a leak with what was coming next.

If this had been a SOG operation, I'd have been fixing things in my mind. Ready for the inevitable inquest.

But it wasn't, so I didn't.

With phase one over, I took cover under the metal stairs leading to the gantry and did a quick ammo and weapons check. Everything was fine. I'd had to change magazines once during the assault, and although the one on the SIG wasn't yet empty, I swapped it anyway.

The workshop was forty yards in length, and I ran up the metal stairs that led into the rest of the complex. Before opening the door, I removed a canister from the top of my backpack. It was what I'd asked Odell to get for me.

Aerosolized o-Chlorobenzylidene malononitrile.

CS gas for short.

I unpinned the canister and threw it into the workshop full of dead men.

I'd trained extensively with CS gas and knew there was only one defense against it: the full-face combat respirator with activated charcoal filters. CS gas is invasive. It sticks to you. You can try holding your breath, but it gets in your eyes. You can try shutting your eyes, but it gets in your nose. And once it's in, it's in. You never forget the first time you're exposed to CS gas. I didn't understand the chemistry behind it, but I knew what it did. Everyone in law enforcement who works with CS gas is required to feel the effects once. Partly so you know what it is you're inflicting on others, and partly to give you confidence in your protective equipment. There's an immediate burning of anything that's wet: eyes, eyelids, nose, throat. The eyes shut involuntarily and stream uncontrollably. Mucus pours from the nose like custard. An uncontrolled coughing and sneezing fit doubles you up. It feels like your lungs are being blowtorched.

It is completely debilitating.

And the only ones Odell had been able to get at such short notice were for *outdoor* use. In big red letters, a warning stated that they were never to be used indoors. There was an exclamation mark after it. "Never" was in bold and underlined. The instructions on the manufacturer's website said it gave "a high-volume, continuous burn that expels its payload in forty seconds through four gas ports at the top of the canister."

Indoors, the concentration would be fifty times stronger. The effects would be brutal, possibly fatal. The Geneva Conventions banned chemical warfare in 1925, but unfortunately for North, I wasn't a signatory.

The canister hit the painted concrete floor. There was a small pause, then the telltale hiss as it discharged its payload. The workshop filled up quickly. A thick cloud of poison. Despite the tight fit of my gas mask, I could still smell the CS gas. My eyes began to sting. It was like I'd just rubbed them after chopping jalapeños. I ignored the pain; it would fade.

When North's outer perimeter sentries arrived back, the CS gas would be impenetrable. They wouldn't be able to enter the workshop. It would be better than having a SOG team watching my back.

I turned to the door, ready to hit the rest of the building. I didn't like how easily I'd slipped into house-clearing mode. It was actually easier here. In the SOG, we were supposed to warn the targets first. All I had to do here was shoot them in the head.

From my brief tour with North, I knew the corridor I was about to step into was a long one. I unpinned my last M84 stun grenade, opened the door, and threw it as far as I could.

CHAPTER 102

The corridor was empty. It had eight doors, four on each side. Opposite each other, like a number four domino. At the end was a bigger security door. The side doors were flimsy and I cleared them without meeting anyone else. All eight rooms were offices. Probably for operational managers. Computers and filing cabinets and pictures of families. Charts and stuff on the walls.

I moved on.

The corridor was the link between the operations side of the business and the corporate side. North had walked me down it when I'd asked to see the workshop. It was carpeted, but with the type that came in easily replaceable squares. Probably had engineers walking on it all day.

The security door at the end of the corridor was controlled by an electronic keypad. I'd watched North punch in the numbers when we'd finished the workshop tour, and I doubted he'd changed them.

Four—two—eight—nine.

The light blinked red, not green. North was more cautious than I'd thought.

That was OK; there's more than one way to eat a pie. And as I'd switched from covert to shock and awe, I didn't need to be subtle. I removed the full magazine from the SIG and replaced it with the half-empty one I'd used to decimate the men in the workshop. I switched the selector to fully automatic and fired three-round bursts at the security door's hinges. The wood around the door exploded. Jaggy splinters bounced off me like darts. One pierced my thigh. I brushed it off. The door fell away from the frame.

I stood back and considered my options. I could only move forward at this point. My rear was covered. CS canisters weren't like normal smokers. The gas hung around. The men from the heliostat field wouldn't be able to join the fight, not without gas masks. I pulled the pin on a new CS canister and lobbed it through the ruined security door. I rolled in after it. Before the smoke filled the room, I scanned the corners. It was empty.

It was a meeting room. I vaguely remembered passing through it the last time I was there. Whiteboards and TV monitors hung from the wall. I figured this was where management and the workforce convened. There were two other doors in the room. Both internal. Quinn's office and the executive dining room were on the top floor and on the left side of the building. I figured that's where I needed to be. I walked over to the door on the right and tried the handle. It was locked. I smashed the glass panel and threw in a canister. Blocked it off with CS gas.

The door on the left was open. It opened onto another corridor, a small one this time. No more than ten yards. It was a connecting corridor as it had no doors to the side. The door at the end was unlocked as well. I threw down more gas, waited, then cleared the room. I was in the complex proper and flying on instinct now. Drop CS, rush the room, clear the corners, on to the next. Run upstairs. Clear floor after floor. Room after room. Leave poison in my wake.

I met no resistance.

Until I did.

CHAPTER 103

North had chosen to make his stand on the top floor. He had to. There were no more floors left. Just the dining room, the boardroom, and the offices of the top men.

I paused. There's an acronym used by the Special Operations Group: JDLR. Just Doesn't Look Right. And the dining room didn't. Despite the noise I'd been making, the door was open. It wasn't even ajar. Every door up until then had been closed. Most of them were locked. It felt like a trap. It almost certainly *was* a trap. If I'd been with the SOG, I'd have withdrawn and called for specialist equipment to get eyes and ears in there.

But I wasn't with the SOG. And turning around wasn't an option.

I was tempted just to do as I had been doing. Lob in a CS canister, give it enough time for everyone inside to be screaming in pain, then go in hard and fast. Kill everyone inside. It was a good option for several reasons, the main one being it had worked up until now. But I had a problem. Unless he was sitting this out, I was getting to the part of the building where North would be. And he'd almost certainly have Martha with him. It would be the sensible thing for him to do. I couldn't risk anything indiscriminate.

Without gas it was then.

When I'd trained with the SAS, they didn't use gas, stun, or frag-mentation grenades on every room. Sometimes diving in at ground level is enough. The human brain is wired to look head high for danger. It's an evolutionary thing. Goes back to our hunter-gatherer days. The fraction of a second it would take someone to readjust to ground level would be all I needed to put two rounds into their head. The longer SIG would be a hindrance rolling on the floor, so I swung it onto my back and unholstered the Glock. Much more maneuverable. Not as accurate but quicker.

I was just about to dive in when I had an idea. An obvious bit of misdirection. If whoever was inside was expecting CS gas, why not give them CS gas? Or at least pretend to. I could throw in the canister without removing the pin. If nothing else, it would draw their eyes away from the doorway.

So that's what I did. I unhooked the last canister from my belt and hurled it hard enough to reach the other end of the dining room. It clattered off the far wall. Something moved inside.

I dived in, hit the floor, rolled, and came up firing.

CHAPTER 104

For the first time since the workshop, someone fired back at me. Or rather they fired at where they thought I was.

A lean, mean thug with a crew cut and a goatee snapped off a burst. By the time he realized I was four yards away from where he'd aimed, I'd put one in his upper chest and one in his shoulder. Neither was a kill shot, but he went down hard and spinning. The floor shook when he landed. The man next to him, frozen in fear, probably drafted in at the last minute, held his gun loosely at his side. I swiveled away from the guy on the floor and aimed at his head.

"No!" he screamed.

My bullet tore his jaw off. He didn't scream anything after that. Just fell over and went still.

The guy I'd shot in the chest and the shoulder was dying noisily. One of my rounds had nicked a lung as he couldn't breathe right. The bullet hole was bubbling with each respiration. A sucking chest wound. Survivable if you have the know-how. I had the know-how, but he'd been trying to kill me. Even so, letting him drown in his own blood was crueler than I needed to be. I raised the Glock and punched a hole through the lower bone of his eye socket. He twitched once, then went still.

The room became eerily silent. The only sound was the *tink* of my barrel as it cooled. I removed my gas mask. Cordite mingled with the CS gas that had stuck to my clothes. It stung my eyes and I blinked away the tears. I backed up to the bar. It was a natural brick wall. It wouldn't stop a high-velocity round, but it was as good a place as any to regroup. Sort through my equipment. Refill my magazines.

I'd made a mistake, though.

I wasn't the only who'd thought being behind a brick wall was better than being in front of a brick wall. A man rose from behind the bar. It was the barman from the night of my dinner.

He was aiming a gun at me.

He fired.

If this had been the first room I'd breached, my instincts would've been too rusty to survive, but by the time he'd pulled the trigger, I was already moving.

The bullet missed my chest and smashed into my left arm.

I'd have been better taking the bullet in my body armor. The pain was immediate and intense, but I still sent three rounds in his direction. They all missed, but that wasn't the point. Being aggressive is how you stay alive in a firefight. You make the other man want cover more than you do.

I stood and fired. My left arm swung uselessly by my side. The man, the first Latino I'd encountered since storming the complex, crouched and ran down the length of the bar, firing over his shoulder. All his bullets missed me, but all mine missed him. My left shoulder was shaking uncontrollably and an inch at my end was a yard at his.

I wasn't concerned. He was going to run out of bar. I would lay down a barrage of fire and make him duck down. I'd then lean over and open up the top of his head. Seemed plausible. It had worked in the warehouse. And I had the whole room to maneuver in; he only had the space between the bar and the wall. I walked toward the end of the bar, firing enough bullets to keep his head down.

But I'd made a mistake. Another one. And because the dining room was big enough to take the noise, when I heard it, the barman heard it as well.

A dead man's click.

Firing on empty.

Bringing a prop to a gunfight.

Whatever you want to call it, the sound of nothing happening was deafening. A rookie's mistake, and one I'd never made before. It wasn't a literal click. The slide holds to the rear on Glocks when the magazine's empty. This was more of a *figurative* click.

The man walked round from the other side of the bar and stood beside a glass cabinet displaying bottles of liquor and expensive cigars. He grinned, calmly raised his revolver, and pointed it at my head. If they'd been told not to kill me, he hadn't got the message. The men I'd just killed were probably his friends. I wondered if I'd feel pain.

The man fired.

And got a dead man's click of his own. Seems I wasn't the only one in the room with poor ammunition discipline.

And now the race to reload was on.

First to finish got to live.

It was going to be very close. He had two hands; I had Urbach-Wiethe.

We both dropped to our knees. He must have been ex-military or ex-cop. Turning yourself into the smallest possible target while you reload or clear a stoppage is second nature to anyone who has been under fire. As he disappeared behind the bar, my right thumb popped the magazine release catch. The empty magazine clattered on to the tiled floor. That was the easy part. The part that could be done one-handed.

My spare magazines were all to hand and I did what I'd been trained to do when you only have the use of one hand: I jammed the Glock into my left armpit. Held it there while I grabbed a fresh magazine from the chest pouch on my body armor. I pressed it home, grabbed the Glock's handle, and thumbed the crosshatched slide release catch. The slide drove forward, picked up the top 9-mil round, and slotted it into the chamber.

I was ready.

The barman wasn't.

He looked at me. "Please," he whispered, pleading for the mercy he hadn't shown me.

I pulled the trigger and he tumbled into the drinks cabinet. It toppled, and mind-numbingly overpriced bottles of tequila slid off their shelf, shattering on the hard floor. The smell of liquor swirled in my nostrils. I stared at the dead barman. Looked at how the blood and brain matter mingled with the oily drink. I wondered what his story was. Wondered why he'd ended up dying in a dining room he'd probably never been allowed to eat in.

It was a distraction and I should have ignored it. I heard the door open behind me, but before I could spin round, a voice said.

"OK, that's enough."

It was Peyton North. He was wearing another lurid yellow suit. He looked unruffled. His sardonic smile was back. He had four men flanking him. One of them was Andrews the giant.

I dropped my Glock. Unfastened the SIG and let it fall to the floor too. He didn't have to ask me.

The knife at Martha's throat had already drawn blood.

CHAPTER 105

North nodded, and three of his men approached me. The giant stayed by North's side. His face was like a totem pole, devoid of emotion.

As North's men approached, I raised my right arm. I couldn't move my left. It was trembling and bleeding, and hurt like a bitch, which was a good sign. It meant it wasn't as badly damaged as I'd feared. The limpness was probably nerve shock. It would wear off. I ignored the men walking toward me and concentrated on making eye contact with Martha. Tried to convey a sense of calm; hoped that, despite how it looked, she'd understand everything was under control.

She stared back with wide eyes, a mixture of terror and confusion. Her high cheekbones and smooth, glowing skin meant she was still as lovely as I remembered. Bit thinner than she'd been in her dorm photographs, but otherwise she seemed fine.

"Ben!" she said in bewilderment.

"Oh, hi, Martha," I said. "Fancy seeing you here."

"What on earth is happening? Where's Dad?"

Before I could answer, the lead man stood in front of me and blocked my view. I tried to twist my head to maintain eye contact, but he was having none of that. He raised the combat shotgun he was holding and smashed the butt into my mouth. The pain was white hot. Fiery bursts pulsated through my head. I stayed conscious but wasn't able to stay on my feet. I collapsed to the floor. He stood over me and jabbed the barrel into my ear. "Give me a reason, asshole," he snarled. "Just give me a fucking reason."

I spat out part of a canine. Ran my tongue over the jagged stump it had left in its place. It was razor-sharp. If I smiled, I'd look like half a vampire.

With the shotgun forcing my head into an expensive-looking rug, I was searched. They found my Fairbairn-Sykes straightaway, which annoyed me. Not because I thought I'd get away with keeping it. It just didn't seem right that people like this should get to own such a piece of history. One of them found the handcuffs in my pack. He examined them. Removed the keys. Tested the mechanism. It was solid.

He held them up so North could see. "Federally issued. Good condition." He was looking at them with nostalgia. I wondered if he'd once stood on the other side of the thin blue line. North nodded, and the man fastened them to my wrists. He closed them as tightly as he could, and I felt an immediate tingling in both hands.

The man with the shotgun still had it pressed into my ear. He was in no mood to be gentle. The rug was exquisite; the colors rich and warm, the pattern intricate. Afghan, I suspected. Certainly Middle Eastern in origin. I'd read somewhere that the great Persian rug weavers deliberately put a flaw in each rug they weave, believing that only Allah makes things perfectly. I wondered if the blood running from my mouth and arm would cover his deliberate flaw.

My head was facing one of the men I'd just killed. The one with the sucking chest wound. Our faces were no more than two feet apart. His lifeless eyes had already clouded over. The bullet hole in his lower eye socket was ragged round the edges. The abrasion ring reddish-brown. It oozed dark, congealing blood.

North left Martha with Andrews, stepped over the other dead man, the one whose life I'd ended with a bullet to the mouth, and approached me.

He stood over me. "Are you finished, Mr. Koenig?" He said it with a certain amount of respect.

Despite the shotgun in my ear, I managed a small nod. The pain in my mouth intensified.

"Good. This ends now."

I knew he wouldn't kill me. Not yet. They needed Spencer Quinn back first.

"You're early," North said.

"And you expected me to be."

He smiled. "I've come to understand you. We knew you couldn't just hand yourself in. It wouldn't be . . . Koenig enough. Kudos on the CS gas, by the way. I hadn't considered that. Very clever. Would have been enough in any other situation, but . . ." He turned and pointed at Martha. ". . . this isn't any other situation. I was always going to win."

I didn't respond.

"Are you ready?" he asked.

I nodded again. Another burst of agony.

"Let's go then." He turned to his men. Pointed at the bodies on the floor. "And clean up this mess."

We were led into the room North had appeared from. It was a plush office and had Spencer Quinn stamped all over it. Antique climbing equipment was displayed alongside photographs of mountains I neither recognized nor cared about. A large teak desk centered the room. Enormous windows afforded panoramic views of both the complex and the heliostat field. The rock face the building pressed up against could be seen out of the left window.

Behind the desk, set against the wall, was a heavy floor-to-ceiling bookcase. It was bespoke and ornate, as if the person who'd made it had a profound love of books. Scenes of the desert were carved into the lightly bleached shelves.

North walked over to it. He knelt down, reached behind it.

There was a mechanical click.

He stood up and gently pulled the bookcase. It wasn't fixed to the wall; it was on rails. It slid noiselessly to reveal a metal door. It was concealed, so it didn't really need a lock, but it had one nonetheless. A handprint ID scanner. Quinn had told me very few people were programmed into it. North was one of them. He placed his palm flat against it. A whirring noise and the door opened inward slightly. He pushed it and gestured us inside.

I walked toward the door, keen for my first glimpse of what all this had been about.

PART FIVE

MAN PLANS, GOD LAUGHS

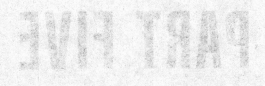

CHAPTER 106

It's not a secret that the gangs that smuggle cocaine for a living have developed increasingly sophisticated ways of getting their product across America's protected borders. Tales of million-dollar submarines and tunnels are so commonplace they don't even make the front pages anymore. It's old hat. Been there, done that, got the T-shirt.

And every time a new way of smuggling is developed, so is a new way of detecting it.

Despite the low detection rates, and the astronomical profits they were already making, to stay ahead, the cartels needed more innovative ways of moving their product. Like it is in any business, if you're not expanding, someone else will. One of their solutions was ingenious. With a simple process, they turned their cocaine into plastic. And that plastic could be turned into anything they wanted it to be.

Like toys.

Or garden hoses.

Or drinking straws.

Or plastic sheeting. Like the kind that protects heliostats on the back of a flatbed.

The process isn't challenging. Cocaine hydrochloride, the powdered version of the drug, is mixed with heated, liquid plastic before being injected into whatever mold is being used. The results, indistinguishable from the real thing, could contain up to 30 percent pure cocaine. The plastic also disguises the smell, making it much harder for drug dogs and chemical scanners to detect. Once across the border, it's a simple job to dissolve the plastic in acid and reverse the process. But . . . once the Drug Enforcement Administration was wise to it, US Customs and Border Protection checked *everything* coming across that had even the smallest plastic component. They routinely took samples.

And so the dance between drug smugglers and the DEA continued.

Once the ants and the cling wrap helped me figure out what they were smuggling from Gauntlet, the question became *why*. Not why convert cocaine into plastic. That was obvious: The profit involved paid for the process many times over. The question was, why Gauntlet? Cocaine couldn't be produced there; it didn't have the right climate. And although cocaine could be transported to Gauntlet in powdered form and turned into plastic sheeting somewhere in the GU complex, why bother? Bringing cocaine across the border to convert it into plastic in Gauntlet made no kind of sense. The hard work had already been done. Border checks were severe. Internal checks were nonexistent. Once cocaine was in the country, getting it to where it needed to be was easy.

Gauntlet made no sense.

Not until the western diamondback spooked those collared lizards.

CHAPTER 107

GU's location had always bothered me. It seemed too twee. Too perfect. The guy who loses his friend and builds up a business in the same location he died. Although I'm not the guy who can't accept people doing things for altruistic reasons, I'd struggled with Gauntlet as a place to open a solar energy business. Commercially, it made no sense. J.T. had told me that. There were better places for a heliostat field. Gauntlet didn't have the infrastructure. There was no ready workforce. No housing capacity. No transportation links. No easy access to the grid.

But Quinn had built it there anyway.

Almost like he had no choice.

So even before I'd made the link with the plastic wrapping, my thoughts had already turned to Quinn and Gunnar Ulrich stumbling across something valuable.

Ore samples assayed as rich in silver.

A cache of looted Aztec gold.

Oil.

Even dinosaur bones.

And for some reason, getting a valid permit hadn't been possible or desirable. Instead Quinn had resolved to remove whatever it was surreptitiously. It had fitted the facts I had at the time. It was also weak and illogical.

If it *were* an illegal mining operation, why bother with the solar energy charade? A simpler cover would have sufficed.

But as soon as I knew what they were doing with the plastic wrapping, what they'd found became easier to figure out.

I hadn't had to approach it laterally. The collared lizards, escaping into the cracks and crannies and crevices around J.T.'s bluff when the diamondback returned, had slapped me in the face with the answer.

Spencer Quinn and Gunnar Ulrich hadn't found precious minerals on that rock face. They hadn't found oil, and they hadn't found Aztec gold. In fact, when Gunnar had driven his SLCD into that rock face and made his discovery, the two young men had in fact found nothing.

A massive amount of nothing.

The discovery of a lifetime.

Because context is everything, and Quinn, studying international economics at Georgetown, understood there were people out there who would pay extraordinary amounts of money for the right amount of "nothing."

But only if they had sole and exclusive access to it. And Gunnar, all environmentally friendly and full of the wonders of nature, wasn't going to let such an amazing discovery be sullied that way. He'd protested and was thrown off a rock face for his troubles.

The way was then clear for Quinn to approach a cartel. He was limited to only one. I'd asked Jen to check if one specific cartel had seen their stock rise since GU went into business. The way it would if, say, 100 percent of its drugs was getting across the border.

She confirmed it had.

As cartels don't like to share, Quinn had needed to take safeguards to protect his discovery. That was why he'd hired the digital death email providers. He had emails set to go to thirty different addresses. Law enforcement agencies, the National Park Service, journalists, anyone who might take an interest. The cartel either accepted his 5 percent distribution fee or they got nothing.

A deal was struck.

Investments were sourced.

Infrastructure was put in place.

Operations commenced.

A multimillion-dollar industry arose from the dust of the Chihuahuan Desert.

And people started to die.

All because of a cave . . .

CHAPTER 108

Long cave systems aren't unheard of in North America. They aren't common, but they certainly aren't rare. Mammoth Cave in Kentucky is over four hundred miles long. Jewel Cave in South Dakota is almost two hundred. Some already cross the United States–Mexico border. These are well-known and strictly regulated.

It was Gunnar, who'd been testing his weight on the SLCD, who had found it. He'd just fitted it into a crevice on the rock face they were scaling. It had come out and taken a large lump of rock with it. That wasn't unusual. It was why you tested it. But what *was* unusual was that behind the space the dislodged rock had occupied was a hole. Perhaps a bit foolishly, considering rattlesnakes love making their dens in rock faces, Gunnar had reached inside. He'd found he could push his entire arm in. He called Quinn over, and the two young men chipped away at the fragile stone, widening the hole until it was big enough to squeeze through.

Previously unknown caves are sometimes named by the people who discovered them, and they had nothing more than that in mind when they'd crawled inside to see how big it was. They'd been equipped for climbing, not caving, though, and could only go so far before darkness forced them to turn round. They finished their climb and vowed to return the next day with the right equipment for cave exploration. Flashlights, spare batteries, food, and route-marking aerosol paint. Even sleeping bags.

What they'd assumed was going to be a nice diversion for the day turned into something else. Instead of the cave being a small local system, it appeared it had once been an underground river. Probably a feeder for the big river that had forged the valley and basin that Gauntlet sat in.

The cave system was a mixed bag. There were easy walking sections, as round and as smooth as a hamster's tube. In other places it was flat, wide, and tight like a cheese press. And there were caverns. Cathedral-sized echo chambers that had clearly been underground lakes at some point. And although it twisted and turned, it kept a steady north-south bearing.

It had been near the end of the second day when Quinn had opened his last bag of dried fruit. He'd suggested they turn round, but Gunnar wanted to keep going. He reckoned they'd been walking up a slight incline for the last mile. If the cave was going to come out somewhere, it would be soon. And Gunnar, whether through luck or something intrinsically Scandinavian, had been right. They hadn't walked much farther when a crack of light lit up the cave ahead. After crawling forward for a few more hundred yards—the cave had started to narrow again—the light was strong enough to turn off their flashlights.

The exit hole was little more than a crack, like the slot in a piggy bank. It was directly above them. At its narrowest it was less than an inch, at its widest no more than six. As they'd expected to have to move rock at some point, they'd brought mountaineering axes with them. With Quinn on Gunnar's shoulders, he'd got to work and soon created a big enough gap to squeeze through.

Blinking like a mole in the bright sun, Quinn had tried to get his bearings. He was in a rocky outcrop, surrounded by low shrubs and stunted trees. There was no sign of human habitation. He turned back to the exit hole and worked on widening it for Gunnar. From the top it was easier, and he soon had enough of a hole to allow the bigger man to join him.

Breathless, the two young men shook hands and hugged each other. They hadn't seen any diverging tunnels, and as both the entrance and exits had needed to be developed to climb in and out, they knew it was an undiscovered cave system. They good-naturedly argued about whose name would go first. Quinn argued it should be the Quinn-Ulrich Cave because he was the one who'd exited first, and Gunnar argued it should be the Ulrich-Quinn Cave because he'd discovered it in the first place.

After exploring their immediate surroundings, they set off to find somewhere to grab a meal and maybe a bus back to Gauntlet. It was five miles before they saw signs of human habitation.

It wasn't what they'd expected.

The first hint they'd crossed the border, and were maybe somewhere they shouldn't be, was when they saw a man nonchalantly carrying an AK-47. They skirted round him and walked until they found a small town with a bar. After loading up on enchiladas and cold beer, and using their limited Spanish, they discovered they had crossed the border. They were in the Mexican state of Coahuila. The municipality they were in was controlled by a small cartel known as the Bandoleros. The man with the AK-47 had been patrolling their outer borders.

They had briefly considered hitching to the border and throwing themselves at the mercy of the US Border Patrol. There were two reasons they didn't. One, the only explanation they had for being on the wrong side of the fence was that they'd been caving and got lost. And they didn't want to reveal the cave's location. Not until they'd registered their find. And more importantly, they were right in the middle of cartel country. There were no guarantees they'd even reach the border. The cartels knew that DEA agents took many forms, and just because the boys knew they weren't federal agents, it didn't follow that the cartel would see it that way. Better to slip out the way they'd come in.

They loaded up on water and fiery jerky, avoided the men with AK-47s, and went back through the caves.

Quinn had been less convincing while revealing when he'd first thought about a more insidious use for the cave. I suspected it was because he didn't really know. What was clear, though, was that by the time they'd made it back to the Gauntlet cave entrance, his plan was fully developed.

Although the manufacturing and distribution of cocaine was illegal, it was still vulnerable to large business economics. The cartels needed to move their product, and there were any number of reasons why the smaller cartels struggled. They didn't have the resources to develop sophisticated ways of getting their drugs over the border. They were landlocked, so they didn't have ready access to the forty million square nautical miles some of the bigger cartels did. They couldn't afford to bribe the right people. They couldn't afford the *sicarios*—hired killers—to keep what they had.

A guaranteed distribution network would be worth every percentage point they paid.

Quinn had initially insisted Gunnar's death was an accident. Said he fell on the descent. Landed on an outcrop and died instantly. When I pointed the Glock at his groin and increased the pressure on the trigger, he decided he valued his dick more than his pride. He admitted to having manufactured Gunnar's fall by levering out his SLCD with his mountaineering axe. When he'd reached the bottom himself, Gunnar was still alive.

While he waited for the boy to die, Quinn got busy setting up a false rock climbing accident on a completely different face, well away from the cave entrance. He knew there'd be an inquiry and that Gunner's death would be checked. He climbed up to ensure there were scuff marks. He left some of Gunnar's equipment up there and collected some of his blood to spread on the ground.

It took eight hours, Quinn told me, for Gunnar to die after he was pushed. Quinn then dragged him to Gauntlet and started spinning tales of tragedy and misadventure.

Quinn wasn't stupid. He knew the value of what he had, and he knew cartels didn't play well with others. Before he approached anyone, he made sure he had documented evidence that, if he died, the GPS coordinates of the cave system, including detailed descriptions of the entrance and exit holes, would be passed to everyone on the distribution list managed by the two emails-after-death providers he'd hired.

Some research on the Bandoleros revealed who was senior, but not so senior they couldn't risk talking to an American. A *sicario* named Pepe was the man he targeted. He was a white Latin American, spoke flawless English, and had a penchant for yellow suits. Pepe was one of the more intelligent psychotics in the trade. He was a huge soccer fan, and had named himself after his hero, the Portuguese hard man who had played for Real Madrid. Eventually Quinn discovered the Bandoleros bar where he preferred to watch his games. He knew that when Real Madrid played their archrival, Barcelona, Pepe would be there.

On the day of the game, Quinn arrived an hour before kickoff. Pepe turned up half an hour later and ordered a bottle of tequila. The men who'd been sitting at the best table in the bar vacated it. Pepe sat in front of the TV, lit a cigar, and settled down to watch his game.

Quinn knew he'd be better off speaking to him before the game started, so he made his move immediately. He brought over an empty shot glass and, pulling up a seat, sat next to him. He pushed his glass toward the bottle. Like a pebble dropped into a pond, a hush rippled through the bar. Pepe glanced at the American, raised an eyebrow, but poured him a drink.

"Talk," he'd said.

After ten minutes both Quinn and Pepe left the bar. The game had just kicked off, and the patrons were unsure whether or not the table in front of the TV was free again.

In the end, they decided not to risk it.

Over the next few months, approval was sought and gained from the upper echelons of the cartel. Plans were refined, profit sharing was agreed upon, and financing from a cartel-controlled bank was sourced.

Pepe, name now changed to the more Stateside-friendly Peyton North, managed the cave development. Parts needed to be widened, and two pieces of additional land needed to be acquired, one to sit over a newly drilled, two-inch-wide ventilation shaft and another to cover the Mexican entrance. Nondescript buildings were built over both holes to disguise their true purpose. A series of safeguards were put in place to make sure the cave couldn't be rushed from either end.

While North was busy developing the cave, Quinn managed the installation of the solar energy company. Land was purchased and licenses secured. The headquarters building was built flush against the rock face so it concealed the entrance hole.

Eighteen months after Gunnar Ulrich was pushed to his death, the first cocaine shipment was taken into the cave system. It was turned into plastic in one of the giant caverns, now a fully functional processing plant. It was then taken to Gauntlet as a spool of plastic sheeting.

When the first repair truck made its way to Austin and the sheeting was turned back into cocaine, North and Quinn opened a $700 bottle of tequila and toasted their success.

In total, the cartel had invested $30 million.

They made it back within eight months.

CHAPTER 109

I'd sort of expected the entrance to the cave system to be dank and dark and wet. Cobwebs and bats and dusty air. I don't know why. North and Quinn had been running a multimillion-dollar business, and the entrance was clean and smooth. I stepped onto a well-lit metal walkway that worked as a bridge between Quinn's office and the rock face. It had a slip-resistant tread. A raised pattern of diamond shapes. I felt the insubstantiality of the bridge and peered over the edge. It wasn't a bridge; it was a raised aerial work platform. One of those with crisscrossing metal plates that act like scissors when it goes up or down. The kind air-duct engineers use to work safely at height. The gap between Quinn's office and the cave entrance was well lit with industrial lighting. I peered over the edge of the platform. Various pieces of equipment were on the ground and pushed up against the rock face. There was also a secure double door. The entrance to the factory floor, no doubt.

Access to the platform from the ground floor was by a portable staircase, the kind airports use to take passengers off the runway and onto the airplane. Passenger boarding ramps, I think they're called. It was a big one. Probably used for something like the Airbus A380. It meant the platform didn't have to be lowered every time someone needed to get up to where we were. The platform was probably only used for heavy or large cargo like equipment or spools of plastic sheeting. Which made sense. They wouldn't want men in overalls and hard hats tramping through the CEO's office, and they wouldn't want men in $3,000 suits walking through a dirty workshop.

The rock face was concave, like the inside of a spoon. The back of the GU building sealed it off completely. GU's builders must have thought they'd been putting in an emergency exit in the back of Quinn's office. One that people on the top floor could use in the event of a fire. With a business like solar energy, I don't imagine that raised any alarm bells.

At its widest the concave space was about ten meters deep. More than enough for what they needed, and not so wide that it needed anything complex to bridge it. I looked up. GU's roof extended out from the building to seal everything in. It wasn't straight-edged like the building; it had been designed to perfectly fit the contours of the rock face.

The entire complex was nothing more than camouflage. Its primary purpose was to hide the entrance to the cave and provide easy and secure access to it. Sure, the building had other uses: It was where they received the plastic cocaine and wrapped up the heliostats bound for Austin, and it gave everyone a reason to be where they needed to be, but essentially it was only there to hide a cave.

At the other end of the raised platform was another metal door. It was embedded into the rock face itself. It was one of those watertight ones used to compartmentalize sections of submarines. The door was locked by a plate-sized handwheel. No need to guess what was behind it.

North spun the handwheel and opened the door.

And revealed the cave in all its glory.

I stepped through the door onto solid rock. We were in an open area. It was smooth, and it looked like a lot of work had gone into making it so. I could see the tool marks in the rock. Three quad bikes waited for us. They were small, like they were made for children. Each one had a trailer. Again, it made sense. A cave system that ran all the way into Mexico needed a transport system. Rough-terrain quads would be perfect. They couldn't be used end to end, though. Quinn had told me parts of the cave had been left purposefully narrow to avoid being rushed by another cartel. They had four different sets of quads that were used in relays like the pony express.

"In," North said, pointing at the middle trailer. While Martha climbed in gracefully, I had a bullet in the arm and was handcuffed to the rear. The only option I had was to fall in.

"You OK?" I asked Martha.

She nodded but said nothing. Probably in shock. I didn't know what she'd seen since she'd been abducted, but witnessing the violence in the executive dining room had to be up there with the worst.

As soon as the front and rear quad bikes were full, North gave the signal to drive off. I concentrated on the route. Tried to remember the forks and detours and pinch points. Anything that might prove useful later.

After we'd traveled less than one hundred yards, the cave veered to the right and it became a cave in the true sense of the word.

The quads' headlights barely penetrated the impenetrable, chilling blackness. Some small loose stones littered the floor, but otherwise it was remarkably clean. It was generally ovoid in shape. The cave slinked and twisted like an abandoned snakeskin, like the water that had forged it didn't give a rat's ass about straight lines. It didn't smell damp, only earthy with a tinge of chemicals and gasoline.

The telltale signs of man-made improvement were everywhere. Bends were widened to allow the quads to turn. Parts of the roof still bore tool marks from where it had been raised. Heavy power cables ran along both sides like handrails. At no point did the height get above five feet. Walking upright or sitting on adult-sized quads would be impossible. Another of North's security features, no doubt. Hard to aim a gun when you're bent over like the hunchback of Notre-Dame. We passed the occasional natural alcove. Some had equipment stored in them. Most of them didn't.

I shivered. The heat of Texas didn't reach this far down, and I wasn't dressed for a cave. Martha was wearing a thick coat. It seemed we were headed for wherever she'd been held captive all this time.

The quads wormed through another two hundred yards of nothingness before there were signs of activity. Noise and light. The lead quad slowed as it entered a large cavern. It took a left and parked. The other two parked beside it.

The cavern was about the size of a basketball court. The roof was high enough to hang lights, the kind that came in wire cages. A small number of men were working. They barely glanced at us. I could see large bits of equipment. I didn't recognize most of the machines, but their purpose was obvious. This was where raw cocaine was mixed with liquid plastic before being turned into the polyethylene sheets. One machine I did recognize. It was an extruder, an all-in-one production line that received raw plastic at one end and turned out sheeting at the other. It had a large, square funnel at one end. A man was feeding it bits of lumpy plastic. They looked normal enough, but as this was the end of the process, not the start, the plastic would already be infused with the cocaine. I watched the plastic travel down a pipe. From what I understood about extruders, it was here that the plastic would be heated gently and joined together, before being squeezed and drawn through a series of presses. It was like a pasta machine, only automated and a thousand times bigger. At the end was a spooling machine. It was turning slowly and looked to be about halfway to being done.

A million-dollar bale of plastic wrapping.

Extraction fans with pipes leading into an industrial-sized ductless fume cupboard meant the cocaine factory was completely self-sufficient. The filters in the fume cupboard would need to be changed occasionally, but other than that they could be working for as long as they had the raw material.

Impressive. Three giant spools were already stacked on a pallet, and I understood why all three quads had trailers. They wouldn't be going back empty.

The tunnel that continued toward Mexico didn't look to have power cables or be as well-developed. Don't suppose it needed to be. A man with a flashlight could carry through packages of cocaine. And keeping the tunnel dark and tight from the factory area onward made sense security-wise. Easier to defend if worst came to worst.

The cavern had sections blocked off with prefabricated panels to form rooms. The door to one was open, and I could see bunk beds. Some of the men obviously slept there. Probably did shift work.

"Impressed?" North asked.

I nodded. Couldn't help myself.

North grinned and turned to Martha. "Won't be long now, Martha. We'll need some assurances, obviously, but you should be home soon."

She shrugged dismissively. It was clear she didn't believe a word. North turned to me. "I don't suppose you'll tell me where the boss is yet? We could use the honor system."

I ignored him.

He looked at his watch. "Your transport won't be here for a few more hours, so I'm afraid you'll have to enjoy our hospitality a bit longer, Miss Burridge. Mr. Koenig, of course, is going nowhere."

Martha jerked her head in my direction and stared. I shook my head slightly. Gave her the impression North had misspoken. She wasn't fooled.

"Put them in the hold," he said to two of the men who'd traveled down with us. He pointed at me. "And make sure he's secured. He doesn't get to roam around." Then to me, "Anything happens, either here or up top, she gets the first bullet. Are we clear?"

I agreed that we were clear.

Martha struggled free of her captor and haughtily walked toward one of the portioned-off rooms. She waited by the door. The same guy frog-marched me to the same place. He opened the door and pushed us both inside. There was a cot, a bucket, and a table with some food and books. A portable heater. A fluorescent lamp lit the room. It was flickering. The floor looked like the bottom of a cave. Funny that.

"I'd like to see the manager, please," I said, nodding at the light. "That'll give me a headache."

"Turn round," one of the henchmen said. My right hand was freed from the handcuffs. I flexed it. It began stinging with pins and needles.

"Sit," he said, pointing at the iron bedstead. I sat on the mattress.

"On the floor," the man grunted.

I moved to the ground, and the man refastened the cuff behind me, making sure I was also secured to the bedstead. He tugged at the hand-cuffs, ensuring they were tight. They were. The hand that had only just started to get some feeling back began to go numb again.

At least it was taking my mind off the pain of the gunshot wound. After the initial numbness had left my arm, I'd been tensing it, trying to see what damage had been done. The wound was purple and lumpy, and although I'd lost a bit of blood, I didn't think any bones or tendons had been damaged. A clichéd flesh wound. Not usually a problem. Clean it, pack it, bind it. Still hurt like hell, though. But as bad as it was, it wasn't a touch on my mouth. The shotgun had caused serious damage. I ran my tongue over my teeth. One had shattered down to a needle. The one beside it was cracked. Split. Deep enough to expose the nerve. The white-hot pain was verging on unbearable. I tried to ignore it, but each time cold air passed over them, it was all I could do to stop crying out.

Our captors turned their attention to Martha. Even though North hadn't told them to, they zip-tied her to the other end of the bed. Neither of us could now move. It didn't matter. One way or another, it would all be over soon.

As soon as they shut the door, I smiled.

I was a quarter of a mile underground. I had no way of summoning help or letting anyone know where I was. My weapons had been taken from me and I'd been shot. Armed men were outside and I was handcuffed to a metal bed frame.

So far, so good.

CHAPTER 110

After an hour, I was thirsty. I kept hollering for a drink until the door opened. A man stepped in, a rat-faced idiot with pockmarked skin and a mouth full of crude fillings. He'd been with North in the executive dining room.

"I'd like to see the wine menu, please," I said with a smile.

"This ain't a goddamned hotel," he snapped.

"Just get us a drink. You're nowhere near high enough up the food chain to know what's really happening here, and you don't want to be the person who has to tell North his prisoners have passed out through dehydration."

Evidently he agreed. Without a word, Rat Face walked to the table, filled a glass with water, and held it to my lips. I hadn't been joking—lugging weapons, grenades, and all the rest of the equipment I'd been using had taken it out of me. I'd also lost a lot of blood. I needed the fluid and I gulped it down greedily. The water passed over the exposed nerves of my damaged teeth. I grunted in pain.

When I'd finished, Rat Face refilled the glass for Martha, but she refused. He left without speaking.

"I think you're really going to have to tell me what you're doing here, Ben," she said as soon as we'd been locked in again. She'd asked earlier, but I'd kept quiet. I assumed they were listening. It's what I'd have done.

"Rescuing you," I replied.

She looked down at me, handcuffed to a bed and bleeding. "And how's that working out?"

I tried to grin, but it hurt too much. Ended up in a creepy grimace.

"Did my dad send you?"

I nodded.

When it was clear I wasn't going to add anything, she said, "What did Peyton North mean when he said you were early?"

"I wasn't supposed to hand myself in until nine o'clock tomorrow night."

Her nostrils flared and I realized my mistake. "What do you mean, hand yourself in?" she said. She crossed her arms and glared. Waited for an answer.

"I've agreed that at nine o'clock tomorrow, you'll leave here on a helicopter." It was an answer, just not to the question she'd asked.

"And why would they let me do that?"

"Because as soon as you're safe, I'll give them the location of their chief executive."

"Spencer Quinn? You have Spencer Quinn?"

I nodded.

"Where is he?"

I shook my head. "Loose lips sink ships," I said.

Martha considered this. "Well, I hope you bloodied his nose."

I didn't answer. We settled down to wait. Martha told me how she'd ended up where she had. "I wanted a project to do for my end of semester paper," she said.

"The one for Professor Marston?"

"You've met him? He's a bit arrogant, but he's the authority on forensic accounting. I hope he's not worried about me."

"He's dead."

"Oh, no!" she gasped.

"I probably should have handled that a bit more sensitively, huh?"

"You think?!"

"Sorry."

"How?"

"Shot by someone working for Quinn and North. She got a campus cop too."

She gasped again. "She?" she asked eventually.

"Female contract killer. Unusual but not unheard of. She's dead too."

"You?"

"No. Someone I've been working with."

"A friend of yours?"

"That's a good question, Martha. To be honest, I have absolutely no idea. On the balance of probability, I'd say no, she isn't my friend."

"I don't understand."

"Neither do I," I admitted. "But I'm starting to build up a picture."

She stared at me, but I didn't elaborate. "Why do you think Professor Marston was killed?" she said after a few beats.

"Because I went to visit him."

"And why did—"

"He wouldn't share the subject matter of your paper with the cops. I was trying to change his mind. If he'd handed everything over when he was asked, the stupid man would be alive now."

"Stupid man," she echoed.

"Your paper was about Spencer Quinn?" I said in an attempt to get her mind off Marston.

"He and Gunnar used to be in the same dorms as me. I thought it would add a personal touch if I examined the business model of a local success story."

"You found something?"

Martha nodded. "There was something off with the bank, I thought. They'd never invested in solar energy before. It was just a small thing, but I'm training to look for the small things."

Quinn had said the same. After 9/11 all cash payments of over ten thousand bucks had to be reported to the IRS. That meant an audit trail. It meant all large purchases had to be funded cleanly.

"Anyway," she continued, "I'd thought there was bound to be a logical explanation—it's solar energy, for God's sake—so I asked a few questions. Eventually I called Banco Nacional de Coahuila and asked to speak to the person who approved the loan. Next thing I know, I'm out on my morning run and I'm bundled into a van and driven all the way here. Today was the first time I've been out of the cave since I was abducted."

When the immediate information exchange petered out, we settled into semi-silence. I busied myself with judging the capability of our make-shift cell. It was probably designed as a storeroom. Anyone able to move about freely could open the door with an enthusiastic shoulder charge. Of course you were then in the middle of a workshop filled with armed men, miles into a complex cave system. But one step at a time.

Martha was staring into space. She looked worried. I'd have liked to tell her to be calm, that things were better than they looked. But I couldn't. So, when she asked me what the plan was, I replied, "We wait."

If we did have eavesdroppers, "We wait" wouldn't raise any eyebrows. North and I had agreed on a timetable. It was why he'd taken me underground. To wait. He knew I wouldn't reveal anything about Quinn's whereabouts until I knew Martha was safe. But as soon as she was gone, and as soon he had Quinn back, I'd be in for some rigorous questioning. Who else knew? Who had I told? Was there anything else that put them at risk? It was why North had been expecting me before the agreed time. He knew I'd try to avoid the car batteries and the chain saws and the baseball bats.

So we waited.

North was waiting to get Spencer Quinn back. Martha was waiting for a helicopter out of here.

And me? Well, I was waiting for something else.

CHAPTER 111

North's men had removed my watch and I needed to know the time. It was important. I asked Martha if there was a set pattern to shift changes, but she didn't think there was.

"Sometimes the same man would look after me for days on end, then I wouldn't see him for a week," she said.

Which was sort of what I'd have expected. Cocaine smuggling is a 24/7 business. North's men were probably doing a week on, week off. Slept and ate down here until they were relieved. The more illegal the role, the less exposure to the outside world they would have. I thought most of the men involved in the actual production of the cocaine-infused plastic would come and go from the cartel-controlled Mexican side. The Gauntlet folk working the solar energy plant wouldn't even know of the existence of the shadow business they were all working for.

The steady hum of men working machines could be heard through the door. North might be gearing up for whatever came next, but he wasn't letting it interfere with business. I wondered how much shutting down for even one day would cost them. Six figures? Seven? The profit margins on cocaine were astronomical.

"Are you hungry?" I asked Martha.

"You kidding?"

"I'm going to start yelling for food. When they bring it in, they'll remove your cuffs so you can feed me. I need you to do me a favor when they do."

"Oh?"

"I need you to get a look at Rat Face's watch."

"Why?"

I ignored the question and started hollering again. Rat Face opened the door and stuck his head in.

"What now?"

"I want food."

"You do, do you?"

"Doesn't need to be fancy. The same swill you guys are eating will be fine."

"Asshole," he muttered, closing the door.

"I get that a lot," I said to Martha.

Rat Face came back with a tray of food around fifteen minutes later. As I thought he would, he cut Martha free but left me cuffed to the bed. He pointed at me and said, "If he wants to eat, you feed him."

The second he left, Martha said, "Sorry, Ben. I couldn't see his watch. I'll get it when he comes back for the tray, even if I have to grab his wrist. It'll be easier now my hands are free."

Neither of us was hungry, but I needed the fuel. I told Martha to eat what she could as well. I didn't explain why, but she seemed to be happy to take her cues from me for the time being. We shared a plate of sandwiches, potato chips, and lukewarm Sprite. She fed me like I was a toddler.

A short while later Rat Face returned. He secured Martha to the other end of the bed and then, probably trying to prove he wasn't a fool, rechecked my cuffs to make sure she hadn't somehow managed to undo them. While he did, I glanced at Martha. She nodded.

Rat Face picked up the tray and left the room.

"It's ten minutes to six, Ben," Martha whispered the second the door was closed.

Which was much later than I'd thought.

The waiting was about to end.

"Whatever happens, Martha, you stick to me like white on rice. Do you understand?"

"Just what is about to happen, Ben?"

"Do you *understand*, Martha?"

"I do."

"Good," I said. "This'll soon be over. Now, do you want to see my party trick?"

"Your party . . ."

I twisted my arms against each other. Strained until it felt like my muscles were about to tear off.

The right-hand cuff sprang open.

CHAPTER 112

Sheriff Long had asked why I continued to carry around my old government-issue handcuffs, handcuffs that could only land me in trouble. She'd assumed I'd been clinging on to part of my past life.

She was wrong.

When I'd first been given control of my SOG team, an unofficial role I'd taken on was that of quartermaster. On one occasion, Matt Westerhoff, a corn-fed man-mountain from one of the Midwest farming states, had come to me with a set of handcuffs he claimed were faulty. He'd handed them over. I tested them but could see nothing wrong. The key wasn't loose in the lock, and the ratchets on the arms were sharp. I pulled it as hard as I could but couldn't break them open. I'd looked at him quizzically.

"Watch," he'd said.

He handcuffed himself to the front so I could see. His wrists were almost as big as my biceps and the cuffs barely fit. The Marshals had only just switched from chain handcuffs to the rigid-bar version, and we hadn't yet sourced an approved and reliable provider.

Matt strained his arms until the veins in his forehead looked fit to burst. At the same time he rotated his arms against each other.

The right cuff sprang open.

I'd looked at it in stunned silence.

"There's a fault with one of the rivets," Matt had explained. "It's not long enough. If you rotate your arms in opposite directions, it pops out and creates enough lateral movement for the pawl to slip the ratchet."

The pawl is the part of the mechanism that locks into the tooth of the ratchet. There is only one way to unlock a handcuff. You have to disengage the pawl. That's what the key does. Fortunately, Matt had discovered this during a training exercise. If it had been during a live operation, the results could have been disastrous. Potentially fatal.

Matt and I checked the rest of the stock held at Camp Beauregard. Out of nearly one hundred sets of handcuffs, we found only one more with the same fault. I discovered later that a small number of twelve-millimeter rivets had gotten mixed up with the fifteens. I'd called the head of operational support personally, and the contract was canceled. I arranged for the entire stock to be returned. We couldn't run the risk of them getting mixed up with the new stock when it arrived, but somehow the original pair, the ones Matt had used to demonstrate the flaw, had missed the recall. They were still in the bottom of my desk drawer. I hadn't noticed them until much later, and by that time it was too late to do anything about it. I didn't throw them away, though. It was possible someone, somewhere down the line, would notice there was one pair missing, and I didn't want to be fifty bucks out of pocket. I put them in an old kit bag and forgot about them.

And when the Russians came knocking, in my rush to pack enough to get a head start on the road, I'd picked up the kit bag and started throwing stuff in. I didn't discover the handcuffs until I'd bought a proper backpack and was transferring the contents. I'd almost thrown them away. I was traveling light. For the first few weeks, at least, I would be avoiding public transport and walking everywhere.

But something made me keep them.

Eventually they became like a high-end disentanglement puzzle. When I was bored, I'd try to do what Matt had done. I was always careful to handcuff myself to the front and would always have the key in an accessible place. Eventually I managed to unspring them, and as with anything else, as soon as I'd done it once, the next time it was easier.

As a way of killing time, it was OK. But I quickly realized there was another possible use for them. At some point, someone would catch me.

The money was too good for people simply to give up. Through sheer dumb luck or something I'd not considered, I would end up in a situation like this.

And I figured there wasn't a vindictive person alive who wouldn't enjoy the irony of using someone's own handcuffs against them. Particularly when they looked as solid as the rigid ones we'd been issued. They even had "US Marshals" engraved on them.

It was just a theory, though. A bit of human psychology.

And like any theory, it needed to be put into practice before it could be proven.

CHAPTER 113

Martha stared, open-mouthed, at the sprung handcuff. To her credit, she didn't make a sound. I was grateful she'd inherited Mitch's common sense. Behind my back, I carefully flexed my right hand until the circulation flowed again. The pain was outrageous, but I kept my expression neutral. I didn't think anyone was watching, but there was no point risking it. I also tested my left arm. I could form a fist and bend my elbow. It seemed to be working again.

I figured it was almost time. Things were either about to happen or they weren't. If they did, I could move on to the next stage. If they didn't, then I was a dead man.

Martha whispered something to me, but I shook my head in frustration. We were too far down to hear what I hoped was about to happen, but I hoped to hear the *reaction* to what was happening. That would happen right outside where we were now.

For five long minutes nothing changed. Men continued to talk in hushed tones. Machines hummed and whirred. No excitement. All routine. We were left alone.

The first indication something was wrong was silence. Everyone outside our room stopped talking at the same time. The second indication was shouting and the sound of men panicking and running. I waited a full minute, desperate to get moving but knowing I'd ruin everything by going too early. There'd been men out there with guns and I needed to wait until most of them had left.

On the count of sixty, I stood up, put my hand in my pocket, and retrieved one of the trick coins I'd bought at the arms fair. Feeling a bit like I was in an early James Bond movie, where the one item Q gives Bond at the start is the exact item he needs at the end, I exposed the blade and cut the plasticuffs from Martha.

"I'm about to smash through this door, Martha, and I'm going to kill anyone who gets in my way. Do you understand?"

She nodded.

"Do you know how to fire a gun?" I asked.

She nodded again. Of course she knew how to fire a gun. She was Mitch Burridge's daughter.

"Hopefully it won't come to that. If I've timed it right, anyone capable of fighting is making their way to the surface right now."

"But what's happening?" she asked.

We crept to the door.

"Listen," I said.

We leaned forward and pressed our ears against the thin wood.

There were a lot of scared people, all talking at the same time. One word was being repeated over and over again.

"Sinaloa! Sinaloa!"

Martha turned to look at me in astonishment.

"You knew the Sinaloa Cartel were coming! How?"

But the men outside were wrong. It wasn't the Sinaloans who were coming.

It was the Russians.

CHAPTER 114

The plan had never been a smash-and-grab. Shooting my way in like John Wick, snatching Martha, then shooting my way out wouldn't work. I'm good, but I'm not invincible. Even if I'd triumphed against the overwhelming odds, I couldn't be sure Martha was still being held in the cave. And even if she was, Quinn had already told me the entrance was protected by palm-print technology.

So, despite the terms I'd negotiated with North, I knew they were never going to let Martha go. They couldn't. They'd known her long enough to know there was no threat that would guarantee her long-term silence. Like father, like daughter, she'd talk. And although she might not know everything, she knew enough. She knew what she'd been doing when she'd been snatched, she knew who some of the key players were, and she knew she'd been in a cave. A team of federal agents, the likes of which had never been seen before, would come crashing down on the house of GU Solar Energy Systems.

No criminal enterprise survived a disproportionate response like that.

Someone would flip. The tried-and-true "whoever talks first gets the deal" routine was tried and true because it worked. Declarations of loyalty are all well and good when everything's going well, but when you're looking at a deuce and a half for people you've never even spoken to, talking to the feds suddenly isn't that abhorrent. And once they have one, the race is on. Nobody wants to be without a chair when the music stops.

Sure, North's men would have taken her anywhere I'd stipulated. But as soon as I'd received the call she was OK, she wouldn't have been. They would have tracked her and found a way to take her out. Martha was never leaving Texas alive.

And neither was I.

So, what do you do when the rules of the game don't allow you to win? You cheat, of course.

By storming the complex twenty-four hours earlier than I'd been expected, I'd convinced North I'd been doing exactly that. That I was cheating. I made him think I understood the rules and was trying the only thing I had left. That he'd expected it was immaterial. I'd seen the look in his eyes after the carnage of the executive dining room. He was disappointed. He'd expected more. He thought he'd overestimated me.

But the attack on GU had been nothing more than misdirection.

Because the other way to beat a rigged game is not to play it.

Instead you change it to a game that's rigged in your favor.

The Solntsevskaya Bratva had been losing ground for nearly five years. I knew this because I kept tabs on them. If they got too small, the price on my head became less of an issue. Would-be bounty hunters would worry about not being paid. Even the dumbest hitman can do a simple cost-benefit analysis.

Unfortunately, their downward trend had stabilized. Natural aggression, uncompromising bosses in the motherland, and a willingness to commit appalling acts of violence meant that they were always going to be earning money. But the timescale was interesting. I calculated the Bratva's troubles started around the same time that Quinn and North's first shipment left Gauntlet. My check with Jen had confirmed that the Bandoleros had become the major supplier to the Five Families in New York. They had less overhead than their competitors. They had a secure transport system. The wholesale price had come down. Profit margins increased for the Bandoleros and everyone they did business with.

To put it bluntly, the Russians were being priced out of the market. The cartel they dealt with couldn't compete with the Bandoleros' prices. They were reduced to scrambling around for scraps. Selling a more expensive product in areas they didn't control.

It was on J.T.'s bluff that I realized what I had.

To the right person, the knowledge of what was happening in the cocaine-smuggling world was worth millions of dollars. Hundreds of millions of dollars.

But I didn't need money. I needed something else.

So I called Yaroslav Zamyatin and convinced him that, contrary to recent reports, I was still alive.

I then offered to level the playing field for him.

CHAPTER 115

My offer had been reasonable. I didn't beg for my life. I didn't ask for the contract to be canceled. All I did was offer to make the Solntsevskaya Bratva competitive again.

My price was that at 6 a.m. exactly, as many of their men as possible would assault GU Solar Energy Systems headquarters. I didn't explain why. Told him nothing about a cave system or an abducted girl. Just said that if he did this, the Bandoleros would be finished on the American side of the border. And when the bigger cartels found out what they'd been up to, they'd be finished on the Mexican side as well.

I told them I'd have softened their approach. Taken out as many of North's men as I could.

As far-fetched as it sounded, I could tell that once the wily old Russian believed I was alive, he believed what I was telling him. He promised to check with his superiors.

I hoped I'd made them an offer they couldn't refuse.

Judging by the panic outside our door, it didn't look as though the Russians had refused. Time was a factor now. North's men wouldn't be able to hold off a determined attack from battle-hardened Russians. When they realized they were heavily outgunned, they'd retreat to where they'd feel safe. The cave.

Back toward me.

I turned to Martha and said, "You follow me, you hear?"

She nodded, scared but defiant.

I stepped back to the opposite end of the room and ran at the door. All my pent-up fury went into the shoulder charge, and the door disintegrated. My momentum carried me through and I ran headfirst into a man holding a clipboard.

He grabbed me in panic, but I slammed his head into the cave wall until he went limp. I hoped he wasn't dead. These were poor workers, little more than farmers. There under the promise of silver or the threat of lead. If they left me alone, I'd leave them alone. I stood and got my bearings. By then, only five men remained in the workshop. None of them looked like fighters.

"Gun?" I yelled.

They didn't answer and I shouted it again, louder this time.

"Ben!" Martha screamed.

I turned.

Rat Face had just sprinted into the cavern. He skidded to a halt while he took in what he was seeing. I'd misjudged him. I'd assumed he was a sidekick. A sniveling bully, happy to spit and sneer when the other guy was in handcuffs, but someone who would run at the first sign of trouble.

He did run.

But not back through the tunnel like I'd expected. He ran straight at me. Caught me in my midriff and we both fell to the floor. He didn't waste his breath on words, just started pummeling me. Not a problem normally, but my hands were still numb and my punches weren't landing right. His were, and I was beginning to weaken. In the end, I had to grab his head and force my thumbs into his eyes. He screamed and wrenched his head free. I followed it up with a jab to his throat, which put him down. I got to my feet and kicked him as hard as I could in the head. Heard the popping sound of his neck breaking. He wasn't dead, but he wouldn't be playing basketball anytime soon.

I turned and smiled in surprise. Unless I was mistaken, Samuel's Glock was sitting on top of a pile of technical manuals. No sign of my SIG or my Fairbairn-Sykes, but I couldn't have everything. I checked the magazine was full and press-checked to make sure there was a bullet in the breech. There was. I tightened the sound suppressor. Now I didn't feel so exposed. The keys to my handcuffs were in a small ashtray. I unlocked my left hand and ignored the pins and needles.

My body armor was hanging off the back of a molded plastic chair. I checked it for anything useful, but it had been rifled through and was empty. I put the handcuffs and keys into the large front pocket and said to Martha, "You're wearing this. No arguments."

There was no answer.

I spun around.

Martha was missing.

CHAPTER 116

"Where is she!" I frantically screamed.

The remaining workers in the cavern stared at me in horror. One of them looked at Rat Face and crossed himself. It was obvious they hadn't seen anything. One of them would have pointed. I didn't have time to force the issue. They were scared of me, but they were also scared of North. Even if they told me, I wouldn't be able to rely on what they said.

The tunnel only had two directions. One led back to GU; the other led to Mexico. It was a coin toss. A fifty-fifty choice. Only it wasn't. Not really. Whoever took her wouldn't know it was the Russians attacking. I'd heard them shouting about the Sinaloa Cartel not five minutes ago. If that were the case, the Mexican side of the tunnel would be under attack too—or worse, they were facing a joint DEA–Mexican law enforcement operation. And if the DEA knew about the GU entrance to the cave, it would be fair to assume the Mexican National Guard knew about the one on their side. When I considered the choice from the point of view of North's man, the Mexican side of the tunnel was out. Nothing good was waiting for him at that end. He would have to head back to GU. Hope North could use Martha to bargain their way out.

I climbed on to a quad, turned it so it faced GU, revved the engine, and began racing back up the cave tunnel.

* * *

Debris blew and swirled alongside me. The air had been still on the way down, but a draft was running through the cave system now. Both ends must have been open. The workers were fleeing to Mexico, and North's *sicarios* would be joining the fight against the Russians.

I forced myself to take it slowly. If I went too fast, I risked overturning the quad taking a corner too quickly. Even so, the return journey only took ten minutes or so. When I could see a pinprick of light in the distance, I braked and turned off the engine. I would cover the last bit on foot.

I got off the quad and jogged the rest of the way, my Glock held out in front like a divining rod. The tunnel veered left, then straightened. I stopped. I was almost at the cave entrance. The light coming from the lamps above the aerial platform washed the last few yards of the tunnel like stage lights. The metal door that protected the cave entrance hung open. So was the door to Spencer Quinn's office, the one behind the bookcase. The bookcase was halfway along its rails, like someone had squeezed through in a hurry. It meant most of Quinn's office was hidden to me, but it also meant no would see me as I crossed the aerial platform.

And I could still hear gunfire. That was good. It meant the majority of North's men would be focused on the Russians. They'd have their backs to me. I stepped on to the platform and shut the cave door behind me. I spun the handwheel and locked it. The gunfight had almost certainly reached the ground-floor workshop by now, and I didn't want North's men trying to escape via the portable stairs leading to the cave. I used the platform's rails as leverage and kicked at the portable stairs. They toppled over and wedged against the rock face. I grabbed my handcuffs and used them on the platform's control panel like a lump hammer. I didn't know if there was also a control panel at the bottom, but if there wasn't, no one was getting to the aerial platform without a ladder.

I press-checked. I figured North would be somewhere in the middle of the building. He'd have chosen somewhere close enough to the battle to direct it, but not so close he couldn't escape if it turned against him. I figured he'd be on the floor below me. He'd have Andrews with him. The giant wouldn't leave North's side now. It was what personal bodyguards did. In high-risk situations they didn't leave their principal's side.

And that was where I'd find Martha. The man in the cavern would have delivered her to Andrews, and Andrews would have taken her straight to North. And when he realized how quickly his house of cards was collapsing, he'd want her as a bargaining chip. A way to negotiate a safe passage back to Mexico.

My job now was to make sure it never got that far. I pulled the bookcase along its rails and stepped across the threshold into Quinn's office.

And saw Andrews.

CHAPTER 117

North's giant was waiting for me.

I could also hear the familiar screech of a helicopter engine warming up. North had never planned to use Martha to negotiate his safe passage. It was too late for that. He was going to fly to Mexico. Straight as the crow flies. He wouldn't pass go, he wouldn't collect $200, but he would live to fight another day.

Martha wouldn't, though.

As soon as he entered Mexican airspace, North would discard her like the liability she would immediately become. He wouldn't land; he'd just open the door and hurl her into the pine and oak forests that covered the Sierra Madre Oriental mountain range. Her body might be discovered one day, but it probably wouldn't be. Black bears, coatis, and coyotes all lived in the Sierra Madre Oriental. None of them would turn down a free meal.

I'd been around helicopters long enough to know I had less than five minutes to get to the roof before it took off. North would wait for Andrews, but not for long. The two of them would have an implicit understanding: North's safety was paramount. Andrews wouldn't expect him to wait. As soon as the helicopter's engine lights all turned green, North would order the pilot to take off.

Andrews was wearing black-and-white camouflage pants, desert combat boots, and an olive green tank top. He had a tattoo on the knotted muscles of his right deltoid: a black owl below a parachute. The insignia of the urban warfare company of the French Foreign Legion's 1st Foreign Parachute Regiment. A tough unit.

He was standing still and expressionless, like a golem. He was holding a FAMAS in his left hand, but loosely. It was pointing at the floor. The FAMAS is an assault rifle designed and manufactured by the French. Fires over a thousand rounds a minute. French troops call it *le clairon*, as the over-sized handguard makes it look like a bugle. It is a good weapon but useless pointed at the floor.

I didn't understand why he hadn't already killed me with it.

And then I did. Andrews raised his right hand and beckoned me forward. He didn't want to shoot me; he wanted to fight. He wanted to fight and I had a Glock. I guess North was the brains of the outfit. I raised my gun, pointed it at his face, and squeezed the trigger.

There was a click.

Another dead man's click. The second time I'd heard it in twenty-four hours. I stared at the Glock in confusion. It was loaded. I'd press-checked before climbing the stairs. And I knew it worked. I'd already killed with it.

Andrews grinned. The first time I'd seen him show emotion.

I'd never had a dud round before, but I'd spoken to people who had. The primer cup can be too far into the casing. The primer mix may have cracked and moved away from the anvil. A dozen other reasons why a man-made thing can fail. I'd even known a guy who'd had a hang fire, a delay between the trigger being squeezed and the ignition of the propellant. He'd shot his pinky toe clean off his foot. Walked with a limp ever since. Sniper's nightmare, his friends called him. But it was statistically unlikely. Around one round in three hundred thousand is a dud.

I racked the slide and ejected the unspent round anyway. Heard it clatter against Quinn's desk. But even before I'd squeezed the trigger again, I knew it hadn't been a dud. Andrews's grin was fixed. He was enjoying himself. He reached into his pocket and held something up for me to see.

It was a firing pin. It was *my* firing pin.

I'd ignored my golden rule: I'd used a weapon I hadn't personally tested. In my haste, I hadn't stopped to consider why my Glock had been waiting for me. Nothing else had been, not the SIG MPX-SD and not the

Fairbairn-Sykes. But my Glock had been there. Sitting where I couldn't miss it.

North really was very clever. Just because he couldn't see how I could escape, it didn't mean he believed I couldn't. So he'd bought himself a little insurance. He'd swapped my firing pin for one with the nub filed down. Unless I fired a test round in the cave, there'd be no way to tell. I'd have needed specialist gauges or dummy rounds with wax-filled primers.

Andrews put his FAMAS on a nearby seat and beckoned me forward again. He still wanted to fight. I couldn't beat him. I knew that. He had no obvious weaknesses and I had a bullet in my arm. He was stronger than me and he was bigger than me. Fighting Andrews wouldn't be a two-way exchange of attacks. He wouldn't have to devote any energy stopping himself from getting hurt. He could put 100 percent of his energy into attacking me. And while his training with the 1st Foreign Parachute Regiment wasn't as comprehensive as mine, it was good enough. He was like the Maginot Line, the impregnable fortifications the French built to deter a German invasion, the ones the Germans bypassed by invading through the Low Countries. But I couldn't bypass Andrews; I'd sabotaged the aerial platform.

The pitch of the helicopter engine increased. I calculated I had three minutes until Martha was gone forever.

Tick-tock.

Andrews mimed a helicopter taking off, then ran a finger across his throat. He seemed to have a sign language all of his own, but that didn't matter. The meaning was obvious: As soon as North was airborne, he planned to slit Martha's throat.

I put my head down and ran at him.

CHAPTER 118

Andrews smiled as I ran toward him. He rolled his shoulders and cricked his neck. I feinted left, but he didn't go for it. His eyes stayed locked on mine. I flicked at them, like I was getting water off my fingers. Nothing. He didn't even flinch.

He'd fought to the death before.

I swiveled round to his right and hit him on the side of his neck. Put everything I had into it. Any punch is a matter of percentages. There are too many flexibilities in the body to deliver the full potential energy of a blow every time. But I'd gotten this one right. Everything was where it had needed to be. The mechanics and the timing and the point of impact were perfect. My fist bounced off him like I'd punched a run-flat tire. I kept the momentum going and crashed my elbow into the back of his head. He took a step forward to absorb the blow, then swung a giant fist right back at me. I threw up an arm and took it in the shoulder. If it had connected with my head, it would have killed me. I felt the shock wave in every bone of my body.

"You punch like an old lady," I grunted, darting back in and throwing a strong jab at his throat. He dipped his head and my hand hit his chin. Drew some blood. Andrews licked it from his lips and smiled again. I shot my right foot out, slammed my boot into the side of his knee. He staggered a bit but didn't go down. It should have put him on the floor. I'd hit the joint perfectly. I stepped back and thought again. I wasn't hurting him. His muscles offered too much protection. He was impregnable, like he was wearing a blast suit. The kind the bomb-disposal guys wear when approaching IEDs. I could go for his eyes, but that would mean getting in close. And getting in close was what Andrews wanted. He wasn't interested in a sparring match. He didn't want to trade blows. He wanted to crush me to death. Look me in the eyes as I took my last breath.

I glanced over his shoulder. The helicopter's rotor system was now moving fast enough to kick up a cloud of dust.

Tick-tock.

I ran in, ducked under his outstretched arms, and gouged at the soft tissue around his eyes. I drew blood, but it wasn't enough.

Andrews caught the back of my shirt, spun me round. Grabbed me from the front like a sumo wrestler. I felt my ribs crack. I couldn't move my right arm—it was pinned to my side—and my left had a bullet hole in it. He held my eyes as he began to squeeze. He wasn't gloating. It was more like he was inquisitive, like he'd always wondered what it was like to be on the other side of one of his bear hugs. I scraped the outer edge of my boot down his shin, then stamped on the instep of his right foot. He staggered back and took me with him, like we were doing the Viennese waltz. I leaned in and bit his ear. My mouth filled with coppery blood. He bent forward and shook me off, and I took the opportunity to reach down and grab his balls. Wrenched down and twisted as hard as I could. He opened his mouth and let out a silent roar. If he made any sound at all, it was in an octave only dogs could hear. He then crashed his head into the middle of my face. It was like he'd just slammed a bowling ball into my skull. It crushed my nose and loosened the rest of my teeth. Blood spurted from my nostrils like I'd squeezed it from a ketchup bottle. I went limp, but only for a beat.

I flung a headbutt right back at him, mashed my forehead into the side of his head. A solid blow, one he'd feel all the way to his inner ear. I felt his cheekbone compress and his jaw unhinge. Hospital injuries, but nothing that would move him from his winning strategy. It was like he was a python. Every time I exhaled, he squeezed a little bit tighter. It was like I wasn't even involved anymore.

My eyes began to blur. The first sign my body oxygen wasn't getting to where it needed to be. Compressive asphyxia, it's called. Next my airways would start to foam. Then the capillaries in my eyes would burst. I'd look like one of those tree frogs, the red-eyed ones only found in rainforests. I had to do something before my skin turned blue. If my skin turned blue, it was game over.

I reached up as far as my bullet wound would allow and grabbed a handful of his hair. Ripped it right out of his head. But Andrews kept squeezing. I did it again and he still didn't react. Pain like that was acute. You couldn't ignore it. But Andrews did. He just carried on staring into my eyes. Emotionless.

My eyes were too blurry now to see properly, but the pitch of the helicopter changed again. Went from whine to screech. I figured I had less than a minute. Sixty seconds to turn this around.

Tick-tock.

Suck it up, marine! The memory resurfaced, insidiously, like a fin in a calm sea. A retired Marine Corps master sergeant had screamed this into my ear once. I'd been doing LINE training with him for three weeks by that point, and I wasn't getting it. LINE is an acronym for Linear Infighting Neural-override Engagement. I didn't ask why it wasn't called LINOE and he didn't offer to explain. It's a close-quarters fighting system designed for combat troops. The master sergeant had yelled "Suck it up, marine!" as I'd questioned how ethical it was. I thought it was too brutal. Too animalistic. LINE was designed to meet four main principles: It couldn't be vision dominant; it should be effective against asymmetrical odds; marines should be able to use it even when fatigued; and, finally, proper execution of the techniques should cause death. I was a serving law enforcement officer. I didn't want to learn a bunch of death blows. But I was told to suck it up, marine.

It took me ten seconds to realize I was in the exact situation LINE was designed for. Another ten to figure out a move I could try. It wouldn't be one I'd been shown, but I thought the master sergeant would have approved anyway.

I angled my head, like I was going in for a kiss. Andrews jerked back in surprise, and I bit into his throat. Clamped down as hard as I could, like a cheetah on an impala. A suffocating bite. My sharpened and broken teeth stuck in like marlin hooks. The windpipe doesn't have natural protection, and even a mute giant will stop fighting if he can't breathe.

The change in Andrews was immediate. He went crazy with panic. Started to buck and thrash like a landed fish. But he was tethered to me now. The only way he could break free would be to rip out his own throat. Instead he redoubled his efforts to suffocate me by crushing. But it was a binary thing. Either I could breathe or I couldn't. He didn't have the option of making me not breathe even more.

Now we were both suffocating. Now we would see who handled the air hunger the best. Andrews was wild-eyed. Scared. He kept trying to shake me off his throat. Which was stupid of him. He should have just waited it out. I was already two-thirds empty. He had a full tank. But he didn't wait it out. He kept burning up his oxygen like he had a limitless supply.

He loosened his bear hug. Changed his grip from a hug to a push. Tried to force my head from his neck. I wrapped my arms around his waist and clung on tight. Now it was about timing. The chair with the FAMAS was on the wall opposite the big window. I took the weight off my left foot. Instead of a back-and-forth, push-and-pull struggle, we started to move in a circle. As soon as his back was to the window, I opened my mouth and let go of his waist. I fell back like I was spring-loaded. I landed on the floor. I rolled twice, then came up holding the FAMAS. Andrews held his hands in front of his face and charged me. Like he was a rhino and I was a safari tour guide. I selected fully automatic and squeezed the trigger; 5.56-millimeter bullets aren't known for their stopping power, but they'll go through most things and that includes a giant's hands.

Momentum kept him running, but by the time he fell at my feet, he was mostly dead. In my experience, 5.56-millimeter ammunition is usually neat. It leaves a small entrance hole and a slightly bigger exit wound. But these bullets had been through a hand first. They had tumbled. Changed the precision ballistics. Two had hit Andrews side-on. Made a hell of a mess. The bottom half of his face was missing. His tongue was hanging down like a necktie.

I pressed the muzzle against his head and put five more rounds in him.

The master sergeant would have been proud.

CHAPTER 119

I switched the magazines on Andrews's FAMAS and sprinted out of Quinn's office. I didn't know where the door to the roof was, but I knew it wasn't anywhere I'd already been. And the roof had fixtures and fittings that would require regular maintenance; both workmen and GU executives would need access to the roof, and that meant the door needed to be accessible to both. Someplace where neither group would bother the other. And it couldn't be at the part of GU that pushed up against the cliff face. There was nothing underneath that part of the roof. Not even a working aerial platform now. It wouldn't be in the middle either. That was where the helicopter landed and took off. It wasn't at the front as it would spoil the geometric lines of the building. That meant it was at the far end of the building. The executives would take the light-filled corridor I was in now; the maintenance guys would use the rear stairs.

I turned a corner and saw a door with two illuminated signs above it. They were both green with white writing. One said EXIT; the other said HELICOPTER LANDING AREA. There was a picture of a helicopter above it. It looked like a picture of Harold, Thomas the Tank Engine's helicopter friend. I ran at the door and it burst open.

A long-haired man I recognized from the cavern stared in astonishment. It was probably he who'd snatched Martha while I'd been fighting with Rat Face. He was armed but had been using his hands to protect his face from the swirling dust cloud the helicopter was kicking up. He reached for his weapon, but mine was already raised. I sent two three-round bursts into his upper torso. The sights weren't zeroed for me, and my shots were higher than I'd planned. My rounds stitched across his neck like a sewing machine. He fell back without even bending his knees. Hit the roof with a thud I couldn't hear above the helicopter. His body stopped moving, but his head didn't. It rolled back another foot. My two bursts had decapitated him. Bad news for him, good news for me. Meant I didn't have to check his vitals as I ran past him. It happens sometimes. Shot a guy with a combat shotgun once, blew his head clean off his shoulders.

The helicopter was off the roof now. The pilot was doing his hover check, the one they did immediately after liftoff. It was too high for me to reach the door and drag the pilot out. I could see North in the back. He was holding on to Martha. Making sure I didn't have a clear shot. There was an old Mexican guy with wet eyes in the seat next to the pilot. I figured he was a senior cartel member. Probably Quinn's right-hand man. He looked terrified.

North didn't look terrified, though. North was smiling. He thought he'd won.

But he hadn't. Not yet. A helicopter is a delicately balanced machine. Most of its weight is concentrated in the main rotor engine. It's why they need tail rotors. The tail rotors apply a counteracting torque to the body of the helicopter. Without that torque, the whole helicopter would spin round. The tail rotor engine is much smaller than the main one. If it wasn't, flight would be impossible.

Tail rotors are vulnerable.

CHAPTER 120

I snapped off two three-round bursts at the tail rotor. Nothing. I heard a *ping*, but the rotors kept spinning. The blades were too heavy for the 5.56-millimeter rounds. They were being batted away. Like grit thrown into a desk fan.

I fired again, but this time avoided the blades and aimed slightly to the right, where I figured the fuel line would be. Squeezed the trigger and kept it depressed.

This time there was a shriek, then a bang, and then a flame, hotter than the afterburner on a fighter jet, shot from the tail-rotor cowling. Everything I'd read about bringing down a helicopter said that once the tail rotor was busted, the rest came down hard and fast.

Which is what happened.

The helicopter pitched erratically and began to vibrate, like it was trying to shake itself apart. The cabin started to spin. The pilot lost yaw control. It only had five feet to drop, but it made a hell of a noise when it crashed and slew across the roof. The round bubble window shattered. A main rotor spun into the air and disappeared over the side of the building. Bits of helicopter shrapnel flew through the air.

The engine whined and got louder and louder. Sounded like I was standing under a 747. Then it jammed, clunked a bit, and everything went quiet. Just a few cooling plinks and the screams of a terrified pilot. I didn't know if he was a player or not. But I did know he was flying a cold-blooded killer and his hostage away from a firefight. I raised the FAMAS again and shot him in the head. Bullet went right through his earpiece. Knocked his helmet and shades off. The old guy next to him didn't need a bullet to the head. His head was at right angles to his shoulder. A snapped neck. I didn't know who he was, but I suspected he'd gotten off lightly.

I press-checked. The chamber was loaded. I didn't know how many rounds I'd used to bring down the helicopter, and because the FAMAS's rate of fire was so high, it was possible that I was down to my last bullet.

It was a moot point, though, as when North clambered out of the wreckage, he was holding Martha tight in front of him. He was busted up and limping a bit, but he was alert and dangerous. He wasn't stupid enough to look over Martha's shoulder. Gave me nothing at all to aim at. I got the impression she wasn't his first human shield. He had his left arm across her chest; his right was holding a knife to her throat. My Fairbairn-Sykes. It had already drawn blood. Other than that, Martha looked to have escaped the helicopter crash with just a cut to her forehead.

"Seems we have a bit of a situation, Mr. Koenig," North said.

"No situation, Peyton," I said. "I'm going to kill you, and then I'm taking Martha back to her daddy."

"You seem very sure."

"I'm here, aren't I? Your men are dead. I've killed your giant. Spencer Quinn bled out last night. I brought down your helicopter. I really don't know what else I can do to convince you I'm serious about Martha's safety."

North said nothing.

Martha said, "You killed Andrews? How?"

"Bit his windpipe, then shot him in the head with his own gun."

She paused, then said, "Guess Mr. North is screwed then."

"I'm walking off this roof and I'm taking this bitch with me!" North snapped. "If you try to stop me, she gets a wet neck."

"And if you *do* get off the roof, then what?"

"And then I let her go."

"And we agree to go our separate ways?"

"Yes! Taking Miss Burridge was a business decision. Nothing more. Now you've put an end to that business, it is of no consequence to me whether she lives or dies."

"What do you think, Martha?" I said. "Do you want to go with Mr. North, or do you want to go home?"

"I'd like to go home, please."

"Sorry, Peyton. We don't accept your offer."

"It's not an offer, you crazy bastard; it's a reality. Unless you're going to shoot through her, this conversation is over."

"Do you trust me, Martha?" I said.

"I guess."

"No, Martha. Do you *really* trust me?"

"I do, Ben," she said. Her voice was clear and steady, and I could see that she meant it.

"I need you to stand very still then."

She did. I think she even stopped breathing.

"OK, Peyton," I said.

"OK what?"

"I'll shoot through her."

So I did.

CHAPTER 121

I'd worked with the Secret Service a few years back. The president had been in Boston, and I'd gotten roped into some outer-cordon bullshit. Lots of cops and marshals and a whole other bunch of law enforcement guys had their leave canceled. All for some moron who kept going on TV and trashing us.

The agents who protect the president are always polite and they're always professional, but they make no bones about it: They *will* shoot through you to kill someone threatening the leader of the free world. If they had a list of the things they considered when there was a threat to the president's life, not shooting cops wouldn't even make the top ten. Maybe not even the top one hundred. If you're near the president when someone pulls a gun, the best thing you can do is hit the deck and watch the show.

So shooting through someone was a concept with which I was familiar. And I knew most gunshots are nonfatal. Some parts of the body are better than others, obviously. The hand is better than the head. The foot is better than the chest. The knee is better than the stomach.

The shoulder is somewhere in the middle. Not the worst, not the best. It has the subclavian artery. It has the brachial plexus, a big network of nerves. A complex set of bones. Four of every five gunshots to the shoulder are nonfatal. Eighty percent survival rate. Or, if you're a glass-half-empty kind of guy, 20 percent of shoulder wounds are fatal.

But North was a psychopath and he was desperate and he had a knife to Martha's throat. I figured those odds were way worse than 20 percent.

I switched the FAMAS's selector to single shot and aimed an inch below the top of Martha's right arm. There were no major blood vessels there, and I was pretty sure the brachial plexus was lower down. And I figured the top of Martha's shoulder would be the middle of North's. I hoped I'd maybe chip a couple of Martha's bones but put the bullet in the middle of North's brachial plexus. See how he held a knife after that. I controlled my breathing. Wondered if this was a step too far. That my Urbach-Wiethe was going to cause another death.

And then I squeezed the trigger.

CHAPTER 122

A complicated sequence of events followed me squeezing the trigger. It was all about potential energy being turned into kinetic energy. The sear released the hammer, which pivoted violently on its axis and struck the firing pin, which struck the primer, which sent a jet of flame through the flash hole, which ignited the propellant, which turned into expanding gas that split the bullet from the cartridge and sent it down the barrel at nine hundred meters a second. All that happened in less than two milliseconds, twenty-five times faster than a diamondback can strike.

The bullet hit the top of Martha's arm. I saw the puff of blood and a bit of bone. She yelled in pain and collapsed in a heap. Looked like she'd tried to sit on a chair that was no longer there.

North yelled in pain too. He also spun around like clay flung from a potter's wheel. He hit the tarmac roof and rolled a bit. The Fairbairn-Sykes flew out of his hand and clattered against an air-conditioning unit. He tried to scramble to his feet, but his shoulder wasn't working anymore. He fell back. Turned on his back and propped himself up with his good arm.

"Step away from Mr. North, Martha," I said.

She got to her feet and followed my instruction. She clutched her right shoulder with her left arm.

"Are you OK?"

"Not really," she said. "Some idiot's just shot me."

"Yeah, sorry about that. Had to make a judgment call." I paused. "But if Mitch asks, say it was your idea."

She laughed. One of those short barks that has nothing to do with finding something funny and everything to do with getting rid of pent-up terror. "Guess I'm sitting out rowing this season." She glanced at North, quickly, then looked away. "What are you going to do with him, Ben?"

I didn't answer. While North lived, she would always be looking over her shoulder. The Texas DA might make a murder charge stick, but he might not. North would lawyer up and claim he was just a solar energy employee. Nothing more. He'd say he was unaware of Spencer Quinn's main business. And I'd killed everyone who could contradict that. He might walk.

No, this needed to end now. I collected my Fairbairn-Sykes and walked over to North. He tried to scramble out of my way, but he had nowhere to go. Solid rock on one side, a sheer drop on the other. I reached down and grabbed him by his hair. He didn't say anything and he didn't deserve any last words. I pressed the tip of the blade against the soft part of his chin and drove it deep into his brain.

It was over.

CHAPTER 123

Almost over.

Gun-toting Russians would still be crawling around GU's complex looking for people to kill. Poking their noses into the cartel's drug business. The best thing we could do was find somewhere safe to hole up until they left. The Russians wouldn't stay forever. The cops would show up soon. But until they did, the roof was as safe as anywhere. I could block the door and wait it out.

I was about to explain this to Martha, but she had closed her eyes and tilted her head to the side. She had heard something. I hadn't, but her ears were younger than mine.

Someone shouted. I heard it this time. It was faint, like it was a couple of floors below us. It didn't sound Russian, although I couldn't make out the words. Martha's eyes snapped open. The fear and fatigue drained from her face.

"Daddy!" she screamed. She leaped to her feet, twisted out of my grip, and sprinted for the roof door.

"Martha, wait!" I shouted after her. She didn't stop. I doubted I'd catch someone who was a varsity athlete at both track and field, but I followed her off the roof and into the GU complex anyway. She was scampering down the corridors into the workshop part of the building. Oblivious to the lingering

CS gas, she powered through room after room, hurdling dead bodies rather than going round them. I did my best to keep up.

The voice grew louder, and I knew what it was that had gotten her so excited.

Mitch was calling for his daughter. His voice a mixture of hope and desperation.

Eventually Martha's own cries of "Daddy" must have been heard as Mitch's shouts got more urgent.

After a few moments I heard squeals of joy.

I sank to my knees in exhaustion.

Job done.

There's a saying the British Army use that dates all the way back to the 1860s: "No names, no pack drill." It means that if names aren't known, punishments can't be dished out.

I didn't know for sure how Mitch knew to be there, but he was an agency director and no doubt had access to intelligence of which I wasn't even aware. Or maybe Jen had told him. None of this explained how he'd managed to arrive at the exact time as the Russians, and I didn't much care. Questions like that could wait. The problem I had was that he would be effusively grateful. He wouldn't know how to thank me. He would want to take me back to DC for a debrief. Some of my actions had been . . . questionable. I'd killed people. Some of them had been trying to kill me, but some of my kills had been little more than summary executions. Best if I simply disappeared back into the shadows. And also, I'd just shot his daughter. I didn't want to have to explain that either.

There was a more urgent reason I needed to slip away: the situation with my contract. The Russians now knew I was alive, and despite me having taken out a major competitor for them, the situation with them would be complicated. Nothing had changed. I'd still killed a boss's son. I'd also faked my own death and stolen five million bucks from them. That's how they would see it. They didn't care about an agency director's daughter. All they cared about was how it would look.

Moving now would be better than waiting. At some point Mitch would take off his father's hat and wear his marshal's one. He'd have to call it in.

The FBI, the DEA, even Homeland would turn up. Processing one of the biggest crime scenes in their history. A shootout over the control of an unregistered, cross-border cave system.

I needed to be someplace else when they arrived.

CHAPTER 124

My damaged arm made the climb up to the bluff more difficult than it ought to have been, but at least I could see the nooks and crannies this time. It had been blind on the climb down. One last effort saw me crest the ridge.

J.T.'s observation post was not as I'd left it.

Spencer Quinn's corpse was gone. So was the sedan. The gear I'd left behind wasn't there either. Someone had cleaned up after me.

And Jen Draper was standing there. Calm as she liked. She was talking to Yaroslav Zamyatin.

Two other men stood by two black SUVs. They were nonchalantly holding weapons, but there was nothing nonchalant about them. I didn't know them, but I knew the type. Intelligent muscle. Good men skilled at violence. Retired special forces. SEALs or Delta probably.

Jen turned as I clambered to my feet. She said, "Ah, Ben, I'm glad you could join us. We were running out of things to talk about."

The Russian grunted, although he didn't look too displeased. I said nothing. Jen and I needed to have a discussion.

"Martha's back with Mitch?"

"She is," I said. I ignored the unpleasant taste talking to her brought and added, "Spencer Quinn?"

One of the ex–special forces guys pointed toward a shovel lying on the ground. Didn't need to say anything. Nothing was open to interpretation. Quinn was in a hole somewhere. He wouldn't be found.

Jen turned to the Russian. "Now to the business of the day."

Zamyatin frowned. "I do not understand."

"Yes, you do," she said. "Mr. Koenig's contract. It was paid in full after he was killed. I don't want it reinstated in light of his miraculous resurrection. You're five million dollars out of pocket, but you'll make that back in three months given what's happened here today. Are we in agreement?"

"I'll need to make a phone call," Zamyatin said. "I do not think this will be an insurmountable problem, though. As you say, because of Mr. Koenig's actions, our product will be competitive again."

"Go make it then," Jen said.

He walked away to make his call.

"I'm sure this will—" she started to say.

"Some people died during this who had no need to," I cut in. "My friend J.T. The truck driver Ned Allan. That idiot Marston and the campus cop. I'm not giving the five million back. It goes to their families. And a lot of people rely on the solar energy plant now. Despite the reasons it was built, it can't be allowed to fail. The town doesn't deserve that. These are my terms and they are nonnegotiable. You will arrange all this."

Jen flushed. I'd given her an order. From what Samuel had told me a couple of days back, that wouldn't be something she was used to. Her response was put on hold. Zamyatin had returned.

"We good?" she said. "The bounty for your son won't restart?"

"*Da.* It is canceled," Zamyatin confirmed. He didn't look happy and I didn't think this was about his dead son.

"But?" I said.

"But it seems the man I report to is not happy you stole our money. He says he cannot forgive this debt. That people cannot think it is OK to steal from us. So *da*, the contract for my son is canceled. The contract for stealing our money starts at midnight. Same terms as before."

"And what would happen if I dropped you right here, Zamyatin?" I said, raising the FAMAS. "I'm in a killing mood and it could hardly make things worse."

"Oh, I think it could be a lot worse, Mr. Koenig," Zamyatin chuckled. "You still don't understand our organization's mindset. We're like the Hydra. You kill me and someone takes my place. And just like the Hydra, the next iteration is worse than the last. So, I suggest you don't kill me. My replacement favors boiling people alive in acid."

I lowered the FAMAS. "Just go," I sighed. "Just get in your car and go away."

Zamyatin did. He got into the passenger seat of a black SUV, and it backed out of the bluff. I'd really hoped to get that monkey off my back. Maybe move back to Boston and pick up my old life. Parts of it anyway. Some of it was gone forever.

I turned the FAMAS on Jen. The two special forces guys stiffened and reached for their own weapons.

"You guys look as though you know what you're doing," I said. "But I've just killed a bunch of bad guys. A couple more aren't going to bother me. Either of those muzzles points my way and Spencer Quinn won't be the only man buried in the Chihuahuan today."

Jen waved her hand and they relaxed. One of them took some gum out of his pocket and offered a piece to his friend. They walked out of earshot.

"What's happening, Ben?" she said it like she was asking how I was finding the meal I'd ordered in a mid-priced restaurant chain. "It seems you're a little hot under the collar."

"How did you find me?" I said.

CHAPTER 125

"You know how I found you," Jen said. "My Stingray is LoJacked and the GPS it uses is accurate to three meters. I knew where you were at all times."

I nodded. I'd expected her to say this. It's what she'd told me in the motel that night, the one I'd stayed in after my first day's drive to Gauntlet. She'd called the clerk the moment I'd arrived and shouted at me for stealing her Stingray.

"I remember," I said.

"Then why are you ask—"

"Only I spent a few hours going over your Stingray that night, Jen. The clerk you called loaned me the handyman's toolbox. And guess what? No LoJack."

Jen said nothing. She looked thoughtful, though.

"So I called Samuel," I continued. "Asked him to look into something for me. I even told him what he'd find."

"And what was that, Ben?"

"I told him that he should be looking into how an employee of a private intelligence company could track an individual over two thousand miles and eight states. That didn't make any kind of sense. Not if you were who you said you were. Tracking someone like that takes drones. At least four to ensure constant surveillance."

"Have you any idea how crazy that sounds, you egocentric asshole?" she said. "News flash. No one gives a shit what you're doing, Koenig. The only reason I'm here now is to get my fucking car back."

"Four drones," I carried on. "One acquiring intelligence, the second flying back to base to refuel, the third refueling, and the fourth flying out to relieve the first. It's how you knew where I was at all times. It's how you knew when to turn up on the bluff and when it was time to tell Mitch where his daughter was. You watched me assault GU in real time."

Jen sighed. "That's a nice story, Ben," she said. "Total bullshit, of course. But a nice story nonetheless."

"Anyway, it took Samuel a few days, which was unusual in itself for someone with his skills."

"And what did Samuel find, Ben?"

"You aren't employed by the Allerdale Group, you *are* the Allerdale Group. The cabin, the Porsche, the whole damn company. It all belongs to you."

She sighed. "I really should offer Samuel a job," she said. "He's far too good to be doing all that shady shit."

"He wouldn't accept," I said. "It may not look like it, but Samuel has a strong moral compass. He wouldn't work for you. Not for any salary."

"I committed the sin of omission, that's all. So yes, I own the Allerdale Group, but I'm also an employee. It's more tax efficient that way. And you murdered someone in cold blood on that roof. Neither of us are angels."

"But even that doesn't make sense," I said. "Because no private company in the world has access to military-grade drones like you were using to keep tabs on me."

"What are you saying, Ben?"

"You know what I'm saying," I said. "The Allerdale Group isn't a private intelligence company at all. It's a CIA front."

I let it hang in the air. Didn't think it needed punctuation.

Jen barked a laugh, then shook her head. "How can someone be so intelligent, so intuitive, yet still be so wrong?"

"You're telling me you're *not* CIA?" I said. "Because I know you were. I know you were transferred Stateside after you got caught up in some really nasty stuff. You still being CIA is the only explanation that works all the way to the end."

"I'm not CIA, Ben. Not anymore."

"Then who are you?"

"I'm the girl who lost everything," she replied. "And for a long time I blamed you."

CHAPTER 126

"What did Samuel tell you?" Jen asked.

"That when you were overseas you'd been involved in some dark shit," I said. "Extraordinary renditions. Black sites. Enhanced interrogation that wasn't in any CIA manual. You went too far, even for the coldhearted bastards who run this stuff. You got caught and you were sent home in disgrace. You were seconded to the Marshals so if your crimes came to light, the CIA could say they'd already gotten rid of you. Is that close enough?"

Jen nodded. "I did all that and more. I put those poor people onto planes knowing full well that when they landed they were going to have holes drilled into their knees. I sat in on some of these sessions to ensure our friends, and I use that term very loosely, were asking the right questions. It was policy. I was following orders. We were in a war, and anyone who spoke out against it was unpatriotic. An appeaser."

"So what happened?"

"There was a guy. A boy really. He didn't speak a word of English and the people questioning him didn't speak his language. They thought he was lying. They thought he *did* understand the questions. Things got ugly. Acid was used. I tried to stop it." She raised her sleeve. Showed me a patch of mottled skin. "This is from the acid burn I got in the struggle."

"You said you got that when your kettle exploded."

"I lied," she said. "Anyway, when I got back to base, I went to see the guy in charge. He listened to what I said. Told me he'd look into it. Next thing I know, I'm being accused of the exact thing I'd tried to stop. I was on a plane back the very next day. Busted right down and banned from working overseas."

"The director out there was covering his back?"

"He was a powerful guy, and he wanted to make sure I was never in a position to contradict his version of events."

"So why not kick you out?"

"Because he wasn't the only powerful guy in the CIA," she said. "There were people who knew what had happened. They couldn't speak publicly, of course. That would expose what the US had been up to. But they could offer me the chance of redemption."

"Which was?"

"There was this guy DARPA was interested in. You know, the research guys who work for the Department of Defense?"

"I know who DARPA are."

DARPA is the Defense Advanced Research Projects Agency. It is responsible for emerging technologies. A fictionalized version of DARPA used to crop up on *The X-Files* every now and then. They were always the bad guys.

"Anyway, this guy was a US Marshal," Jen said. "Apparently he couldn't feel fear. He was about to be given a desk job, but his director had asked around. Wanted to know if anyone could think of a way to keep him in the field. So a deal was done. This marshal could stay with his unit, but it was under DARPA and CIA supervision. DARPA was interested in this marshal's condition as they work toward helping our troops recover from PTSD. I guess the CIA just wanted to see what he was capable of."

"The CIA arranged my training?"

"They did. Mitch didn't have those kind of contacts. And DARPA oversaw everything."

"I was your guinea pig."

"You were an asset. A valuable investment. And I was your handler. You just didn't know it."

"Did Mitch?"

"He suspected. He was never told, though."

"And how was I doing?"

"You'd exceeded expectations."

"And then I disappeared off the face of the earth."

"Yes, you did. And that was the end of my CIA career. 'A complete failure of objectives,' my discharge papers said."

"So, you resented me because you had to babysit me," I said. "And then you blamed me for ending your career."

She shrugged. "What can I say, I'm a complex gal."

"But you're a successful businesswoman now. To build a company like the Allerdale Group from scratch, you must have gotten lucky straightaway with government contracts."

"There were people in the CIA who knew I'd been unfairly treated," she said. "They threw contracts my way. Kind of like a payment in kind. Or at least that's what I thought."

"What does *that* mean?"

"Someone somewhere has plans for you, Ben," she said. "And somehow I've gotten dragged into it all."

CHAPTER 127

"I got the call when you were arrested in DC," Jen said. "DoD and the CIA both have your fingerprints flagged. They'll show up as unknown, but will ring all sorts of silent alarm bells."

"It was *you* who busted me out?"

"Not me. My old colleagues arranged it. Pulled the right levers, whispered in the right ears. That type of thing."

"I assumed it had been Mitch."

"He doesn't have the clout. I was told where to collect you and what to do if someone tried to stop you."

"They knew someone would try to kill me?"

"They were monitoring it all very closely. I was asked to find out why you had resurfaced and then to offer you any assistance."

"But only if I asked for it, right?"

"How did you know?"

"After you and Samuel helped me fake my death, Samuel said he'd stay and help. I could tell he didn't want to, but he offered anyway. You didn't even offer. That never sat right with me. The Jen I knew was an asshole, but she never shirked a fight."

"I was ordered back to DC. Given access to the drone feed and told to watch and wait."

"But not to help."

"Strict instructions not to. I think they saw your battle with Spencer Quinn and Peyton North and an entire fucking cartel as some sort of field trial."

"Why you, though?" I said. "You tell me you're a private citizen. OK, I believe you. But the CIA doesn't work like that. They don't share their toys and they certainly don't share their intelligence."

"I was your handler once," she said. "It seems it's a role I'm destined to play once more."

"I don't think so," I said.

"And I don't think either of us has a choice. I'm under no illusions: If I don't agree to this, my government contracts will all be canceled and the Allerdale Group will be put on a watch list. I have almost three hundred employees now. All of them rely on me for a living."

"They have no hold over me, though," I said. "I can't be compelled to do anything. They couldn't find me for six years. What happens if I walk out of here and disappear for another ten?"

"Nothing good," she said. "I'm told that they'll find a predatory prosecutor in DC and charge you with murder two for the guy you killed in that DC cell. They'll then pick apart your actions here and see what they can make stick. I know you've disappeared before, but never with every cop in the country looking out for you. Face it, the same people who screwed me over have now screwed you over. They are the fight we cannot win."

"What do they want?" I sighed.

Jen shrugged. "That's just it," she said. "They don't seem to want anything. Not yet anyway. I suspect, although I'm not in this loop at all, that you're insurance. A final throw of the dice if something has gone very wrong. We're an expensive but ultimately expendable asset. It's probably why they don't mind you being out there, getting into bother, messing with cartels and Russian gangsters. All that does is make the cover story more believable. But until that day occurs, their only stipulation is that you and I remain in touch by email at least once a month. Same way we communicated on your journey down here. Drafts that don't get sent."

"That's it?

"That's it," she confirmed. "Agree to monthly email check-ins and you can do what you want. They won't monitor your whereabouts and they won't put you on any databases. You'll be a ghost. Just like before."

I didn't respond. I closed my eyes. I could have gone to sleep right there, right on J.T.'s bluff. I could have crept under one of the ebony trees, curled up into a ball, and slept for thirty-six hours.

"What's it to be, Ben?" Jen said. "They're expecting an answer."

I grabbed my backpack and hoisted it onto my shoulders. Tightened the straps.

"You can go to hell," I said. "You can *all* go to hell."

I turned my back on her and started to walk.

To where, I didn't know.

ACKNOWLEDGMENTS